DETAINED

OTHER BOOKS BY DON BROWN

• • •

DETAINED

The Navy JAG Series

BOOK 1

DON BROWN

ZONDERVAN
Detained
Copyright © 2015 Don Brown

This title is also available as a Zondervan e-book. Visit www.zondervan.com.

Requests for information should be addressed to:
Zondervan, *Grand Rapids, Michigan 49546*

Library of Congress Cataloging-in-Publication Data
Brown, Don, 1960-
    Detained : the Navy JAG / Don Brown.
        pages ; cm. — (The Navy JAG series ; Book 1)
    ISBN 978-0-310-33805-5 (softcover : acid-free paper) 1. False arrest—Fiction. 2. False imprisonment—
Fiction. 3. Guantanamo Bay Detention Camp—Fiction. 4. Political fiction. I. Title.
    PS3602.R6947D48 2015
    813'.6—dc23   2014040330

Printed in the United States of America

15 16 17 18 19 20 / RRD / 20 19 18 17 16 15 14 13 12 11 10 9 8 7 6 5 4 3 2 1

This book is dedicated to:

Judith & Marvin Miranda of Prosper, Texas

&

Star & Peter Miranda of McKinney, Texas

My "Texas Family"

"There is a friend who sticks closer than a brother."
Proverbs 18:24 (NKJV)

In Loving Memory:

First Lieutenant Darwin W. McCaffity, Unites States Army
February 3, 1928 – December 31, 2012

Who, after his service as a United States Army artillery officer, coached the Jamesville High School Red Devils, then became a Doctor of Dental Surgery, and then devoted his life to his family, to Barton College in Wilson, North Carolina, and to the Christian Church, Disciples of Christ.

&

Lieutenant Colonel Eual J. Landry, Jr., United States Air Force
October 7, 1932 – February 12, 1997

Who, after service as a jet pilot in the United States Air Force, flying numerous missions over Southeast Asia in time of war, returned to his native Louisiana and devoted his life to his family, to his church, and became a loyal servant of public education through his dedicated service as a member of the School Board of Saint Charles Parish.

PROLOGUE

• • •

EL-MINA, LEBANON
CORNER OF AL ISTIKLAL AND MAR ELIAS
NORTH GOVERNORATE, TRIPOLI DISTRICT
15 MILES SOUTH OF THE SYRIAN BORDER
85 MILES NORTH OF BEIRUT

The cool gust was pleasant, heavy with the smell of salt water from the Mediterranean Sea. But when the wind subsided, it yielded to an angry sun that again beat down, relentless and unmitigated, ending the temporary relief from the scorching conditions. Thousands of men, women, and children were crammed tight like cattle, with sweat drenching their clothes, faces, and underarms.

A mishmash of El-Mina police officers and Lebanese soldiers pushed against the crowds, waving them off the streets.

The man and his son had jammed themselves in the sea of humanity, hoping for a fleeting glimpse of the ambassador.

They stood behind the portable waist-high aluminum fencing that stretched along each side of the boulevard. The fencing posed a theoretical yet ineffective barricade designed to deter the crowds from spilling into the thoroughfare as the motorcade approached.

Armed officers positioned themselves in groups of two, spacing themselves every hundred yards or so on each side of the boulevard.

1

The authorities had their guns and the light aluminum fencing to restrain the crowds.

But the crowds possessed overwhelming numbers.

If the crowds mobbed the motorcade as it rolled by, the people outnumbered the bullets that could stop them.

The emotions of the crowd soared hotter than the scorching midday sun. Angry throngs had come to protest the American ambassador, to shake their fists and bathe his car in spit.

Those on the opposite side of the debate, though fewer in number, had come to show their appreciation.

From the swarming crowd, hatred boiled as if in a hot cauldron, spewing into the air:

Hatred for the ambassador.

Hatred for America.

Hatred for Israel.

Hatred for Assad of Syria.

Hatred for the Shiites.

Hatred for the Palestinians.

The ambassador had been warned to stay away. But stubbornly he had accepted the joint invitation from the president of the National Orthodox College and the bishop at Saint George's. As if he had some point to prove.

Overhead, three pale-green military helicopters, like giant locusts buzzing in the light-blue sky, roared in a sonorous cacophony.

One helicopter flew circle patterns out over the Mediterranean about a hundred yards from the shoreline. A machine gun was pointed out from the cargo bay, keeping guard against any intruder who might approach from the sea.

Another helicopter hung over the T intersection of Al Istiklal Boulevard and Mar Elias, over the motorcade route beside the National Orthodox College.

The third flew a few blocks inland, over Mar Elias, where the motorcade would pass on its way toward Saint George Cathedral, where the ambassador would meet with the Greek Orthodox Patriarch of Antioch and address the crowd.

Each of the helicopters had on its fuselage an inverted white triangle with a red border, like a yield sign. The image of a cedar tree—the symbol of Lebanon—graced the middle of the inverted triangle.

Five uniformed policemen quick-stepped along the side of the boulevard with bullhorns in hand, barking instructions to the crowd gathered on the edge of the campus of the National Orthodox College.

"Stand back! Stand back!" a policeman barked in French. "The ambassador's limousine is approaching. Make no unusual gestures!"

A second police officer repeated the instructions in Arabic.

Along the street, the shouting grew louder, as if challenging the roar of the helicopters.

Hasan Makari put his arm around his son, Najib, and pulled him tight. The boy had complained that morning when Hasan had gotten him out of bed so early.

Today the boy's youth would not allow him to understand. But one day Najib would remember that on a scorching-hot day in July, his father brought him to witness history.

"I'm hot, Papa," the boy protested yet again.

Hasan bent down and spoke into the boy's ear, his voice competing with the roar of the three helicopters. "The ambassador will be here soon. This will be spectacular."

A moment later, sirens could be heard coming from the direction of Al Istiklal, the seaside boulevard that curved around the peninsula on which the city of El-Mina was located.

"The motorcade!" someone shouted.

Dozens of police motorcycles, their mufflers rumbling in a steady roar, rolled into view from around the bend on Al Istiklal.

Paired in twos, the white Harley-Davidson bikes sported twirling blue lights on elevated poles behind the seats. Mounted on the cycles were elite police officers of the Lebanese Internal Security Forces. The

ISF officers sported helmets, black visor-shields over their eyes, spit-polished black boots, and sidearms, their grim faces with jaws of steel giving them an intimidating appearance.

As the motorcycle escort approached the T intersection where Mar Elias dead-ends at Al Istiklal, Najib put his hands over his ears.

"The ambassador!"

Fingers pointed away from the motorcycles on Mar Elias and down toward Al Istiklal.

A black limousine, a Cadillac with headlamps burning, came into view from around the bend in the road. The flags of the Republic of Lebanon and the United States of America flew on small poles over the left and right headlights. The limousine tailed close behind a police car, flanked by police motorcycles. Forming a human buffer between the limousine and the motorcycles were eight armed soldiers carrying assault rifles walking beside the limousine, four on each side.

Another police car followed behind the limousine. More police motorcycles followed the squad car.

Hasan bent down and spoke in Najib's ear. "The ambassador is coming!"

"Where, Papa?"

"Over there. Keep watching."

The limousine rolled into the T intersection, about to make its left turn onto Mar Elias.

The motorcade halted, with the limousine stopped in the left-turn lane.

Another cool gust from the sea brushed the crowd. The sight of the American flag fluttering in the wind incited the crowds on both sides of the parade route.

Jeering, cheering, clapping, and fist shaking greeted the black car, which was stalled right under the traffic light in the turn lane from Al Istiklal to Mar Elias, waiting for the motorcycles to move east down Mar Elias.

Hasan took Najib's hand. "Come. Let us get closer."

They pressed forward a couple of feet, squeezing through narrow gaps between the shoulders of the spectators, pushing up to the edge of the boulevard.

From here, Hasan had a clear view of the intersection to his right and of the boulevard in front of him. At the moment he reached the aluminum barricade, the ambassador's car turned onto Mar Elias, only a few yards in front of Hasan and Najib.

As the car passed by, the chanting from the crowd intensified.

"Allahu Akbar!"

"Death to America!"

"Allahu Akbar!"

"God bless America!"

"Allahu Akbar!"

Hasan would keep his true feelings quiet. He could not join in with any chants, lest he be spotted and raise suspicions.

He wanted the boy to see this. Yet he also had to protect the boy.

The motorcade inched forward, having turned from the route that was parallel to the sea, and headed east, leaving the sea behind.

As the limousine rolled in front of Hasan's position, he strained for a look into the back to see the passenger. But a motorcycle officer blocked his view. Then the motorcade stopped again.

From his position along the sidewalk, he now stood no more than ten feet from the ambassador! But still he could not see.

Craning his neck to the right, Hasan waited for the motorcycle officer to move forward.

A brief glimpse opened up, but a foot soldier blocked his view.

The processional started moving again, and the soldier stepped forward, giving Hasan a clear view.

The windows were tinted, but not so much that Hasan could not see inside.

The ambassador wore a dark-blue suit with a red tie. His thick white hair matched the shine of his teeth. He smiled, waving at the crowd, even at those shaking their fists and holding "Death to America" signs.

Hasan threw up his hand and gestured.

That seemed to catch the ambassador's attention. For a split second, eye contact!

Through the tinted glass, the ambassador looked at Hasan, smiled broadly, and waved. Hasan would never forget this providential moment—a moment of eternal destiny!

In the rush of adrenaline, Hasan's heart pounded like a jackhammer. "He sees us! He sees us!" Hasan said as the ambassador's eyes darted elsewhere.

The limousine rolled on, picking up speed, then hitting its brakes again. The ambassador had passed. But Hasan stood still.

Watching.

Waiting.

About a hundred feet down the road, as the car passed, someone waved a solitary American flag. More screaming followed the sight of the flag.

The brake lights flashed on and off again.

A thunderous blast shook the earth.

The blinding explosion from the back of the limousine sent soldiers and bystanders diving to the street.

Screams.

Chaos.

Pandemonium.

Hasan shielded Najib from flying glass, but not before he himself had been struck on his cheek, just under his eye.

Sirens blared.

Crowds knocked down the flimsy barricades, pouring onto the boulevard, swarming the burning limousine.

"*Allahu Akbar!*"

"*Allahu Akbar!*"

From the angry fireball inside the car, orange flames danced above the roof. Thick black smoke engulfed the car.

Police rushed in to pull back the throngs as the helicopters converged in a triangle overhead. Medics ran through the chaos with empty stretchers.

Hasan took the boy's hand, yanking him away from the carnage. It was time to go.

CHAPTER 1

● ● ●

MEDIA CENTER
USS *ABRAHAM LINCOLN*
ATLANTIC OCEAN
45 MILES EAST OF HILTON HEAD, SOUTH CAROLINA
11 YEARS LATER

In a room about half the size of a tennis court, a dozen American sailors, most wearing standard-issue blue-gray camouflage Navy working uniforms, stood in line, waiting for a seat to open up at one of thirty computers lining the bulkheads.

"Now hear this. This is the executive officer. Set condition River City in five minutes. Repeat. Set condition River City in five minutes. This is the executive officer."

The announcement did not sit well for the sailors in line. Some crossed their arms. Many cursed under their breath. Others cursed aloud. A few checked their watches. Others eyed clocks on the bulkhead.

The Navy used the term "River City" for a communications blackout regardless of reason. The XO's announcement meant that a communications blackout with the outside world was about to take place. For those standing in line, hoping to drop a hello to a spouse or a child or a parent or a girlfriend, the dreaded fear was that the blackout would come before they could get to a terminal.

Although a powerful supercarrier like the USS *Abraham Lincoln* possessed tremendous broadband capabilities, most of its broadband remained devoted to the ship's war-fighting capabilities.

"Come on, man!"

"Hurry up."

"We got family too!"

Some of the more sanitary comments coming from several of the waiting grumblers were exhorting their shipmates to hurry along.

"Now hear this. This is the executive officer. Set condition River City in three minutes. Repeat. Set condition River City in three minutes. This is the executive officer."

"I ain't got time for this." The chief petty officer, who was next in line, checked his watch and cursed. "Good luck, bud," he grumbled at the aviation boatswain's mate third class standing behind him.

Just then the Marine corporal sitting at the far right terminal stood, prompting the duty officer to ask, "All right, who's next?"

"That would be me, sir!" The sailor next in line waved at the duty officer.

"Make it fast, Makari," the duty officer said. "Lights out in less than three."

"Yes, sir. Just need to check my e-mail, sir." Najib Makari made a beeline for the vacant terminal at the end of the line.

He sat, tapped the Enter button on the right of the keyboard, then typed the URL for his e-mail.

Connecting . . .

Connecting . . .

"This is the executive officer. All hands prepare for communications blackout in sixty seconds."

The inbox popped onto the screen.

Najib pressed the Control and *P* keys at the same time, sending the e-mail to the laser printer.

"This is the executive officer. Set condition River City in three . . . two . . . one . . . All hands to duty stations. Communications blackout is in effect."

Thirty monitors in the media center went black, prompting a collective groan from those sailors still in the middle of their personal business.

Although his screen had blacked out, Najib's printer kept printing. The message had reached the printer's memory cache before the blackout.

When the printer stopped, Najib retrieved the message from the outbox tray.

From: hasanmakari@beirut.com
To: nmakari@Cvn72.navy.mil
Subj: Visit to America

Najib,

This will confirm my flight to America in two days, arriving in Philadelphia on May 1. From there, I will catch another flight to Norfolk and await the arrival of your ship. I will contact you in Norfolk.

This will be a glorious occasion! The most glorious since the morning we went to see the ambassador!

God is great!

I shall look forward to our experience together.

With love,
Your Father

"All hands. This is the captain. Prepare to resume flight operations in fifteen minutes. All hands report to your duty stations to resume flight operations. AIRWING, stand by for further instructions from the CAG commander. This is the captain."

Najib's heart leaped with excitement. Indeed, God was great! Just as his father had taught him all those years ago.

He folded the message, stuck it in his shirt pocket, and headed up toward the flight deck.

• • •

BRITISH AIRWAYS FLIGHT 442
15-MINUTE FLIGHT TIME TO PHILADELPHIA INTERNATIONAL AIRPORT
MAY 1

"Ladies and gentlemen," the voice announced in a heavy British accent, "the captain has turned on the Fasten Your Seat Belt sign. We should be on the ground in Philadelphia in less than twenty minutes."

From the back right window seat of the 757, just two rows in front of the rear toilets, Hasan Makari fished for his seat belt buckle to comply with the captain's instructions.

There. Found it.

As he brought the canvas belt across his waist and clicked it, the giant 757 passenger jet banked in a slow swoop to the right.

The open blue water below gave way to a long, sunlit, green-colored coast off to the right of the plane.

The shoreline of America!

Goose bumps crawled up his arms as he stared out the window in a near-paralyzing amazement, transfixed at the sight of the American Atlantic seaboard.

To many around the world, America no longer represented the shining city of freedom that she once was.

But to Hasan, America had never lost her luster. Not as a boy. Not as a young man. Even now, as he approached his fiftieth birthday, the dream that America represented, the dream of freedom from religious persecution, that dream had never died.

Hasan had studied American geography since his childhood. His mother was given an atlas of the United States by Christian missionaries from America, Carol and Eugene Allison.

Eugene Allison always took time to visit with Hasan. When the Allisons were called from Lebanon by their missionary organization, they presented the Makari family the atlas and a Bible as gifts of remembrance.

"Please make good use of these books, especially the Bible,"

Eugene told Hasan and his mother and brother around the dinner table on the night before they left Lebanon.

The departure of the Allisons left a painful hole in Hasan's heart. Eugene Allison had served as a surrogate father figure for Hasan, whose own father had been caught up in the cross fire of a battle for which he did not pick sides. The elder Makari left the small family flat one morning to buy vegetables at the market. He would never return. Mohammed Makari was killed by a stray mortar shell fired by pro-Syrian forces against anti-Assad rebels in Tripoli. As a seven-year-old boy who idolized his father, Hasan was crushed by Mohammed's death. For weeks he grieved the loss.

Eugene Allison had five children of his own, most of them adopted. When the Allisons arrived in Lebanon just months after Mohammed Makari's death, Eugene took to the Makari brothers as if they were his own. Hasan's older brother, Jamal, was seventeen. Hasan had just turned seven.

Hasan gravitated toward Eugene Allison, who read to him, played games with him, and told him stories about America and about Jesus.

Eugene also taught Hasan about American football. On Saturday afternoons, Eugene and his sons, Joel and David, would pick up Hasan and drive down to the "corniche," the two-mile stretch of palm-tree-lined, wide, flat beach along the Mediterranean that stretched around the thumb-shaped peninsula and the old city of El-Mina.

They all played "tag" football, as his American friends called it, on a sandy beach in northern Lebanon. Proclaiming himself to be a lifelong Washington Redskins fan, Eugene pretended to be someone named "Joe Theismann." Hasan played the role of a person called "Art Monk."

Hasan never acquired the knack for throwing the awkward, oblong-shaped football. But as it turned out, he became the best receiver of the bunch, earning himself the American nickname "Art."

Sometimes the Allisons called him by his Lebanese name, Hasan, and sometimes by this bestowed nickname, Art.

Hasan loved the nickname. It gave him a sense of identity, making him feel a little bit part of America.

"Here, my son." His mother came into his bedroom the morning after the Allisons left. "Eugene wanted you to have it. Take this." She handed him the atlas that the Allisons had given the family. "There's a note on the inside cover."

Sitting on his bed, Hasan took the atlas, stared at it, and then, with a slow reverence, opened it to the inside cover. His eyes fell on the handwritten note penned by Eugene Allison.

> To Hasan "Art" Makari.
> We love you and will miss you. I will miss our talks and our football games!
> Please keep this atlas of America as a remembrance of our time together. I hope that one day we will see each other again.
> Perhaps in America!
> Remember Romans 10:9.
>
> > With much love,
> > The Allisons

From that day forward, Hasan had kept the atlas in his bedroom and opened it almost every night for the next two years. Years after he lost touch with the Allison family, he still treasured the atlas and had become a self-taught expert on American geography. Not long before the assassination of the ambassador, Hasan presented the atlas to Najib.

As the British Airways plane crossed the shoreline, jetting west over the mainland, Hasan remembered the atlas and let his mind wander.

Below them, the state of New Jersey.

Out to the right, just out of sight beyond the horizon, loomed the great New York skyscrapers.

Somewhere off to their left, a hundred miles or so away, was the American capital city, Washington, DC, with the White House, the Capitol, and all the great monuments of marble to the great American presidents.

Washington was three hours by car from Norfolk. Before he

returned to Lebanon, he and Najib would rent a car and visit the world's greatest capital.

Perhaps they could see the stadium where the Redskins play!

That brought another smile to his face.

The plane began its descent. Pressure mounted in his inner ears.

Hasan popped two sticks of gum in his mouth and started chewing, which at least seemed to neutralize the buildup.

Closing his eyes, he uttered a silent prayer of thanks to God.

• • •

FLIGHT DECK
USS *ABRAHAM LINCOLN*
ATLANTIC OCEAN
62 MILES EAST OF CAPE HATTERAS, NORTH CAROLINA

The warm summer breeze gusted onto the great ship's flight deck, carrying with it a distinctive salty smell that reminded Najib of the ambassador's assassination. For on that day, all those years ago, in the minutes leading up to the killing, sporadic sea breezes had blown in from the Mediterranean, giving relief to the crowd from the oppressive heat.

He was a boy then.

Now he was a man.

But eleven years later, Najib Makari—now Aviation Boatswain's Mate Third Class Najib Makari, United States Navy—still had four indelible memories from that fateful day:

The scorching heat on his head and shoulders.

The salty smell of the Mediterranean breeze.

Bright orange flames engulfing the ambassador's limousine.

The sound of sirens and helicopters.

Even now, sometimes when Navy Seahawk helicopters performed touch-and-goes off the flight deck, or with the salty smell of a gust from the ocean, he experienced chilling flashbacks to that fateful hot summer day.

Najib's father had taught him about America from the time he could walk.

"America is a place for freedom. There we can play, speak, and worship without fear of persecution," the elder Makari had told his son.

On the morning that the ambassador came up to El-Mina from Beirut, his father had gotten him up early.

The new American president at the time, Mack Williams, had reached out to Christians in the Middle East, reversing a heavy-handed pro-Islamic policy embraced by some of his predecessors. The ambassador had come to meet with the patriarch John X of the Greek Orthodox Church.

Williams's "fair and balanced approach" started with America extending a hand of friendship to the Greek Orthodox Christians of northern Lebanon and Syria.

And so on the day that Najib would never forget, the American ambassador arrived in a gesture of friendship, to show America's respect for Christianity in the Middle East, to address the perception that some earlier administrations had become too Islam-centric.

Despite Najib's initial nightmares and the sense of horror that had haunted him after witnessing the explosion at such a tender age, he had in time overcome the nightmares and fears because of the encouragement of his strong-handed, stable father.

Over the years, Hasan Makari had never wavered in his support for the American ideal of freedom of the individual, and a commitment to Christianity remained at the core of Hasan Makari's household.

When Najib learned of a program that would allow him to further his education through an educational visa to the United States, his father had approved of the plan. Then, when he learned that he could speed his quest for United States citizenship by enlisting in the United States Navy, Najib, with the help of a crack immigration lawyer from church, withdrew from his classes at George Mason University. The lawyer helped him get a work permit that he used to secure work as a janitor at a local church, and then a permanent resident card. One month later, he took an oath of allegiance to the United States.

He had joined the Navy to chase away his own fears and to fulfill his dreams and his father's dreams.

And now, a world away and a lifetime removed from that day of the ambassador's death, here he stood in protective helmet and jacket on the flight deck of a nuclear-powered aircraft carrier, one of the most dangerous yet exhilarating work environments in the world.

Despite the temporary flashback evoked by the scent of the ocean breeze, he could not dwell in the past.

Not even for a second.

The steel deck of an aircraft carrier might resemble an ordinary land-based runway, but because of its much smaller size, launching and recovering Navy jets at sea made the deck a much deadlier environment than any land-based airport.

With flight operations under way on this late spring afternoon sixty-some miles off Cape Hatteras, planes launched from and landed on USS *Abraham Lincoln*'s flight deck at a furious rate in the limited space.

Crew members on the flight deck, wearing a variety of different colors depending on their job, had been selected based on testing, psychological maturity, and motor-skills coordination.

Under windy skies, Najib wore his green jacket and helmet, signaling his status as an enlisted member of the "catapult crew." The other crew members wore jackets of blue, purple, red, green, brown, or white to signify their jobs on the flight deck.

The Navy handpicked each flight deck member, emphasizing no room for a slipup. In one careless moment, the twin jet engines of an F/A-18 fighter could suck somebody into the back of a jet or blast a crew member off the deck into the Atlantic.

Najib's catapult crew operated the giant steam-compression-powered steel catapult. When launching aircraft, the catapult crew performed the most important job on the flight deck.

Because the carrier's runway is not long enough for a jet aircraft to take off on its own, Navy jets are literally thrown off the end of the carrier's flight deck by the giant steel catapult that the crew attaches under the nose of the plane. Then the jet's twin engines provide the forward propulsion as the jet climbs sharply into the sky.

In simplistic terms, the catapult system serves as a giant slingshot. The steel cable acts like a giant rubber band, with an F/A-18 "Super Hornet" fighter playing the role of the stone being shot from the slingshot.

"One minute to launch. All nonessential personnel, clear the area."

The announcement echoed across the steel flight deck. Crew members not needed for the launch scrambled back, away from the ship's forward section.

Najib stayed in place, as green- and yellow-jacketed air-handling officers and plane directors moved to the front of the runway alongside the jet out to the left.

The jets roared with a shrill whiney sound that could bore a hole through a man's eardrums if it weren't for special protective gear worn over the ears.

Standing between the plane's left wing and the ship's edge, under brisk winds blowing off the bow, Najib watched as the jet blast protector, the garage-door-sized steel section of runway rising up from the deck at an angle, was pushed up by hydraulic steel arms behind the jet's twin turbo fans.

The blast protector inched upward, rising into place at an angle about forty-five degrees off the flight deck.

As steam seeped up through the catapult track, sweeping across the deck in a fleeting wisp, Najib held his right hand in the air and commenced a clockwise swirling motion, signaling that the jet blast protector was in place, ready for launch.

The pilot, Lieutenant Mark "Maverick" Garcia, nodded at Najib from the cockpit, gave a confident thumbs-up, then turned his head to look straight ahead.

Everything was a "go."

Hearts pounded. Adrenaline spewed like exploding lava. This moment washed away memories of that fateful day in El-Mina all those years ago.

Najib and four fellow catapult crew members took several steps back as the jet's engines roared to a deafening pitch.

The "shooter," the yellow-jacketed catapult crew officer, got down on one knee by the jet's nose. In a quick motion, he pointed his finger straight out front, off the bow of the ship.

More steam oozed up through the flight deck.

The thirty-seven-thousand-pound jet moved forward . . . faster . . . faster . . .

Then, like a slingshot shooting a rock, the giant steel catapult slung the jet fighter out over the water.

Twin afterburners kicked in from the jet engines, shooting angry orange plumes of fire behind the plane.

But even with the twin jets firing, something seemed wrong.

The jet veered to the right, then dropped quickly.

The splash into the Atlantic, off to starboard, sent plumes of water exploding into the sky.

Sirens sounded. Loudspeakers boomed all over the ship.

"Aircraft down! Starboard, forty-five degrees! All rescue teams to the flight deck. Prepare to launch choppers."

Najib and other members of the catapult crew ran across the deck for a better look.

The gray jet was floating at an angle, the cockpit submerged. Waves were lapping against the aircraft. Like the back end of a seesaw, the twin turbofans at the aircraft's rear rose above the waves. Black smoke plumed up from the turbofans.

As the USS *Abraham Lincoln* began a sweeping right turn in the ocean, cutting a protective circling pattern around the sinking jet, two SH-60B Seahawks flew into position over the crash site.

Within seconds, the turbofans slipped under the water. Then the twin tail fans disappeared, leaving only a trail of jet fuel and oil pooled on the surface.

Two Navy frogmen in black wet suits and wearing oxygen tanks dropped feetfirst into the water from one of the Seahawks.

Then two frogmen plunged into the water from the other helicopter.

Despite the roar of the helicopters, the swoosh of the rushing breeze, and the steady hum of the carrier's nuclear-powered engines, a stunned silence settled over the ship. All eyes focused on an empty spot in the water—on a pool of rippling waves and floating jet fuel where the jet disappeared.

The heart-stopping moment took Najib back in an instant—again—to the day he had stood paralyzed, watching the ambassador's car consumed by a leaping, angry fire. Perhaps he would still be standing on the side of that street to this day, all these years later, had his father not snatched him by the hand.

But today no one snatched him away by the hand.

How had this happened?

Had he done something wrong? His mind ran through a mental checklist, but he discovered no answers.

There was nowhere to go, nowhere to run. Najib could only breathe, watch, and pray.

Two more helicopters joined in the rescue effort. One dropped a raft into the water. From the other, two more frogmen dove into the Atlantic.

It seemed like only seconds had passed since the jet plunged into the sea. But in witnessing events that meant life or death, time often became suspended, without measuring sticks. As Najib remembered from that fateful day years ago, the difference between an hour and a minute became meaningless.

"It doesn't look good," said the chief petty officer who was standing near Najib.

"No, it doesn't," said the lieutenant who had been the plane's "shooter." He was standing beside Najib and the chief.

"Look!" A petty officer pointed out to the area.

"Have they got somebody?"

"I think they've got him!"

A head popped above the surface, but the back of the head was to the ship. The frogman turned in the water, his arm in a vise-like grip around the pilot.

Cheering and applause rose from the flight deck. Other frogmen joined in the rescue. One boosted himself into the life raft and helped to pull the pilot into the raft. The cheering turned to silence.

"Is he alive?" somebody asked.

"Hard to say. Somebody better say a prayer."

"This is the captain." An announcement over the 1-MC, the ship-wide public address system. "All hands stand by. Clear all passages. Stand down for emergency medical personnel. Medical staff, prepare to transport the pilot to sick bay. Father Maloney. Report to the flight deck. Repeat. Father Maloney to the flight deck."

"They're calling the Catholic chaplain."

"Is Lieutenant Garcia Catholic?" the lieutenant asked.

"Yes, sir," Najib answered. "I've talked to the lieutenant about his religion. He is Catholic and has a wife and two young children."

"Oh, man." The chief winced. "I hope they're not calling the chaplain up to read him his last rites."

A metal stretcher, dangling from a steel cable below a chopper, was slowly lowered over the life raft, like a ball at the bottom of a pendulum.

A frogman reached up from the raft, grabbed the dangling stretcher, and pulled it in.

The wind was whipping up, and the orange life raft rode the waves. A diver bent down and started mouth-to-mouth resuscitation. Chest compressions followed, then more mouth-to-mouth.

As one diver continued the CPR, two others strapped the pilot's feet, then his legs, onto the stretcher.

The diver administering the CPR backed off, and another diver fastened a waist belt around the pilot. The second diver gave a thumbs-up, and the motorized winch aboard the Seahawk lifted the stretcher skyward.

The pilot's hand flopped over the side of the stretcher as the Seahawk reeled him up, higher and higher. Seconds later, airmen aboard the chopper reached out and pulled the stretcher in. The gray chopper turned, dipped its nose, and flew back toward the *Abraham Lincoln*. As it touched down on the carrier's fantail, two Navy doctors and four hospital corpsmen pushed a mobile stretcher to the cargo door. The Catholic chaplain, Lieutenant Brian Maloney, trailed a few feet behind the medical team.

The chopper's cargo bay door slid open. Two airmen from the chopper stepped out to the flight deck. They turned and pulled the stretcher basket carrying the pilot out of the chopper. They grabbed the head of the basket, and two hospital corpsmen grabbed the other end, then lifted the stretcher-basket onto the rolling gurney. A doctor started chest compressions while two corpsmen cut Garcia's flight suit away from his chest, their scissors glistening in the sun.

The medical team worked quickly, ignoring the sailors, including Najib, who had gathered behind them in a hushed semicircle.

The doctor switched to mouth-to-mouth resuscitation as the two corpsmen removed the cut-up flight jacket from the pilot's chest.

The doctor came up for air and waved for two other corpsmen. One approached with a satchel and held it up as the doctor extracted two electrical pads attached by cords to an electrical defibrillator inside the case.

The doctor touched the pads together, then placed the paddles at an angle on Garcia's chest. He nodded at the corpsman controlling the defibrillator. Garcia's chest jumped in reaction to the powerful electric jolt.

The doctor felt Garcia's throat. He motioned to another corpsman standing a few feet away. The second corpsman strapped an oxygen mask over the pilot's face. The lead doctor motioned, and the corpsmen rolled the stretcher away from the chopper. The pilot's hand dangled off the side as they pushed the gurney across the flight deck, finally disappearing inside the superstructure.

For a long time, the men stood on the flight deck enduring a whipping wind, staring in silence, unable to muster words. All thoughts were on the fate of the pilot.

Najib, too, could find no words to say. First the ambassador. Now this. Was his fate in life to witness sudden and unexpected tragedy?

"This is the air operations officer. All hands remain at your stations. Flight operations will be suspended until we can check the catapult to ensure full operational capacity. Stand by."

Tragedy was best forgotten by getting back to work. But another stand-down would delay even that.

This was the nature of the Navy. Hurry up and wait. What if they discovered a deficiency in the catapult system?

And what about the pilot, Lieutenant Garcia? What if he did not survive?

The situation looked bleak, but Najib could not worry about that now.

The pilot's fate, and his own, remained in God's hands.

• • •

BRITISH AIRWAYS FLIGHT 442
FINAL APPROACH TO PHILADELPHIA INTERNATIONAL AIRPORT
MAY 1

If there had ever been a moment of greater excitement in all of his life than this very instant—except for when his son, Najib, was born—Hasan could not remember it.

He looked out in amazement as the British Airways jet taxied toward the terminal.

Out to the left, under sunny blue skies and wispy clouds, airplanes attached to Jetways were docked in front of long terminals. Their fuselages featured the painted markings of the great airlines they represented.

US Airways.

American.

United.

Southwestern.

Air Canada.

Delta.

But it wasn't the sight of the aircraft that saturated his body with amazement. He had seen airliners before at Beirut International. Rather, it was the realization of where he was.

America!

Here there would be no mortars flying.

No more grenades exploding.

No more booby traps blowing off children's legs as they played in a park.

No more radical Islamists firing AK-47s into the air on public streets, indifferent to where their bullets fell.

Here little boys didn't worry about their fathers being shot dead on a trip to the market, gunned down in a civil war over religion.

America!

The land of the free!

He thought of his wife, Sabah, who died last year after a short bout with breast cancer. He had always hoped that when he first visited America, she would be with him. How he wished she could be here to share in this moment of excitement.

The first teardrop left a wet streak down his cheek. His right eye had also flooded. He wiped both eyes with his hand, hoping no one would notice.

The plane rolled to a stop. After the sound of a single electronic bell in the cabin, passengers stepped into the aisles and began popping open overhead bins, retrieving bags, laptops, and other items that were stowed in the overhead.

Hasan did not like being jammed shoulder to shoulder in crowds. Crowds brought horrible flashbacks from the day the ambassador died. He tried avoiding crowds. The good thing about sitting in a window seat near the back was that it allowed him to wait until everyone else cleared out.

After all, the sun was shining on a new day. A strange warmth overcame him. It felt as if finally, he was home.

He uttered a silent prayer of thanks. When his eyes opened again, the space around his seat had cleared.

Hasan exited the plane, stepping into the Jetway, quickening his step toward the terminal, which was off in the distance, over the shoulders of a few passengers walking out in front of him.

Approaching the end of the Jetway, he checked his shirt pocket to make sure his passport, visa, and tickets were in place. His connecting flight to Norfolk was in two hours. He would have to find the US Airways terminal, but that would give him at least an hour and a half to explore the airport after he cleared customs.

He stepped out of the Jetway into a flood of blinding lights, forcing him to squint his eyes.

Were those television cameras off to the left?

"Hasan Makari?"

He looked to his right.

"Freeze! Federal agents! TSA! Hands in the air! Don't move!"

There were four agents, three men and one woman. They wore black pants, sky-blue shirts with shiny badges, black neckties, and shoulder boards. On the black shoulder boards, the letters TSA were embroidered in white.

Each agent, with both arms extended, gripped a black pistol pointed straight at his head!

"Hands up and freeze, terrorist punk!" A blinding light beam hit Hasan in the eyes.

He squinted, blocking the blinding light with his hands. "I am sorry. I do not understand."

"Hands up, punk, or I blow your brains out!"

Had the plane turned around? Flown back to Beirut?

A hard blow to his stomach sent Hasan to his knees, gasping for breath.

"Federal agent! TSA!" Someone jammed a gun to his temple.

Someone else grabbed his arms, shackling his wrists behind his back with cold steel handcuffs. "You will follow instructions when given instructions by United States federal agents. Is that clear?"

"Yes, sir."

"Good! Now move! There are people who have a few questions for you. You have some explaining to do."

They grabbed him by the arms, pulled him up from his knees, and shoved him forward.

The blinding lights obscured his visibility, but Hasan by squinting could see they were rushing him down a roped-off corridor in the terminal.

People were lined along the roped-off barriers on each side of the corridor. Armed police officers were standing at regular intervals. Camera flashes exploded as the federal agents rushed him past the crowd.

"Terrorist!" someone shouted from the crowd.

"Murderer!" from a woman's voice.

"Burn in hell, Muslim pig!" a man's voice from off to the right yelled as another flash went off.

"Stand back! Stand back!" a TSA ELITE agent yelled. The agents cleared a path through the bystanders.

"This way!" another ordered.

They stepped off to the left, through a set of large double doors, and were out of the main terminal.

The windowless hallway had narrow concrete walls and steel beams overhead.

Angry shouts of the crowd gave way to clicks of the agents' boots echoing off the concrete floors.

Suddenly, they stopped.

Hasan heard a clinking. One of the agents was fiddling with a large ring of keys. He inserted a key into a large steel door, then pushed the door open. The room was dark, chilly.

The agent flipped on a fluorescent light, revealing an empty room with concrete walls.

"Get in there!" They shoved him inside, slammed the door, and locked it.

Hasan was alone.

• • •

71261 ENGLISH IVY WAY
OFF OLD KEENE MILL ROAD
WEST SPRINGFIELD, VIRGINIA

To any Washington insider, the phrase "inside the Beltway" referred to living inside the "Capital Beltway," meaning any geographic location within the city of Washington, DC, bordering out to the great sixty-mile freeway loop around the city known as Interstate 495.

The upper crust of Washington, from diplomatic officials to high-ranking federal workers to top military brass, often sought a prestigious address "inside the Beltway" in the affluent neighborhoods of Georgetown, Rock Creek Park, Bethesda, Arlington, and Alexandria.

Yet despite the allure of the "in-crowd" cocktail circuit, which ordinarily required residence in a blue-blooded community like Georgetown or Arlington or Alexandria, not all high-ranking officers of the United States military were enamored by the prestigious addresses of back-slapping cocktail sippers.

In the modest nineties-vintage three-story brick townhome off Old Keene Mill Road in West Springfield, Virginia, in a townhouse community called Millwood in an area located *outside* the Beltway, a slender redheaded woman in her early forties, wearing a navy-blue spandex workout suit and white Nikes, stood at her kitchen bar stirring a cup of hot green tea.

The woman had herself once been a naval officer, and a good one. If anyone had attained the professional and personal pedigree to occupy a more prestigious "inside the Beltway" address, it was she.

She attained the rank of lieutenant commander, becoming one of the best-known officers in the Navy JAG Corps. Her father was an admiral in the surface fleet. And now her husband served as a three-star vice admiral at the Pentagon.

But her husband never cared for fancy parties or political butt kissing. They lived where they lived because he had bought this townhouse as a junior officer on an earlier tour at the Pentagon, and when he came back as judge advocate general of the United States Navy, though he could have afforded almost any respectable neighborhood inside the Beltway that he chose, he refused to waste the money.

"If my men can't afford 'inside the Beltway,' and if it's too expensive for our junior officers and enlisted men, then why should I separate myself from them?" he had asked her upon receiving news that he had been selected by the secretary of the Navy to return to Washington as judge advocate general. "And why spend the money?"

Her husband was a leader, yet a man of the people. Brilliant, yet unpretentious. Passionate, yet cool under fire.

Handsome.

They began as bitter rivals, both as Navy lieutenants, fighting like cats and dogs. He won, and the electricity of opposites had left him irresistible to her. That enraged her—at first. But finally, Diane Colcernian, then a lieutenant commander in the United States Navy, surrendered her resistance. That cleft in his chin had sent her over the cliff. They were meant for each other.

And in the Rose Garden at the White House, in a surprise ceremony before the president, he had married her.

Even now, with her quadriceps aching from her vigorous daily workout, she remembered him and smiled. Still. After all these years.

Lights flashing from the flat-screen TV mounted on the kitchen wall caught her attention. TSA agents were leading a man in handcuffs through a tunnel of flashing lights. A message scrolled across the bottom of the screen: "Fox News Exclusive: Suspected terrorist arrested at Philadelphia International Airport."

She reached for the remote and unmuted the TV. The voice of the venerable, long-standing Fox broadcaster Tom Miller filled the open-air townhouse.

"This is Tom Miller with this exclusive, breaking Fox News special report. Fox News has learned that US Homeland Security officers, primarily TSA officers, have arrested a suspected terrorist at the Philadelphia airport.

"The suspected terrorist has been identified as Hasan Makari, who, according to TSA officials, is a suspect in connection with the murder of US ambassador to Lebanon George Madison, murdered by a car bomb in El-Mina in northern Lebanon eleven years ago."

The screen switched to split shots, with a file photo of Ambassador George Madison on the left and an Arab-looking man on the right identified in a caption as "Hasan Makari."

The screen switched back to footage of the handcuffed Arab-looking man being hurried along a corridor in an airport terminal.

Tom Miller's voice again: "Now Fox News has learned that Homeland Security and TSA agents intercepted Makari as he entered the country on a British Airways flight from Lebanon. We are told that the TSA has been investigating this case for some time, although we do not have more details. No comments from the White House, the State Department, or the Justice Department in connection with the capture of what we are told may be a high-profile suspected terrorist. Fox News will bring you more information as soon as we have it. And now we're joined by terrorism expert Edward Lyons, who . . ."

Diane hit the Mute button. Her instinct as a former prosecutor screamed that something seemed fishy.

She picked up her iPhone and punched the first number on her autodial.

Voice mail.

She punched the second number.

Two rings.

"United States Navy. Office of the judge advocate general. Captain Foster speaking. You are on a nonsecure line subject to monitoring. May I help you, sir or ma'am?"

"Kirk?" She was talking to her husband's chief of staff, Captain Kirk Foster. "This is Diane Brewer. Is the admiral available?"

"Afternoon, ma'am," Foster said. "He's on the phone with the secretary of the Navy. Would you like me to interrupt him?"

"Oh no. Just tell him I—"

"Hang on, ma'am, I think he's wrapping up right now."

"Okay."

"Here you go, ma'am."

"Hi, baby." The voice that still made her knees shake. "Sorry I couldn't answer. Had SECNAV on the line. What's cookin'?"

"Have you seen this breaking news story on Fox about an arrest of some suspected terrorist at Philadelphia International?"

"Hang on." A pause. "Kirk, could you pass me that laptop, please?" A briefer pause. "Sorry, Di. No, I haven't seen the report, but the secretary just mentioned it."

"I don't know what, but something seemed odd about it."

"Sounds like the trial lawyer coming out in you. What's odd about it?"

"I don't know." She sipped her tea. "It seemed so orchestrated, so contrived." Another sip. "I mean, why have cameras there at the moment of an arrest? Can you imagine if SEAL Team Six had aired a live broadcast of the raid on bin Laden?"

"No kidding. But you know these federal agent types. Especially TSA. They wish they were SEALs. Heck, they'd even give their left arm if somebody would call them FBI. Hang on a second. I'm going on the Fox website." A second later. "Okay, I see it now. You're right. Something does seem kind of odd about it. Smells like some publicity-loving bureaucrat tipped off the media."

"I know," she said. "I think I hate bureaucrats worse than my daddy did."

"Spoken like a true admiral's daughter."

"How about like an admiral's wife?"

"Now you're talking about the luckiest admiral in the history of the US Navy."

"Ha!" She sighed. "What time will you be home?"

"Let's see . . . around eighteen hundred? That okay?"

"How about I thaw out a couple of rib eyes?"

"Get 'em thawed out. I'll throw them on the grill," he said. "Well done for you. Medium rare for me."

"Can't wait to see you, Admiral Brewer," she said.

"You too, baby!"

• • •

TSA INTERROGATION ROOM
INTERNATIONAL TERMINAL
PHILADELPHIA INTERNATIONAL AIRPORT

Hasan sat alone on the concrete floor in a corner opposite the door. The calendar showed May 1, a season when the warmth of spring should have bloomed in the air outside.

But in this cinder-block windowless cell, hidden in the midst of a major American metropolitan airport, they had jacked the air-conditioning down so low that he was shivering.

His stomach ached with soreness from the punch he had taken. He could not even fathom the treatment he had received. Wasn't this America? The land of the free? The home of the brave?

Thirty minutes had passed since they threw him in this place. He knew this because although they had taken his passport, his visa, his wallet, and his boarding pass for his connecting flight to Norfolk, and although they had not removed the steel handcuffs—for whatever reason—they had not taken his watch. He had set his watch's alarm to go off at the top of the hour to help him remember the time for catching his next plane to Norfolk.

Above his head, in a panel in the ceiling, three fluorescent tubes buzzed, casting a white light in the room. It was the only sound.

Were they watching him?

He scanned the walls and the ceiling, searching for a small hidden camera. He saw nothing.

What a nightmare to start his visit to the land he had dreamed of. Hopefully they would clear this up and let him catch his flight to Norfolk in time for the *Abraham Lincoln*'s return from sea.

But what if they did not have it cleared up in time?

How would he get word to Najib?

The sound of shoes . . . boots . . . *click-clicking* against the floor outside. The clicking grew louder. Now more. The sound of multiple boots!

Perhaps they had the place bugged.

Perhaps they had heard the watch go off.

Jingling of keys.

The doorknob turned.

With a grating squeak from its hinges, the door opened.

He could see three or four in the hallway, milling about, talking. He could not hear what they said. They wore the same uniforms as the agents who confronted him when they threw him in this place—sky-blue shirts, dark pants. They all had guns.

A fat woman with short, cropped hair walked in carrying a metal folding chair.

She unfolded the chair and placed it in the middle of the room. "Stand up and sit in this chair." Her voice was low, deep—a voice that sounded almost like a man's. Her eyes were a pretty shade of green, set in a chubby, stoic face that showed no emotion.

"Yes, ma'am."

He tried to get up, but with his hands cuffed behind his back, he lost his balance and fell down hard on the concrete floor.

"All right," the woman said, "I'll uncuff you. But don't try anything stupid. We've got a dozen armed agents outside. If you try anything, you're a dead man. Do you understand?"

"I will cooperate. But I do not understand why you are holding me."

"I don't care what you understand. Are we clear?"

"Yes, ma'am."

"Roll over and lay on your stomach."

"Yes, ma'am." Hasan twisted himself around, belly down, his lips touching the cold concrete floor. Tears formed in his eyes.

"Martin," the woman snapped. "Come help me."

"Be right there."

More footsteps.

A gun to his head.

"All right, Mohammed," the woman said, "I'll take your cuffs off long enough so you can get up. But Sergeant Johnson here is going to keep this gun on you, and he will pull the trigger if you try anything."

Hasan wanted to plead and tell her that this was a mistake. But something told him to remain silent.

She grabbed his wrist and fiddled with his handcuffs. Then the handcuffs unclasped.

"Okay. Push yourself up and go sit in the chair."

He got on his feet, then sat in the chair.

As Hasan sat, the guard with the gun stepped back, keeping his gun pointed at Hasan.

"All right, Mohammed," the woman said, "put your hands behind the chair."

"My name is Hasan. Not Mohammed."

"You're all Mohammed," the woman sneered. "I don't have time to debate with you about your name. Put your hands behind the chair or I'll arrange to have your hands put anywhere I want them."

"Yes, ma'am."

Before he could comply, she grabbed his arms with a vise-like grip. Her hands seemed too powerful for a woman. She clamped the handcuffs back onto his wrists.

"We're ready, gentlemen."

Two men wearing TSA uniforms rolled a cart into the room from the hallway. A medium-screen television sat on the cart.

As the two men were setting up the television, a third walked in. He carried a clipboard, and his uniform pants were tucked into black combat-looking boots.

"Are you Hasan Makari?"

At least he had gotten the name right. "I am he."

"Tell me, Mr. Makari," the man said as he glared at him, "are you Shiite or Sunni?"

"I am neither," Hasan said. "I am not Muslim."

"What are you?" the man snarled. "Are you Hindu?"

"I am Christian."

"Don't lie to me, terrorist!" The TSA officer grabbed his pistol and whacked it across Hasan's face.

"Aaaahhhhh!"

Hasan jerked his head back. His nose throbbed. Blood ran down his lips and into his mouth.

"Clean the blood off his face," his interrogator ordered.

The fat woman came toward him with a white rag in a gloved hand. He jerked back as she started to wipe off his face.

"Be still, Mohammed." She put a hand on the top of his head and held him while she wiped the cold, wet rag across his face. When she pulled it away, it was drenched in blood. "There. That's got it." She walked out of the room, holding the rag in her hand.

The agent who struck him with the pistol said, "Do we have an understanding that it's not wise to lie in response to my questions, terrorist?"

"I did not lie. I am not a terrorist."

Slap!

Hasan saw stars after the open-handed slap to the left side of his face. The room started spinning.

"Hit him with smelling salts!" The man's sharp voice cut through the fog.

"Hey, Mohammed! Wake up!" It was the voice of the woman again, sounding wavy, as if passing through water.

The smell of ammonia drifted up his nose.

Hard, instinctive coughing popped his eyes open. He blinked hard, gasping for air.

The grogginess evaporated. The room stopped spinning. The man's piercing eyes glared at him.

"Now that we're awake," the man said, "we should become acquainted with one another. I am Inspector Gordon. Federal agent.

United States Transportation Security Administration, United States Department of Homeland Security. I must confess, this is the first time I have ever ordered smelling salts for a terrorist and a murderer. I'd rather shoot a terrorist than revive one. So I must admit my disappointment in ordering smelling salts to your nose rather than a bullet to your brain."

"Please. This is a mistake. I am no terrorist. I love America."

A prolonged belly laugh from the interrogator. "You love America? Now that is funny!" More laughter. "I tell you what. If you love America, then you love movies. Do you not?"

Hasan silently prayed for wisdom. The wrong answer could provoke another pistol-whipping. Perhaps worse.

"Well?" the TSA interrogator pressed. "Do you like movies?"

"Some I like. Some I do not care for."

"Well, then," Gordon said, "since you claim you have not had an opportunity to see many movies, I have some good news for you." He paused, as if expecting Hasan to respond. "The United States government is going to help you make up some lost ground in the movie department. Sergeant?"

Another TSA officer aimed a remote control at the TV.

"I will be interested in hearing your comments about this movie," Gordon said. The screen lit up.

A black limousine.

Motorcycles.

A parade route.

Lebanese and American flags.

Dear God, no! Hasan thought.

"Do I detect a look of recognition in your eyes, Hasan?"

"I remember this day." His stomach knotted.

"I am certain that you do remember this day." The interrogator sneered.

Hasan did not want to look. But he could not take his eyes off the screen.

The footage showed the ambassador's limousine with the Lebanese and American flags flapping over the headlights as it moved along Al Istiklal Boulevard, approaching Mar Elias.

Cold sweat beads formed on his forehead.

On the screen, in slow motion, the ambassador's motorcade approached the intersection of Al Istiklal Boulevard and Mar Elias.

Hasan's heart pounded.

Why would God allow this to happen?

On the screen, the car turned from Al Istiklal to Mar Elias.

Hasan tried not to look. Yet he could not take his eyes off the screen. The shot panned to the crowd. Then a closer shot.

"Freeze it!" Gordon ordered. He stepped to the screen with a pointer. "Closer." The image enlarged. "Still closer!" The picture on the screen enlarged again.

The TSA officer stared at Hasan. "Tell me, Hasan Makari, do you recognize the individual right here standing beside this boy?" He tapped at the screen, pointing at the frozen shot of Hasan and Najib, both of whom were standing under the hot sun in the midst of the crowd, between two men carrying two signs proclaiming "Death to America."

"Yes, I do," Hasan said.

"So am I correct in assuming that this man, at the end of my pointer . . . that this man is you?"

"Yes, that is me."

"And this boy"—*tap, tap*—"do you know this boy as well?"

"Yes. I know the boy."

The TSA officer glared at him. "Who is he?"

"He is my boy, Najib."

"And this is the same boy who now has infiltrated the United States Navy as a petty officer on board the USS *Abraham Lincoln*?"

"Najib is proud to serve in the US Navy. He enlisted legally with the help of a retired US Navy captain that he met at his church. I respectfully disagree with your characterization that he infiltrated the Navy."

Gordon drew his hand back in a striking position, and Hasan instinctively jerked back.

"You aren't here to argue with my word choice. You are here to answer questions. Do you understand?"

"Yes, I understand."

"So. It is true, therefore, is it not, that you and your son were there, and present, at the site, at the time and moment of our ambassador's assassination?"

Hasan nodded.

"Don't nod your head! Speak up! We are recording your statement. Our recorder cannot pick up a nod."

"Yes!" Hasan said. "We stood there alongside the road. We came to greet the ambassador. To welcome him to Tripoli and El-Mina."

"Hmm." The interrogator crossed his arms and stared down at Hasan. "And I take it you came to 'greet'"—he made quotation marks with his fingers—"the ambassador along with your friends? Did you?"

"I am sorry," Hasan said. "I do not understand."

"Your friends!" Gordon snapped. "The ones here. The ones carrying the signs saying 'Death to America.'"

"I do not know those people. I swear it."

"You don't know these people?" Gordon raised his voice. "They are standing beside you! One sign to your left and one to your right! For someone you do not know, you seem cozy with these two."

Hasan did not respond.

"You know, this will go much easier for you if you come clean." A pause. "Tell me, Hasan, the one on your left. What's his name?"

"I do not know him."

"You were standing right with him the whole time."

"No. Not the whole time. He happened to be there."

"Aw, come on. Who is the one on the right?" Gordon tapped at the other man, shown screaming and holding a "Death to America" sign. "Who is he?"

"I do not know."

"Liar!" The veins on each side of his head bulged. "You expect me to believe that moments before our ambassador is killed, you just happened to be standing between two angry Muslims holding 'Death to America' signs, and you can't remember either one of their names?"

"There were others in the crowd holding pro-American signs," Hasan said.

"Ah." This time the TSA investigator wagged his finger in the air. "But you were not holding a pro-American sign, were you? You instead chose to align yourself with someone calling for the death of our ambassador."

"I could not hold any signs, sir. I had my son with me. I could not lose track of him, lest he become lost in the crowd."

"Ha!" Gordon sneered. "So your testimony is that you needed your hands free to keep track of your son?"

"My testimony?" Hasan said. "Am I on trial, sir? Many in the crowd that day did not hold signs."

The TSA investigator leered at him. "Tell me, Hasan. Were there many in the crowd that day giving hand signals to cue a rocket attack on the ambassador's car?"

Hasan hesitated. He prayed silently for wisdom. "I do not understand your question."

"Ah! The same old terrorist refrain. 'I do not understand,'" Gordon said with a tone of mocking sarcasm. "Perhaps this will jar your memory. Roll the tape," he commanded. "Slow motion. Close up."

"Yes, sir."

The image, frozen on the screen, moved again in slow motion.

The ambassador's car turned left from Al Istiklal onto Mar Elias.

As the car turned, another close-up of Hasan flashed on the screen.

How he remembered the excitement of that moment. How proud he felt to be so close to the great American!

The slow-moving image showed Hasan throw his arm up, beginning a frantic wave at the American ambassador. What a happy moment that had been before . . .

"So, Hasan, how do you explain within seconds of your hand signals, the ambassador's limousine exploded?"

"Hand signals?"

"Yes. Hand signals," Gordon said.

"Those weren't hand signals. I was waving at the ambassador."

"Freeze the screen."

The officer froze the screen.

"Close up!"

Another close-up frame showed Hasan pointing straight out.

"I see you are pointing at something. Perhaps signaling something?"

Hasan did not answer.

"Tell me, Hasan. Who are you signaling here? Or rather, what are you signaling?"

Hasan thought. "Wait a minute. This photograph is taken out of context. If you look at the film clip in its context, you will see that I am waving most of the time."

"Oh, I can see that you are waving up to a point," Gordon said. "But then you begin to point. Am I correct?"

Hasan did not respond.

"Well?" Gordon snapped. "Do you deny that you are pointing? Or are we imagining things as we look at the screen?"

"I do not deny what we see on the screen," Hasan said. "But I deny that I remember pointing. I do remember waving at the ambassador just before he died. It has been years."

Gordon nodded and toyed with his chin. "Just waving, and conveniently you do not remember pointing?"

"That is right, sir."

"Then tell me, Hasan, how do you explain this?"

He hesitated, then said, "Explain what?"

"Pull back on that angle and roll the tape, Sergeant."

"Yes, sir."

The screen flashed to a wide angle, still showing Hasan in the picture, his finger pointed out. The screen rolled again, in slow motion. Now in slower motion.

"Freeze it."

As the screen froze again, the tips of three rocket-propelled grenades, airborne, could be seen streaking in from the right side of the screen followed by three trails of smoke.

"Wider angle!"

The image on the screen morphed into a wider view.

On the screen, three RPGs flew at the limousine from the right side of the screen, just as Hasan had pointed from the left side of the screen.

"Okay, roll it."

A TSA guard pressed the remote control, and on the screen was the image as the ambassador's car exploded.

Hasan turned his head, wincing. Watching the explosion again, even on a screen eleven years later and 5,700 miles away, still cut to his core like a knife.

For the moment, the excruciating sensation of reliving that moment proved every bit as painful as the thug tactics that the buffoonish TSA agents had thrown at him the last thirty minutes.

"Do not feign horror with your facial gestures, as if the event that you signaled is now somehow displeasing to you. No one will fall for your hypocritical theatrics."

"I . . ." Hasan hesitated. He had read the words of Solomon, that even a fool appears wise when he remains silent.

"Well," Gordon demanded, "what do you have to say for yourself?"

Hasan did not answer.

The punch across his jaw sent the room into a tailspin, generating a starburst across his eyes.

"Get him up!" someone said. They yanked him up by the arms, pulling him to his feet.

"Get him to the plane!" Gordon's voice was like an echo through a fog.

"Where are you taking me?"

The TSA officers started to rush him back to the hallway.

"Hold him there," Gordon said as he walked over to face Hasan. "You are going to a place where you will have far less incentive to stonewall when you are questioned by a federal agent."

They shoved him along, back down the hall. They reentered the main terminal and were stopped by a wall of blinding lights and camera flashes.

"Stand back!" The TSA officers formed a human wedge and, pushing through the reporters, shielded Hasan in the midst of the wedge.

"Officer! Who is this man?" a reporter shouted.

"Officer, is this man a terrorist?"

"Where are you taking him? What will you do with him?"

"No comment," Gordon snapped.

"Officer. We've heard unofficial reports from some in the TSA that this man killed Ambassador Madison. Is this true?"

"No comment," Gordon snapped again.

"Just one question for the prisoner? Sir, were you involved in the plot to kill the ambassador?"

"Did you kill him?"

"Murderer!"

"I killed no one!" Hasan shouted at the blinding television lights as the TSA masters shoved him through the crowd.

A hand grabbed his mouth. "Shut your mouth, Mohammed."

They crossed to the other side of the terminal and pushed through a set of double doors onto a concrete platform outside.

A gust of warm air and the whine of jet engines greeted them. Hasan squinted in the bright glare of the sun, and as he regained his vision, an officer pointed to a portable aluminum stairway leading down to the tarmac, where a white jet waited.

On the side of the jet, in dark blue, were the words "Department of Homeland Security—United States of America."

"Down the steps. Move!"

Two TSA officers grabbed his arms and pushed him toward the stairway.

"Down the steps, Mohammed!"

Hasan started down the stairway toward the tarmac, but on the fourth step, his foot got caught. He instinctively tried jerking his hands to grab the handrails. But with steel cuffs clasping his wrists behind his back, he fell headfirst down the stairs.

His face smashed into the lower steps. Jets of sharp pain shot through his face and nose and teeth as he lay there, unable to move.

"Get him up!"

They grabbed his arms and yanked him down to the tarmac. His face scraped against the concrete.

"Mohammed, I'm going to uncuff you so you can get up. Don't try anything."

Hasan heard a *click*. A gun barrel was jammed against his head, then the handcuffs slid from his wrists.

"Push yourself up!"

"Please," Hasan said as he pushed against the concrete, trying to get himself up. His eyes locked on the black front wheel of the big Homeland Security jet in front of him.

Two men grabbed him under the arms and yanked him to his feet. Blood was running down his face. He saw only a bright, unfocused swirl of sunlight, airplanes, blue sky, and men rushing about.

"Hey, wipe that blood off his face. The press could be filming this."

"I've got a handkerchief."

"Okay, wipe his face!"

A hand swiped a white handkerchief against his nose.

"Aaaahhhhhhhhhhhhhhhhh!"

"I think he broke his nose. All right. That's the best I can do with the blood, boss."

"That'll do. Get him in the plane."

"Yes, sir. Move, Mohammed. Up the steps."

• • •

DEPARTMENT OF HOMELAND SECURITY
NATIONAL CAPITAL REGION HEADQUARTERS
ST. ELIZABETH'S CAMPUS
ANACOSTIA NEIGHBORHOOD
WASHINGTON, DC

The middle-aged man, slightly portly and balding, crossed his arms over his belly and spun around in his chair. A large window behind his desk gave him a view of his vast brick and electronic kingdom. Beyond that, across the sparkling waters of the Potomac to the shores of Virginia, on the long runways of Ronald Reagan International Airport, a jumbo jet touched down under the sunny Virginia skies.

The Chicago-based architectural firm of Perkins and Will had designed the secretary's office with one of the best views in Washington.

The battle over the construction of this massive project had divided along partisan political lines on Capitol Hill, with Democrats in Congress siding with the Obama administration to build it, and Republicans siding with former House Speaker John Boehner, branding it an expensive waste.

Not that it mattered now.

His kingdom was established. And though the man with his hands folded over his belly was a registered Republican, he smiled, knowing that in this case the good guys—the Democrats in Congress—prevailed, and Congress had spent the money to construct this state-of-the-art facility.

Fallington Strayhorn had registered as Republican because all career Washington insiders had to be registered to one party or the other. But the best career insiders understood that the camaraderie of bureaucratic philosophy that united them extended far beyond the nominal differences relating to the name of their political affiliation.

The role of the bureaucrat wasn't to be political. Both parties had funded his kingdom. Republicans established it under Bush. Democrats expanded it wildly under Obama.

Strayhorn gazed across the Potomac River.

The Reagans and Clintons and Obamas and Mack Williamses and Douglas Surbers and other flavor-of-the-day, flash-in-the-pan politicians would come and go.

Some, like Reagan and Williams, threatened to cut the Washington apparatus. Recently, the trend had gone too far in the wrong direction, with a bunch of budget-cutting garbage rhetoric from Congress and the new administration.

In public, Strayhorn always nodded, appearing to be in agreement with his bosses at the White House. His private thoughts, however, did not match his public comments.

But he knew that in the end, the money faucets were always reopened. Career Washington insiders would remain forever.

The construction of the new Homeland Security headquarters overlooking the Potomac, built on the site of the old St. Elizabeth's Hospital, was a victory for government expansionism and, whether they understood it or not, a victory for all Americans.

"Mr. Secretary?"

Strayhorn wheeled around from his view of the river to pick up the phone on his desk. "Yes, Carol."

"The TSA director is here to see you, sir."

"It's about time he got here. Send him in, please."

"Yes, sir."

The secretary of Homeland Security rose to his feet as an aide pushed open his office door for the arrival of the administrator of the Transportation Security Administration.

"Come in, Billy," Strayhorn bellowed and reached out to shake the hand of his subordinate Billy McNamara, a tall, slender, balding man in his forties and the nation's newest TSA administrator. McNamara, career Civil Service, had proved himself as a loyal TSA man since the Obama administration.

"Thank you, Mr. Secretary," McNamara said. "I'm sorry I'm a bit late, sir. We were finishing the white paper that you had requested."

"Have a seat, Billy."

"Thank you, sir."

"Before we get to the white paper, it looks like your people have done a decent job with the situation in Philadelphia. I've been following some of the events on Fox and CNN. There seems to be some positive publicity so far. We need all the positive publicity we can get. You know as well as I do that some of our renegade Tea Party Republicans are talking cuts again. Our House leadership is having a hard time keeping them under control."

"I'm well aware, sir. We've gotten a slew of congressional inquiries in the last week alone. Some are even talking about defunding or eliminating TSA. Congressman Barnes from Texas is on a rampage."

"Barnes is out of control," Strayhorn said. "I wish the president would call him on the carpet."

"Where does the president stand on all this budget-cutting talk from these Tea Party types?" McNamara asked.

"Hard to say, Billy. He's new. He's got other fish to fry. He's a hard-liner in the War on Terror and on China. He's big on defense but talks a fiscal conservative line on domestic programs. If push came to shove, I've got a feeling he might side with some of these Tea Party kooks. That's why we have to walk a fine line here. We have to make it appear on the outside that we're toeing the party line with the president while at the same time protecting the interests of the department."

McNamara nodded. "Agreed, sir."

"Tell me"—Secretary Strayhorn took a sip of coffee—"what's our current situation in Philadelphia?"

"The ground officer in charge is Inspector John Gordon, one of our more experienced armed air marshal officers. All of the officers on the ground handling the Makari arrest are armed air marshals. As you're aware, sir, air marshals are currently the only regular TSA agents authorized to carry weapons."

"Hopefully, that changes soon."

"Agreed, Mr. Secretary. Gordon and his men better keep everything under control. I hear they're getting this Hasan Makari on the plane as we speak, sir. Our PR people have slipped talking points to the press, along with mug shots of Makari, with the credit line 'photo courtesy of TSA.'"

Strayhorn nodded. "Nice touch. I like it. Keep the agency's name in front of the voters and in front of Congress."

"Thank you, sir. Our PR people are on top of it. We have a presser scheduled at TSA headquarters in one hour. As the cabinet member over the agency, you're welcome to join me at the press conference, Mr. Secretary."

Strayhorn crossed his arms. "Since the public sees this as a TSA operation, let's not obfuscate things. No, I think it's best if you appear alone as TSA administrator. There's a time and place for me to appear in the future, but not now. Not yet."

"Very well, Mr. Secretary."

"Now, about this white paper. You say you have it?"

"Yes, sir."

"And you're sure you've maintained absolute secrecy on this?"

"Yes, sir."

"Because you know, if this thing leaked, with this Makari arrest going on, we'd have a colossal disaster on our hands."

"Yes, sir. Understood. At this point, only three members of the general counsel's staff have seen the document, and they were involved in drafting it with my input. Then there's me and now you, sir."

"Very good," Strayhorn said. "Tell you what. Why don't you head back to TSA to prepare for your press conference? You can leave the paper with me, I'll study it, and we'll discuss it in a day or so."

"Yes, Mr. Secretary." The TSA administrator stood up, pulled a package from his briefcase, and laid it on Strayhorn's desk.

"You're still planning to do the other press conference in the morning?"

"Yes, sir. We want to give the networks the chance to digest the news of the arrest today. We'll announce tonight that we will have an important press conference in the morning. Word will get out, and members of Congress will tune in. Our PR people are telling us the presser will have maximum impact by letting the media chew on it all night."

"Excellent thinking, Billy. We need to milk this for all it's worth."

"Thank you, sir."

"Anyway, good luck with your press conference today." Strayhorn grasped the hand of his subordinate. McNamara's handshake was the wimpish fish shake of the professional bureaucrat.

But that was exactly why Strayhorn handpicked him. McNamara's lack of ambition and his team-player mentality would advance the dual interests of the TSA and of Homeland Security. Plus, McNamara would keep his mouth shut. The Navy's famed saying "Loose lips sink ships" also rang true within the federal bureaucracy.

Loose lips and self-appointed whistleblowers had brought great embarrassment upon the State Department in the wake of the terror attacks on Benghazi.

He thought of the traitorous insiders who had brought great embarrassment upon the IRS's auditing practices during the Obama administration, including the grilling of one of its directors by irate members of Congress.

Confidentiality and information control were essential to the effective operation of any agency. That meant selecting trustworthy bureaucrats who lacked personal ambition, aside from the ambition of drawing a paycheck and perpetuating the agency.

Strayhorn personally selected these personality types to work under him. In this way, he would avoid the type of personal embarrassment that had befallen former secretary of state Hillary Clinton and former IRS director Steven Miller.

He would not tolerate traitorous information leakage at Homeland Security. His secret historic plans for the department—to make it the greatest, most powerful department in the executive branch—demanded confidentiality!

He would succeed with bureaucrats like McNamara. Effective. Unambitious. Tight-lipped with expert paper-pushing abilities.

Strayhorn opened the packet McNamara had left on his desk and pulled out the document.

Confidential White Paper
United States Department of Homeland Security
Transportation Security Administration
Overview of the SITUS Project
Proposals for Logistical Implementation

TOP SECRET
Eyes Only Approval by the Secretary

He smiled. Goose bumps crawled over his shoulders and arms.
His great vision would soon become reality.

. . .

71261 ENGLISH IVY WAY
WEST SPRINGFIELD, VIRGINIA
1 HOUR LATER

Diane Brewer, dressed in a white tennis skirt and pink polo shirt,
checked her watch as she stepped out onto the front stoop of the townhouse. If she hurried, she could make it to Macy's to purchase a few
items before heading to Arlington for a tennis date with Admiral
Lettow's wife at Fort Myer.

The lime-green summer dress on sale was to die for. And Zack
loved her in green. He said it brought out the color of her eyes. She
had just called. One remained in a size 4 and would be gone soon if
she didn't hurry. She wanted to surprise Zack when he got home. That
thought brought a smile to her face.

If she left now, she could grab the dress, try it on, and buy it, but
she would be late for her tennis match.

Maybe she should phone in her credit card and tell them to hold
the dress.

But what if it didn't fit?

She made a command decision. She'd stop by the mall.

Besides, it wasn't like Admiral Lettow had more stars on his collar
than Zack. Their husbands were both staff officers—Zack, the head
of Navy lawyers, and Jeff Lettow, the chief of chaplains. No need for
either admiral's wife to kowtow to the other.

Besides, Crystal Lettow was perpetually late. And Crystal would
never pass up a deal at the mall, especially not for a tennis match.

Diane slid into her Audi convertible, cranked the engine, and opened the top, relishing the sun and the warm breeze caressing her forehead and flowing through her hair.

She backed the Audi out her driveway and turned down English Ivy.

Just as she reached the entrance of the neighborhood, before she turned onto Old Keene Mill Road, she remembered.

"My tennis racket."

She pumped her brakes, swinging the Audi into a tight U-turn. Zack would have to wait on the sundress surprise. Oh well. She had a couple of other options in the closet that he'd not seen in a while.

Not to worry. Zack adored her even if she wore the same thing for a solid month.

She smiled.

Wheeling the Audi into the driveway, she got out, slipped the key in the front door, opened it, and punched in the code to shut off the irritating *beep-beep-beep* of the alarm system.

She stepped into the townhouse, jogged up two flights of stairs to the cathedral-ceilinged master bedroom, grabbed her tennis racket from the closet, then ran back down to the main deck.

The image on the flat screen stopped her in her tracks.

The words on the bottom of the screen proclaimed, "TSA Administrator McNamara Addresses Press on Arrest of Terrorist."

She watched the wimpish-looking bureaucrat with pale skin standing behind the podium. *This must be the new TSA administrator,* she thought.

She picked up the remote and unmuted the TV.

"This is a great day for the TSA and a great day for America. Today the agency has proven its value in maintaining security at the nation's airports and as a crack investigative agency to be deployed in the War on Terror. Like Osama bin Laden, Hasan Makari has been on the terror watch list for years. What a watershed day for TSA, and for the entire nation. We take great pride in knowing that TSA cracked the case. I'd like to thank . . ."

Her phone rang.

Zack.

She muted the TV.

"Hi, Zack."

"Hi, sweetie. What's up?"

"I was headed out to play tennis with Crystal and forgot my racket. When I came in, this new TSA guy is on the tube claiming credit for the biggest arrest since bin Laden. These wimps make my skin crawl. I'm so glad I'm married to a handsome he-man." She chuckled.

"Listen, baby, I'm afraid your handsome he-man won't be home for dinner."

"Really?" What now? She couldn't contain her disappointment. "What? The secretary of the Navy again?"

"I wish. I'm going to Norfolk."

"On such short notice?"

"Afraid so."

"Are you driving down?"

"No, we're taking the chopper."

"Are you taking Kirk?"

"Yep. Kirk and Commander Melesky."

They'd been married for eight years now, but even still, it crushed her when they were apart. "You can't stop by for a few minutes first?"

"I wish."

"I'll make it worth your while."

He laughed. "Don't tempt me."

"But I *love* tempting you."

"I know you do. But this is a hot matter, and I have to deal with it. I'll be back as soon as I can, Diane. I'll miss you."

"I love you."

"Love you too."

The line went dead.

Diane looked up at the flat screen and cut the power.

Time for tennis.

• • •

They had shoved him into a small jump seat and chained his cuffs to a bar bolted into the bulkhead. Then they cut all the lights in the cabin and closed the door.

At least they had not hit him since the flight took off from Philadelphia. But the deep, painful throbbing in his face and nose reminded him of their brutality.

How long had he been strapped in the plane? He guessed at least three hours because he knew his body could last only two and a half hours without a bathroom break.

The sharp pain in his bladder had become unbearable some time ago. He finally had lost control, relieving himself in his pants. Now the throbbing in his head and nose had subsided a bit.

About twenty minutes ago, after the accident in his pants, the plane had gone through severe turbulence. The bumping started as sporadic, then became more violent. In the dark cabin with no visibility, each hard bump, each sudden drop in altitude, each rattling sound seemed magnified.

Jets of pain shot through his mouth. The TSA bullies had broken a tooth when they punched him.

Through the darkness, he saw a jump seat in front of him and a small solitary red light, about the size of a Christmas tree light, burning up in the forward section of the plane, over what appeared to be the closed entryway to the cockpit.

The Americans had transformed this jet into a dark prison plane.

With the plane flying smoothly again, his mind wandered back to the days of his youth, to the stories Eugene Allison had told him about the great apostle Paul being held in prison for his faith. Eugene Allison had warned him of the cost of following Christ.

He remembered the words of the missionary even to this day.

"Hasan, the time is coming when they'll imprison us for our faith in Christ and torture us. And not just in places like Iran or Lebanon. I'm talking America too. So if you accept this Jesus, you need to know that doing so could come at a heavy cost."

"I want to accept him, knowing all the costs," Hasan had said that night. The missionary had led him in something called "the sinner's prayer" and given him some Bible verses.

Years later, memories of that night had never faded, and Hasan never forgot what Eugene Allison had told him about Paul being in prison. Hasan went on to memorize portions from the apostle's letters about imprisonment.

Was this, now, his personal punishment for embracing Christianity? His price for following Christ?

That made no sense.

His interrogators had referred to him, sarcastically, as "Mohammed" and accused him of being Muslim.

"Jesus, what's going on? Please help me!"

Najib!

Wherever they were taking him, it probably was not Norfolk. Najib would sail into port, and he would not be there.

How would he get a message to Najib?

Even if the face bashing he had taken had broken his nose, his tear ducts had not been damaged. Thinking of Najib standing alone, searching for him, not knowing his fate . . . Cool tears flowed across his bruised cheeks, accentuating the throbbing pain.

Najib was all he had here on earth. In the dark reality of this, the darkest hour of his life, he could not stop thinking about his son.

He had replayed the scene in his mind a thousand times—and now a thousand and one. He had planned on shooting Najib a smart salute the moment he stepped off the ship. Then he would hug him and not want to let go.

But now, in this dark prison plane, Hasan wondered if he would ever see Najib again before they met in heaven.

His throat thickened, signaling the onset of more tears.

For the moment, the darkness in the plane was a blessing. They could not see him cry. Still, he sensed their evil presence, like predators hiding in the shadows.

Hasan closed his eyes and prayed. Perhaps he could sleep.

A change in the whine of the engines was followed by pressure in his ears. The high-pitched sound of the engine morphed into a muted garble. The pressure intensified, as if someone had connected a pressurized tire pump to his head.

Hasan tried working his jaw to relieve the tightening, but the pain in his jaw would not permit it.

The pressure sharpened, like someone pushing a power drill in each ear. His head was like a balloon about to explode. He winced from the pain, and then . . .

Pop . . .

Pressure relieved. Thank God.

The sound of the jet engines returned, at least halfway, and then his stomach jumped up as the plane dropped.

Another drop. Then another pressure-relieving *pop* in his right ear, leaving his right ear liberated. His left ear was still half plugged.

A whining sound: the plane's landing gear activating.

His prayer was whispered. "Lord, whatever happens to me, please protect Najib. Please be with him."

Another *pop*. This time in his left ear.

A bumping jolt. The thudding sensation of rubber wheels on a concrete runway. A reverse swooshing from the engines, then braking.

"The Lord is my shepherd; I shall not want. He maketh me to lie down in green pastures: he leadeth me beside the still waters . . ."

The plane rolled to a stop.

Bright lights flooded the cabin, blinding his dilated pupils, sending his eyes into a protective squint.

"Okay, Mohammed, we're here." The gruff voice came from the back of the plane. "We're home."

Hasan looked up. Two TSA guards stood in the aisle. One stepped past his seat and leered down at him with piercing black eyes.

"Hold your hands out," the other said. But the guard's demands were impossible, since Hasan's hands were chained to the bulkhead.

Hasan remained silent.

The guard reached over him and inserted a key in the dead-bolt lock. The chains fell to the deck of the aircraft. The guard did not unlock the handcuffs.

"Okay, get up." The guard tipped his head back, displaying a cocky-looking smugness on his face.

Hasan pushed up with his legs and discovered that his right foot was asleep.

"Move to the back of the plane," the guard ordered.

Hasan stepped into the aisle between the empty seats, but his right foot had not recovered sensation. Unable to brace himself because his hands were cuffed behind his back, he stumbled to his knees.

"What's the matter with you, Mohammed?" The guard grabbed him by the collar, yanking him to his feet. "You'll have plenty of time to pray to Mecca where you're going."

"I am sorry. I stumbled."

"Move!" A hard shove in the back.

Hasan stepped forward. An armed TSA agent standing in the back of the plane, in front of the rear restroom, pushed open the door of the cabin. Sunlight flooded the back of the rear cabin.

The TSA guard behind Hasan said, "Keep moving."

Halfway down the aisleway, Hasan caught a whiff of warm, moist, salty air, which brought back memories of that day in Tripoli, in El-Mina.

"Keep moving."

Hasan reached the tail section of the aircraft, where the rear guard pointed out the door. "Out of the plane!"

He stepped out onto the top of the portable Jetway. The airstrip lay on a narrow peninsula, with aqua-blue water on both sides.

Several US Navy and US Coast Guard planes sat on the tarmac. At the bottom of the stairway, a group of armed men in light-colored camouflage military uniforms, wearing caps and boots, stood in a semicircle. On their sleeves they wore armbands with the initials "SP." A tan Humvee sat parked behind the men.

"Okay, down the steps. Those men waiting down there are US Marines. When you reach the tarmac, if you know what's good for you, you will do what they tell you to do."

"Yes, sir."

The salty breeze whipped up again as Hasan took his first step down into a sun-drenched late afternoon. With his hands remaining cuffed behind him, Hasan proceeded carefully. He stepped down the portable stairway with his left foot, then his right.

"Get a move on!"

He took another step. Then another. The tropical breeze caressing his face was refreshing. He was grateful to be outside.

The TSA officers up in the plane behind him barked at him a couple more times, but he paid them no mind and stepped down onto the tarmac.

A uniformed man stepped forward.

"Mr. Makari. I'm Captain Roger Kohlman. United States Marine Corps. If you would follow me please, sir, we're going to have you take a seat in the back of this Humvee over here. A couple of my men will be riding with you."

"Certainly, Captain," Hasan said. He walked toward the Humvee with the two Marines, one on each side.

A Marine opened a back door and directed him into the seat. Hasan noted the difference in how they treated him. They had a matter-of-fact, polite professionalism. They were US Marines.

This brief handover from the TSA to the Marines gave him hope that the United States military, of which his son was a member, was way above the TSA gangsters.

A Marine guard, a pistol in his side holster, got in the backseat beside Hasan. Another armed Marine got in on the other side of the Humvee, squeezing Hasan into the middle of the backseat.

Captain Kohlman got into the front seat, beside the driver.

They remained silent as the Humvee moved forward.

As they pulled away from the plane, Hasan looked over his shoulder. Another Humvee full of Marines followed close behind. He had not noticed this second Humvee when he stepped off the plane.

They drove past the terminal, leaving the runway behind.

The large sign posted beside the terminal sent his body into an instant chill.

Welcome to
Leeward Point Field
United States Naval Station
Guantánamo Bay, Cuba

• • •

FLIGHT DECK
USS *ABRAHAM LINCOLN*
APPROACHING NORFOLK NAVAL STATION

The long string of warships, a tapestry of battleship-gray lined up along the four-mile waterfront of the Norfolk Naval Station, represented the mightiest display of concentrated firepower of any place on earth.

A quarter mile out, in bay waters that were beginning to stir, a long, sonorous blast from a navigation tug off to the starboard of the supercarrier USS *Abraham Lincoln* signaled that the concentration of firepower along the world's largest naval base would soon grow greater.

All along the perimeter of the *Lincoln's* flight deck, more than a thousand sailors stood shoulder to shoulder at parade rest in white uniforms and Dixie cup hats.

Along both sides of the carrier, four navigation tugs pushed the great ship toward Pier 12, to be moored alongside her sister ship, USS *George H. W. Bush.*

Petty Officer Najib Makari, standing along the starboard of the ship, held his shoulders back and jutted his chin out. Keeping his head straight in the afternoon Virginia breeze, he allowed his eyes to wander to the left and right, scanning the large crowd of well-wishers and family members down along the pier.

He bit his lower lip to suppress his smile. Warriors weren't supposed to smile, which would prove unmilitary if his father happened to be watching him through binoculars. Najib would look the part of the brave, disciplined American sailor to make his father proud.

Of course his father, whether he had spotted Najib yet or not, was out there smiling, taking pride in the accomplishments of his son. Neither father nor son would ever forget this day, and never had Najib been prouder to be a member of the United States Navy.

For the moment, anyway, the mishaps that had plagued the ship for the last couple of days—the loss of a jet in the Atlantic, the still-uncertain fate of the pilot, Lieutenant Mark Garcia, whose plane had plunged into the ocean on takeoff—faded in the pageantry of the moment.

Najib found himself lost in it all. He could not wait to see the look on his father's face when they were reunited.

The navigation tugs pushed the *Lincoln* up against Pier 12 as Najib stood on the starboard edge of the flight deck, the side facing the cheering crowds down on the pier.

He searched along the pier, hoping to catch a glimpse of his father. Amid the cheering throngs and smiling faces, dozens of signs were held by loved ones hailing the return of the great ship.

Welcome Home, Petty Officer Martinez!
We Love You, Daddy!—Helena and John Paul
Lieutenant Evans—Welcome Home and Roll Tide!
Chief Gimler and the US Navy! #1 in Our Hearts!

Hundreds of signs were interspersed in the crowd of several thousand. Between the signs, throughout the crowd, camera strobes exploded, and television crews stood along the dock, determined to cover the triumphant return on the evening news.

On the other side of Decatur Avenue, across the street from Pier

12, the base McDonald's had a sign draped on it that read "Welcome Home, USS *Abraham Lincoln*."

The signs provided no clue as to the whereabouts of Hasan Makari in the crowd. Najib's dad was too reserved for such attention-getting flamboyance.

Down below, on the hangar bay, as the Navy band transitioned from "Anchors Aweigh" to "God Bless America," sailors threw ropes at shore station crewmen on the pier.

Pier crewmen started moving catwalks into place. A few minutes later, Najib's shipmates began walking across the gangplanks, stepping on the pier to a sea of hugs, kisses, high fives, and handshakes.

One major advantage of being assigned to the honorary deck detail on the flight deck was that the high vantage point allowed one to see everything down below as the ship pulled into port.

The biggest disadvantage—the deck detail would disembark the ship last. Witnessing the joyous family reunions down below, Najib wished he had not been selected for deck detail, as his heart pounded with the excitement of being with his father again!

His mind wandered to the coming evening. He would take his father out for a big, fat, juicy American steak at the Norfolk Chophouse, the highly popular, long-standing steak house near the main gate of the naval base.

Najib loved the Chophouse. Fabulous food. A reasonably priced menu fitting the budget of a third-class petty officer.

"Petty Officer Makari."

Najib turned around. The ship's executive officer, Commander Hugh Bennett, was walking out from the superstructure. This marked the first time the XO had ever called his name.

"Yes, sir."

"Would you step over here, please?"

Two men in dark shades and navy-blue civilian suits stood beside the XO, along with Master Chief Martinez, the ship's master at arms.

Najib broke from the ranks and walked across the flight deck toward the XO.

"Sir." Najib popped a salute at Commander Bennett.

"Petty Officer." Bennett returned the salute. "Please follow us."

"You want me to fall out of formation, sir?"

"You heard me, son. Fall out and come with us."

"Yes, sir."

Najib swallowed hard and followed the men to the ship's towering steel superstructure looming over the flight deck, referred to as the "Island."

Something felt odd. Who were these men in navy-blue suits?

They stepped inside the main doors of the Island. Bright fluorescent lighting flooded the large steel interior spaces. Only a skeleton crew remained inside, as most of the ship's crew members had gathered on the deck and were now forming into lines to cross the catwalks for liberty.

The XO directed the two men to walk over to his left. Then he looked at Najib. "Petty Officer Makari, this is Special Agent Harry Kilnap of the Naval Criminal Investigative Service."

One of the blue-suited men stepped forward and stood just in front of Najib. "Aviation Boatswain's Mate Third Class Najib Makari?"

"Yes, sir."

"I'm Special Agent Harry Kilnap, a federal agent. Naval Criminal Investigative Service." Kilnap glared angrily with piercing eyes. His salt-and-pepper hair sported a grayish streak. His baritone voice revealed a twisted Yankee-sounding accent like that of the sailors from Long Island.

Najib stood still, at first unable to speak. Then he managed to say, "Yes, sir."

"It is my duty to inform you that you are under arrest."

"Under arrest? For what?"

"Master Chief," Kilnap said, "please cuff the prisoner."

"But—"

"I'm sorry, Makari." The master at arms stepped behind Najib, grabbed his arms, and cuffed his wrists behind his back.

"Petty Officer Makari," Kilnap said, "it is my duty to inform you of your rights under Article 31 of the Uniform Code of Military Justice and the Fifth Amendment of the United States Constitution.

"You have the right to remain silent. If you give up the right to remain silent, anything you say can and will be used against you. You have the right to speak with an attorney, and to have an attorney present with you during questioning . . ."

• • •

HEADQUARTERS
MID-ATLANTIC REGION LEGAL SERVICE OFFICE
DEFENSE SERVICE OFFICE SOUTHEAST
US NAVY JAG CORPS
US NAVAL BASE
NORFOLK, VIRGINIA

The United States naval officer, decked out in his comfortable working khaki uniform, wore the two silver bars of a Navy lieutenant on his right collar and the millrind insignia of the US Navy JAG Corps on his left collar. He leaned back in his chair, kicked his feet up on his desk, and watched the clock on his wall *tick-tick-tick* toward 1700 hours.

He was listening to the carryings-on of his latest dalliance, Lieutenant Commander Amy Debenedetto, who at that moment sat at her desk at the Regional Legal Service Detachment at Oceana Naval Air Station, some twenty miles away.

They had dated twice, secretly, in the face of the institutional military taboo against dating senior officers. Frankly, their dates had been out of this world.

Amy sizzled. But why did they all want to get so serious so fast?

"Talk to me, Matt," she said. "What are you afraid of?"

"Me? Afraid?" He chuckled. "You know I'm not afraid of anything, ma'am."

"Stop calling me ma'am. You don't have to do that in private. You weren't doing that on your sailboat last Friday night."

He smiled. "I guess you've got a point about that."

"That's part of the attraction." A flirtatious yearning saturated her voice. "You're the only Navy JAG defense lawyer who lives on a sailboat. How can a girl not be attracted to that?"

He chuckled again and looked out his window at the sparkling waters of Hampton Roads. "That I plead guilty to, ma'am."

"I told you to stop calling me ma'am!" A short pause. "You make me sound like your grandmother!"

"Okay! Okay! To the charge of being the only JAG officer who lives on a sailboat, I plead guilty." A pause. A smile. "You're a great-looking sailor!"

"I like that." A thrill in her voice. "That's more consistent with your sailboat language, if I recall correctly."

"Oh, I'm sure you recall correctly," he said. "Just make sure I don't slip up with that in public."

"Oh, I don't envision any slipups from you. Besides, you know I'm just one pay grade above you, Matt. I'm not that much older, so it's not like an admiral dating an ensign or something. One pay grade difference can work. Besides, we're not even in the same chain of command. That could be raised as a defense if anybody said anything."

Matt shifted his feet, from right over left to left over right. "No, we're not in the same chain of command. At least not yet. Right now, you're in charge of helping sailors with wills and powers of attorney. But if they make you senior trial counsel at Oceana, like they've discussed, then you become a supervising prosecutor, and we'd have a direct conflict of interest. And you know it."

Silence.

"Also," he added in the face of her silence, "although it's true that we're only one grade apart, with me being a lieutenant and you being a lieutenant commander, you know as well as I do that you're up for the next promotion board to commander, and if you get picked up, there will be two full pay grades between us. A lieutenant and a lieutenant commander is one thing . . . but a lieutenant and a full commander? Please. Tell me that won't bring out the fraternization nannies."

Three sharp raps on his door.

"Hang on, Amy." He put his hand over the phone. "Come in."

The door opened.

The sudden sight of high-ranking brass.

"Attention on deck!"

Matt slammed down the phone and shot up from his chair, coming to full attention.

For the first time in his young naval career, he was speechless. Of course, this marked the first time that a three-star admiral had paid a visit to his office with a full-bird navy captain.

His mind flew into instant hyper-gear. Why were they here? How had he screwed up?

He must be busted. That had to be it. Someone had blown the whistle. People talk. Maybe someone saw Amy come onto his sailboat down at the marina. He should have known better. Women talk.

The scuttlebutt got out. NCIS probably followed her to his sailboat. They probably had pictures and a full report.

He tried to think. Had he closed the curtains over the portholes? He couldn't remember. Sweat beaded on his forehead.

Now his commanding officer and the judge advocate general of the Navy had come to personally bust him. Perhaps take him to admiral's mast here on the spot. Or even worse, announce that they were convening a summary court-martial against him for unlawful fraternization.

Why did he have to like an older, higher-ranking woman?

"Captain Rudy. Admiral Brewer. To what do I owe this honor so late in the afternoon?"

"Are you saying, Lieutenant Davis, that our presence here is an honor only because we are here at a time, as you describe it, that is 'late in the afternoon'?"

The words of the admiral stunned him again. Matt Davis stood in awe of only a handful of people. But the judge advocate general of the Navy, Vice Admiral Zack Brewer, was in that group.

Admiral Brewer's sudden presence in his office was the JAG Corps equivalent of Moses descending from Mount Sinai.

Matt's tongue froze, then unthawed again. "Sorry, sir. No, sir. Of course it's an honor to have you here any hour of the day. A Freudian slip, sir."

"Nice recovery, Lieutenant," Brewer said. "Listen, son, the captain and I need a word with you. And for your sake, it would be better if what we have to say is not broadcast to the public. But if we have to stand out here in the passageway and tell you what we have to tell you through this open door, there's no telling who might hear."

He was cooked. He knew it. "My apologies, Admiral. Captain. Please come into my office. But my office is small. Perhaps there's another place that's more comfortable for you. Perhaps you would wish to chat in the captain's office or somewhere else?"

Brewer looked at Rudy. "What do you think, Captain Rudy?"

"The lieutenant's office is fine with me, Admiral. As far as I'm concerned, the sooner we get this done, the better."

"Agreed." Brewer stepped in and motioned for Rudy to follow him. "Captain Foster?"

"Yes, sir." Another officer stepped into view in the hallway. Captain Kirk Foster was Brewer's chief of staff.

"Would you get the door, please? We need some privacy with Lieutenant Davis."

"Certainly, Admiral." Foster closed the door, leaving Matt alone with Brewer and Rudy in the small office.

"Sit down, Lieutenant," Brewer ordered.

"Yes, sir."

"Mind if the captain and I also sit?"

"Not at all, sir. Please, have a seat."

"I think we'll take you up on that." Brewer sat in the chair on the left facing Matt's desk. Rudy took the chair on the right.

"So," Brewer began and held Matt's eyes with a penetrating stare, "I hear you live on a sailboat, Lieutenant Davis."

They knew.

Brewer in his day was the best trial lawyer in the Navy. In fact, perhaps the best in the world. And he had proffered the question with the savvy of a skilled cross-examiner about to pounce on his helpless prey.

Matt cleared his throat. "Yes, sir, Admiral. I keep her moored over at the Little Creek Marina."

"Good choice." Brewer nodded. "Tell me about her."

"Thirty-foot sloop. Manufactured by Alpha out of Seattle. She runs a mainsail and a jib under way. Makes for a great place to bunk out during the week, sir. Sure beats paying rent, sir."

"Sounds sleek," Brewer said. "What did you name her?"

Matt looked away, then looked back at Brewer. "Well, sir . . . I . . . I named her *Not Guilty*, sir."

The admiral raised an eyebrow. "So did you name her that because of your string of 'not guilty' verdicts in the last ten general courts-martial you've tried? Or because of your supreme confidence in your own abilities as a defense counsel?"

Matt looked down. "Sir, I christened her *Not Guilty* when I found out they were sending me here from the Justice School to be a defense counsel. So at the time I had no 'not guilty' verdicts under my belt. So, to answer your question, Admiral Brewer, I suppose the name had more to do with my confidence than with my track record. Because at the time, I had no track record, sir."

Brewer chuckled. "I like a little cockiness in a trial lawyer. Of course, sometimes that cockiness can get you into trouble. Did you know that, Lieutenant Davis?"

"I don't understand, sir."

"How many portholes have you got on that boat?"

"Four, sir." Matt thought. "Two on the port cabin. Two on the starboard."

"Sounds about right," Brewer said. "Tell me, Lieutenant. You keep the curtains drawn over the portholes while you're in port?"

"Sir?"

"You know"—Brewer toyed with his chin—"might not be a bad idea. You know, for security purposes. I mean, there's light security around these public marinas. You never know who might be lingering around."

"Yes, sir."

"You know, you aren't the first JAG officer I've known to live on a sailboat."

"Sir?"

"Back when I was a young Navy prosecutor in San Diego, we had a defense counsel. A Lieutenant Morris. A kind of freewheeling, non-conformist type, pretty good in a courtroom. Morris tried all kinds of off-the-wall tactics. The kind of stuff that drove the commands crazy. Know what I mean?"

"I think so, sir." But Matt was lying.

"Anyway, Morris bought a sailboat and kept it moored at the San Diego Yacht Club down near Shelter Island. He lived on it when he became a defense counsel at the Defense Command in San Diego." Brewer crossed his arms. "Know what turned out to be his downfall?"

Matt caught himself bouncing his knee under his desk. "Ah . . . no, sir."

"Women," Brewer said matter-of-factly.

"Women?"

"Yep. Seems like ole Lieutenant Morris had a thing for a couple of good-looking enlisted paralegals. Started taking one of 'em out to that sailboat of his. Got busted."

Matt's heart pounded like at the end of a hundred-yard sprint.

"Went to admiral's mast, if I recall," Admiral Brewer added. "Then disappeared."

Brewer stopped talking, then glanced over at Captain Rudy, who shook his head.

Matt decided not to speak unless ordered to speak. If ordered, he might invoke his rights under Article 31.

"Anyway," Admiral Brewer said, "we're not here to talk about your sailboat."

Matt exhaled. "You're not?"

"Why would you think we would be?"

"Aah . . ."

"I'm here to talk to you about a sensitive special assignment that I'm going to order you to take."

Matt sat back, unsure of what to make of it all. Brewer had a reputation for making people squirm. Had he heard that right? A new assignment? Perhaps Adak, Alaska. The ultimate dreaded duty station in the Aleutians that all JAG officers tried to avoid.

"Tell me, Lieutenant . . . how do you like cold weather?"

No doubt.

Adak.

They were transferring him as far away from Amy as possible.

"I'm prepared to serve wherever my country needs me, sir."

"I'm glad to hear that, Lieutenant. But you didn't answer my question."

"Permission to speak freely, sir?"

"Of course," Brewer said. "Not that you've asked permission for anything else recently, but go ahead."

"Well, sir. I don't do well in cold weather. But I am happy to execute any orders you have for me."

"Well, today is your lucky day, Lieutenant, because this time, I'm not sending you to Adak."

"Thank you, sir."

Brewer was toying with him. "In fact, where I'm sending you, not only is the weather gonna be a ton hotter than Adak, but your assignment will be even hotter, from a professional standpoint." Brewer leaned back in his seat. "Son, get ready to pack your bags. You're going to Guantánamo Bay."

Matt hesitated, and then the admiral's words hit him. "GITMO?" Matt looked at Captain Rudy. "Am I being transferred to the detachment down there?"

"Not permanently. But your assignment could be prolonged and high profile," Captain Rudy said.

"I don't understand, sir."

Admiral Brewer stared at him for a moment, as if deciding whether to say anything else. Or perhaps he would change his mind about Adak.

"Are you familiar with the Guantánamo Military Commissions?"

"You mean the terrorist court at GITMO, sir?"

"Some people might call it that, I suppose," Brewer said.

"I'm somewhat familiar with it," Matt said.

"What do you know about it?"

"Let's see." Matt scratched his chin. "Top-secret court. Veiled in secrecy. Established during the Bush administration at the US Naval Base in Cuba so accused terrorists could be tried outside the United States. Part of the reason was to keep terrorists off of US soil. But another part of the reason was to try these cases outside of the US so that these defendants would not have the benefits of the constitutional rights afforded to Americans in a court of law."

Brewer nodded. "How much have you been paying attention to the news the last couple of days?"

"I'm afraid I've gotten behind on my web browsing the last couple of days, sir."

"Yes. I understand you've been detained by other matters," Brewer said. "But if you had not been detained, you'd know that the TSA arrested a Lebanese national at Philadelphia International Airport—"

"Oh yes," Matt said. "I saw the Google headline on that but didn't get a chance to read much in detail. Something about this guy they're accusing of having something to do with the assassination of the US ambassador a few years ago?"

"Maybe you haven't been as distracted as I thought, Lieutenant." Brewer looked at Rudy. "Captain, pass me that dossier, please."

"Aye, sir." Captain Rudy pulled two manila folders from a brief-case and handed them to the admiral.

"Lieutenant," Brewer said, "this is the dossier on a Hasan Makari. Here's all I know about him. He's a Lebanese national. He was just arrested by the TSA at Philadelphia International. Now TSA ran this investigation from start to finish. That's a little unusual, because apparently the TSA now wants into the business of investigating and tracking terrorists overseas."

"Sounds like an agency turf war to me," Captain Rudy remarked.

"Ya got that right, Captain," Brewer said. "Anyway"—he looked back at Matt—"Lieutenant, I have no idea whether this guy is innocent or guilty as sin. I have an inherent distrust for the TSA. For the time being, there are two things you should know about him. First, he's been transferred to Guantánamo Bay, where he's facing a trial before the Military Commissions Tribunal."

"I don't remember reading that on the Google news report, sir."

"That's because it hasn't been announced yet," Brewer said. "That'll be out soon enough."

"Understood, sir," Matt said. "You said there was something else I needed to know?"

"Right." Admiral Brewer glanced at Captain Rudy, then back at Matt. "The other thing you need to know, Lieutenant, is that this Hasan Makari, whom the TSA claims is the biggest terrorist since Osama bin Laden, is now your client."

"Excuse me, sir?" Had Matt heard that right? "Did you say this man is my client?"

"You got a problem, Lieutenant? Some conflict of interest or something? Or maybe you don't want to defend someone accused of terrorism?"

"Ah, no, sir, Admiral. That's not it. But——"

"But what, Lieutenant?" Admiral Brewer glared across the desk with angry green eyes. "Spit it out."

"But, sir, I thought as a JAG officer, my obligation was to defend only active-duty military."

Brewer leaned back and crossed his arms. "Lieutenant, as a naval officer, your duties are to obey the lawful orders of your superiors. Not to question those orders."

"I wasn't questioning my orders, Admiral, I——"

"And secondly, your question reveals a lack of understanding of the history of the GITMO commission. Because if you'd studied the operation of the commission in any significant detail, you would know that several senior military officers—JAG officers from various branches—have been appointed to defend a number of these detainees, and that there has been a mix of civilian and military defense counsel involved in the defense of these matters."

"I should have known more about the commission. My apologies."

"No apologies necessary, Lieutenant. In fairness, most of the JAG officers appointed in these situations—Commander Walter Ruiz and Lieutenant Colonel Sean Gleason—were senior officers. You're the first junior officer appointed to defend one of these guys."

Matt responded in a disbelieving voice. "Why me, sir?"

"Because you may be a royal pain in the rump, and you know what I'm talking about. But you're the best defense counsel we've got right now."

"Thank you, sir." He tried to absorb it all. "I'm stunned. I don't know what to say, sir. I've never defended a civilian, let alone a foreigner."

"Well, if it makes you feel better, Matt, this civilian foreigner won't be your only client when you get down there."

"Sir?"

"This Hasan Makari has a son who's in the US Navy. As a matter of fact, the son is stationed on the USS *Abraham Lincoln* right here in Norfolk."

"The *Lincoln* returned today from a Med cruise," Matt said.

"Yes, they did. And as soon as they tied up to the dock, NCIS arrested BSM3 Najib Makari on charges of terrorism and murder." Brewer checked his watch. "He's probably boarding a jet right now for GITMO." He looked at Matt. "Lieutenant, you're also Petty Officer Makari's lawyer."

"I'm representing both of them?"

"That's affirmative."

"But . . ." Matt found himself tapping his fingers. "Isn't that a potential conflict of interest, sir? I mean, if the son has incriminating information on the father, or the father has stuff on the son, how do I represent them both?"

"I can't answer that. I can say the conflict of interest rules don't apply in Cuba. Neither do a lot of other rules designed to protect civil liberties in American courts." Brewer checked his watch. "Matt, enough chitchat. Pack your seabag and prepare to move out. Your plane for Cuba takes off from Oceana in two hours. Now if you'll excuse us, we've got other duties to attend to."

Brewer rose, and Matt shot to his feet and came to attention.

The admiral turned, waiting for Captain Rudy to open the office door. Rudy stepped outside into the hallway, and Brewer turned around. "You know, Matt, I almost sent you to Adak. But you're the best I've got. Go down there and do your job, and let the chips fall where they may. Got it?"

"Aye, aye, sir. Got it."

"Very well." Brewer stepped out of the office and closed the door.

• • •

BUILDING AV624
UNITED STATES NAVAL STATION
GUANTÁNAMO BAY, CUBA
30 MINUTES LATER

Above the tall palm trees, the sky had turned a deeper blue, and the clouds seemed puffier, taller, threatening to waltz into the formation of a squad of afternoon thunder boomers.

Based on the downward trek of the sun, Hasan estimated that thirty minutes must have passed by now. In that time, they had gone nowhere.

Instead, they sat in the Humvee, parked with the motor running, in front of the two-story, white cinder-block building down the road from the terminal with the sign welcoming visitors to Guantánamo Bay.

The building resembled some barracks or military housing complex. Over the main entrance, a painted sign declared Building AV624. Under that, the phrase "Honor-Bound to Defend Freedom."

Captain Kohlman had left the vehicle and walked inside the building to "take care of some paperwork," leaving Hasan with his three Marine guards.

The guards remained silent, sitting there motionless, their eyes scanning the area outside the vehicle.

At least the Humvee had an air conditioner.

And no one had struck him or spit on him or cursed at him.

Not yet, anyway.

Military trucks and Humvees with US Navy markings zoomed along the two-lane asphalt road in front of the cinder-block building.

Three large jets, two white ones with US Navy markings on the side and a green one with MARINES painted on the side, had landed over on the airstrip in the time that the Humvee had been sitting in the parking lot.

"Here comes Cap'n Kohlman," a Marine said, breaking the silence.

Hasan looked to his right. Captain Kohlman, with an envelope in hand, was walking back toward the Humvee.

Kohlman got into the Humvee. "All right. We're good to go," he told the driver. "Just like I thought. They're taking him to Camp Delta. Let's roll, Corporal."

"Camp Delta. Aye, sir." The Humvee rolled forward, turning left onto the two-lane asphalt road. As the Humvee pulled onto the road, Hasan saw a street sign: First Street.

As they proceeded along First Street at a slow pace, off to the left the rolling, scruffy hills rose above the naval base. To the right, they drove parallel to the runway. Off beyond the runway, the aqua-blue waters of the Caribbean Sea were mixed with the late-afternoon orangish tint of the setting sun.

How could a place with such a sinister reputation for torture look so enticing?

They drove down a small strip of land extending into the water. The base runway occupied most of that strip.

When the Humvee reached the point of the road opposite the end of the runway, the road angled to the left about forty-five degrees.

They rolled forward another hundred yards or so, and the Humvee came to a stop. The land had run out. There was water on three sides. They were sitting on a point beyond the end of the airstrip.

To their right was an old military jet, restored and propped up on four steel poles. Three artificial palm trees rose over the jet, resembling something in an old aviation museum. A green three-leaf clover was painted on the tail.

Just off to the left was a wide asphalt parking lot leading to a dock. Above the dock was another sign with navy-blue lettering:

Guantánamo Bay Ferry Terminal
United States Navy

Captain Kohlman checked his watch. "He's running late again."

"With respect, sir," the driver quipped, "if the Marine Corps were running that ferry, she would be on time every time."

"Ya got that right, Corporal. But if we were running the ferry service, that'd be a bruising blow to the Navy's ego. They already have an inferiority complex."

"Roger that, Cap'n."

"Here she comes, sir." The Marine sitting to Hasan's right pointed out to the bay.

A gray ferry sitting low in the water was heading toward the dock.

When the ferry turned, they could see the number 91 in white on the bow.

The vessel looked to be about sixty or seventy feet long and had no vehicles on it.

The ferry captain guided the ferry between two concrete docks extending out into the water. A US Navy sailor, wearing a light blue shirt, dark blue pants, and a white Dixie cup hat, walked down the ramp from the ferry and motioned for the Humvee to pull forward.

"That's our signal, Corporal," Captain Kohlman said.

"Aye, sir. Roger that."

The sailor stood on the asphalt, just beside the steel bridge, and like a traffic cop in Beirut, signaled the move-forward motion as the Humvee edged up to the adjustable ramp, then rolled onto the deck.

One other Humvee followed them onto the ferry.

The ferry's engines revved, and it soon had backed out into the blue waters of the bay.

Hasan looked back. The old jet and three palm trees grew smaller as the ferryboat churned toward the middle of the bay.

Hasan turned and faced the open water ahead.

His heart pounded. What would he face on the other shore?

• • •

MID-ATLANTIC REGION LEGAL SERVICE OFFICE DETACHMENT
OCEANA NAVAL AIR STATION
BUILDING 320
VIRGINIA BEACH, VIRGINIA

Lieutenant Commander Amy Debenedetto, JAG Corps, United States Navy, sat alone at her desk in the Command Services section of the Mid-Atlantic Region Legal Service Office Detachment.

With the clock approaching 1800 hours, most people, except for the command duty officer up front and a couple of sailors, had left the building.

Her stomach had suddenly turned chaotic.

First, she'd gotten a text from Matt about forty minutes ago: THEY KNOW. CAN'T TALK RIGHT NOW. TTYL.

After the text, she had gotten a call from Captain Rudy with ominous instructions. "Amy, I'm instructing you to remain at your post until we can talk. Admiral Brewer is in town. We need to speak with you about a personal matter."

The one-two punch of Matt's text—proclaiming "they know"—followed by Rudy's call could spell nothing but trouble.

"They know" translated into this: they knew about her tryst with a junior officer. In situations like this, the senior officer always got punished. The junior officer would often skate. Or if they did not, there would be a private slap on the wrist in a manner that would not totally damage the JO's career.

That's how they would paint this, even though Matt threw the first flirtatious glances, flashed that candle-wax-melting irresistible smile, and dropped those close-to-the-line flirtatious comments that could be considered borderline disrespect.

She liked the comments so much—even though she should have reprimanded him—she wanted more.

"No way you're old enough to be a senior lieutenant commander, ma'am."

Or . . .

"Ma'am, can I volunteer to transfer to your command and become your personal assistant? I'll work hard for you and take care of all your professional needs."

She should have stopped him right there. She knew it.

But when he shot those blue eyes and that hopelessly enticing smile at her, her resolve melted in the Atlantic breeze. Matt was her Kryptonite.

Their relationship smoldered on and on, nuclear hot under the surface, obvious to them but not to the rest of the Navy.

Her good judgment failed. She accepted his invitation to dinner. And then, next time, to his boat.

He would prove to be her undoing.

She read Matt's text message again. THEY KNOW. CAN'T TALK RIGHT NOW. TTYL.

Can't talk right now?

Really?

The heck with that.

Who was the superior officer here, anyway?

She punched the Call button.

One ring. Two rings. Three rings.

"You have reached Lieutenant Matt Davis, United States Navy. I'm unable to take your call, but—"

. . .

HEADQUARTERS
MID-ATLANTIC REGION LEGAL SERVICE OFFICE
DEFENSE SERVICE OFFICE SOUTHEAST
US NAVY JAG CORPS
US NAVAL BASE
NORFOLK, VIRGINIA

Matt checked the caller ID: "LCDR Amy Debenedetto."

"Not now, baby. Not enough time," he mumbled and returned his eyes to his computer screen.

A headline popped up:

GITMO Defense Counsel Accuses Government of Spying, Censoring E-mails.

A new bombshell revelation surfaced today at the controversial military tribunal trials at Guantánamo Bay. Defense lawyers assigned to defend high-profile terror suspects accused the government of illegal censoring and, in fact, in many cases reading sensitive e-mails which go to the defense of their clients' cases.

According to one source who spoke on condition of anonymity, the government planted listening devices in attorney-client meeting rooms, disguised as smoke detectors, and then spied on confidential conversations between defense attorneys and their clients. Defense lawyers also claim that the government has illegally accessed their e-mails and servers, giving the prosecution an unfair and illegal advantage in trial preparation.

Then another headline:

Letter to Obama Could Land Famed GITMO Lawyer Six Months in Prison

Clive Stafford Smith, the most distinguished of the civilian defense lawyers representing detained prisoners at the US prison facility in Guantánamo Bay, has been accused of "unprofessional conduct" by Pentagon officials monitoring communication between GITMO prisoners and their lawyers. Defense lawyers have sided with Smith, arguing that confidential communications between Smith and his client Binyam Mohamed are illegal. Yet now, according to sources, Smith faces a possible six-month jail sentence because he wrote a letter to President Obama detailing his client's allegations of torture by US agents.

Then another:

Guantánamo Detainee Lawyers Accuse Government of Harassment

A federal investigation is now under way over allegations of US government harassment of defense lawyers representing terror suspects at the US Naval prison facility at Guantánamo Bay, Cuba. At the center of the investigation is prominent "GITMO" defense lawyer Clive Stafford Smith who has already been "investigated" at least four times for a variety of allegations, from rules violations on handling classified information to smuggling contraband to his clients.

Mr. Smith denies all the allegations, calling them government attempts to intimidate defense lawyers. Smith reports that he and other defense lawyers working at Guantánamo Bay have received numerous threats, including anonymous death threats, made simply because the lawyers are trying to do their jobs.

Thus far, no arrests have been made of anyone making the death threats, and the government investigation continues.

"What?" Matt mumbled. "Death threats?"

Another headline claimed even more intimidation of defense lawyers:

GITMO Standoff: Prosecutors Threaten Defense Lawyers, Courtroom Cleared

By James Bell, June 21, 2013

A military judge cleared the courtroom at Guantánamo Bay, Cuba, today, in the midst of death penalty proceedings against five Guantánamo Bay detainees convicted of terrorism. The judge, Colonel James Pohl, stopped proceedings when a defense counsel's cross-examination of former GITMO prison commander Rear Admiral David Woods led to a heated exchange between prosecutors and defense attorneys. Commander Walter Ruiz, a US Navy JAG officer, and appointed defense counsel, had been questioning Woods about his knowledge of CIA control over the detention center, and CIA restrictions on defense counsel having access to clients. When Woods claimed lack of knowledge about CIA involvement, Ruiz pressed the matter further, asking about other intelligence organizations that were operating at GITMO.

Ruiz's questioning prompted an angry response from Justice Department prosecutors, who threatened that Ruiz was "playing with fire" by pressing the matter with Woods.

When Ruiz responded that he would not be threatened by the prosecution, Judge Pohl cleared the courtroom and convened a secret, closed-door session to take the matter under advisement. No details were made available about what happened in the secret session, and the death penalty hearing later reconvened in open court.

Matt shook his head.

The ramifications of what he had just read were clear. If Justice Department prosecutors tried intimidating Commander Walter Ruiz, a career officer two full pay grades above Matt's rank, think of what they would try with a mere lieutenant like Matt.

Perhaps that's why he was chosen—perhaps this had nothing to do with his abilities as a defense counsel. Perhaps they were theorizing that a junior officer defense counsel would not question high-ranking DOJ prosecutors like a higher-ranking officer such as Commander Ruiz had questioned them.

If this was their assumption, they would soon find out that they were wrong.

Still, these allegations of threatening intimidation against defense counsel within a constitutional republic were troubling.

He conducted another Google search. "I can't believe this," he mumbled, reading the next search result on the screen.

Was Former Guantánamo Bay Defense Attorney Murdered?

The body of Andy P. Hart, 38, a lawyer from Toledo, Ohio, who had defended notorious Guantánamo Bay detainee Mohammed Rahim al-Afghani, was found today in his Ohio apartment. Cause of death was a single gunshot wound to the head.

Authorities claim to have discovered a "suicide note" with the body, along with a computer thumb drive containing Hart's client files, including sensitive client information for al-Afghani. The government claimed that Mohammed Rahim al-Afghani was Osama bin Laden's personal translator and a high-level al-Qaida operative.

Mr. Hart's death comes in the wake of numerous death threats to several Guantánamo Bay defense attorneys, including prominent civilian defense attorney Clive Stafford Smith and others.

In recent weeks, Mr. Smith and others had complained about anonymous death threats and direct threats from the government, which Mr. Smith referred to as "intimidation tactics."

US Navy JAG officer Commander Walter Ruiz, one of the senior military JAG officers assigned to defend Guantánamo detainees, accused Department of Justice prosecutors of openly threatening him in court, suggesting that he was "playing with fire" by pressing a witness, Rear Admiral David Woods, about Woods's knowledge of secret government agencies asserting control of the Guantánamo Bay prison facility.

In the wake of all those threats, now comes news of the death of Andy Hart, who had shown no suicidal tendencies in the weeks leading up to his death. And while authorities were very quick to dub Hart's death as a suicide, without any meaningful investigation, considering the multiple threats made to GITMO defense counsel, that fast-trigger determination will raise more questions than it answers.

"This sounds fishy." Matt clicked the next set of search results.

Andy P. Hart: Suicide or Murder?
Guantánamo Prisoners' Attorney Andy P. Hart: Suicide or Murder?

A cold fear cascaded through his body. Something smelled.

A knock on the door.

"Enter."

"Excuse me, Lieutenant."

Master Chief Ronnie Lewis, in a working khaki uniform resplendent with seven rows of service ribbons on his chest, stood at the door.

"Master Chief."

"Sir, I understand you've got a plane waiting for you at Oceana. The skipper asked me to give you a lift."

"Ah, yes." Matt tried to ignore the dead GITMO defense counsel. Was this his punishment for fraternization with a senior officer? He should have volunteered for captain's mast. Even a court-martial. At least he might escape alive.

"Be right there, Master Chief. Also, I need you to stop by the boat so I can pick up a few things for my trip. Not sure when I'm coming back." *Or if I'm coming back.*

His cell phone rang again: "LCDR Amy Debenedetto."

They'd gotten in this together, toying with forbidden fruit, playing with dynamite.

He wanted to hear her voice. To sail with her up Chesapeake Bay in his boat. He started to pick up, then changed his mind.

The master chief stood outside the door. Best to stay quiet, especially if they were building a case for fraternization.

"Okay, Master Chief. Let's roll."

"Aye, sir."

• • •

MID-ATLANTIC REGION LEGAL SERVICE OFFICE DETACHMENT
OCEANA NAVAL AIR STATION
BUILDING 320
VIRGINIA BEACH, VIRGINIA

Why wasn't he answering? This wasn't like Matt. They must have gotten to him.

Perhaps they ordered him not to speak. In fraternization cases, they always approached the junior officer first. They considered the junior officer the "victim" in such cases.

Amy knew the fraternization drill. As a former Navy trial counsel, she had prosecuted three fraternization cases. She once prosecuted a navy commander, the former executive officer of the naval air station, for an affair with his staff judge advocate, a woman who was a senior lieutenant.

In every case, they called the junior "victim" to testify against the senior officer, always considered the "aggressor."

The facts did not matter. Even in a military court. Oftentimes the agenda trumped the facts.

And in difference-of-rank fraternization, the agenda was always the same: blister the senior officer.

They made every JAG officer study the case of the USS *Chief*, the 225-foot minesweeper out of San Diego. The Navy had relieved the commander of the minesweeper for fraternization with his female second in command.

In that case, Lieutenant Commander Laird, the executive officer, had been fired for "misconduct" after "an investigation into a violation of the Navy's fraternization policy."

Such punishment ends a naval career.

And what a career hers had been. Years ago Amy served as the enlisted legalman for Admiral Zack Brewer, back when *Lieutenant* Brewer was a rising star in San Diego. As Brewer's paralegal, she helped him gather evidence in the court-martial titled *United States v. Olajuwon*, a case that made international news when Brewer prosecuted three Navy chaplains for treason.

As a result of her work in that case, they commissioned her as an ensign in the Navy JAG Corps and put her through law school.

Now, after all that, to throw it all away.

Zack Brewer went on to become judge advocate general of the Navy.

And she rose through the enlisted ranks, then into the officer ranks, and then into the JAG Corps.

Theirs was once a special professional relationship. Not the type that would bust her career—like her relationship with Matt—but the relationship of proud mentor and eager student.

She remembered the case of the USS *Chief* and then considered her own case. In the case of the *Chief*, the two officers were of the same rank. A lieutenant commander in a relationship with another lieutenant commander in the same chain of command.

But her situation proved more egregious. Her case involved a lieutenant commander in a relationship with a lower-ranked lieutenant in the same chain of command.

The phone rang. Her pulse accelerated. The caller ID showed RLSO Duty Officer from the Regional Legal Service Office.

"Lieutenant Commander Debenedetto."

"Ma'am, this is Lieutenant JG Anderson at the duty desk."

"How can I help you, Lieutenant?"

"Ma'am, the skipper called. He and Admiral Brewer are at the main gate of the air station. The skipper asked me to relay this message. He and the admiral will be at the RLSO in five minutes. Meet them at the OIC's office."

Amy hesitated. "Thank you, Lieutenant. I'll be right there." She hung up. Now there was no doubt. She was about to get blasted. The skipper had sent instructions through an officer two grades below her. A classic power move.

What would she do? Of course there would be no prison sentence, but they would demand her resignation. Her best-case scenario? A reassignment, followed by being passed over for commander.

Then they would drum her out of the Navy by a Selective Early Retirement Board—well short of her twenty years. Then she would have to look for a legal job with a law firm or a district attorney's office with a starting salary below her current pay and without her military pension. If they asked for copies of her military record and discovered that she had been kicked out for fraternization, her job hopes would vanish. Maybe she could start her own practice, which would prove challenging, considering the civilian economy and the glut of lawyers being churned out of those warehouse-on-the-corner-turned-law-schools.

"Get hold of yourself, Amy," she muttered. "Just keep your cool."

She stood, checked her watch, and headed out of her office for her meeting with the admiral and the captain.

Stepping into the passageway from her office, she heard another text signal. She reached into her purse to check her phone.

Text from Lieutenant Matt Davis.

CHECK THAT. NOT SURE THEY KNOW. I THINK THEY PROBABLY KNOW. CAN'T SAY FOR SURE THAT THEY KNOW. MAYBE THEY DO. MAYBE THEY DON'T.

"What? What are you talking about, Matt? Do they know or not?"

Frustration flushed her body, mixed in with all the twisted anxiety in her stomach. She tried calling Matt again.

One ring.

Two rings.

Voice mail again.

"Come on, Matt." She hung up and walked toward the OIC's office to await the admiral and the captain—and her fate.

• • •

UNITED STATES NAVAL STATION
GUANTÁNAMO BAY, CUBA
US NAVY FERRY
APPROACHING FERRY TERMINAL

Under an orange glow and long shadows on the sparkling blue waters from a setting sun, the US Navy ferry containing the Humvee with the four US Marines and Hasan Makari approached the ferry terminal opposite the side from which they had departed.

Not a word had been spoken in the twenty minutes or so that Hasan had estimated the ferry ride to have been.

But as they chugged in close to the terminal, it became clear that the most active side of the Guantánamo Bay naval base was on the other side of the bay, the side they had just left.

Under palm trees swaying in the late-afternoon breeze, the approaching shoreline featured a small harbor with docks and piers, mooring a number of small craft that were rocking from the light swells. Out to the left, two sleek-looking identical gray US Navy warships floated at anchor.

As the ferry swung around for a final approach to the landing, he saw a large sign behind the piers:

US Naval Station Guantánamo Bay
Welcome to the Windward Side

The Windward Side.

It hit him. He had read an article several years ago in the *New York Times* about the Guantánamo Bay hunger strike put on by prisoners stationed there. Now the article was like a searing memory he could not shake.

The Guantánamo Bay Prison Camp, with its dreaded torture

chambers, was located on what was called the "Windward Side" of the base.

Some of those who were tortured he knew were bloodthirsty terrorists from places like Afghanistan, Yemen, and Pakistan. Others were innocent, having been rounded up like herds of cattle, having done nothing against the United States.

Hasan felt like a man condemned to the gallows, having finished his last meal, being led by his executioners to the wooden trapdoor platform, where a noose of large, coarse rope would be tightened around his neck.

He wished he could choose the hanging.

If he were hanged, at least the pain would be short. Tomorrow his suffering would be over.

But the excruciating torture he now faced could last for months, even years.

The ferry inched into the port terminal, then came to a stop.

With a humming mechanical sound, the ferry's bow opened for the vehicles to exit.

A sharp clang followed. The sound of steel against the dock.

"All right, Corporal, get ready to move out."

"Aye, sir." The driver started the Humvee's engine. Another sailor stepped out in front of them and, playing the role of traffic cop, motioned the Humvee forward.

The driver pressed the accelerator, and they drove down across the steel ramp, onto the concrete driveway at the end of the pier.

"Okay, Corporal. Take us to Camp Delta. Camp 1."

"Camp 1, sir?" The corporal raised an eyebrow.

"You heard me, Corporal."

"Camp Delta. Camp 1. Aye, sir." The Humvee turned right onto the main two-lane road outside the ferry landing.

Hasan's forehead grew clammy, then his hands did. He wanted to heave, to vomit right there in the vehicle. He bowed his head, whispering, "Our Father, who art in heaven, hallowed be thy name . . ."

• • •

MID-ATLANTIC REGION LEGAL SERVICE OFFICE DETACHMENT
OFFICE OF THE OFFICER-IN-CHARGE
OCEANA NAVAL AIR STATION
BUILDING 320
VIRGINIA BEACH, VIRGINIA

Amy sat alone in the waiting area of the OIC's office, checking her watch. They were two minutes late, probably a deliberate tactic designed to accelerate her heart, to torture her breathing, and to compound the cold sweat beads that had formed on her forehead.

How had she gotten into this mess?

"Attention on deck!" The command came from the hallway, from the duty officer.

Amy rose as her old friend Vice Admiral Zack Brewer and her commanding officer, Captain Rudy, strode one behind the other into the office.

"Follow us, Commander," Rudy said. "And close the door behind you. We have some sensitive matters to discuss."

"Aye, Captain." She stepped in and closed the door.

Admiral Brewer was sitting behind the desk normally occupied by Commander David Reams, the JAG officer who was officer in charge of the legal service detachment. Captain Rudy pulled up a chair next to the desk.

Amy stepped in front of Brewer's desk and came to full attention.

Silence and cold stares followed.

"At ease, Commander," Admiral Brewer said.

"Thank you, sir."

"Pull up a chair if you'd like," Brewer said. "There's no point in making you stand for this."

"Thank you, sir."

Amy sat down across the desk from the JAG.

Brewer flashed those famous hazel eyes at her and held his stare.

She wanted to look away, to stare at the clock on the wall as his eyes bore down on her. But looking away would prove guilt, and weakness, a sign of capitulation.

This she had learned from the great Zack Brewer himself. She even remembered his words: *"If you blink first, you look weak."*

"Amy, you and I go back a long way."

"Yes, sir."

"In a way"—he steepled his fingers together and spoke in that distinctive Tar Heel accent—"I'd say both of our careers got launched at the same time. Wouldn't you say?"

She nodded, remembering that she first fell for Matt because he had reminded her of a younger Zack Brewer. A confident, young, swashbuckling naval officer from the Carolinas. Zack was from Plymouth, North Carolina, and Matt from Rock Hill, South Carolina.

Truth be known, she'd gotten into trouble because Matt fulfilled that long-ago infatuation she had with Zack Brewer himself.

Zack never knew.

Why couldn't the self-discipline she exercised as a junior petty officer have followed her throughout her career?

"What? You don't agree?"

"Sorry, sir. I was distracted. Yes, sir. I think that's fair to say, sir."

"Remember the first case we tried together, with me as lead prosecutor and you as my legalman paralegal?"

"Yes, sir. How could I ever forget?"

"Remember the defendant's name?"

"Of course, sir. Petty Officer Antonio Blount, US Navy SEAL. Accused of raping Ensign Marianne Landrieu at the North Island Naval Air Station. Ensign Landrieu, the niece of a prominent United States senator from Louisiana. Chairman of the Senate Armed Services Committee, as I recall. You were under tons of political pressure to deliver a conviction. And, of course, you delivered, sir. And then you turned around and delivered when you prosecuted the case of the three Islamic chaplains."

Admiral Brewer nodded at Captain Rudy. He looked back at Amy. "You remember well, don't you?"

"Yes, sir, I do."

"And you mentioned the case of the Islamic chaplains."

"Of course, sir. It was the highest profile case in the world."

"Yes, well." Zack seemed to ponder his thoughts. "Those guys were not only terrorists, but they were masquerading as officers. It's a shame when someone wearing a naval officer's uniform makes the officer corps look bad."

Ouch.

"Do you know what I mean, Commander?" His reversion from calling her "Amy" back to the more formal "Commander" signified a less-than-friendly change in tone.

"Yes, sir." She maintained eye contact but tried to project softness, not defiance, in her eyes and her speech.

"Sometimes this job is pleasant. Sometimes it's unpleasant. And sometimes whether it's pleasant or unpleasant depends on the parties involved. On their goals. Their objectives."

She nodded.

"The Navy has invested a lot of money in you."

"Yes, sir."

"Tell me, Lieutenant Commander Debenedetto, what had you hoped to achieve in your naval career?"

Hoped to achieve? I'm already toast. "Sir, my greatest hope is to serve my country."

Zack's face twisted into a pained, somber expression. "Well, I regret to say, Amy, that if you continue to serve your country, it won't be here."

His words gut-punched her. She felt breathless.

"Captain Rudy is here because he is your commanding officer." A pause. "Effective this afternoon, you are relieved of your duties."

Her lips trembled. She wanted to cry, but that would never happen. Not here.

Not now.

She would cry in front of them when hell froze over.

Captain Rudy nodded and said, "We'll miss you around here, Lieutenant Commander Debenedetto."

"It's been an honor to serve under your command, sir. I hope that I haven't let you down." She paused. "I suppose I'll need to vacate my office."

Brewer nodded. "Yes, Amy. The sooner the better."

The lump in her throat swelled to grapefruit size. Matt's instincts were correct.

They knew.

"Sir, would you like me to take leave and get out of the way for the time being?"

"Leave?" Brewer raised an eyebrow. "You think we could let you off that easily, did you?"

Here came the news. She faced a court-martial. The admiral was about to read her her rights. "I understand, sir."

"You cannot remain here, at the RLSO."

"Understood."

"We're transferring you to Guantánamo Bay, where you'll be detailed to the prosecution team against two accused terrorists who were arrested within the last couple of days, one being a US Navy member."

"Sir?"

"You heard me. Get packed. Be ready to move out in two hours."

"But, sir?"

"Something wrong, Commander? Would you prefer some other options that I have in mind?"

"No, sir."

Brewer's hazel eyes bored right through her. "You know, Amy, sometimes second chances come by tackling tough assignments."

"Yes, sir."

"Good. Then get out of here before I change my mind."

"Yes, sir." She commenced a quick about-face and walked straight to the door.

"Amy!" Brewer's voice stopped her.

"Yes, sir."

"About-face. There's a little matter I forgot to take care of."

She turned around.

"Attention on deck!"

She jumped to attention.

"I'm sorry about this. But this isn't a matter of transferring out of here and leaving it at that."

He walked over to her. Close to her. So close that she caught a whiff of his cologne.

Still Geoffrey Beene. Grey Flannel. After all these years.

He took hold of her right collar, then proceeded to unpin and remove the gold oak leaf that signified her rank as lieutenant commander.

Of course.

She should have expected this. She would face admiral's mast and receive a demotion in rank. Still, this was preferable to a court-martial.

At least there would no longer be a rank difference between her and Matt, which meant they could resume their relationship and avoid fraternization charges.

"You know I'm doing you a favor, don't you?"

"I trust your judgment, Admiral. I always have."

"Lieutenant Commander Amy Debenedetto, United States Navy. It is my duty to inform you that you have been deep-selected for the rank of commander, United States Navy. And therefore, I am frocking you to the rank of full commander, United States Navy, effective immediately."

Before his words sank in, he had reached into his pocket, retrieved a silver oak leaf, and pinned it on her collar in place of the gold oak leaf that he had removed.

He wagged his finger in her face. "Do not blow this. Understand me?"

"Aye, sir."

She could no longer choke back the tears.

"Get out of here, Debenedetto. Before I change my mind again."

"Aye, sir."

• • •

UNITED STATES NAVAL STATION
GUANTÁNAMO BAY, CUBA
APPROACHING CAMP DELTA

The change in the landscape, or rather the change in the types of buildings along each side of the two-lane roads, signaled that they were entering a different sector of the base.

The base McDonald's, the Navy Exchange, the residential communities alongside the road, the military barracks and ball fields—all these were left behind. Now, as the Humvee slowed, they were passing a steel chain-link fence with sharp barbed wire coiled at the top. Signs along the fence declared "Guantánamo Bay Detention Center—Keep Out."

The prison sat on a bluff overlooking the Caribbean, an isolated corner of the remote US Naval Base at Guantánamo Bay.

Hasan knew in his gut, by the Humvee's change in speed and the somber looks on the faces of the Marines guarding him, that his time was short.

The Humvee slowed again, then turned left and came to a stop outside a gate with a guard tower looming over it, reminiscent of the design of the guard towers at Nazi prisons in World War II. Draped under the guard tower observation post hung an American flag.

A white sign on the fence with a graphic of the Pentagon was to the left of the locked gate:

Camp Delta
JTF Guantánamo
Honor-Bound to Defend Freedom

Dark-green boards had been placed all along the chain-link fence to block any view of the interior.

Two armed Marine guards came from inside the compound and unlocked the gate.

As the twin steel-caged doors swung open, the Humvee rolled onto the grounds of the prison camp. Marine guards shot sharp salutes to Captain Kohlman, who crisply returned the salutes.

The Humvee rolled a hundred yards or so inside the compound, then stopped.

Hasan looked off to his right. There were four of them. They wore dark blue pants and blue T-shirts. Stenciled in gold were the words "TSA ELITE Forces."

The phrase "ELITE Forces" on their T-shirts was new to him. He had not seen it on the uniforms of the TSA officers back in Philadelphia.

The ELITE Forces each wore aviator-style shades, Ray-Bans style, and they each had an assault rifle slung over a shoulder.

Like the four horsemen of the apocalypse, they marched toward the Humvee.

"Here they come," the driver said.

"Yep," Kohlman said. "Right on time."

"I guess having just the CIA and the FBI in here wasn't enough for 'em."

"Typical civilian bureaucracy," Kohlman said. "Everybody wants a piece of the pie. Everybody wants their day in the sun. Show off to Congress what they can do to justify more money. That's the end game. Money. They spend some money for new T-shirts and a couple of he-man training manuals and call themselves ELITE Forces." The disgust in his voice was clear. "I guarantee you none of these ELITE boys would last a week at Parris Island." Kohlman removed his sunglasses. "Well, let me deal with these cats. Then we can go home, get some shut-eye, and start all over again tomorrow."

Kohlman stepped out of the Humvee. "Gentlemen," he said as the foursome approached.

"Captain," the man in front said. "Special Agent Ira Jacobs, TSA. I'm the new chief investigator on the ground here. These gentlemen are my assistants."

"Welcome to GITMO, Mr. Jacobs."

"That's Special Agent Jacobs."

"Excuse me. Special Agent Jacobs," Kohlman said with a tinge of disgust.

"If you will hand over the prisoner now, Captain, you are relieved of your duties in this matter."

"Mr. Jacobs. We will deliver the prisoner to you. But let me be clear. The only ones who can relieve me of my duties are the commanding general of this base, the commandant of the Marine Corps, or the president of the United States himself. I don't see any stars on your collar, sir, and I do not, and never will, work for the TSA or Homeland Security."

"Whatever, Captain. You're wasting my time. Now surrender the prisoner."

Kohlman turned around. "Corporal. Sergeant. Produce the prisoner."

"Aye, sir."

"Let's go, sir." The sergeant opened the back right door of the Humvee.

His hands still cuffed, Hasan slid along the seat to the open door, pivoted on his butt, and stepped out of the Humvee.

"Okay, we've got him now, Captain," the TSA agent said as two other agents grabbed Hasan by the arms. "That will be all."

"This is still a military base," Kohlman said, "not a TSA compound. I'll decide when 'that will be all' only by a lawful order from a superior officer."

"The military isn't equipped for this," Jacobs shot back. "I'll see you next time, Captain."

"Yes, you will."

Jacobs turned his back on Captain Kohlman. "Let's get this terrorist to his cell. We'll give him a taste of the consequences of terrorism against America."

. . .

Ever since the federal government bailed out General Motors, US government agencies had been instructed to purchase GM products as a means of trying to protect the government's tax dollars investment.

As part of that boondoggle, the Navy, known for huge gray ships and black submarines, to the extent that it needed automobiles for its shore stations, fell under the "buy GM" mandate. That mandate had trickled down to the Navy Regional Legal Service Office in Norfolk.

Matt Davis didn't care for the notion of being seen in a Chevy Malibu. If he was going to be seen in public in a General Motors product, that class of vehicle would include only a convertible Corvette, like the brand-new limited-edition Corvette C7 Stingray, with a sweet 450-horsepower, LT-1, V-8 engine under the hood, painted in garnet and black in honor of his beloved South Carolina Gamecocks.

In the final analysis, it wasn't his sailboat that persuaded Amy to risk her career for him, but rather that powerful, sleek driving machine of a gorgeous sports car that he raced about in. He saw it in her eyes the first time he opened the door for her.

She never would have admitted it, but if the truth were told, his Stingray cast a psychological and physical spell on her.

And then there was the spell she had cast on him.

She had shown up in civilian clothes, trying to disguise herself. White Bermuda shorts, designer sunglasses so big they could have passed for something Jackie O would have worn. She was drop-dead stunning, especially when she loosened her shiny blonde hair from that military-style bun, freeing her locks to bounce so teasingly onto her shoulders. What an oxymoronic paradox she became, a conflict of regulation against free spirit, a juxtaposition of precision in the day against flowing lava in the evening. His chest pounded like a driving bass drum at the sight of her.

In retrospect, he messed up by lowering the top.

Of course, every girl likes riding in a sports car convertible in the summertime with the top down.

But having the top down made them vulnerable to getting spotted.

He knew this at the time, but the daredevilish rush of flirting with detection ran through his veins, fanning the excitement of it all.

Matt would rather think all day about Amy than anything else.

But the sight of the twin-engine US Navy C-26 Metroliner, its engines running, brought Matt back to Andy Hart, the GITMO defense lawyer mysteriously found dead. The death-by-suicide version reported by the press smelled rotten.

Interesting how people who got too close to the truth always seemed to "commit suicide" or suffer from a death-producing heart attack. Or in some instances, they were just murdered.

From Lee Harvey Oswald, shot in the stomach by Jack Ruby to keep Oswald from talking, to Jimmy Hoffa who disappeared from the planet, to former Clinton commerce secretary Ron Brown who "died in a plane" even though military investigators found a bullet hole in his head, to former White House counsel Vince Foster who allegedly put a gun in his mouth and pulled the trigger, to Andrew Breitbart who suffered a fatal "heart attack" days before he threatened to release damaging information on President Obama, and to Andy Hart and another case of a press-reported "suicide" by a lawyer. All these cases had this in common: each of these men died under mysterious circumstances, and they all died with knowledge that, if exposed, could have been extremely embarrassing to some very powerful people.

Matt had a feeling of foreboding that he would soon discover something that some people would not want exposed. The more he thought about it, the more the names of the dead flashed through his mind: Oswald, Hoffa, Brown, Foster, Breitbart, Hart.

All too close to the truth.

All stone-cold dead.

"You okay, Lieutenant?"

The master chief's question brought him back into the moment.

"I'm fine, Master Chief. Just a last-minute mental checklist."

"Your first trip to GITMO, sir?"

"Is it that obvious?"

"You'll be fine, sir. Just do your job. They pick the best for a reason, sir." He pulled the Malibu to a stop a few feet from the plane. "I'll get your bags on the plane, Lieutenant."

"Thanks, Master Chief. But no point in you grabbing all that stuff by yourself."

Matt hadn't packed much. Seabag. Computer. Suitcase. Uniform bag. He reached into the backseat and grabbed his computer and seabag, and the master chief grabbed the rest.

As they reached the stairway heading up into the plane, Matt turned around.

"We'll miss you, Lieutenant. Go down there and do us proud." The master chief saluted. "Knock 'em dead, sir."

Matt returned the salute. "I've got a feeling somebody's going to knock somebody dead. I'm not sure who's going to be left standing."

"You'll do great, Lieutenant. Fair winds and following seas."

"Fair winds to you too, Master Chief." Matt turned and boarded the plane.

• • •

GUANTÁNAMO BAY DETENTION CENTER
CAMP DELTA
UNITED STATES NAVAL BASE
GUANTÁNAMO BAY, CUBA

The TSA agents grabbed Hasan's arms, squeezing so tight he winced in pain as they rushed him down the center of the dusty prison courtyard. He was sure that their vise-like grips would leave dark bruises on his upper arms and shoulders.

Like tentacles stretching from an evil amoeba, several long caged entrances jutted about twenty feet or so into the courtyard from the cinder-block prison facility. These cages each had a metal canopy to shield occupants from direct driving rain but were otherwise open-aired on the sides—like a kennel where impounded animals awaited either their masters to come rescue them from captivity or the moment when, abandoned, they were "put down" by an executioner's injection.

Guarding the entrance of the cages were armed military men in fatigues who looked like US Marines.

Several more armed guards had joined their security detail and had moved into a circle around him, much like they had done at Philadelphia International Airport.

Hasan thought perhaps they were leading him to the back of the prison to be shot in the head.

If only he could be so lucky.

"Move!" a TSA ELITE agent shouted. They jerked his shoulder, yanking him off to the left toward one of the extended walkway cages. They passed the first cage, then the second, third, and fourth.

The fifth caged walkway, like the others, was framed in wickets of coiled stainless steel barbed wire. An agent punched some numbers on a combination pad on the gate, triggering a sinister-sounding *click*, followed by a *clank*. Then two more, *clank*, *clank*.

With a humming buzz, the steel-caged door swung open.

"Okay, move!"

They shoved him forward into the walkway cage. But because of its narrowness—barely enough room for three men to stand abreast—the TSA ELITEs were forced to realign themselves to fit in the cage with the prisoner. Two stepped in, single file, ahead of Hasan. The others shoved him forward and followed him into the cage.

A tropical breeze gusted through the open steel wires of the cage, providing relief from the heat. The breeze would have refreshed his face, but the heaving convulsions and contorted twisting in his stomach nullified its benefits.

A steel *clank* sounded behind him. The door locking them in.

"All right, let's move," an agent said. They started forward again but had gotten no more than a couple of steps when a loud, shrill whistle pierced the air, surrounding them.

In an instant, all activity froze.

Then the shriek of the whistle stopped, and the still air yielded to the blare of an almost eerie-sounding bugle call. The bugle produced a haunting call, with a tune sounding almost like taps but not quite. A bit more lively.

"Colors," one of the agents mumbled, obviously disgusted.

"What a waste," another said. "These military types waste so much time with their stupid patriotism crap and garble about the Constitution."

Marines and sailors stood at attention, salutes flashed toward the large flagpole in the middle of the courtyard.

At the base of the flagpole, a Marine honor guard worked furiously to bring the American flag down for the evening as dozens of other Marines paid reverent homage.

For Hasan, this sight brought comfort in the midst of his nightmare. The reverence shown by the US military for the flag that stood for freedom represented what Hasan had always associated with America. His heart told him that the military officers he had seen and these TSA ELITEs were not the same.

The words of the Lee Greenwood ballad came to mind. "The flag still stands for freedom. God bless the USA."

He prayed, *God bless America again. I don't know what's happening here, and I don't know what will happen to me. But please restore America as a beacon of true freedom, and please protect my son.*

Forced to wait for the bugler to stop, a couple of agents cursed under their breath, disgusted by the interruption of their routine.

The flag reached the bottom of the pole, and the Marines folded it sharply, tucking it into a red, white, and blue cloth triangle. The bugle call faded. The whistle blew again.

The pause ended, salutes were dropped, and activity returned to GITMO.

"All this for a dang flag," an agent said.

"All right. Enough of that," Jacobs said. "We've wasted enough time. Let's move."

Jacobs took the lead. The TSA ELITE entourage, with Hasan jammed in their midst, walked down the caged corridor to a steel door to the main prison. Jacobs punched some numbers into a combination box, causing more electronic buzzing and clinking.

"Step back," Jacobs ordered.

The steel door swung out slowly, revealing a long, dark hallway.

"Let's go."

Jacobs stepped in first. Hasan's bodyguards pushed him in next.

The long hall felt humid and had a musty smell. The floor was concrete. The cinder-block walls had no windows or doors. Lightbulbs hung from the ceiling every ten feet or so. Sweat beaded on his face. He felt short of breath.

They walked under a sign that said "Welcome to the Corridor of Freedom," and just past that sign they came to another hallway off to the left.

"This way," Jacobs barked.

They turned, and about twenty feet beyond the turn was a set of yellow steel double doors.

And another sign:

High Security Area
Solitary Confinement

Jacobs punched a security code, and the doors slid open like elevator doors.

"Let's go." Jacobs motioned for his men to enter the secure area with Hasan.

Inside, three US Marines in camouflage uniforms manned a guard station. One of the Marines looked up as the TSA group entered. "May I help you, sir?"

Jacobs flashed an identification badge.

"I'm Special Agent Jacobs, TSA ELITE Forces. Who's in charge, Sergeant?"

"Right now, that would be First Lieutenant Elliot, sir."

"Where is Lieutenant Elliot right now?" Jacobs snarled.

The duty sergeant cocked his head with a quizzical look. "He's out making rounds at the moment, Mr. Jacobs. He should be back in about ten minutes."

"That's Special Agent Jacobs to you, Sergeant. And I don't have ten minutes."

"I'm sorry, sir, that's what he said."

"What about 'I don't have ten minutes' do you not understand, Sergeant? Do you know who this man is?" He pointed at Hasan.

The sergeant shot a glance at Hasan, then turned to Jacobs. "Sorry, sir. I don't recognize him."

"Well, this happens to be Hasan Makari, one of the most sought-after terrorists in the world. He's the guy who murdered our United States ambassador eleven years ago in Lebanon. What do you expect me to do? Stand in the hallway with the world's most notorious terrorist while I wait on your lieutenant to return?"

The sergeant looked at Jacobs. "With respect, Agent Jacobs, we—"

"That's *Special* Agent Jacobs."

"Excuse me. But with respect, sir, we have a bunch of the world's most sought-after terrorists in this wing. The CIA has been bringing these guys in here for years. They don't snap their fingers and demand that we change our military procedures when they show up."

"Well, that's not good enough, Sergeant!" Jacobs snapped. "From here on, you're going to be dealing with me. And TSA ELITE is not CIA. We have our own unique procedures. We don't tolerate the inefficiencies tolerated by the CIA or the military. Am I clear?"

The Marine hesitated. "I hear you, sir."

"Well, hear this! Call your lieutenant to the guard station. Now."

The sergeant studied Jacobs's face for a second, then picked up his walkie-talkie. "Lieutenant Elliot. You have a visitor at the guard station."

A second later, "Elliot here. What's up, Sergeant?"

"Sir. Sorry to interrupt. There's a Special Agent Jacobs, an ELITE TSA special agent, with a new prisoner. The prisoner is a Mr. Makari."

"Oh yeah. Captain Kohlman warned me about this guy. I'll be right there."

"Aye, sir."

Jacobs stepped closer to the Marine. "What did the lieutenant mean by that remark?" he snarled.

"What remark, sir?" the sergeant asked.

"About Captain Kohlman warning him about me?"

"I have no idea, sir. You'll have to ask him when he gets here."

"I intend to do that."

Seconds later, a Marine wearing fatigues walked around the corner. "I'm First Lieutenant Elliot," the officer said.

"I'm Special Agent Jacobs, Lieutenant. TSA ELITE Forces. I overheard your comment on your sergeant's walkie-talkie. What's this about Captain Kohlman warning you about me?"

"Sir, I'm not in a position to discuss any conversation with anyone in my chain of command."

"We'll see about that, Lieutenant," Jacobs said. "I work for the director of TSA, who works closely with the secretary of Homeland Security. Rest assured, your remarks will be passed on to the highest echelons of power in DC."

"Report whatever you'd like, Special Agent Jacobs," the lieutenant said. "If you are ready, you may move your prisoner to cell 4. Down the passageway here to your right. The sergeant here and the corporal will accompany you.

"Once the prisoner is contained, you will have to clear these immediate spaces. As you know, there are other spaces in the prison that you may occupy for whatever you have planned. But these are military-only spaces."

"I don't think I like your attitude, Lieutenant."

"That's your privilege, sir," Elliot said. "Sergeant? Corporal? Please accompany Mr. Jacobs and his crew with the prisoner to cell 4."

"Aye, sir."

"Aye, aye, Lieutenant," the sergeant said. "This way, sir."

They walked down the hall to an area marked "Isolation Inmates." They passed three steel doors on the right, then the sergeant held up his hand. "This is it."

He inserted a large key into a dead-bolt lock and turned the key to the left.

The door swung open with an eerie creaking, like something from a haunted house. "Okay, Makari, inside," Jacobs said.

Hasan stepped into the small cinder-block cell. There was no bed, no furniture, no chair. Only a toilet. In the back of the cell, he noticed another door, which had no window, only a small trapdoor cut into the bottom of it, about a foot wide by six inches high. Perhaps a feeding door to slip him food? *How odd*, he thought. *A cell with two doors.* The one linking to the guard station had a square Plexiglas window covering the vertical bars that were at head height in the door.

A video camera was mounted next to the ceiling in the back right corner.

"Aren't you going to uncuff him?" Lieutenant Elliot had followed the group down the passageway.

"We'll decide how we deal with our prisoners," the TSA chief said. "He's lucky we haven't amputated his hands after what he did."

"I suggest you uncuff him," Elliot said. "What you or the CIA do with him one-on-one might be your business. But here in our presence, until he gives a reason to act otherwise, I'm instructing you to uncuff him before we close the door."

"How dare you!" Jacobs fumed. "This is a TSA ELITE operation. Not CIA."

Elliot said, "US Marines don't violate the Geneva Conventions. Now either carry out my instructions or we'll take matters into our own hands."

Jacobs cursed under his breath. "Gentlemen, draw your weapons on the prisoner. Unless the lieutenant here objects to that too."

"Just don't get trigger-happy," Elliot said.

Three TSA ELITE guards jammed their pistol barrels against Hasan's head. "Fuchs, step into the cell. Uncuff him. If he makes a break for it, kill him."

"Yes, sir," Fuchs said as he walked into the small cell. "Turn around, Makari. Put your face against the back wall until the cuffs are removed and you hear us close the door behind you. Do you understand?"

"Yes."

Hasan turned around, walked to the back wall, and put his nose against it.

Fuchs gripped the cuffs and unlocked them. The cuffs dropped to the concrete floor, freeing Hasan's hands, but he didn't move. He heard shuffling behind him, and a moment later he heard the cell door slam.

Hasan turned around. He stood there. Alone.

Someone slid a metal blind down over the Plexiglas iron-barred window, blocking his view of the hall area. Now he could see no one and nothing.

The trapdoor at the bottom of the back door opened, letting in some light. A paper was pushed onto the floor.

A voice over a loudspeaker said, "Hasan Makari. We are special agents of the United States Transportation Security Administration— ELITE Forces. If you wish to save your life and your son's life, you will cooperate . . . sooner rather than later.

"What we are seeking from you is simple. Tell the truth. Confess to your crimes. Acknowledge your fault, and you may live. If you fail to do that, you shall die.

"On the floor before you is a simple statement for you to sign, acknowledging your guilt. Acknowledgment of guilt is the first step toward restoration.

"Pick it up, read it, and let us know when you are ready to sign it."

Silence.

Hasan reached down and picked the document up off the floor.

I, Hasan Makari, a citizen and resident of the Republic of Lebanon, do hereby acknowledge my involvement in the following acts, and I make this acknowledgment to United States Transportation Security Administration ELITE Forces, to whom I confess the following acts:

I did conspire and participate in the criminal operation causing the assassination of the United States ambassador, the Honorable George Madison.

My involvement consisted of, but was not necessarily limited to, the following acts:

- Communicating with unnamed coconspirators armed with rocket-propelled grenades, knowing that my coconspirators would launch an attack against Ambassador George Madison's motorcade in the city of El-Mina, Lebanon, at the corner of Al Istiklal and Mar Elias, in the North Governorate, Tripoli District.
- Assisting in this operation by serving as an active lookout, whereby I provided manual hand signals as the ambassador's motorcade rolled by my position to initiate the fatal rocket attack against the ambassador's motorcade.

I now confess, without reservation or hesitation, that I aided and abetted the assassination by giving hand signals to fire the rocket that killed the ambassador.

I further confess that my son, Najib Makari, assisted in the planning and execution of this operation to assassinate the ambassador.

Moreover, my son, Najib Makari, procured a fraudulent enlistment into the United States Navy for the purpose of perpetrating acts of terror against United States forces, and I have entered the United States to conspire with Najib Makari to perform further acts of terror against the United States.

I make this confession freely, voluntarily, and not under any undue influence or force of coercion.

Signed,

Hasan Makari

Hasan looked into the camera mounted up in the corner of the cell. "This statement is not true. There is nothing true about it. I cannot sign it."

The cell went dark.

He waited for his eyes to adjust.

A voice in the dark.

"That's a foolish choice, Mohammed."

The cell had been sealed from the outside, leaving him in total darkness.

What to do? Hasan reached out into the dark space, trying, against a swelling sense of panic, to feel for something to touch. The darkness enveloped his body like a suffocating blanket, with a noose of claustrophobia around his neck.

He took a step, both hands out in front of him.

Then another step.

Another.

The coarse surface of the cinder-block wall felt damp, almost cold.

He could not understand the sense of relief he felt, but he was grateful that somehow the panic had drained from his hands and into the concrete walls.

With both hands against the wall, he slid to the floor. He turned and sat, resting his back against the wall.

He closed his eyes, and when he did, there seemed to be more light against the backs of his eyelids than in the darkness of the room.

CHAPTER 2

• • •

HEADQUARTERS
US TRANSPORTATION SECURITY ADMINISTRATION
OFFICE OF GENERAL COUNSEL
ARLINGTON, VIRGINIA
THE NEXT DAY
8:00 A.M.

"Are you getting excited, Em?"

Emily Gardner smiled at her exuberant young colleague who stood at the door of her office. She removed her reading glasses and swiped a lock of brunette hair from her forehead. She smiled.

"Willie, why is it that when you greet me in the morning, you remind me so much of my little brother, Chuck?"

The young lawyer at the door sported a starched white shirt and power-red tie. He flashed a mischievous grin. "Maybe it's because you're struggling all night long with an overwhelming urge to date me. Maybe if you convince yourself that I'm your little brother, Chuck, this fleeting illusion helps you fight your overwhelming desire to date me. After all, you wouldn't want to kiss someone you imagined was your brother.

"Of course, you'll soon realize that I'm nothing like your brother. All your resistance will melt, and you'll surrender to your burning desire to date me, marry me, and have babies with me, babies who will grow up to become brilliant TSA lawyers like their mommy and daddy!"

Emily chuckled. "Now that last thought is scary."

"So the part about dating me and marrying me sounds good?"

She balled up a piece of paper and threw it at him. "Get out of my office, Willie, before I run the risk of getting arrested for indecent liberties with a minor."

"So if I don't get out of your office, you mean you might change your mind?"

"Okay! Okay! Coffee! Next week!" She threw up her hands. "But just coffee. Okay? You win. Now out of my office."

"Yessssssssss! There is a God." He turned to go out with a jig in his step.

"Close the door behind you before I change my mind."

"Yes, ma'am."

The boyish grin proved irresistible.

"And cut out the ma'am stuff. I'm not in the Navy anymore. I'm sensitive enough about going out with a guy who looks like he could be my son."

"With pleasure, ma'am." Willie Roberts moved out into the hall, blew her a kiss, and closed the door.

Emily turned around and looked out the window.

Thirty minutes to the press conference. The director wanted her there, standing behind him, available for an immediate consultation should any legal questions arise as he faced the press on national television. Or, if necessary, to step in and field questions.

She had never appeared on national television before, not even as a backdrop.

By all accounts, this should be a crowning and glorious moment in her professional career—her opportunity to shine in the limelight, with the full confidence of the director of the TSA. Only she and the chief of staff, Trevor McCorkle, would accompany the director.

Even if she merely stood there in her sharp power-red dress, new off the racks from Nordstrom, and was asked no questions, she would be noticed.

The PR offensive called for the director to be proactive with the press over the next few weeks as the program was unveiled with appropriations requests to Congress.

She had been told by the director to be ready, that he wanted her there, at each of the ten initial appearances planned, even the appearances scheduled before the Congress.

"I want you with me, Emily," Director Billy McNamara, the nation's newest TSA administrator, had told her. "Before this is over, you'll be promoted from deputy general counsel to general counsel. From there, the sky's the limit."

McNamara's obvious preference for Emily had ruffled some feathers within the general counsel's office. That she was, more or less, handpicked to be his protégé, ahead of a handful of attorneys more senior than she was, had not been well received.

The general counsel, Nick Miller, would retire in less than a year and seemed oblivious to the McNamara-Gardner axis.

But the four senior deputy general counsels, three being women, were all one level above Emily on the bureaucratic chain. All harbored ambitions of becoming general counsel. All were cold and backbiting.

"Hell hath no fury like a woman scorned." Emily had experienced for herself the truth of the statement. In this stormy turf war, Emily had become target number one by the "first rungers," as the senior deputy general counsels were called, especially the three female "first rungers," known collectively around the office as "the three witches of Eastwick."

As for McNamara, his intellect proved attractive. Emily could tolerate his less-than-macho stature, as she always had a thing for brainier types. A little more machismo would make him wholly irresistible.

McNamara's wimpy physical appearance was in sharp contrast to the boyish young staff counsel, Willie Roberts, a marathon runner whose wide smile, sparkling blue eyes, and flowery flattery captivated her imagination. Willie reminded her that she still had it, even after a contentious divorce, even with a guy seven years her junior.

Still, she had tried keeping Willie at bay. No need for more office talk. No need to rock the boat with the director, if there even was a boat to rock.

Things were happening so fast.

Why was she feeling queasy? Unsure?

She ticked off her bio. Only daughter of a Presbyterian preacher from meager beginnings: full scholarship, then valedictorian at Queens University in Charlotte. Law Review and summa cum laude at Campbell Law School. Rising through the ranks as a Navy JAG officer. Then to the general counsel's office at TSA. Now about to take the national stage.

Workaholism cost her a marriage. Or . . . not workaholism so much as Joe's young, blonde, miniskirt-wearing, gum-chomping paralegal at Furman & Watkins named Tiffany.

Whatever.

What scared Emily the most was that she had not cared when she discovered the text messages. At least there were no children involved.

Twenty-five minutes until the presser.

She glanced at her notes.

The phone on her desk buzzed.

"Yes, Kate."

"Miss Gardner, the director is on the line for you."

She smiled. "Punch him through, please."

"Yes, ma'am. You're connected."

"Morning, boss."

"How's my number one hotshot lawyer this morning?"

"Your number one hotshot lawyer stands ready to support the most brilliant administrator in the United States government, sir."

"Excellent answer, Emily. And not only the most brilliant administrator but the best judge of legal talent too."

"You're making me blush, sir."

"Anyway, are you ready for the presser?"

"All ready, Mr. Director."

"Billy."

She hesitated. "Of course. Billy. Will the secretary attend the presser?"

"No. We talked about it. Secretary Strayhorn's presence would take the spotlight off TSA. If the TSA is going to be the flagship agency of Homeland Security, we want the light shining on us. So at the presser, it's gonna be me, you, McCorkle, and Special Agent Bob Nolan."

"Hmm. Is Nolan speaking too?"

"Well, since we will be revealing to the public the formation of TSA ELITE Forces, it's possible that he could get questions about his role as operational head of TSA ELITE Forces, like you could get legal questions. I'll introduce him like I'll introduce you . . . but his instructions are to defer questions to the director . . . and that would be me.

"But like you, his principal role will be to serve as a human backdrop. Although I'm sure the ratings will be much higher on the left side of the screen, where you'll be standing."

She smiled. "You're going to make me blush, Director."

"Billy."

"Yes, of course. Billy."

"Okay, listen. We've got to get moving. Come up to my office. We'll spend a few minutes getting ready, then we'll walk down together."

"I'll be right there."

The phone went dead.

She took a deep breath, stood up, and checked herself in the mirror. She pushed a lock of hair back out of her eyes and said a final prayer before leaving her office. "Lord, please keep my hair in place and help me if they ask questions."

Time to go.

With purpose in her step, she walked out of her office, closed the door behind her, strode past her secretaries and paralegals with a confident smile, then headed to the elevators to go up to the director's office.

Today would be the day that would begin to define the rest of her destiny.

• • •

BUILDING AV624
UNITED STATES NAVAL STATION
GUANTÁNAMO BAY, CUBA
8:43 A.M.

Lieutenant Matt Davis, electing to wear his summer khaki working uniform rather than the hotter Navy camouflage uniform, stood with briefcase in hand on the gravel drive in front of his new temporary home, otherwise known as Building AV624.

The sun had risen ten degrees above the horizon. Already the temperature had closed in on eighty degrees. The first tropical gust from the Caribbean provided welcome relief.

He checked his watch: 0843.

His ride from Navy Defense Command GITMO, over on the Windward Side, was late.

In most of the Navy, "zero eight thirty" meant "zero eight thirty."

But he had been warned that at GITMO, there seemed to be an unofficial suspension of the Navy's strict adherence to punctuality.

Part of it, apparently, had to do with the whole Caribbean nonchalance about time, which seemed to have somehow bled across the borders of the barbed-wire fencing separating the American base from the rest of Communist Cuba.

A bigger part of it, however, or so he had been told, revolved around the erratic ferry schedules. While the ferries were supposed to run on time, circumstances, he had been warned, often prevented it.

Special flights with VIPs, press members, and high-ranking brass demanding immediate access to the Windward Side all gave reason for the ferry not to be on time.

The Windward Side was the main part of the base, separated from the Leeward Side by a bay two and a half miles across. Matt was on the

Leeward Side, the more desolate side of the base, with the airstrip and the spartan government barracks where they had stuck him last night.

It appeared, following a second check of his watch, that Lieutenant JG David Rusotto, JAGC, USNR, had been detained by ferry service delays, or something else had come up.

The beep of the horn brought his eyes off his watch. The approaching jeep was driven by an officer in working khakis with a single silver bar on one collar and the millrind of the US Navy JAG Corps on the other. The officer had a receding hairline, looked goofy, but had a friendly grin. "Lieutenant Davis?" the officer called out from his open window.

"You Rusotto?"

"That'd be me, sir." Rusotto kept grinning. "Need a ride?"

"I thought you forgot me."

"No, sir. Ferry schedule problems. Sorry, sir."

Matt hopped in, and Rusotto wheeled the jeep out of the gravel parking lot.

"Welcome to GITMO, Lieutenant."

"Thanks, Rusotto. At least I think thanks," Matt said as Rusotto turned onto the two-lane asphalt road so fast, squealing the tires, that Matt was slung to his right.

"Slow down, Rusotto."

"Sorry, sir. Don't want to miss the ferry. How was your flight?"

"Peachy."

"Sorry for speeding. But the ferry captain said if we hurry, we can catch the ferry straight back to the Windward Side and not get stuck over here for another thirty minutes."

"By all means. If you have to drive like Earnhardt Junior to get us on that ferry, go for it, as long as the Shore Patrol doesn't ticket you. Last thing I need is to waste another thirty minutes."

"Aye, sir."

"So, Rusotto. Where are you taking me first?"

"The RLSO detachment, sir."

"That's great. But when do I get to see my clients?"

Rusotto pulled into the ferry parking lot. The gray ferry was still at the dock, but sailors appeared to be getting her ready to sail. "We'd better hurry." He gunned the accelerator, now pushing Matt back in his seat. "Sorry, sir," Rusotto said. A sailor in a Dixie cup hat and light blue service work shirt and blue-jean dungarees was directing traffic onto the ferry. He held up his hand in the universal halt motion. "Whew. Looks like we're going to make it."

"Great driving, Lieutenant JG Rusotto. Now, what about me seeing my clients?"

"Not sure. That can be a problem."

"What do you mean—that can be a problem?"

"Well, sir, I've been here at the detachment for six months, but from what I'm told, the agencies tend to determine when defense counsel can have contact with clients."

"Agencies?"

"Yes, sir." The sailor directing traffic waved the jeep onto the ferry. Rusotto drove forward, up onto the deck. "DOJ. CIA. Now, most recently, the FBI. They always seem to want to control everything. It's a big sticking point with defense counsel."

The ferry started backing out, away from the dock. Matt slipped his Ray-Bans out of his pocket as he looked at the bright waters of the bay. "That's better. Anyway, I remember reading about Commander Ruiz getting into it with the DOJ when he asked the former commanding admiral at a hearing about all the agencies that have been down here."

"Exactly, sir," Rusotto said. "Ruiz is a defense legend. I never met him. Wish I had."

"Yep," Matt said. "I read an article in the *Miami Herald* about the flap. Something about the DOJ lawyer claiming Ruiz was 'playing with fire,' and Ruiz saying he wasn't gonna be threatened."

"From what I hear," Rusotto said, "Ruiz doesn't take junk from anybody. His clients had been tortured, and he wanted to know what federal agencies were responsible. "

"Was Ruiz right?"

"Right about what, sir?"

"Right about that comment on 'playing with fire' being a threat."

"No doubt, sir. They threaten defense attorneys all the time. That 'playing with fire' comment happened to go viral. But most of their threats never see the light of day. The government doesn't want anyone to know that these terror trials are kangaroo courts. Threatening defense counsel is one of their tactics. You heard about Andy Hart, didn't you?"

"The civilian defense attorney from Ohio? Yes, I read that," Matt said. "Paper said he committed suicide."

"Well, let me tell you something, sir. Nobody here, none of the JAG defense lawyers, are buying the suicide story any more than anybody thinks Vince Foster committed suicide or Andrew Breitbart died of a heart attack."

Matt let that sink in.

"Too much information can be dangerous. If you know what I mean, sir."

"I think I know what you mean, Rusotto."

The ferry engines revved, and the ferry, transporting two jeeps and a truck, churned into the bay.

"Want to step out of the jeep, sir?"

"Sure, that'd be great. I could use some fresh air."

Matt stepped out onto the deck. Out on the bay, the ferry was gliding across the amazing aqua-colored water, so distinctive of the Caribbean. He walked over to the railing on the starboard side and leaned into a cooler breeze from across the bay, from the Windward Side.

Somewhere over there, his clients awaited him. The twisting in his stomach told him that somewhere over there mortal danger lurked.

"Lieutenant?"

Matt looked around at Rusotto. "What is it?"

"Sir, I know you outrank me, but would you mind if I offer you some friendly advice?"

The bubbly smile on Rusotto's face had turned stone cold.

"Sure, Rusotto. I'm not above taking advice from anybody."

Rusotto looked off to the side, his face toward the sea, to the breeze now blowing in from the mouth of the bay. "Well, sir, if I were you, I would be careful."

"What do you mean, Rusotto? Do you know something that I need to know?"

Rusotto looked at him. "That's all I can say, sir. Please. Watch your back."

• • •

DEPARTMENT OF HOMELAND SECURITY
NATIONAL CAPITAL REGION HEADQUARTERS
WASHINGTON, DC

The six flat screens in Strayhorn's office were preset to the networks whose coverage would interest him.

Fox.

CNN.

MSNBC.

CBS.

ABC.

NBC.

Each network had a talking head or two babbling about what to expect in the press conference, all spouting off as if they knew something. In reality, none of them knew anything.

All but one of the screens had been muted. Only the CBS News video stream could be heard. Aside from the fact that he viewed Fox, CNN, and MSNBC as too political, in one direction or the other, and viewed CBS as more of a bureaucrat's network, his longtime affinity for CBS went back to his boyhood crush on Lesley Stahl, who at the time could have been his mother, but still remained for him the hottest creature on the planet, even in the twilight of her career.

A knock on the door.

"Come in."

"I prepared a few goodies for you for the press conference." His longtime secretary, Carol Gibson, wearing her middle-aged beauty with an attractive charisma, stepped into his office with a silver tray full of cookies, donuts, coffee, and orange juice.

"You're gonna make me fatter, Carol." He picked up a chocolate chip cookie and took a big bite.

"Just trying to make sure my boss is happy."

"That you do, my dear."

"It's my pleasure, sir." As she poured him a glass of orange juice, all six flat screens cut away from their network talking heads and gave a widescreen view of the pressroom at TSA headquarters.

The press hounds were all there, all in their seats, the backs of their heads showing in the camera view. All eyes were glued to the empty podium in front. Were it not for the absence of the presidential seal on the podium, the image could almost pass for a briefing at the White House pressroom.

Good, Strayhorn thought. The Homeland Security PR team had done a marvelous job.

The double doors behind the podium opened. Billy stepped up to the podium. Strayhorn recognized Bob Nolan, lead TSA ELITE special agent, who walked in just behind McNamara.

But the brunette in the red dress with him? He wasn't sure who she was.

McNamara looked out over the crowd of reporters, with his two escorts flanking him.

"Good morning," McNamara said. "I'm Billy McNamara, the director of the United States Transportation Security Administration. I have with me this morning, to my left, Special Agent Bob Nolan, chief special agent in charge of our new TSA ELITE Special Forces, a new and special law enforcement component which will be instrumental to the United States in our continued War on Terror. Bob will be pleased to provide more information on this exciting new organization." McNamara nodded at Nolan.

Nolan, wearing the standard light-blue shirt and dark-blue pants of regular TSA officers, except that his shirt had a patch saying "TSA ELITE," stepped forward, nodded and waved, then stepped back.

"And to my right, I would like to introduce an invaluable member of our legal staff. This is Emily Gardner, deputy general counsel for the agency. Emily has been instrumental in providing legal guidance on a number of issues."

The lady in red stepped forward, nodded, smiled, then stepped back.

"Emily Gardner," Strayhorn said to himself.

"As you know, yesterday at Philadelphia International Airport, officers of the Transportation Security Administration arrested a suspected terrorist, a Lebanese national named Hasan Makari, who is suspected to have ties in connection with the murder of United States Ambassador George Madison.

"Additionally, yesterday at the Norfolk naval base, authorities arrested Mr. Makari's son, Najib Makari. Najib Makari enlisted in the United States Navy. Based upon evidence gathered by TSA ELITE Forces, he is allegedly involved in the conspiracy with his father, Hasan Makari, to commit acts of terror against the United States. TSA reports that this father-son terror cell planned terror strikes within the United States military. Najib Makari is suspected of sabotaging a United States Navy jet that plunged into the sea while taking off from the aircraft carrier USS *Abraham Lincoln*, the ship to which Najib Makari had been assigned as a petty officer.

"If unchecked, we believe Najib Makari would have attempted further acts of terror within the US Navy. Even worse, as an aviation mechanic working on attack jets, he had opportunities to commit sabotage causing great loss of life."

The TSA director took a sip from a glass of water.

"Special Agent Nolan is our lead TSA ELITE special agent. As such, he is the operational officer, reporting directly to me, heading up a new special investigations and law enforcement unit which we believe is the finest in the world.

"TSA ELITE Special Forces, which we are announcing today, is comprised of the best and brightest law enforcement and investigative officers the United States has to offer and will enable our agency to provide a higher level of security to the American people.

"Heretofore, the mission of the Transportation Security Administration has been to protect the nation's transportation systems to ensure freedom of movement for people and commerce.

"Our agency, since our inception in the wake of 9/11, has carried out this mission superbly. Now, with the addition of TSA ELITE Special Forces, our agency will be able to acquire investigative and offensive capabilities to prevent terrorism, both foreign and domestic, including terrorism from right-wing groups and others, before that terror can even germinate.

"Think of it this way. My doctor friends tell me the best attack against a cancer cell is to eradicate it when it's still a cell, before it metastasizes, before it goes anywhere.

"And so it is with the cancer of terror. When it comes to protecting the nation's transportation systems, we intend to eradicate terror at the early cancer stage, before there is an opportunity to create significant damage, as we have done now with the arrests of these terrorists.

"I am pleased to report that TSA ELITE Forces were active not only in the arrests of these terror suspects but also in the investigation and planning.

"In announcing these benchmark arrests, we are placing on display the employment of a new doctrine, a doctrine we call 'Seek Out and Destroy,' whereby we seek out and destroy terror cells before these terror cells, like malignant cancer cells, have an opportunity to metastasize and cause great harm to the American people.

"And in discovering and quashing this Makari cell, we have stopped the work of these cells and, in doing so, have saved the lives of thousands of American citizens—American men, women, and children—who would have died in acts of terror had these terrorists not been stopped.

"These arrests not only mark the beginning of a new strategic doctrine being employed by your TSA, but also the unveiling of a new strategic force."

McNamara looked around the room, then continued, "These TSA ELITE officers will comprise an armed, truly elite force operating in the venues already controlled by TSA at our nation's airports, as well as some train stations and bus terminals, and they will now be directing missions at undisclosed locations as well.

"The mission of TSA ELITE is one of moving forward. In this case, our motto is 'Forward Prevention.' Our agency, like our nation, must move forward. Never backward.

"And now, I will be happy to answer any questions you might have."

Hands flew up all over the room, most of them waving like a group of first graders trying to get the teacher's attention.

"Here in the front."

"Elisabeth Miller. NPR Radio."

"Morning, Elisabeth."

"Director. It now appears that TSA is transitioning from an agency that is unarmed to an agency that is armed. Most Americans remember when TSA was created after 9/11 that an army of blue-shirted agents were deployed to the nation's airports and that those agents were unarmed. Now, under this new policy, you've described a sudden shift designed to make TSA into a nationwide armed police force, rather than simply a force to protect Americans at airports. When did this sudden shift of the TSA's mission take place?"

The camera caught McNamara sipping water. "First off, Elisabeth, I'd point out that we will still have a lot of unarmed officers in airports and other public transportation venues. But to answer your question, the strategic shift goes back to 2013, when the TSA, under the Obama administration, purchased 3.5 million rounds of .357 caliber ammunition under the Visible Intermodal Prevention and Response Program, otherwise known as 'VIPER.' That program, established under President Obama, has deployed teams of armed TSA officers to railroad stations, bus stations, ferries, car tunnels, ports, subways, truck weigh stations, rest areas, and special events.

"And, as many of you know, Homeland Security purchased ammunition during the Obama administration to prepare the government for the inevitable battle of the domestic terror onslaught here on the American homeland. In the year 2013 alone, the department purchased over two billion rounds of ammunition, and for good cause. As President

Obama once said, we need new and enhanced civilian law enforcement forces, even forces that rival the military, to protect the homeland.

"So to answer your question, I'd say that the TSA ELITE Force is a natural extension of that philosophy, and of the VIPER program, and in reality, being armed is nothing new at all. Next question."

"Javier Perez, CBS News."

"Go ahead, Javier."

"Sir, our ambassador was assassinated eleven years ago. Why has it taken so long to bring Hasan Makari to justice? And second, is it a negative reflection on the CIA and our military that they haven't been able to grab this guy for all these years? Yet this new TSA ELITE Force located this terror cell and made the arrests in short order. What did this TSA ELITE Force do that the CIA could not?"

McNamara forced a wry smile. "First off, Javier, the yeoman's work of our TSA ELITE Forces in apprehending these terrorists is by no means any reflection on the fine work done by other US agencies, such as the CIA and the US military. We're all on one federal team. We all support one another.

"I can't go into a lot of detail, but knowledge of Hasan Makari's involvement with the conspiracy to assassinate the ambassador surfaced recently, and our people were in the right place at the right time." He pointed to another questioner.

"Director, John Haynes, MSNBC. Can you share anything about the specific terror plots that were foiled by these arrests?"

"Thank you, John. I wish I could go into detail, but I can't, for security purposes. I can say, however, that we believe the younger Makari, who enlisted in the US Navy, attempted to sabotage a US Navy jet. It appears that he may have taken action that caused it to abort on takeoff and crash in the Atlantic."

"Angela Johnson. European News Service. Sir, can you confirm any loss of life as a result of this terrorist incident with the Navy jet?"

"Angela, we're hearing that the pilot is in stable condition."

"Sir. Anthony Taylor. Skynews. As I understand it, the elder Makari flew to the US from Lebanon. If that's the case, since the elder

Makari is a foreigner, doesn't that make this a case within the jurisdiction of the CIA rather than the TSA? It's my understanding that
the CIA oversees foreign surveillance and counterterrorism overseas.
And has President Surber been briefed on all this?"

"Good questions, Anthony. First off, it's my understanding that my
boss, the secretary of Homeland Security, Secretary Strayhorn, either
has briefed or will be briefing the White House. Second, you're correct about the CIA primarily having jurisdiction over foreign matters.
But in some cases, there can be some overlap. And while in this case
it's true that the elder Makari's flight to the US originated in Lebanon,
the case came under our jurisdiction before then, when the younger
Makari entered the United States, making this a domestic rather than a
foreign issue. So we opened it as a domestic case. Our investigation into
Lebanon sprang from the domestic surveillance of the younger Makari,
that is, Najib Makari. So we retained jurisdiction of the case."

"Sir. Jeff Cullipher. *Washington Post.* Could you comment on where
the terrorists are being detained?"

"Yes. We've transferred the terror suspects to the US Navy detention facility at Guantánamo Bay."

"Anne Brown. Reuters legal correspondent. Director, we've seen
plenty of precedent for foreign terror suspects being transferred to
Guantánamo. But the precedent so far seems to have been to try military terror suspects in military courts-martial. An Army court-martial
prosecuted Bradley Manning. The Army also prosecuted Major Nidal
Hasan, the Fort Hood shooter.

"Isn't it true that members of the United States military are entitled
to a trial by their peers in a military court-martial? Consistent with the
Sixth Amendment right to trial by jury?"

McNamara seemed to hesitate at that question. He turned to
the woman to his right and whispered something in her ear, which
brought a nod from her, then a short smile. Then he turned back to the
questioner.

The whole off-the-record conversation lasted only a couple of seconds, but to Fallington Strayhorn, watching the screen in his office, the interaction between the bureaucrat and the brunette seemed like a slow-motion blur.

"Anne, you ask a great question, and since that's a legal and a constitutional question, I'll defer to Emily Gardner on this one." He turned to the brunette. "Emily?"

"I'm Emily Gardner, TSA Office of Legal Counsel. You're correct, Miss Brown, that both the Uniform Code of Military Justice, or UCMJ, and the Sixth Amendment guarantee a right to trial by jury, and the UCMJ, with which I'm familiar as an ex-JAG officer, ordinarily affords a military member the right to trial at a military court-martial.

"You've correctly cited two other military-terrorist cases, the Manning court-martial and the Hasan court-martial, as examples of that. We also considered the example set in the successful prosecution of the three Navy chaplains for treason a few years ago, prosecuted by the current judge advocate general of the Navy, Vice Admiral Zack Brewer.

"So we took a look at all that as precedent. But in the end, our legal recommendation hinged on factual factors which set this case apart from those. First, unlike those cases, where service members were American born, Petty Officer Makari was born in Lebanon. Therefore, we say that he's not entitled to the same Sixth Amendment protection for a right to trial by jury as US citizens.

"Also, we noted that this conspiracy to commit acts of terror started before he enlisted in the Navy. Therefore, we took the position that the enlistment was based on a fraudulent conspiracy, meaning that the younger Makari was never legally part of the US military and therefore not entitled to the right to trial by a military court-martial."

"But, Miss Gardner, isn't that a tenuous position? I mean, shouldn't a judge or jury decide that the enlistment was fraudulent?"

The gorgeous lady smiled, brushing back her hair. "No. If Makari were being prosecuted for fraud, then I suppose I could see that point. But since he is not, we feel that we can make that determination administratively."

"What is the Navy's position on all this?"

McNamara stepped back up to the podium. "I'll take that. Thank you, Emily." The woman stepped back to her place. "All federal agencies, including the Navy, have been cooperative. Now, if you'll excuse me, that's all the time we have for questions, as we have a lot of work to do in follow-up."

McNamara, Gardner, and Nolan turned, all waving, and stepped away to a howling chorus of questions being yelled at them. The screen shot back to the studio. Secretary Strayhorn punched the Mute button to end the idle chitchat from the talking heads.

He picked up the telephone and buzzed his secretary.

"Yes, sir?"

"Carol. Get Barry Samuels on the phone for me, please."

"Certainly, sir."

Strayhorn leaned back in his chair and tapped an ink pen against his large mahogany desk. He needed a smoke. The pack of Marlboro Menthol Blend No. 54, just purchased on the way to the office that morning by his driver, sat in the front pocket of his short-sleeved white shirt.

He popped a cigarette in his mouth and caressed the filter with the tip of his tongue. He fished in his pocket for the lighter, and within seconds, a satisfying, warm nicotine cloud filled his windpipe and lungs.

Sweet relief!

Carol Gibson had had to put up with his smoking all these years. So what?

Strayhorn ignored the widespread antismoking campaign waged by the surgeon general, for he believed that in the halls of power, powerful men could smoke, and the smell of cigarettes was a powerful aphrodisiac.

His desk phone buzzed.

"Yes, Carol."

"Mr. Porter is on the line, sir."

Strayhorn took another drag and set the cigarette in an ashtray. His reliable right-hand man, Barry Samuels, on whom he had bestowed the title of "special assistant to the secretary—Department of Homeland Security," could wait another second or two.

In Washington the party with the ability to force another party to wait demonstrated a subtle but clear show of power in a city where the chain of power took a backseat to nothing.

Never be too anxious—nor too quick—to answer the call of a subordinate on hold. But a modicum of common courtesy mandated that a subordinate not be placed on hold so long as to waste excessive time—just long enough to remind the subordinate, ever so subtly, that your time was more valuable than his.

He picked up the phone. "Morning, Barry."

"Good morning, sir. How may I be of service to you today?"

"Did you see McNamara's presser?"

"Yes, sir. I think everybody in the department did. Big day for the department, sir."

"What did you think?"

"From my standpoint, it went well."

"This new lawyer that Billy had with him . . . what's her name?" As if he didn't know.

"Gardner, sir. I believe her name is Emily Gardner."

"Yes, that seems right. Anyway, what do you know about her?"

"I understand she's new to the legal staff down there at TSA. She's supposed to be a rising legal star at TSA. I've never met her."

"She handled herself superbly when she got put on the spot by Anne Brown."

"Yes, sir," Samuels said. "Anne Brown can put anybody on the spot. I agree. Gardner responded superbly."

"Yes." Strayhorn toyed with his chin. "Anyway, I want you to run a full background on this new legal beagle, Emily Gardner. Include everything in the TSA file and more. I want that report on my desk by the end of the day."

"Certainly, Mr. Secretary."

"And, Barry?"

"Yes, sir."

"Listen. This is between us. Don't let anybody know I've ordered this background. And don't let Billy McNamara know that his boss is snooping around on his new legal star. No point in bursting the boy's bubble."

"Acknowledged, sir. All intel on this Emily Gardner stays between us, Mr. Secretary."

"Excellent." Strayhorn smiled and leaned back in his chair. He took one last drag from his cigarette and then crushed out the glowing end. He rubbed the butt to a pulp and dropped it in the ashtray. "Now get to work."

"Yes, sir."

CHAPTER 3

* * *

"Welcome to the Windward Side, Lieutenant." Lieutenant JG David Rusotto pulled the jeep into the sunny gravel parking lot of the Navy Legal Service Office. "And welcome to the RLSO. This is where you'll set up operations.

"I'll take you to your offices, let you get settled in. Then Lieutenant Commander Bob Petronio, the senior defense counsel, will stop by and talk to you about getting in to see your client." Rusotto brought the jeep to a stop.

"Where's Commander Petronio now?"

"Department meeting. All the JAGs are tied up for the next thirty minutes. I got lucky I got drafted to go pick you up. I hate those meetings."

"So I've got to wait thirty minutes before I can even start finding out how to get to my clients?"

Rusotto looked at him, and Matt noticed, for the first time, that his bushy eyebrows ran together. Sort of a unibrow look. "Sorry, Lieutenant, I don't make the rules. I do what I'm told."

"No problem, Rusotto."

"Anyway, want to go see your office?"

"Sure. Why not? I can go to my new office and hurry up and wait. Like I've been doing all morning. It's the Navy way."

They got out of the jeep and walked toward the Navy Legal Service Office building, a one-story yellowish stucco structure nestled in a grove of palm trees, sitting about a hundred yards off the road in an area of lush green grass. A dozen cars, all with silver-and-black US government plates, sat in the parking lot.

Two flags were mounted on the exterior wall flanking the entrance, the flag of the United States of America and the flag of the US Navy.

As they approached the entrance of the RLSO, something ran across his foot. He jumped back, his heart in hyper mode.

"What the—" Then three more large, yellowish rats scampered across in front of them. "What the heck?"

"Sorry, sir. Forgot to warn you." Rusotto reached down, picked up a rock, and threw it at the rats. "Get out of here!"

The squealing rats raced across the parking lot and disappeared behind the hedges of shrubbery up against the building.

"Banana rats," Rusotto said. "They're everywhere down here. They're scarce elsewhere in Cuba, but we have an overabundance of them at GITMO because the animal rights wackos back in the States won't let us clear 'em out, even though they're a royal pain.

"They're mostly harmless. But they get big and brazen. The Cubans eat them, so they're scarce outside the base. But this base is infested with thousands of them, hanging in trees, crawling all over the place. They aren't deterred by humans."

"Looks like I should have brought my sidearm."

"Shooting one of the suckers might be the quickest way to get you an audience with your clients," Rusotto quipped. "I'm not so sure which is a tougher terrorist group to deal with—al-Qaida or PETA."

"If it takes shooting one of those yellow rats to get to see my clients, I'm all in," Matt said.

"Hopefully it won't come to that." Rusotto pushed open the front door for Matt to step inside.

"Master Chief, Lieutenant Ernie James, this is Lieutenant Matt Davis," Rusotto said to the command duty officer and the chief of the watch, who wore working khakis and sat at two separate desks in an open-door office to the left.

"Welcome, Lieutenant," James, a lanky, mustached officer, said.

"I'm taking Lieutenant Davis back to his office," Rusotto said. "If you see Lieutenant Commander Petronio, please let him know Lieutenant Davis is here."

"Roger that, Rusotto." James looked up from his computer screen, making eye contact with Matt. "Welcome aboard and good luck, Lieutenant Davis."

"Appreciate it, Lieutenant," Matt said.

"Down this passageway, sir," Rusotto said.

"After you, Rusotto."

They headed down a long hallway that ran from the quarterdeck like a spoke extending from a wheel. The floor tiles were a dark green, perhaps black, giving the hallway a bit of a dim, shadowy appearance. The closed doors to the left and right bore the names of the Navy defense counsel who occupied the offices.

The third door on the right displayed the nameplate of LCDR Bob Petronio, JAGC, USN—Senior Defense Counsel.

"So nobody's in these offices at the moment because of the defense meeting?" Matt asked.

"Right, sir. You'll have the wing all to yourself for a while. Your office is the last on the right. Here we are, sir."

The closed door bore the nameplate "LT Matt Davis, JAGC, USNR—Special Detailed Defense Counsel, US Military Commissions Court."

"How nice," Matt said. "My own nameplate already."

"Commander Petronio doesn't miss much, sir." Rusotto opened the door. The darkness from the hallway faded in the bright morning light streaming through the three large windows in the office. "What do you think, sir?"

"Not a bad view," Matt said.

"Not if you like grass, palm trees, and a road full of military vehicles going back and forth," Rusotto said.

"I've seen worse," Matt said.

"Yes, sir. Anyway, this is it. If you're looking for the head, it's down the passageway, port side."

"I saw it when we walked by."

"Also, the coffee mess is down by the quarterdeck. Chief Richards makes a mean brew. Lots of battery acid and caffeine."

"Great to know," Matt said.

"Make yourself at home. I have to attend to some other business, but I'm sure Commander Petronio will be by soon."

"That's great, Rusotto. Thanks for everything."

"My pleasure, sir." The unibrowed junior grade lieutenant stepped into the hall and disappeared.

Matt turned his back to the door, crossed his arms, and looked outside. Something felt strange, but he could not tell what. Something odd, sort of like the old Jim Carrey movie, *The Truman Show*. What was that fictional, surrealistic town where Truman lived? He walked to the window, craned his neck, looking to the left and the right. Then it hit him.

Seahaven.

From a natural-setting standpoint, GITMO's beauty featured swaying palm trees, luscious green grass, flowers in pink, yellow, and white, and aqua-blue water.

Yet GITMO also had a plastic, Seahavenish, superficial veneer about it. The plastic feeling reeked in the air despite the undisputable beauty of the place's natural setting. The strange aura had something to do with the GITMO detention center and the Military Commissions Tribunal. From the publicized treatment of defense counsel practicing before the commission, to the strange death of Andy Hart, to Rusotto warning him to watch his back, something didn't feel right.

Oh well.

As a defense attorney and a naval officer, Matt had sworn oaths to the Constitution in both capacities, and he had pledged to perform his duty to the best of his ability in the case of each.

Whatever his gut was screaming, he would not allow the weird feeling to interfere with the performance of his duty.

Time to get to work, at least to the extent that he could get anything done before he met Hasan Makari or his son, Petty Officer Najib Makari.

Matt turned his back to the window and pulled out the leather chair from behind his desk and sat down, happy to get off his feet.

A to-do list. That's where he needed to start.

He spun his chair to the left and pulled open the metal file cabinet. "Okay. Legal pads. Check. But where are the doggone pens?"

He spun the chair back around. "Maybe they're in here." He pulled open the center desk drawer. A single white envelope, standard business size, lay in the drawer, addressed to "LT Matt Davis, JAGC, USNR."

Matt picked up the envelope, opened it, and read the undated handwritten message.

> Welcome to GITMO, Lieutenant Davis.
> Check your e-mail.
>
> > All the best,
> > Andy Hart

"Andy Hart? What the—" Cold chills cascaded down his back, the instant effect of receiving a letter from a dead man. Was this the very office where Hart had worked?

He punched the power button on the desktop computer.

The computer fired up.

Instantaneous Internet connection.

With his heart pounding, he typed in the URL for his e-mail.

No delays. Instant access.

The first e-mail in his inbox flashed the sender's address as *andyhart@springgrovecemetery.com*.

"Dear Jesus." Matt clicked on the e-mail.

DETAINED

Dear Lieutenant Davis,

Welcome to GITMO!

You join a long line of dutiful defense counsels representing the world's most unique criminal clients, making you part of a small, unique fraternity of attorneys whose place will be assured in history.

I hope you will find your stay here comfortable and that, unlike mine, your life following your service here will be long and fruitful.

You are occupying the office that I once occupied. You are sitting in the chair that I once sat in.

The issue is whether you will now meet the same fate that I met.

For here you have a glorious opportunity for permanent fame and an elevated respect within the legal community, provided you do not blow it, like I did.

You have been selected for this post by the same governmental organization that is prosecuting the terrorists you are defending. I represented many of these. Now you have been preordained to represent two more.

Let the press see that you are going through the motions. But understand that there is a limit beyond which you should not ask questions. There is a point that you should not press further.

There is a preordained verdict already destined that you should not disturb nor refuse to accept.

Do these things and you will be handsomely rewarded.

Refuse, and you will meet the fate that I met and join me where I am.

> Andy P. Hart, Esq.
> Spring Grove Cemetery
> 4521 Spring Grove Avenue
> Cincinnati, Ohio
> Counsel for the Defense
> January 19, 1975–April 25, 2013
>
> *Annuit Coeptis*
> *Novus Ordo Seclorum*

"What? What kind of a sick joker is behind this bull? And what's with this Latin *Novus Ordo Seclorum* stuff?" The e-mail sent his heart racing. But the accelerated heart rate came more from anger and adrenaline than fear. "Bunch of classless bull. Draft a classless letter from a dead man. You want to play ball like this?" He was speaking to an empty office. "Fine. Go for it."

Matt hit the Control button, followed by the Print button, and hoped the message would finish printing before Commander Petronio showed.

He snatched the message off the printer, folded it, and stashed it in his briefcase.

He could do nothing but wait.

• • •

GUANTÁNAMO BAY DETENTION CENTER
CAMP DELTA
UNITED STATES NAVAL BASE
GUANTÁNAMO BAY, CUBA

The darkness.

It proved overwhelming. When Hasan opened his eyes after sleep, he would stare into the blackness, straining to detect even a particle of light. He felt like a thirsty man in the desert, salivating at the mirage of a watery pool.

Sensory deprivation, whether deprivation of water or of light or of sound, could within a short time drive a man mad.

Hasan had learned that the best mode of defense against the madness was to keep his eyes closed, which fooled the body into believing that it was time for bed, making the unbearable shroud of darkness a tad more bearable.

He opened his eyes, facing the darkness with Scripture. "I will fear no evil, for thou art with me; thy rod and thy staff they comfort me."

Thank God Eugene had encouraged him to begin memorizing Scriptures all those years ago. The Word of God gave him light in the darkness.

He spoke again, from memory: "In the beginning was the Word, and the Word was with God, and the Word was God. He was with God in the beginning.

"Through him all things were made; without him nothing was made that has been made.

"In him was life, and that life was the light of all mankind.

"The light shines in the darkness, and the darkness has not overcome it."

What? Was he seeing a change in color in the cell?

The blackness morphed to a dim purplish glow.

He looked above and squinted his eyes.

No.

Yes.

They were tampering, somehow, with the lighting in the cell. Perhaps with black light. Or dim fluorescents. Something.

"Hasan Makari. Hasan Makari." A woman's voice. Low in pitch. Almost sultry.

The purple light came up a bit more. They started mixing a dim reddish hue in with the purple.

"Do you hear us, Hasan Makari?"

"I hear you. What do you want?"

"All we want is for you to tell the truth."

More red light. More purple light. He could see the outlines of his hands and arms.

"I always tell the truth."

A high-pitched squeak from across the floor. Not so loud, just high-pitched. Then another squeak. And then another.

"Good. Then there is the small matter of the confession you refused to sign earlier. You know, they say confession is good for the soul. And they also say the truth shall set you free."

The squeaking grew louder. Like a chorus of chirping crickets or something. He could not be sure.

"The truth may set you free," Hasan said, "but I will not and cannot turn the truth into a lie, nor a lie into the truth."

More squeaking. The blackness morphed to a dim glowing red, and then the red became slightly brighter. Then they filled the cell with a purple and red light mix, like a haunted house at a cheap carnival.

"Once again, your choices are unfortunate. Perhaps some of our friends can persuade you that your wisest choice for freedom would be to come clean. Sign that confession, Hasan Makari."

"I cannot and will not."

Across the room, the trapdoor opened.

A sheet of white light shone across the floor, like a white glowing carpet stretched under the canopy of red and purple.

More squeaking. Like a chorus of angry chimpanzees. But not chimpanzees. Smaller vocal cords. High-pitched. Chirping. Angry.

A long shadow appeared down the middle of the white-carpeted light.

Something black, a shadow, was in the center of the trapdoor!

It turned. The silhouette of a long tail stretched across the opening.

The head curved down into a pointy nose.

A rat!

It turned, faced him, and started crawling under the trapdoor into the cell.

Another black ball was at the trapdoor.

Then another.

And another.

Dozens of nibbling rodent faces crawled into the cell as the lights came up more.

Hundreds more followed the first wave. They inched across the floor toward him, their noses twitching, like a slow, black tide rolling across the beach—an army of rodents, coming toward him like a tsunami breaching the bulkhead.

"It is not too late to change your mind, Hasan Makari. The truth. That is all we seek."

Hasan pushed himself into the corner of the cell as the squeaking of hundreds of rats echoed against the concrete walls.

"What do you say, Hasan?"

He felt a rat nibbling at his foot.

"I cannot."

"Don't be foolish. You do not have to subject yourself to this."

Then onto his hands.

"I will not lie."

He held his breath as rats swarmed up his pant legs, then up his arms, and then . . . the first reached his neck. Then another.

Hasan closed his eyes and remembered the words of Isaiah the prophet:

> *The wolf also shall dwell with the lamb,*
> *and the leopard shall lie down with the kid;*
> *and the calf and the young lion and the fatling together;*
> *and a little child shall lead them.*

But the words of Scripture did not stop the rats from advancing on his body. They crawled up onto his neck and face and into his hair.

"Take me, Jesus! Take me!"

CHAPTER 4

· · ·

HEADQUARTERS
US TRANSPORTATION SECURITY ADMINISTRATION
OFFICE OF GENERAL COUNSEL
SPECIAL DEPUTY COUNSEL EMILY GARDNER'S OFFICE
ARLINGTON, VIRGINIA
11:08 A.M.

"You were great, Em!"

"Thanks, Willie." Emily smiled, watching the excitement of the cute face of her devilish-looking young admirer. "But I didn't say much. Director McNamara gets all the glory on this one."

"It isn't how much you said." Willie sat back in the chair across from her, stretching his hands behind his head. "It's how you said it. You know, Lincoln said less than anybody else at Gettysburg, but nobody remembers anything except what Lincoln said."

"Oh, stop it, Willie."

"You know I can't stop it, Em. I'm in love." An irresistible grin. "Besides, I have to hand it to him. Director McNamara's no dummy. He knows what drives TV ratings up. Sharp. Smart. Colorful. Sex appeal."

"Willie."

"You know what worries me most?"

"What's that?"

"When we go out, I'll be dating a celebrity and will have to fight off your fans and autograph seekers."

"You're going to make me blush."

"Oh, really? Good. Then you'll match that gorgeous red dress!"

"Willie."

"So when can I take you out?"

"Aaah . . ."

"How about tonight?"

"Well, I need to check my calendar . . ."

"Just one time. Tonight. If you don't have the best time of your life, it's a onetime thing. What do you say?"

She looked at him. His flattering persistence melted her resistance. "Okay, Willie. Seven o'clock. You can pick me up at my townhouse."

"Yes!" He pumped his fist in the air in a sign of jubilation. "There's one problem."

"A problem? What's the problem? I said yes!"

"Problem is, I don't know where you live."

"Oh. That problem."

Her phone buzzed.

"Miss Gardner?"

"Yes, Kate?"

"You have a high-priority call on one."

Willie flashed a curious look.

"A high-priority call?" She picked up. "Who is it, Kate?"

"The secretary, ma'am."

"The secretary?"

"Yes, ma'am. The secretary of Homeland Security."

The announcement stunned her into a moment of breathlessness. Emily had never met any cabinet members or even spoken with anyone in the government ranked above the director of the TSA.

"Are you sure?"

"Yes, ma'am."

What could this be about? Why would the secretary of Homeland

Security be calling her? She set down the phone. "Excuse me, please, Willie. I need to take this."

"Okay. No problem." He stood up, nodded, and stepped to the door. "Want me to close it?"

"Please."

"See you tonight." He smiled, stepped out, and closed the door behind him.

Emily took a deep breath, transitioning into official business mode. She wasn't nervous about appearing on national television. But now, with a member of the president's cabinet on the line, her stomach had double-knotted. She picked up her glass of water, sipped it, and noticed her hand was trembling. She set the glass down on a coaster and picked up the phone.

"Emily Gardner speaking."

"Emily. Fallington Strayhorn here. How are you today?"

She recognized the voice as the same voice she had heard on television a hundred times. Did her boss, Billy McNamara, know about this call?

"I'm fine, Mr. Secretary. And let me say it's an honor to get the chance to speak with you in person."

"Thanks, Emily. Likewise, it's nice to get to chat with you. I've heard great things about you."

Strayhorn's political skills and personal magnetism oozed through the phone. Personality-wise, he was Billy McNamara's bureaucratic opposite. Strayhorn's charm bested Billy's cerebral tin-man demeanor. No wonder Strayhorn had climbed up the ladder of power.

"How may I be of service to you, Mr. Secretary?"

"Well, first off, I wanted to call and congratulate you on your splendid performance during McNamara's presser. You did the department proud, Emily."

"Thank you, sir."

"I loved the idea that that kid's enlistment contract is invalid because of fraudulent procurement. How brilliant!"

"Thank you, sir."

"Was that your baby?"

"My baby?"

"Yeah. Did you think up that argument?"

"Well, yes, sir. But in my case, as an ex–Navy JAG officer, it wasn't that hard to figure out. I used to deal with enlistment contracts all the time."

"You're too modest, Emily. I think your background as a Navy JAG makes you ideal for this job. I hear you were a defense counsel and command services attorney at the Navy Legal Service Office in San Diego."

"You know that about me, sir?"

"Emily." She heard him chuckle. "I am the secretary of the Department of Homeland Security." Another chuckle. "It's my job to know everything about everybody in the country!"

She allowed herself a chuckle, fulfilling her subordinate's duty to feign humor in the remarks, although she found the whole conversation more nerve-racking than funny. "Yes, of course, Mr. Secretary. How could I forget?"

"Anyway, for the record, that was ingenious. We should not give these terrorists the protection of the American courts. They're lucky to get the protection afforded at Guantánamo, instead of eating a missile fired by an unmanned drone."

"Yes, sir." How to react to that? The notion of blind drone strikes turned her stomach.

"Of course, we could have tried him in the once-secret FISA court and burned him and branded him there. But that Judas Iscariot, that Benedict Arnold of a traitor Ed Snowden leaked the existence of that without authority."

"Yes, sir. Snowden leaked tons of classified material."

"Sucker's lucky I wasn't running Homeland Security back then. I'd have had him drawn and quartered. Know what I mean?"

"I think so, sir."

"But back on point. I think we can nail him in the war crimes court. Your work in keeping him out of the military courts was instrumental in that. We don't always get the results we want in the military courts. Like the Bradley Manning case, for example. Another traitor, and that military judge acquitted him of rendering aid to the enemy."

Strayhorn was right about one thing. The military justice system featured a better sense of balance and fair play than most civilian courts. It wasn't even close. But Strayhorn omitted the fact that even though Manning was acquitted of rendering aid to the enemy, he'd been convicted of espionage.

"There's a basic principle, sir, that any contract procured by fraud, including an enlistment contract, can be vitiated."

"I like that word . . . vitiated."

"Thank you, sir."

"There's something I'd like to chat with you about, Emily."

"Certainly, sir. How may I be of service to you?"

"I'd like to chat with you about you."

Had she heard that right? "About me, sir?"

"Absolutely. About you."

"Is everything okay, sir? I'd be happy to answer any questions you may have."

"Super. But this isn't the time or the place. It's confidential."

"Confidential?"

"Very much so. And I don't want you to mention this to anyone. Including Billy McNamara."

"Ah . . . Okay." She had devolved, in a matter of minutes, from showing total command on national television to struggling for the right words. "Would you like me to set an appointment to come to your offices?"

"I'd like you to set an appointment. But not at my office."

"Let me know when and where, Mr. Secretary."

"I'll have a Homeland Security limo pick you up at your town-house tonight. There's a quaint little French restaurant in Georgetown. We won't be recognized. I have an important topic to discuss with you. That okay?"

"Ah. Yes, sir. Do you need my address?"

"I'm the secretary of Homeland Security. Remember? I know where everybody lives. My driver will find you."

"Yes, sir. Of course, sir."

"Good. Then my driver will pick you up at seven. I'll meet you at the restaurant around seven thirty."

"Okay."

"Excellent. See you then."

The line went dead. Emily hung up the phone and leaned back in her chair. Why did her body feel like she'd just finished the last hundred-yard sprint at the end of a half marathon?

The sound of a text message. She reached into her purse for her cell phone.

SO PROUD OF YOU TODAY. LOOK FORWARD TO SEEING YOU TONIGHT. XO.

"Oh, man." She exhaled. What had she gotten herself into? She texted a response.

MY APOLOGIES. SOMETHING'S COME UP. RAIN CHECK?

A moment later, the response. SOUNDS LIKE I'VE BEEN DUMPED FOR A DATE WITH SOMEONE POWERFUL? HA HA. NO PROBLEM. CATCH YA LATER.

CHAPTER 5

• • •

ELECTRIC SHOCK TORTURE CHAMBER
GUANTÁNAMO BAY DETENTION CENTER
GUANTÁNAMO BAY, CUBA

Petty Officer Najib Makari sat alone, mostly naked, tied down to the cold steel chair in the center of the room. He would have been totally naked, except they had allowed him to wear a small pair of white skivvies.

They had braced his head in a metal contraption that would not allow him to move it up or down, and after that, they taped electrodes onto various parts of his body. They taped three electrodes to his chest, one on his sternum and two below his shoulders. His forearms were strapped against the steel armrests, and his legs were bound to the steel legs of the chair. Both his arms and legs were strapped so tightly that his fingers, hands, and toes were going numb.

After strapping down his limbs, they wrapped copper wires around his left pinkie, then his ring finger, then his middle and index fingers, and then his thumb.

The two men then wrapped wires around every finger on his right hand. After they finished with his hands, they started on his toes.

As they bent down, he noticed the odd-looking white patch sewn on the sleeve of their uniforms: "TSA ELITE Forces."

They wrapped his left small toe first with the copper wire, then wrapped the rest of his toes, ending by wrapping wire on every toe on his right foot.

But still they were not finished.

"Hold still" one of the Elitists had snapped, as if Najib could do anything but hold still.

Najib remained silent.

They taped two electrodes on his forehead, one over each eye, and taped an electrode behind each of his ears.

"Hold still! Don't move!" The same command again from the same TSA agent, an Elitist with an obvious need to bark orders.

No response from Najib.

The other one reached down into a large leather-looking briefcase on the floor, retrieving something that resembled a crown. But this was no ordinary crown. This crown had electronic receptacles and blinking lights attached at various points across the cranium plates.

The agent squeezed the headset onto Najib's head, then attached wires to the receptacle points on the helmet. Like tentacles dangling from an octopus, the wires attached to the helmet fed into a centralized plastic-looking receptacle at the end of a long black cord.

Other wires ran from the electrodes attached to his body into centralized cords, which ran to a metal machine with blinking lights over in the corner of the room. The machine resembled a typical office filing cabinet, but it had a control panel and a chair attached.

"Hold still! A couple more!" the TSA guy snapped again.

The other one turned to a table behind him and, in almost ceremonious fashion, slipped thin surgical gloves onto both hands.

He held his gloved hands up against the light, spreading all ten fingers out like a double fan, examining them, like a surgeon about to begin a delicate operation. He then taped a receptor onto the inside of Najib's upper right thigh, so high up that it encroached within inches of his private area. The thug taped a second receptor onto Najib's upper left thigh.

Najib's heart raced. He knew what was coming. Either death by electrocution or torture by electric shock.

He prayed for death. But deep down, he doubted that he could be so lucky.

Sweat beaded on his forehead, but he could not move his hands to wipe away the sweat.

"Open your mouth!" Another command from the command meister.

What?

"I said, open your mouth, Mohammed!"

The punch to the middle of Najib's stomach left him heaving.

With Najib gasping for breath, the ELITE guard put his surgically gloved hand into Najib's mouth and, acting like a dentist about to perform a root canal, pried it open wide. They wedged a rubbery block between his teeth, prying open his mouth even more as they worked.

As he tried catching his breath from the body punch, the TSA guard grabbed Najib's tongue and held it up. A metal receptacle was stuck to the bottom of his tongue with instant-sticking body glue.

They held his tongue up for a few seconds, then released it.

The wire ran from his mouth, like a tentacle from an electronic octopus, out to the centralized cord box, and from there bundled with other black cords running to the control panel.

"There. That should do it."

The TSA guards walked out of the chamber and closed the door.

CHAPTER 6

• • •

HEADQUARTERS
US TRANSPORTATION SECURITY ADMINISTRATION
OFFICE OF GENERAL COUNSEL
SPECIAL DEPUTY COUNSEL EMILY GARDNER'S OFFICE
ARLINGTON, VIRGINIA
11:30 A.M.

Since the telephone call from the secretary of Homeland Security, Emily's stomach had turned to a mushy brew of hot and cold, of excitement and turmoil, of electric ambition and cautious uncertainty.

The call from Secretary Fallington Strayhorn had rendered her unable to concentrate or to engage in anything of meaningful significance, other than answering a few calls and taking a few notes.

A senior-level attorney in a highly profiled federal agency should never be so nonproductive.

Thank goodness her boss, Billy McNamara, had not called. If Billy ever found out about this meeting with Strayhorn, and found that she had not told him in advance, in the worst-case scenario, he might fire her. In the best-case scenario, he would view such a secret meeting as undermining their mutual level of reciprocal confidence.

Why did she feel like such a two-timing traitor? It wasn't like she'd been asked to do something to betray McNamara or anything along those lines.

But a member of the president's cabinet, a man of great power, more powerful than Billy McNamara, had ordered her to keep it quiet.

She checked the clock on the wall. She needed some air. She picked up the phone. "Kate, I'm going to take an early lunch. I'll be back around one."

"Yes, Miss Gardner."

She grabbed her purse and headed out the door.

Out on the sidewalk along 12th Street, she turned right. With sunshine caressing her face, she fished for her designer shades in her purse.

The presence of a retail establishment nearby known as "The Fashion Centre at Pentagon City," shortened to "Pentagon City Mall," made her workplace an ideal location. The upscale Arlington shopping mecca sat two blocks from the tree-lined entrance of TSA headquarters. Sometimes she would just walk the mall on her lunch hour, and sometimes she would frequent the upscale restaurants and clothiers located there.

But despite the refreshing qualities of the breeze and sunshine, her stomach remained coiled like a rattlesnake ready to strike.

She needed somebody to talk to.

Somebody she could confide in.

Only one name came to mind.

Heading toward the intersection of 12th Street and South Hayes Street, near the Pentagon City metro station, she pulled her cell phone from her purse and hit number 4 on her speed dial. After two short rings, she heard the comforting voice that she had known for fifteen years, since their days as junior JAG officers.

"Hello." The woman's voice revealed honest enthusiasm. "You looked great in your national television debut."

"Thanks. I think. I'm wondering if I've bitten off more than I can chew."

"Emily, we've known each other a long time," Diane Colcernian Brewer said, "and I've never known you to tackle anything that you didn't wind up licking. Today the country got a glimpse of what Zack and I have known for years. You are a legal star. And I love that hot little red dress. Let me guess. Nordstrom?"

The pedestrian crossing sign changed from "Don't Walk" to "Walk." Emily stepped into the crosswalk leading to the front of the mall.

"Thanks, Diane, but listen. I need to talk. Do you have a few minutes?"

"For you? Sure. Ex–Navy JAGs always have time for each other. Want to talk now?"

"If that's okay. Are you home?"

"Actually, I'm not far from you."

"Where are you?"

"I was supposed to stop by the mall yesterday before I played tennis with Crystal Lettow, but I got sidetracked. This morning's *Post* showed a few sales at Pentagon City, so I'm a couple blocks from you."

"You're at Pentagon City?"

"I am."

"Me too! Let me buy your lunch. What are you in the mood for?"

"I don't care," Diane said. "I just finished a tennis match with Crystal and I'm hungry. I'm kind of in the mood for a salad and grilled chicken."

"Great. How about Harry's Smokehouse down in the food court?"

"I'll see you in about three minutes."

Emily quickened her step. She needed to see Diane, who was one of the smartest lawyers she knew. Emily knew only one lawyer sharper than Diane, and that was Diane's husband, Vice Admiral Zack Brewer, the judge advocate general of the Navy.

Emily hurried into the mall, then took the escalator down to the food court area.

Harry's Smokehouse, located deep within the food court beside the Pentagon City Metro, wasn't a bad place for a drink, appetizers, or a relaxing conversation. But it lacked the quaint atmosphere of some of the posh little restaurants in Georgetown and Old Town Alexandria.

"May I help you, ma'am?" the greeter asked as Emily walked into the restaurant.

"I'm meeting a friend. She just arrived."

"Ah, yes. Mrs. Brewer?"

"That's her."

"She's in the bar. If you will follow me."

"Thank you."

The gorgeous redhead in the white tennis dress and sweater rose from her bar table and extended her arms. "I want to be the first to hug our new national celebrity."

"Don't be silly." Emily accepted the embrace. "I've got a long ways to go to catch up with you and Zack."

"Yeah, yeah," Diane said. "You want a drink?"

"I wish. I could use one, but I'm working."

"Two soda waters"—Diane held up two fingers at the bartender—"and two menus, please."

"Yes, ma'am."

They sat at a small round bar table, a couple of feet away from each other, and Diane beamed at Emily with those magnetic blue eyes of hers. "Okay, what's the matter? This is not the confident face I saw on national TV a little while ago. What's up?"

"I'm not sure what's up."

"Talk to me."

"I got a strange call today."

A furrowed brow. "A strange call? From who?"

"I'm not supposed to be saying who."

"Okay, that's up to you. But you know whatever you tell me stays here."

"I know."

"Your soda waters, ladies. Are you ready to order?"

"Ah, I think I'll have a grilled chicken salad, please," Diane said. "Oil and vinegar."

"Very well. And you, ma'am?"

"Same thing," Emily said.

"So you received a strange call?"

"About an hour ago, I got a call from Fallington Strayhorn."

"You're kidding!"

"Nope."

"In your office?"

"Yes."

"Does anyone else know that Strayhorn contacted you?"

"I don't think so. Except for my secretary, who passed the call through."

"What did he want?"

"He started off bragging on my performance at the press conference."

"Can't disagree with him there, even though I'm not crazy about your employer."

Emily ignored that comment. "He was over the top. He told me not to tell anyone about the call, including Billy McNamara."

Diane leaned forward. "Really?"

"Yes, really."

"That sounds odd."

"Yes, it does. It gets even odder."

"I'm listening."

"He's sending a Homeland Security limousine to pick me up tonight."

"What?"

"Yep. Wants to meet me for dinner at a quaint little French restaurant in Georgetown."

"Wow."

"I don't know, Diane. I've got a funny feeling about it. I don't have a clue what he's up to, and I don't want to lie to Billy. But this guy is a powerful guy in this town."

Diane sipped her soda water. "He is that."

"What do you think?"

"The whole thing sounds strange to me too. You know, he might be trying to pick you up."

"I get that feeling too, Di. But I can't put my finger on it."

"Your salads, ladies?" The waiter returned with a tray with two grilled chicken salads.

"That was fast," Diane said.

"Yes, ma'am," the waiter said. "Anything else I can get for you?"

"No, I think we're fine," Diane said in a tone of voice that shooed off the waiter.

"So what do you know about this guy?" Emily asked.

"I don't like him. While I'm happy for you, I'm not crazy about TSA or Homeland Security. Zack doesn't like Strayhorn or McNamara, for that matter."

"I appreciate your honesty."

"We've always been honest with each other. That's what friends are for."

Emily started forking her salad. "What should I do?"

She'd barely finished her question before an explosion sent a hailstorm of plaster and glass in all directions, knocking Emily to the floor. She lay flat on her back, the bar table pinning her leg to the floor. A cloud of smoke billowed into the restaurant from the outside food court area. Screams and calls for help came from all over the restaurant. The lights flickered.

"Help!"

"Oh my God!"

"No!"

Screaming. Crying. Wailing.

The mall's fire alarm system was shrieking in an ear-splitting frequency. In the distance, sirens started sounding.

Emily tried pushing herself up, but the table had pinned her right leg. Panic set in. "Dear Jesus, help me!"

"Emily! Emily!" She saw the red hair of her best friend, then Diane's face was over her. "Em, are you okay?"

"I'm pinned. I can't move. This place is on fire! Get out of here, Diane!"

"I'm not going anywhere without you!"

CHAPTER 7

. . .

ELECTRIC SHOCK TORTURE CHAMBER
GUANTÁNAMO BAY DETENTION CENTER
GUANTÁNAMO BAY, CUBA

Five minutes had passed.

Nothing but silence.

Najib needed to relieve himself, but that wasn't possible.

"Petty Officer Najib Makari." A voice over the loudspeaker.

"Wha-at?" Najib struggled to speak because of the metal contact glued to the bottom of his tongue. "Aahh, ahh . . . what . . . you want?"

"We have your father, Makari. We know he's a terrorist, and we know you're a terrorist!"

"Aaah." Najib's pulse accelerated. His tongue froze.

"You love your terrorist father, do you not, Najib?"

"Aaah." Najib's eyes filled with tears.

"We take that as a yes. Good. All this means we are making progress. Surely you would wish your terrorist father to live."

"Aaah. Let! . . . Him! . . . Live!"

"Very good. An excellent response. And there is only one thing you must do to save your father's life." A pause. "Would you like to know what?"

Najib tried nodding his head. But the neck brace under his chin would not allow it. And the neck brace, along with the tongue sensor, shocked his tongue when he spoke. After several heaves and gasps, an "Aaah." And then "Yeees!"

"Very good. All we want is your signature admitting that your father helped murder the American ambassador to Lebanon."

"Aah . . ."

"And in addition, we want a statement of acknowledgment that you were involved in the intentional sabotage of the Navy jet on board the USS *Abraham Lincoln*, and that you and your father came to America to plant Islamic sleeper cells."

"Wah . . . Woh . . . Aah . . ."

"Do this and your father will live. Do this and you will live. We will deport you to your homeland, like we've done with other terrorists. "But if you refuse, we will kill you both."

"Na . . . na . . ."

"Well, what do you say, Najib? Will you save your father? Will you save yourself?"

Najib wanted to answer, but his racing heart, his desperate lungs, and the contraptions on his head and tongue stifled him. His chest tightened. Tears rolled off his cheeks, splashing on his legs, then streamed down and splatted on the floor.

Najib could not live without him. His father had led him to Christ, taught him about America, taught him about American football, and had been there every minute for him.

Najib didn't care what they did to him personally. But he loved his father like he loved no one else.

But would they live up to their word?

Would they save Hasan?

"Well? What is your answer?"

Najib looked into the blinding bright lights. The silhouette of a man appeared near the control panel. The voice boomed over the loudspeaker. Was the interrogator in the chamber? Or somewhere outside?

Sweat beaded on his forehead and dripped down, mixing with the tears still streaming from his eyes. His head throbbed. He had to make a decision.

Najib could not let his father die.

"This is your last chance to respond, Petty Officer Makari."

Najib thought of how the father he had grown to love so much had drilled Bible verses into his head and told him to live by those verses.

"Well, Najib? Will you come clean with your acts? Will you confess?"

"And you will know the truth, and the truth will set you free."

"Nooo!!!"

His answer echoed throughout the room, reverberating back and forth off the cinder-block walls. His ability to answer had been nothing short of miraculous.

The echoes of his response died down, yielding to a hushed silence in the room.

"Your choice has been unfortunate. Prepare to face the consequences."

Najib lost control of his bladder. The sudden jolt of electricity to his cheeks knocked his head back, as if a heavyweight prizefighter had punched him in the noggin with steel-knuckled boxing gloves.

"That was only one shot to one section of the body. We have more, Najib. But there's no point in making this hard on yourself or on your father. Come now. All we're seeking is an acknowledgment of responsibility. That's all. Then at that point, you and your father would be transferred to the general prison population to await your eventual deportation back to Lebanon at some point in the future.

"If you know our history, you know that others have been released alive. Of course, if you love your father, you will want to save him. Otherwise, he will be executed for his crimes by hanging, much as our forces hung the murderous terrorist Saddam Hussein."

Silence.

"You know the next jolt will be more severe than that first one."

More silence.

"So what do you say, Najib? Will you be a good son and save your father's life?"

Najib was panting. His lungs ached. His rib cage tightened. His head throbbed from the first jolt, as if someone had struck him with a rock at ninety miles per hour.

Perhaps he should cooperate. What choice did he have? The public would understand that they coerced his confession, and nobody would believe it.

Or would they?

Or did it matter?

The headache was unbearable. He remembered his father playing American football with him as a boy down on the "cornice," the beach along the Mediterranean in El-Mina, as Eugene Allison had done with his father.

He should relent. His father would do the same to save him. Wouldn't he? Or would he?

His head told him one thing.

But his conscience told him another.

The apostle Paul had been beaten and tortured and imprisoned for standing for the truth of the gospel.

"No! I cannot!"

Silence.

"Very well. You are a fool. Feel the power against those who would commit terror against America!"

The current started in the two electrodes strapped to his chest. At first tingling, then warm, then hot, then red hot, then "Aaaaaaaaaaaahhhh!" The electrodes on his chest had become as hot as cattle-branding irons.

He tried squirming but couldn't. They'd clamped him in too tightly. He could do nothing but feel the red-hot burners cooking into his chest.

And then the electrodes high up on his inner thighs heated up. More heat. Concentrated fire. The electrodes became miniature stovetop burners, branding him like a cow. The fire spread to his head. And then his hands and arms and feet burned like searing coals.

He screamed, his body scorched with white-hot electricity.

. . .

HARRY'S SMOKEHOUSE
BASEMENT
PENTAGON CITY MALL
ARLINGTON, VIRGINIA

"Diane! Please! Get out of here! The smoke's getting thick!"

"No, Emily. We'll stay together or we'll go together," Diane said over the chorus of screaming, crying, wailing, and coughing. "Talk to me. Does your leg hurt?"

Smoke poured into the restaurant from the food court. "Diane, go while you can still breathe. Please! Zack needs you. Our country needs you!"

"Answer me, Em! Does your leg hurt?"

"No! Not at all. But I'm pinned and can't move."

"Hang on." Diane coughed. "I see the problem. The bar was knocked over. It's on the chair that's got your leg pinned. I'll get this bar lifted up to take pressure off the chair. Hang on." More coughing. Sirens blaring louder. "This thing is heavy."

A man's voice on a distant loudspeaker. "This is the Arlington Fire Department. If you can move, evacuate the mall immediately before the smoke makes evacuation impossible. If you cannot move, help is coming."

Another explosion from somewhere in the mall shook the outside of the restaurant. More glass flew. But the second explosion sounded more distant, and it did not sound as powerful as the first.

"I'm dying! Help! I'm dying." A man's voice from somewhere.

"I can't breathe! I can't breathe!"

They could hear the crackling sound of fire, feel the heat radiating in from the food court.

"Diane, please. Go!"

"Let me help." A man's voice. The waiter.

"The bar got knocked over onto the chair, and the chair pinned her leg," Diane said. "If we could get the bar up a bit, I think she could slide out."

"Okay, hang on," the waiter said. "I'll try the bar. You try the chair. What's your friend's name?"

"Emily," Diane said. "Her name is Emily."

"Okay, Emily. I'm Dennis. Do you think you can pull your leg out if we can get that chair lifted a bit?"

"Sure, but promise me you'll get out of here if this doesn't work."

"Listen, ladies. I'm gonna count to three." Another explosion from somewhere in the mall. "Don't worry about that. On three, I'll shove the bar, you pull up on the chair, and, Emily, I want you to pull your leg out. Y'all got it?"

"Got it."

"Got it."

"Okay. One. Two. Three!"

"Aah. It's still stuck."

"Okay, let go," Dennis said.

"I don't know about this," Emily said. "Diane, get out of here. Please. There's no point in us both dying."

• • •

HEADQUARTERS
JUDGE ADVOCATE GENERAL OF THE NAVY
WASHINGTON NAVY YARD
ANACOSTIA RIVER
WASHINGTON, DC

"Excuse me. Admiral?"

Seated at his desk, talking on the phone, his back to the scenic view of the Anacostia River from his office windows, Vice Admiral Zack Brewer looked up and knew something was wrong from the look on Captain Kirk Foster's face.

"Jeff, I think something's up. Can I call you back?"

"You bet. I'll be here."

Rear Admiral Jeffrey Lettow, chief of Navy chaplains, was a long-time friend.

Zack hung up the phone. "What's going on, Kirk?"

"Sorry to interrupt you, Admiral, but there's been an explosion at Pentagon City Mall."

"What? What kind of explosion?"

"It's too early to say, sir. The news is just breaking. But we're also getting reports of explosions in malls in Minneapolis, Dallas, and San Diego."

"Multiple explosions in multiple cities?"

"Yes, sir. Appears to be some coordinated attack."

"A coordinated terrorist attack against civilian targets."

"That's my gut, Admiral."

"Diane!" *Did she say she was going shopping?*

"Sir?"

"Listen, Kirk. Issue an order to all JAG personnel worldwide. Cancel leave and liberty. Call in all nonessential personnel. All personnel report to duty station for further orders. Alert status: high. By order of the judge advocate general."

"Aye, sir."

"Let me know when the order is issued."

"Aye, Admiral."

"Then get the CNO's office on the line ASAP and get me some updated info."

"Yes, Admiral."

Zack picked up his cell phone as Kirk Foster stepped out of the office. He hit the speed dial for his wife with one hand and punched the remote control for the flat screen with the other.

As Diane's phone rang, the muted image on the television screen showed an outside shot of Pentagon City Mall billowing in smoke, with closed captioning scrolling across the bottom, saying, "Emergency workers starting to arrive at the scene."

"Come on, baby! Answer the phone!"

"You've reached Diane Colcernian Brewer. Please leave a message."

"Call me, baby! ASAP!"

He hung up, then hit the speed dial for his friend Rear Admiral Jeff Lettow. After two rings, Lettow answered.

"Jeff, have you heard about an explosion over at Pentagon City Mall?"

"Just heard. They're getting reports of explosions at malls in other cities."

"Where are the girls?"

"I talked to Crystal. She said they played tennis this morning. Then Diane went shopping."

"Where?" He wiped his head. "Did she say where?"

"Zack, she said either Crystal City or Pentagon City."

"Jesus, help me. Look, I gotta go."

"Where are you going?"

"Pentagon City."

"Zack, they'll have that place locked down. You'll never get in."

"Watch me."

"I'll meet you there."

• • •

HARRY'S SMOKEHOUSE
BASEMENT
PENTAGON CITY MALL
ARLINGTON, VIRGINIA

"Get out of here!" Emily screamed as sweat beaded on her forehead from the intensifying heat. "Both of you!"

Dennis looked at Diane. "You go. I'll stay with her until help arrives."

"Like hell I'm leaving her. She's my best friend."

Another explosion somewhere in the mall.

"Secondary gas explosions."

Roaring, crackling flames now overwhelmed the sounds of human moaning and weeping.

Emily closed her eyes. She was going to die.

"I'm going to find something," Diane said. "Maybe there's a crowbar in the kitchen or something."

"I don't know if that's a good idea," Dennis said. "I think we should wait here for help."

"Help might be too late," Diane said. "I'm going back into the kitchen."

"No, Diane," Emily said.

"I'll be right back." Diane disappeared into the dark smoke.

• • •

HEADQUARTERS
JUDGE ADVOCATE GENERAL OF THE NAVY
WASHINGTON NAVY YARD
ANACOSTIA RIVER
WASHINGTON, DC

His heart pounding, Zack ran out into the sunshine, into the parking lot outside JAG headquarters, and raced toward his silver Mercedes parked in the space reserved for the judge advocate general.

The sight of a three-star admiral sprinting into a parking lot had turned a few heads, bringing quick salutes that he didn't return. He reached the Mercedes and reached into his pocket.

"Dag blast it!" His car keys were with his aide. "I should have called Kirk."

Zack pulled his cell phone and hit the speed dial. One ring. Two rings. "Captain Foster."

"Kirk, you got the Mercedes keys?"

"Yes, sir."

"I need 'em now!"

"Where are you, sir?"

"In the parking lot by the car."

"I'll be right out, sir."

Zack leaned against the Mercedes and put his Oakleys on. His stomach churned.

The sound of multiple sirens poured in from the distance. It wasn't that far across the river from the Washington Navy Yard to Arlington and the Pentagon City Mall.

Two beeps from a nearby car brought his head to the right. "Hey, Zack, get in the car."

Jeff Lettow, with windows rolled down, sat in the driver's seat of the gold Nissan Altima.

"Hey, get in the car," Jeff said. "I'll drive you over there."

Zack got into the Nissan. "I thought you were going to meet me over there."

"I changed my mind," Lettow said. "I figured you'd forget your keys."

"You know me, don't you?"

"Yes, I do."

"Hey, there's my aide, Captain Foster. Swing by and tell him you've got me."

"You bet." Lettow tooted the horn, catching Foster's attention. "Hey, Captain, I've got your boss. I'll bring him back in a while."

"Aye, sir." Foster flashed a salute.

Lettow returned the salute, then drove out of the Washington Navy Yard.

"I don't feel good about this, Jeff."

"Let's pray."

• • •

HARRY'S SMOKEHOUSE
BASEMENT
PENTAGON CITY MALL
ARLINGTON, VIRGINIA

"Arlington Fire Department! Anybody in here?"

The man's authoritative voice snapped Emily's eyes open in time to see a flashlight beam streaming across the room.

"Over here!" Dennis yelled.

"What's our situation here?" the fireman asked.

"The bar fell over. Her leg's jammed. She says she's not hurt, but she's pinned."

The fireman let out a shrill whistle. "Sergeant, over here."

"What's up, Captain?"

"Let's give this guy a hand. On three. Ready?"

"Yes, sir."

"One. Two. Three."

Emily felt the chair lift off her leg and she quickly slid out. "It's off! I'm free!"

"Can you walk?"

"Yes, I think so."

"Let's see." The fireman reached down and pulled her up.

"No pain. I'm good."

"Okay, let's go. Single file. Sergeant, bring up the rear."

"Yes, sir."

"Follow us. But keep your head low. Gases up high, oxygen down low. We've gotta get up the escalators before the fire spreads."

"Sergeant! Wait!"

"Can't wait, ma'am. We've got to move."

"My friend. She might still be in here."

"Where?"

"She went to the kitchen to look for something to pry me loose."

"The kitchen of the restaurant?"

"Yes. We can't leave her."

"Okay, I'll send somebody to check it out. But we've got to move right now."

"But—"

"Ma'am. Please. Stop talking. You must conserve your breath. Now listen. If the smoke comes into your face, do not breathe it. We have an oxygen tank that you can breathe from if that happens. Got it?"

The captain, wearing a khaki fire suit with a red helmet, a yellow oxygen tank on his back, stepped out into the food court area. He turned and gestured with his hand. "This way."

Emily and Dennis were right behind the captain, staying close.

They turned left, moving past Harry's on the left and Johnny Rockets on the right. Fire blazed from stores on both sides of the interior of the mall.

Smoke billowed down in the path in front of them.

"Don't breathe it," the captain warned. "Sergeant." He motioned for the sergeant from the rear. They slipped an oxygen mask over Emily's face. "Hold this and walk beside me. We'll take turns till we get through this smoke. You first. Then me. Just don't breathe the smoke. Let's go. Sergeant, help the waiter."

Emily nodded.

"Sergeant, share this oxygen. You know the drill."

"Yes, sir."

The captain put his arm around Emily's shoulder and stepped forward. The oxygen refreshed her lungs, but the lingering hot smoke in her face burned her eyes.

The captain kept his hand around her shoulder. "Stay with me."

The heat from behind and from the sides intensified.

An explosion burst behind them with a *whoosh*, and a wave of powerful hot air knocked them forward. Emily stumbled to the floor. The oxygen mask dropped off her face.

"Backdraft! Get up and run! Run!"

The air swooshed as if from a broiling oven. Emily got up, flailing her hands, desperately trying to push smoke out of her face.

"To your right! To your right!" someone yelled.

Through a gap in the smoke, she saw the escalators, which were not operating.

"This way, ma'am!"

She started climbing the dead escalator. Two Arlington firemen met her midway up the steps. They grabbed her by the arms and guided her up to a clear area on the next level.

"You okay, ma'am?"

Coughing. "Yes."

"Get her out of here," a fireman said.

"Wait! Diane!"

CHAPTER 8

. . .

Matt refolded the bone-chilling message from the dead man and stuck it in his back pocket.

Who could he trust?

Rusotto? Rusotto seemed nice enough. Anyone looking that goofy could not be that sinister. Or could he?

What had Rusotto meant when he warned Matt to watch his back? Was that a threat?

The sick e-mail was an in-your-face threat.

But were Rusotto's comments part of a coordinated effort?

Or had Rusotto spoken a warning out of concern?

Perhaps Rusotto knew the fate of the others who had been assigned to represent these defendants. Perhaps he wanted to warn Matt out of legitimate concern for a fellow JAG officer.

And what about Lieutenant Commander Petronio? The senior defense counsel for the detachment, Petronio, had not even shown his face yet.

Matt checked his watch. Why the delay? What were they talking about? The trial docket in an RLSO detachment on a base that was home port to only a few auxiliary ships could not take that long.

Should he even show the message to Petronio? What if Petronio was in on it?

It appeared that this whole charade was a kangaroo court where they expected a dutiful defense counsel to cooperate if he had any interest in surviving.

A knock on the door.

"Come in."

The door swung open. The short naval officer who walked in wore working khakis with the gold oak leaf of a lieutenant commander pinned to his right collar. His closely cropped black hair matched his black plastic government-issue glasses, known in the vernacular as "BCGs," for "birth control glasses," because of their ugliness.

Petronio looked quintessentially Italian and could pass for a Gambino family member. "Welcome aboard, Lieutenant Davis." His voice was not welcoming in tone. "I'm Lieutenant Commander Bob Petronio."

"Thank you, Commander."

"I think you know your assignment, but there is a technical matter. You're assigned to the Military Commissions Tribunal and technically not part of the RLSO Defense Command. However, you have been assigned to use this office, and because we're all working as defense counsel—you for alleged Islamic terrorists, and us for US Navy personnel—we're here to provide whatever help we can."

"Commander," Matt responded, "it appears that one of my clients is US Navy also, which makes me wonder why he's here."

"Semantics, Lieutenant. Tell me how I can help you."

To tell him or not to tell him about the threat. A snap decision. Best not to talk about it. Yet.

"I need to see my clients."

Petronio grimaced. "You and every other defense counsel they send down here to represent these guys."

"With respect, sir, what does that mean?"

"Do sit down, Matt."

"Yes, sir."

Petronio walked over to the window and looked out, his back to Matt. "Remember that the right to effective assistance of counsel is found in the Sixth Amendment of the Constitution." Petronio kept looking out, avoiding eye contact.

"I understand, sir. That's why I need to see them. So I can prepare the defense they deserve and make the government prove its case."

"That's nice, Matt. You might understand the first part, but you don't yet understand the second part."

"Maybe not, sir. You'll have to elaborate."

Petronio turned away from the window and looked at Matt, who was sitting in his chair behind the desk.

"You're right about the Sixth Amendment right to effective assistance of counsel. But what you don't understand is the Sixth Amendment doesn't apply here. Neither does the First, Second, Third, Fourth, or Fifth."

"I see," Matt said. "I take it you're referring to the Military Commissions."

"Now you're catching on, Matt. Oh, the Constitution applies in our military courts-martial. But these Military Commissions? Where they prosecute these terror defendants? That's some kind of legal la-la land."

"Legal la-la land," Matt parroted Petronio. "Then why am I even here?" He hesitated. "I mean, what's my role?"

Petronio turned back to the window and gazed out again. "That, Matt, is a question that every defense lawyer who's ever been sent here has wrestled with. Clive Stafford Smith. Commander Walter Ruiz. Andy Hart, David Nevin, James Connell, Marine Colonel Jeffrey Colwell. Lieutenant Colonel Yvonne Bradley. The list goes on. You know, in 2010, Colonel Jeff Colwell, as tough a Marine as you'll find, said, 'It is our job to make the government do what the law and the Constitution require.'

"So you'll have to decide on your own, Matt. Why are you here? And what is your role as a lawyer? And what is your role as a naval officer? This assignment will test you at the core, force you to examine who you are as a man, examine what you believe and how much you want to risk."

Matt considered that. "If you don't mind answering, Commander, what do you mean by that last comment?"

"About how much you want to risk?"

"Yes, sir."

"You have to decide how much you want to risk professionally and how much you want to risk personally."

Was this a threat? Or a warning?

"Commander, I did my homework the best I could after I got here. I've read the reports about defense counsel intimidation. Even saw the reports about the questionable death of Andy Hart. Are you telling me, sir, that you believe that stuff is true?"

"Lieutenant, I'm a naval officer," Petronio said. "And I'm a defense counsel. My job is to obey the orders of my superior officers the best I can and defend my clients to the best of my ability.

"It isn't within my job description, nor is it appropriate, for that matter, for me to offer my opinions on certain matters, particularly when those opinions might be construed as critical of anyone who might be above me in my chain of command." Petronio glared at Matt, a perturbed look in his eye. "Were my previous comments ambiguous?"

"No, sir. Understood, sir."

"Now . . . you were asking about wanting to interview your clients?"

"Yes, sir."

"I'm afraid that's going to be easier said than done."

"What do you mean? They have a right to counsel."

"That's what you think. And that's the same position taken by every defense counsel who's been assigned down here. At least at first. But there are others who don't believe these guys have a right to counsel."

"Really?" Matt said. "Then, again, why am I here?"

"You've hit on the real question. Some would say you're here for show. Others would say you're here to defend these guys. The political types running the prison would say that you're merely window dressing. And they're determined that you'll see your clients only when they decide you'll see them."

Matt was instantly angry. "That's a bunch of bull!"

"I'm not arguing with you about that," Petronio said. "Remember, I said there are two philosophical camps here—those who say you're window dressing and those who think these guys have a right to counsel. I personally don't fall into the window-dressing camp."

Matt examined Petronio's face. His eyes flashed a glint of sincerity. "So if I'm reading between the lines here, there are certain forces on the other side that don't want me to see my clients at all, but if I do get to see them, they don't want that to happen until after they have had the first shot at my clients."

"Now you're catching on."

Matt looked out the window. "So is there anything we can do?"

"There is no 'we,' Matt. You are the detailed defense counsel."

"All right then. Is there anything I can do?"

"Look," Petronio said, "they're basically telling you that you can't see your own clients until they're ready for you to see them. The same thing they've tried with every lawyer they've brought down here. So they're going to force you to file a motion with the Military Commissions to gain access to them, like they have with every other defense counsel. Mind if I sit?"

"Please, sir."

Petronio walked around in front of Matt's desk, pulled up a chair, and sat.

"Sounds like they toy with defense counsel right from the get-go," Matt said.

"You said it."

"Almost like a rite of initiation."

"You said it," Petronio said again.

"So what tactic have other defense counsel used with this initial round of motions? Claiming that the delay amounts to ineffective assistance?"

"You're on it."

"So what can I expect the Military Commissions to do?"

"Well, you can expect a vigorous challenge from the government. Then, eventually, the Commission gives in. You understand how the process works?"

"About as well as I can after cramming on two days' notice."

"All right. Here's some background. The secretary of defense appoints the chief judge of the Military Commissions Trial Judiciary. Right now, that's Colonel Bob Kinsley, an Air Force guy. The chief judge, Colonel Kinsley, then details a military judge to each case referred to trial.

"So each military commission consists of a military judge and at least five members, so from that standpoint, they're constituted like the military courts-martial that you're familiar with. Of course, in a case in which the accused might be sentenced to death, which is the case for both of your guys, there's a minimum of twelve members, and unanimous agreement is required."

"Of course," Matt said, "I take it it's going to be judge alone for the motions."

"That's right," Petronio said. "All preliminary matters before trial are just you, the government's lawyers, and the military judge."

"Well, at least it sounds like a format I'm familiar with."

"You might think you're familiar with the format," Petronio said, "but when you get in there and realize they're not applying the Constitution or the Rules of Evidence, you might think you're in Russia. By the way, are you familiar with the case of *Boumediene v. Bush*?"

"You mean the Supreme Court case that held these guys are entitled to *habeas corpus*?"

"I see you've done your homework, Matt."

"I try."

"Well, you've got that as an option, I think, especially with the kid they plucked off duty."

"No kidding. If Nidal Hasan could get a military court-martial for mass murder at Fort Hood, it seems like an active-duty Navy guy should at least be entitled to the same."

"Agreed," Petronio said. "I think their argument is that this guy has vitiated his enlistment contract. Their calling him a terrorist is a bunch of malarkey."

"Agreed, sir."

Petronio's cell phone rang. "Hang on a second." The chubby officer punched a button on his cell phone. "Lieutenant Commander Petronio." A pause. "What?" Another pause. "Where?" Another pause. "Okay, I'll be right there." Petronio ended the call.

"Something wrong, sir?"

"Looks like a coordinated terror attack in the States."

"What? Where?"

"Bombs in civilian malls. DC area. Dallas. San Diego. The chief wasn't clear."

Matt wanted to get up. To go somewhere. To do something. He remembered where he was on 9/11 all those years ago. Now the feeling of bricks in his stomach returned.

But what could he do?

Amy!

His mind rushed to her. "Any military facilities hit?"

"No. Just malls. I gotta go, Lieutenant."

"Do we have any orders, sir?"

"GITMO and all naval facilities are on high alert. But you have your orders. Those orders are to defend these two individuals about to be prosecuted. If I were you, I'd stay here and concentrate on that. Get those motions prepared. You can file them today. All you have to do is walk in the courthouse and file them. I'll have Rusotto drive you over. Then you can make an appearance in the morning."

Matt stood up. "You're right, Commander. I'll get started right away. You'll let me know if my orders change?"

"You bet, Matt. Good luck." Petronio stepped out of the office and into the hallway, then stuck his head back into the office. "Matt."

"Yes, sir?"

"Watch your back."

CHAPTER 9

• • •

"My friend's still in there! She's in the kitchen! I'm going back in!" Emily yelled as an Arlington EMT and three police officers pulled her by the arms out the front entrance of the mall, onto the sidewalk, to a wall of flashing blue lights from police cars barricading the street.

Several helicopters roared overhead, making it almost impossible even to hear her own voice.

"You don't understand! She went into the kitchen! Into the kitchen at Harry's! We were in the basement! Where's the captain? The waiter? He stayed with me!"

"Ma'am," the police officer said loudly enough to be heard over the hovering helicopters, "nobody can go in there. Not now. If your friend is still in there, our firemen will find her. Please let the EMTs check you out."

"I'm fine!"

"Please, let us check you out, ma'am!"

"No! I'm fine. Just swallowed a little smoke. Please. Find my friend!"

"Emily!" She heard a man's voice that sounded familiar to her. She looked over her shoulder. Two United States Navy admirals, a three-star vice admiral and a two-star rear admiral in summer whites, were crossing South Hayes Street.

Unlike others who were being kept away by police, the admirals were waved through the barricades.

"Admiral Brewer!"

"Emily? Where's Diane?"

"Inside!"

"Where?"

"In the basement. I was pinned down. Diane went to the kitchen to find something to pry me loose."

"What kitchen? Where?"

"Harry's Smokehouse. I was pinned under a chair. The bar fell on the chair. My leg was pinned at an angle. I couldn't get it out. Smoke filled the basement. Di went to the kitchen to find something to pry off the chair. The firemen came. I told the firemen. They said they would look for her."

Zack took off.

"Admiral, where are you going?"

"To find my wife!" Zack yelled back.

"Stop! You can't go in! Orders of the Arlington Fire Department! There are backdrafts in there, Admiral!"

"You wanna stop me?" Zack said as he ran to the entrance of the mall. "Shoot me!" Zack darted into the smoke and was gone.

The second admiral, whom Emily recognized as the chief of Navy chaplains, took off, sprinting toward the entrance.

"Admiral, stop!" the policeman yelled.

"I'm going with him!" the admiral said. "He needs prayer."

"Ma'am, let me check you," the paramedic persisted.

"No. I'm fine. Please. Go help those who need you."

The paramedic looked at the fireman, who nodded and said, "Go."

"This is the FBI!" a voice boomed from the helicopter overhead. "By orders of the secretary of Homeland Security, you are ordered to evacuate the premises. Evacuate the premises!"

Most people standing around the outside of the mall ignored the order.

A loud siren came blaring up South Hayes Street. Then another.

A red ladder truck rolled up and parked on the street.

"If you're going to stay here, you have to stand back, ma'am." The policeman pushed Emily back several feet as a platoon of firemen wearing oxygen masks dismounted and rushed with a long fire hose into the mall.

Paramedics and police were hauling people from the mall out on stretchers. Some were in body bags. The first four bodies were lined up on the cement in white body bags to the left of the Hayes Street entrance. Emily just stared at them in shock. "Dear Jesus, please save Diane. Please save Zack. Keep them safe. Please don't let that be Diane."

Paramedics rushed out of the mall with two more filled body bags and laid them down on the sidewalk beside the four already there.

The wail of more fire trucks arriving.

More squealing police cars.

More helicopters overhead. Military helicopters. Police helicopters. The chopper from WUSA Channel 9.

More orders from an FBI chopper. "By orders of the secretary of Homeland Security, evacuate the premises. There may be poisonous gases in the area."

Screams and panic from civilian bystanders followed the announcement about poisonous gases, sending a mad, sprinting horde scrambling back on 12th Street, toward TSA headquarters, to get as far away from the mall as possible.

The sight of stampeding crowds reminded Emily of the people running from the collapsing debris in the streets of New York when the World Trade Center towers collapsed.

But poisonous gas or not, and fire and smoke or not, Emily wasn't going anywhere. Unless someone forcibly removed her. Not until she knew the fate of Diane.

• • •

HEADQUARTERS
US TRANSPORTATION SECURITY ADMINISTRATION
ARLINGTON, VIRGINIA

Billy McNamara sat at his desk, watching the flat-screen televisions mounted on his office wall, all showing live aerial images of smoking, smoldering shopping malls.

The live shots were being beamed from helicopters flying over four American cities. One screen contained a subscript proclaiming, "Fashion Valley Mall, San Diego." Another stated, "Live Aerial Footage of the Shops at Legacy, Dallas." One read, "Arlington, Virginia—Terrorist Attack on Shopping Malls."

McNamara shifted his eyes back and forth, from one screen to another. Special Agent Bob Nolan was sitting in a chair, leaning forward, also focused on the TVs.

The desk phone rang.

"Yes, ma'am."

"Mr. Director, Secretary Strayhorn is on the line, sir."

"Punch him through."

"Yes, sir."

McNamara picked up the phone on the first buzz. "Yes, Mr. Secretary."

"You watching all this on TV, Billy?"

"Yes, Mr. Secretary. Special Agent Nolan and I are watching it right now."

"Y'all got everything under control?"

"Yes, sir. I'm going to take a squadron of ELITE Force guys to Pentagon City to inspect the operation."

"That's fine," Strayhorn said. "But the White House called. They want to release a statement, and they're asking us for some information. What do you think, Billy?"

"Mr. Secretary, I'd suggest that the White House issue a statement that the nation is under a coordinated terror attack, and that TSA, working under the auspices of the Department of Homeland Security, is warning all Americans to return home, wait for instructions, and if given instructions by TSA agents or other federal authorities, to follow those instructions without questions. Then I think we should do another press conference at three this afternoon after the initial statement by the White House."

"You think the White House should issue a statement? Or should the president address the country?"

"Good point, Mr. Secretary. On second thought, it wouldn't look good if I am the first government official speaking to the country after a terrorist attack. The president doesn't need to look like he's been upstaged. So let's suggest that the president go on air at two o'clock from the Oval Office and read the statement I suggested. Short. Sweet. He looks presidential and directs the nation to follow our lead. Then at three o'clock, we have our presser to assure the nation that everything's under control."

"Now you're thinking like a politician, Billy." Strayhorn snorted.

"Think the president will go along with it?"

"Oh, I think so. I'll speak with him about it. Plus, if he speaks from the Oval Office, he doesn't have to take any questions. He leaves the details to us. Hey, are you going to make sure there's press coverage of our on-site inspections at Pentagon City?"

"Yes, sir. I've alerted our PR people to contact the networks."

"Good. Stay in touch. Sounds like you've got a busy afternoon. I'll be watching the coverage of your on-site inspection in a few minutes."

"I'll do you proud, sir."

"I know you will, Billy."

• • •

SOUTH HAYES STREET
PENTAGON CITY MALL
ARLINGTON, VIRGINIA

Paramedics, firemen, policemen, and members of the Virginia National Guard were rushing into the mall. Some firemen and paramedics wore gas masks as they rushed in.

But others, Emily noticed, had no gas masks, which seemed odd. Just moments ago the FBI chopper had warned of poisonous gases.

And if that was true, that poisonous gases were in the area, then those brave emergency workers without any protective masks were signing their own death warrants. Was it because of a shortage of gas masks for an emergency of this magnitude?

Emily knew, by remaining, she might be signing her own death warrant. But she wasn't going to leave. Not without Diane. She realized that she had become unnoticed in the midst of the chaos, with rescue workers and law enforcement scrambling to deal with the smoke and fire and to help those who were actually hurt.

She was standing out of the way, away from all the commotion, and none of the rescue teams noticed her. They had more important things to do. Any sane person had already evacuated this hellhole. Anyone left remained at their own risk.

Overhead, a small fleet of drones had joined the sonorous helicopters. One drone circling bore the inscription "NSA." Another had painted on it "Homeland Security."

Movement from the mall.

Two firemen emerged, rolling a body bag out on a stretcher.

Then another.

Followed by another.

Altogether, within a period of thirty seconds, paramedics had rolled eight more body bags out onto the sidewalk.

Police and paramedics unloaded the body bags from the stretchers, laid the bodies on the sidewalk, then returned with gurneys into the mall.

"Dear Jesus. Please not Diane. Please not Zack. Not the chaplain. Please."

She heard a rumbling to her right, coming from 12th Street, down toward TSA headquarters. A man's voice boomed from a loudspeaker.

"TSA ELITE. Stand aside! Stand aside."

A mob of lights and cameras, carried by cameramen, sound engineers, and reporters, was walking in a moving circle up 12th Street, headed toward the mall entrance.

The man's voice from the bullhorn. This time louder. "TSA ELITE. Stand aside! Stand aside!"

The cadre of reporters, with their bright camera lights, walked straight toward the mall entrance. Their cameras and lights were aimed inward, not toward the mall, but at someone in their midst.

Surrounding the reporters and camera crews were fifteen or twenty blue-shirted TSA ELITE Force agents bearing M-16 military rifles, walking in precision military marching style. They wore shiny black storm-trooper military helmets that glistened in the sunshine. They resembled something that could have come from a World War II movie about the Gestapo.

On the front of the black storm-trooper helmets, painted in white, was the phrase "TSA ELITE Force."

"Stand back! TSA ELITE!"

A TSA ELITE agent with a bullhorn, over on the far right, yelled various renditions of his "step aside" order even though the ones "in the way" were emergency workers fighting the fire and rescuing victims. Emily was amazed to see some of the Arlington firefighters and police officers step aside as the federal contingent, representatives of the very agency that employed her, marched down the street. Others, however, ignored the federal "step aside" order and kept rushing into and out of the smoking mall.

The TSA ELITE Forces and the press contingent stopped near the entrance to Pentagon City Mall, about fifty feet from Emily.

The bullhorn guy barked another instruction: "All state and local rescue workers. Continue your operations until further order by federal TSA or Homeland Security officials. Repeat. To all rescue workers. Continue your operations until further order by federal officials from TSA or Homeland Security."

After the announcement, the horde of reporters converged into a tight circle, their microphones and bright lights aimed at one man in the middle.

Emily squinted her eyes and did a double-take.

Was the guy in the middle . . . Billy?

Her boss, the director of the TSA, was staging a photo op right at the heart of ground zero!

She inched in closer. Billy McNamara, without any gas mask, stood at the center of the semicircle of press reporters and photographers. Two flagpoles had been set up, one flying Old Glory, the other flying the navy-blue flag of the Commonwealth of Virginia.

As she slipped in a bit closer, a TSA ELITE guard wearing aviator shades to match his black storm-trooper helmet stepped in front of her. "Sorry, ma'am, but I cannot let you breach this perimeter."

"I'm Emily Gardner, TSA general counsel's office. I work for the director."

"Do you have any identification, ma'am?"

"Of course." Then she remembered that she had left her purse, containing her identification badge, in the restaurant. "I left it in the mall after the explosion . . . I . . . Billy . . . Director McNamara knows me."

"The director is busy at the moment, ma'am. I'm sorry, but with no ID, you can go no farther."

"Well, can I at least stand here and listen?"

"No. You can't stay. Unless you consent to a field search."

She looked over at the mall entrance. Still no sign of Zack or Diane. "Okay. Fine."

"Turn around, ma'am. Hands in the air."

"Fine." She turned around and heard the guard's voice.

"Perkins. Cover me while I search this lady."

"Yes, sir."

Hands, gruff hands, started on the back of her neck. The hands moved down her back, then her front, and, to her disgust, lingered longer in places than they should have lingered.

Just as the cheesy guard removed his hands and told her she could turn around, she heard her boss say, "Okay, I'll take a few questions."

"Mr. Director. What happened here?"

"Too early to say, but I can say two things. First, TSA ELITE Forces have converged on the area, and we have the matter under control. TSA ELITE Forces have also converged on civilian shopping malls in Chicago, Dallas, and San Diego. The public should heed and obey the instructions of TSA ELITE Forces, members of the FBI, or any other federal agencies.

"Second, it's my understanding that the president will be addressing the nation at 2:00 p.m. Eastern Time."

"Mr. Director, would you classify this as an act of terror?"

"I'm not going to classify it as anything. Not yet, anyway."

"Mr. Director. What about reports of poisonous gases? There were reports earlier that poison gas could have been used."

"Yes, I'm aware of that. The FBI released that information. Not the TSA. Unfortunately, the FBI released that information prematurely. That's the FBI's mistake. While there's a possibility that poisonous gases could be inside the mall, TSA has determined that the area outside the mall is free of poisonous toxicants. Obviously, I'm not wearing a gas mask."

"Mr. Director, was this a terrorist attack? And do we know who is responsible?"

"At this time, I am going to neither confirm nor deny anything concerning the classification of this as a terror attack, nor will I provide speculation on those responsible. The president will be speaking to the nation at two o'clock. I'm not going to take any more questions at this time. I will be inspecting the work being done here."

Two navy admirals, their white uniforms smudged with soot, and two paramedics rushed out of the mall. The paramedics were pushing a stretcher carrying a woman with an oxygen mask over her face, red hair fanned out from her head.

"Is that Zack Brewer?" someone asked.

"Diane! Zack!" Emily rushed to the stretcher, but the paramedics ignored her and kept going. Zack did not respond. His face was stern. His eyes were on Diane.

The paramedics rushed to a white ambulance on South Hayes Street with its engine running.

Emily followed.

"Where to?" the driver yelled at the paramedics.

"Bethesda Naval Hospital," a paramedic responded, then jumped in the back of the ambulance and lifted the head of the stretcher as the second paramedic lifted the foot and pushed the stretcher into the ambulance and jumped in.

Zack hopped in right after them. The back doors of the ambulance closed. A blast from the siren cut through the sound of the choppers overhead. Another siren blast, and Emily watched the ambulance pull away, its twirling red-and-white lights flashing.

"Are you Diane's friend?"

She turned around. The two-star rear admiral who had followed Zack into the mall was standing there. His name tag read "Lettow." She noticed the gold cross on his black shoulder board, the insignia of a Protestant chaplain.

"Yes. My apologies, Admiral Lettow. I didn't recognize you. How is she?"

"The paramedics say she suffered smoke inhalation. She's tough. Somehow she'd escaped from the restaurant and made it to the base of the escalator when they found her. If she'd not gotten out of the restaurant, she'd be dead."

"So she was breathing?"

"Barely."

"Is she going to make it?"

"The paramedics didn't say. I'm headed to Bethesda to be with Zack and to pray."

"Emily!" She turned around. "What are you doing here?" Billy was standing there.

"I was in the basement having lunch with a friend when the bomb went off. It was horrible, sir."

"You okay?"

"I'm fine. I was pinned down . . . but my friend . . ." Her voice trailed off.

"Look, I need you to come back to headquarters with me. We've been hit by terrorists. The president is going on air at two o'clock to announce the attack to the nation. Then we're going live at three with more details. I want you there with me. Just like before."

"I . . ." How could she transition like this? "My friend. They took her to Bethesda." Emily wanted to cry but could not allow it. She was deputy counsel for the TSA, for heaven's sake. She just saw the movie *The Iron Lady* on Netflix. Margaret Thatcher, her heroine, would never crack publicly in a crisis. Neither would Emily.

"Excuse me. Miss?"

The chaplain, Admiral Lettow. She had almost forgotten he was there.

"I'm going to check on Diane at Bethesda. If you'd like me to call you, I'd be glad to. I'm sure the director needs you at your post."

"Thank you, Admiral. I . . . I don't have my cards. They're in my purse."

"Here," Admiral Lettow said. "Here's my card. Here's another. If you'd like to write down a number where you can be reached, I'll call you when I know something."

"Thank you, Admiral."

He handed her a pen, and she wrote her name and number, then gave the card back to him.

"Are you ready, Emily?" Billy McNamara asked.

"Yes, Director. Let's do this."

CHAPTER 10

· · ·

NAVY LEGAL SERVICE OFFICE
WINDWARD SIDE
UNITED STATES NAVAL STATION
GUANTÁNAMO BAY, CUBA
2:00 P.M.

"Hey, Rusotto," Lieutenant Commander Bob Petronio shouted. "Get in here if you want to see this. The president's getting ready to come on."

Rumors had surfaced that President Douglas Surber would declare that America was under terrorist attack. But the lockdown order at all US military installations left little doubt about what the president would say.

The military's state of readiness had been elevated to DEFCON 3, or "condition yellow," the highest readiness level since the September 11 attacks.

All the live shots of burning shopping malls, of panicked civilians, of traffic jams and emergency vehicles with flashing lights and body bags brought back memories of 9/11, and a feeling of anger flooded his body. The images, the pain, the crying—Petronio wanted to be home in the States, to do something to help. He wanted to be in Philadelphia, there to protect his elderly parents and younger sisters, not sequestered on a military base in Cuba, ninety miles from American soil.

"Did I miss anything, sir?" Lieutenant JG Dave Rusotto, wearing a short-sleeve khaki uniform, stepped into Petronio's office.

"No, Rusotto. Just images of smoke, fire, and panic." Petronio kept his eyes glued on the screen. "The president's about to come on, though." On the screen was an overhead shot showing smoke billowing from the Fashion Valley shopping mall in San Diego.

The helicopter shot pulled away, and they could see black smoke blowing south over Interstate 8, which ran parallel to the mall. Cars along the interstate had come to a near standstill. No commentary was provided. Only the sound of the helicopter, with a caption that said, "Terrorists Attack Fashion Valley Mall—Live Footage."

A voice said, "This is Tom Miller. Fox News in New York. You are watching live footage of the Fashion Valley Mall in San Diego burning from what appears to be a coordinated terrorist strike against several shopping malls across the United States.

"Although terrorism is suspected, nothing official yet from the White House, where President Surber is about to address the nation from the Oval Office any second." More sound of helicopter rotors. "And now, we switch live to the Oval Office, where I'm told President Surber is about to address the nation."

The screen switched from the image of Fashion Valley Mall burning to the Oval Office, where a somber-looking President Douglas Surber sat behind his desk, looking at the camera, his hands resting on his desk, grasping a sheet of white paper.

"My fellow Americans, the sad and outrageous events of this afternoon have evoked memories of a somber duty carried out by former president George W. Bush, who on September 11, 2001, announced that our nation had been attacked.

"It is my painful duty to announce once again that today our nation has been attacked. In four American cities, Washington, Minneapolis, Dallas, and San Diego, there has been a coordinated attack against defenseless civilian shopping malls.

"This attack against civilians is the epitome of cowardice, the handiwork of yellow-bellied animals who would toss grenades and hide behind rocks, rather than come out and fight like men. They brag about martyrdom, and send others to commit martyrdom for them, but dare not commit martyrdom themselves. For it is easier to persuade the weak-minded to buy their lies than to prove publicly that they believe their own propaganda embracing martyrdom.

"Lives have been lost, and our hearts and prayers go out to the innocent Americans who today were minding their own business, carrying out their daily activities, looking forward to reuniting tonight with their husbands or wives, or parents, or children.

"We don't yet know the number of victims, but we know that tonight will be a time of sorrow for many of our fellow Americans. And as our fellow Americans grieve, we as Americans, each and every one of us, will grieve with them.

"We do not yet understand the cause of this attack, but we know enough to know the motive. I won't go into details, because now is not the time, but you can expect a briefing from federal officials later in the day.

"Effective immediately, I am ordering all flags at federal buildings lowered to half-staff in honor of the dead, and I am ordering a week of mourning.

"My fellow Americans, until we can determine that no more malls or public arenas are in danger, I urge you to obey all instructions from federal and local authorities for your safety.

"But to those who did this, you are warned. Do not mistake our mourning as a message that we are without resolve. For though our sorrow is great, our vengeance for our loss is greater.

"I started by quoting former President Bush. And to those responsible for this rampage of murder, I say, You can run, but you can't hide.

"You know who you are, and we are coming for you.

"God bless you all, and God bless America."

CHAPTER 11

• • •

"Hold still, ma'am." The makeup artist dabbed powder onto Emily's cheeks.

What a surreal experience! Was she really here? About to go on national television again? In a brand-new navy-blue dress that the federal government brought in for her because her red dress had been smudged with smoke? About to stand before the eyes of the nation again with her boss, who was preparing to address the nation in the wake of the emergency presidential address that ended just minutes ago, in the wake of the heinous terrorist attacks against her country?

Or was she still a little girl, asleep in the safety of her bedroom? The daughter of a small-town Presbyterian preacher in Cabarrus County, North Carolina, about to wake up to the smell of pancakes cooking on the stove, with her mother packing a peanut-butter-and-jelly sandwich into the Barbie-doll lunch box that her daddy had bought for her at the Roses Dime Store?

Which was reality? Which was a dream? And what about Diane? If anything happened to Diane . . .

Lord, let me wake up and be that little girl again! Charley and Mary

184

Ann's little girl. In a simpler place. In an innocent place. When the sun warmed my shoulders under Carolina blue skies and the breeze refreshed my face! When America was safe. Before the world lost all its common sense. In a time when right wasn't wrong and wrong wasn't right. When David and Chuck caught tadpoles and pulled pigtails.

"Are you ready, Em?"

The voice of Billy McNamara brought a cold splash of sober reality.

"Ready, boss," she answered.

"Okay, remember this. Same format as before. You flank me on the right. Nolan flanks me on the left. Remember, look somber. We've been attacked."

"Yes, sir. Of course."

"Okay, let's go."

They stepped out of the green room and walked to the back entrance of the pressroom, where Special Agent Bob Nolan waited for them.

"Ready, Bob?" McNamara asked.

"Yes, sir," the grim-faced agent responded.

"Good. Let's do this."

McNamara stepped out into the bright press lights. Shoulder to shoulder, Emily and Nolan followed the director into the pressroom.

Emily fought the natural tendency to squint as she stepped out to her place beside Billy McNamara.

"Good afternoon, ladies and gentlemen," Billy began. "I am Billy McNamara, director of the United States Transportation Security Administration. With me today are, first to my right, Emily Gardner of the TSA special counsel's office, who provides the agency invaluable legal advice on complex terrorism and counterterrorism issues . . ."

Emily nodded, her mind on Diane, her face unable to display anything other than the grim look she had been told to display for the cameras.

". . . and to my left, Special Agent Bob Nolan, chief special agent in charge of our new TSA ELITE Forces.

"An hour ago, you heard the president announce that America has been attacked by terrorists. Our purpose in the next few minutes is to provide additional information to give you a better understanding of what has happened, for the protection of the public.

"Let me first begin by saying, as the president said, that four malls in four cities—San Diego, Minneapolis, Dallas, and here in the Washington area, a few hundred yards from here—have been hit in a coordinated terror attack.

"At the moment we have reports of 245 Americans killed in the attacks and more than 700 more seriously injured. We're concerned that the death count may grow over the next few hours, and our agency, the TSA, will be responsible for providing updates on casualties.

"Now for the question of who is responsible for this and why. I am here to report that we have received a transmission from a group taking responsibility, and our intelligence verifies the authenticity of the claim.

"To the American people, I can assure you that your Transportation Security Administration will be deploying officers and assets to places of public gatherings, to transportation terminals, to shopping malls, to subways, and to airports to ensure your protection.

"The deployment of these assets will be taking place over the next few days, and until deployment is complete, you should remain in your homes and out of public venues.

"We will issue a travel alert for a national all-clear when we are assured that all venues are safe from further terror attacks.

"I have time to take a few questions, and then my colleagues and I must get back to work. Bear in mind that for security purposes, we may not be able to answer all of your questions, but we'll do the best we can. First question."

"Mr. Director. Javier Perez. CBS News. Sir, we note by this press conference that the TSA is front and center with the first agency briefing after hearing from the White House. In the past with briefings like this, we've typically heard from the FBI and/or the Justice Department. You mentioned earlier the incorrect information about the use of chemical weapons released by the FBI. Could you comment on why TSA appears to be taking the lead in this case, and did the mistake by the FBI have anything to do with the fact that you are here, rather than the director of the FBI or the attorney general, as we've seen in the past?"

McNamara looked at Emily, as if expecting her to answer. Then he turned to the CBS reporter. "Javier, first of all, the initial mistaken report of chemical weapons I would categorize as one of those things that can happen in the fog of war, at a time when all federal agencies are attempting to get our arms around the magnitude of the attack, to synthesize what is happening. But that issue has nothing to do with the excellent and unparalleled professionalism of the FBI. And I can assure you that the FBI is working hand in hand with us in a supporting role in this case. We're all on the same team.

"Now regarding your question about why TSA is taking the lead in this case. Well, the reason has to do with venue. As many of you know, TSA exercises primary jurisdiction over venues involving areas of transportation and other public venues. Transportation and public venues include airports, train stations, public interstates, and, in this case, areas of public commerce, such as shopping malls.

"Because the areas of attack involve public shopping malls, the venue is one of primary jurisdiction exercised by the TSA. By having a federal agency focus primarily on these areas of transportation and public commerce, we are able to provide focused firepower in protecting the public against attacks such as this. But I can assure you that the FBI will be providing the finest logistical support to us on this matter. And likewise, in future operations in which the FBI or other agencies take the law-enforcement lead, we will provide manpower, investigative expertise, and firepower to support those operations."

More hands flew up.

"Okay, a couple more." McNamara sipped water. "Yes. Ann."

"Ann Rogers. Fox News. Do you have any indication of the motive behind these attacks, and who has claimed credit?"

Billy took yet another sip of water, gulped it twice, and set the glass back down. "Thanks for your question, Ann, and this will be the last question that I will be able to answer for this session.

"The organization responsible is an organization that we have dealt with before. They call themselves the Council of Ishmael.

"This Council of Ishmael is a radical Islamic group, which, you may recall, has been involved in terror activities in the United States in the past. Closely aligned philosophically with al-Qaida, the Taliban, and Hamas, ten years ago the COI attempted to plant sleeper cells in the United States Navy. The three Navy Muslim chaplains who were executed five years ago were Council of Ishmael operatives.

"Now as you know, earlier in the week, the TSA arrested two Lebanese-Islamic terrorists, one at Philadelphia International Airport named Hasan Makari, and his son, who had infiltrated the US Navy.

"Our evidence shows that Hasan Makari and his son, Petty Officer Najib Makari, were masterminding a dangerous sleeper cell in the United States.

"It appears that this terror group, the Council of Ishmael, is unhappy that we arrested the Makaris and stopped this sleeper cell. They attacked today and say they will continue to attack unless we release the Makaris to them."

Emily reacted with a raised eyebrow. *A ransom situation?* Why hadn't she heard this before?

Billy continued, "They did not give a time frame as to when they would strike again. But regardless, we intend to deploy TSA ELITE Forces and auxiliary paramilitary units into shopping malls, airports, train stations, and on interstates to block any further domestic terror strike. This is why we are urging civilians to go home and remain indoors. We will issue a national all-clear via press release in a few days after we've determined that it is safe for civilians to return to the streets.

"Let me assure you, let me assure the American people, and let me assure the Council of Ishmael that today they have reawakened a sleeping giant. We know who you are. We know where you are. We have the assets and the resources to deal with you, and we will deal with you. That is all."

"Mr. Director?"

"Mr. Director!"

Billy turned to Emily and mumbled, "Let's go."

He stepped away from the podium, and she and Nolan stepped in behind him.

Outside the pressroom, out of the lights and in the hallway area, the three of them huddled. "Okay, Bob," McNamara said. "We need to get TSA forces deployed in force out on the streets. I want you to identify the one hundred largest shopping malls in the United States, and I want our forces out there, armed, and setting up checkpoints for shoppers going in and coming out. I want searches with metal detectors and full-body scanners like we use for airport security all over the country. I want pat-downs of everyone going in shopping malls. You're head of ELITE Special Forces, so you're in charge of this operation.

"In some of the smaller malls, let's utilize the armed AmeriCorps kids who are working under FEMA. Bring them in under our control. Those forces can patrol the malls and show force. But the point is this: by this time tomorrow, I want to show an incredible armed federal force around the country, like something we've never seen before."

"Yes, sir," Nolan said.

"And, Bob, there's one other thing."

"What's that?"

"I want federal roadblocks with TSA set up on major interstates going into and coming out of the top twenty-five cities in the country. Again, we want our presence out there for everybody to see. Code name Operation Lockdown. But hold the code name. We'll coordinate a press release with the PR folks tomorrow. Got it?"

"Yes, sir."

He turned to Emily.

"Emily, we'll need legal backup for all this. The ACLU and all these liberal groups will be squawking as soon as the operation is launched. It'll be the same thing. Fourth Amendment this. Fourth Amendment that. We need to be ready to respond. I need you to get on this and fast. I want our legal response ready as soon as the liberals start complaining. You up to that?"

How is this happening? Please, Lord. Be with Diane. Let her live.

"Emily?"

"I'm sorry. I was distracted. Yes, sir. Fourth Amendment defense positions. I'll work on it."

"Good." He put his hand on her shoulder. "Emily, I know you had a close call. But we've been attacked. We need your head in the game. Are you up for this?" His blue eyes blazed into hers.

"Yes, of course. I'll be fine. I'm in the game."

"Very well. Then let's get to work."

• • •

PULMONARY INTENSIVE CARE UNIT
BETHESDA NAVAL HOSPITAL
(WALTER REED NATIONAL MILITARY MEDICAL CENTER)
BETHESDA, MARYLAND

Zack checked his watch, then ran his hand through his hair for the hundredth time.

A text message. He checked it. Captain Foster.

SIR, SECNAV WANTS YOU, THE SECRETARY OF THE NAVY, THE CNO, AND SEVERAL UNDERSECRETARIES IN HIS OFFICE AT 1640 FOR AN EMERGENCY BRIEFING RE: TERROR ATTACKS. —V/R K. FOSTER, CAPT, USN

Thirty minutes had passed, and the wait had seemed longer than an eternity. From the time they'd found her, lying on the floor at the base of the escalator, there had been no signs of consciousness, and she had shown little responsiveness. How could they expect him to be at the Pentagon in an hour and a half at a time like this?

"Zack." He looked up. His friend Jeff walked into the ICU waiting area. Lettow reached out and gave him a hug. "Know anything?"

"Not a thing, Jeff." Zack stepped back. Even understanding the concept of Christian brotherhood, Zack wasn't comfortable with grown men hugging. "The wait is maddening, Jeff. They're supposed to have their best pulmonary guy working on her. A Commander Berman. He came out and said it's touch-and-go. They're worried about carbon monoxide poisoning. That's what's killed most of the victims so far.

"I'm worried about her. On top of that, SECNAV has been on the phone. They want me at the Pentagon for a briefing on this terrorist attack. I've got JAG officers all over the world depending on me.

"You never realize until it's too late how you've taken someone for granted, even the person you love most in the world. I pray to God she makes it. I'm a tough guy, but I don't think I could take losing her. Not now. It's too soon."

He sat back down on the black leather sofa, feeling exhausted.

Lettow sat down on the other end of the sofa. "Why don't you let me pray for you?"

"I'm always in favor of prayer," Zack said.

"Our Father, we ask that you be with Diane—"

"Admiral Brewer?"

Zack looked up.

Commander Larry Berman, the slightly balding Navy pulmonologist, was standing there in green scrubs, looking grim-faced.

Berman pulled up a chair and sat down. "Sir, smoke inhalation is the number one cause of death related to fires. Eighty percent of fire deaths are the result of smoke inhalation rather than burns.

"Smoke inhalation occurs when the victim breathes in the products of combustion during a fire. Combustion comes from the rapid breakdown of a substance by heat. Smoke is a mixture of heated particles and gases.

"Part of the problem is that it's impossible to predict the exact composition of smoke from the fire. The products being burned, the fire's temperature, and the amount of oxygen available to the fire all make a difference in the type of smoke produced.

"Now, in your wife's case, Admiral, we can't know for sure what she inhaled. They found her in the basement of the mall, where there were several restaurants. Natural gas elements may have exacerbated the flames after the explosion. The biggest unknown here is that we don't know the composition of the explosives used."

"I've got all that, Doctor. I need a bottom line here. What are you doing for her? Is she going to make it?"

"She's sick, Admiral. Her condition's critical. We're treating her for possible carbon monoxide poisoning through hyperbaric oxygenation. She's in a compression chamber. If there's any improvement in her condition, we'd like to try a bronchoscopy. But right now, she's too weak for that. She's strong, and that's why she's survived this long. The next twenty-four hours will give us a better idea of whether she'll make it."

Zack's stomach felt like he had swallowed a cinder block.

"If you'll excuse me, sir, I need to get back to your wife," the doctor said.

"Of course." Zack swallowed hard. "Do everything you can for her. Please."

"I will, Admiral. But may I make a suggestion?"

"Of course."

"While you have the chaplain here, I suggest that you pray, and pray hard. Because the outcome is no longer in my hands."

CHAPTER 12

. . .

HEADQUARTERS
US TRANSPORTATION SECURITY ADMINISTRATION
OFFICE OF GENERAL COUNSEL
SPECIAL DEPUTY COUNSEL EMILY GARDNER'S OFFICE
ARLINGTON, VIRGINIA
4:00 P.M.

Emily sat at her desk, her computer logged on to WestLaw, the powerful but ultra-expensive legal research tool affordable primarily to large law firms and the federal government, both of which could afford the two-hundred-dollar-an-hour online research fee.

Her mind, her heart, and her gut were all torn as she typed in another query, looking for exceptions to the Fourth Amendment in times of national emergency. In this case, her legal brief would focus on checkpoints and searches at shopping malls and along interstate highways.

The cases seemed to be split. Some judges were strict constitutionalists, unwilling to recognize exceptions for warrantless searches under any circumstances. Others took a more expansive view in the wake of 9/11, advocating a "public safety" exception to the Fourth Amendment.

Emily had loved her job. But her gut sided with the strict constitutionalists, holding that searches at airports, in malls, and along the highways would not be permissible without probable cause that a crime had been committed.

With so much swirling within her—her concern for Diane, her own near-death experience in the mall, and now her orders to research and defend a legal position that contradicted her instincts even though she could see both sides—she wanted to throw up.

Could she argue the position Billy wanted? Of course she could. Could she see both sides? Yes. Could she concentrate and deliver given the circumstances?

That remained to be seen. Her stomach twisted in knots. But she was an ex–Navy officer. America was under attack. She had to perform. There were no other options.

She glanced up at Tom Miller on the flat screen on the wall. The script on the screen proclaimed: "Mall Terrorist Attacks—TSA Orders National Lockdown." She picked up the remote from her desk and punched the TV off mute.

"This in from Washington. The TSA, the agency coordinating the federal government's response to today's terror attacks, has ordered a national lockdown. This communiqué from TSA director Billy McNamara, who in addition to having ordered that Americans go home until the dust clears, now says that TSA will be instituting searches in and out of major shopping malls in the United States, and will be conducting roadblocks for an indefinite period of time on inbound and outbound interstates in major American cities.

"Now in the midst of the chaos surrounding today's attacks, the TSA director's announcement raises the question, does TSA have legal authority to do this? And how does all this square with the Fourth Amendment's guarantee of the right against unreasonable search and seizure by the government?

"As the TSA deploys armed agents all across America, we're joined by our legal correspondent Judge Williford Devins and prominent constitutional law expert Gregory Kemp Liles.

"Good afternoon, gentlemen."

"Good afternoon, Tom."

"Thank you for having us, Tom."

"Gentlemen, our nation has been attacked. Americans have died. We don't know how many yet. Our hearts and prayers go out to the families who have lost loved ones. And now in the midst of this tragedy and turmoil, the TSA has rolled out a program whereby an army of federal agents will be pouring into shopping malls and onto interstates and highways to begin searching Americans, all in the name of safety. No question that all Americans want to be safe. But can TSA do this without violating the Fourth Amendment? Judge Devins? Why don't we start with you."

The screen switched from Miller to Judge Williford Devins, a late-middle-aged portly fellow with slicked-back graying hair and a robust voice. "Tom, the short answer to the question is no, they cannot. And the reason is that the Fourth Amendment does not contain a provision where it may be suspended under the guise of 'public safety.'

"Otherwise, all the government would have to do is to claim there's a public safety concern and search all it wants like they do in Communist Russia. The public has a right against unreasonable search and seizure. And, despite some liberal and incorrect judicial rulings, if you read the Fourth Amendment literally, it is never permissible to search without probable cause—a belief that the person being searched has committed a crime. There is no probable cause in mass searching a horde of shoppers entering a mall. You'd need a reasonable basis that each one of those people had committed a crime. Same is true with random searches on the interstate."

"But, Kemp Liles, haven't we seen precedent already? TSA with full-body scanners at airports? Boston police, without warrants after the marathon bombing, kicking people's doors in and conducting warrantless searches?"

The split screen focused on the tall, lanky, distinguished-looking southerner in the seersucker suit sitting beside the portly judge. "Look. I'm sorry about the people who died. But just because Boston police got away with trampling over the Constitution doesn't mean you give a license to the TSA or anyone else to make a mockery of the Fourth Amendment."

Emily's telephone buzzed. She muted the television, picked up her phone. "Emily Gardner."

"Miss Gardner. Secretary Strayhorn is on the line."

"Secretary Strayhorn. Oh my gosh. How could I forget . . . Okay, put him through."

"Yes, ma'am."

A second later. "Mr. Secretary."

"Emily. How are you?"

"I'm fine, Mr. Secretary," she lied.

"I understand you had a close call."

"Yes, sir."

"I understand your friend Mrs. Brewer is in the hospital at Bethesda."

"Yes, sir. I'm worried about her."

"We all are." A pause. "Look, Emily, I know it's been a long day, but I wanted to talk to you about tonight."

How could she have forgotten about tonight? "Yes, sir?"

"I might suggest that we cancel or postpone in light of today's events. But it's precisely because of today's events that we need to meet. Are you going to be up for it?"

Oh, goodness. How can I do this? What if Diane dies? Against everything in her gut, she responded, "Yes, of course, Mr. Secretary."

"Excellent. I'll have the limo pick you up at the time we agreed on."

• • •

BUILDING AV624
UNITED STATES NAVAL STATION
GUANTÁNAMO BAY, CUBA

The ferry ride across the glistening aqua waters of Guantánamo Bay, under the warm orange glow of the sun on its downward trek, with cool wisps of the approaching evening breeze, could pass as a scene from a travel magazine promoting cruises to the Caribbean.

Matt stood outside the jeep, on the deck of the ferry, allowing the breeze to caress his face as the ferry approached the Leeward Side.

His day was a day from hell—long, confusing, troubling, and memorable. He could not sort the jumbled mix of his feelings.

The bone-chilling note from a dead lawyer.

The vague and ambiguous warnings from colleagues in the JAG Corps.

The terror attacks back home.

Then the surprise announcement by the TSA director that the captivity of his clients, Hasan and Najib Makari, had spurred the attacks had complicated matters even more.

Overnight, his clients had become among the most hated men in America and would become more hated in the days to come. The blogosphere screamed for vengeance against the Makaris.

He immersed himself in thought as the ferry crossed the bay. His driver, Rusotto, had likewise been silent, shaken by the news from home. The nation today had been unified in a way not seen since 9/11.

And with the homeland being attacked and the military on high alert, every sailor and Marine and officer stationed at GITMO, it seemed, longed to return to the States to fight for America at home, whatever that meant.

As the ferry approached the dock, Matt glanced down at his iPhone, following a blog called NationalSecurityFirst. The subject of the discussion: the Makari sleeper cell.

"Just string 'em up and save the gov't some $," one blogger said.

"Shoot the Makaris!"

"Waterboard 'em! And waterboard 'em some more!"

Matt put his phone in his pocket. No point in dwelling on the ignorant comments of the ignorant masses. He still wasn't sure about the Makaris.

But this much he did know. In modern America, the truth mattered less than perception and propaganda. His clients might be guilty as sin, or they might be innocent as doves. But the facts mattered not to the ignorant fools in the blogosphere or the immoral grandstanders in the press.

But a good officer heeds the call of duty. And now his duty as a JAG officer was to defend two men accused of heinous terror.

"Ready to roll, Lieutenant?"

Matt's unibrowed friend, Rusotto, was getting into the driver's seat of the jeep. The ferry had arrived on the Leeward Side.

"Ready, Rusotto." Matt got in on the passenger's side. Despite today's attacks back in America, he sensed that tomorrow would bring about a storm of its own before the military tribunal. Already they'd done everything to let him know, without specifically saying it, that they wanted him here at GITMO to act the part of defense counsel, rather than actually being a defense counsel.

In other words, they wanted window dressing for the press.

But Matt Davis would become nobody's window dressing, not when it involved the Constitution.

He would resign his commission first.

The sailor standing on the ramp gave the drive-forward motion, and the jeep rolled off the ferry for the short half-mile ride to the dormitory building. Matt glanced at Rusotto. The unibrow had become more of a furrowed brow. Rusotto looked to be deep in troubled thought.

And why wouldn't he be? It felt like 9/11 had happened all over again.

Rusotto stopped the jeep in front of the barracks. "This is it, sir. The military tribunals open at 9:00 a.m. I should pick you up around zero seven hundred to make sure we get back across the bay to get you to court on time."

"Okay," Matt said. "Seven o'clock it is." He got out of the Humvee, then leaned back in. "You wanna go with me to court, Rusotto?"

Rusotto flashed a nervous grin. "I'd love to, sir, but Commander Petronio has me busy with other things."

"No problem. Just asking."

Matt stepped back and the jeep rolled out, turned left, and headed back down First Street toward the ferry. He checked his watch, 1800 hours. He hadn't eaten, but he wasn't hungry. A twisted stomach killed hunger.

He would head to his room, brew a cup of black coffee, then take out a legal pad and refine his plan of attack before the commission. Yes, he needed to focus. He would hit the government as hard as he could with arguments that he should have immediate access to his clients. The Sixth Amendment would be on the line in the morning.

He stepped into the front of the building, received a nod and an "Evening, sir" from the chief working the front desk, and headed down the passageway toward his room.

"Let's see. What's my room number?"

He fiddled in his pocket and pulled out his key. The key showed room 106.

"Let's see," he said as he passed the room to his right, "100, 102, 104, 106. Here we go."

He unlocked the door, pushed it open, and stepped in.

What?

He squinted for a double take. Were those decorative ornaments hanging down from the ceiling?

Then another double take.

There were two of them. And they hung side by side on twine about two feet long, dangling from a ventilation grill in the ceiling.

Banana rats.

Dead banana rats.

Strung up with twine tied into tight nooses around their necks.

Their tails hung down long, and an index card was stapled to the tip of each tail.

Another index card, with something scribbled on it, had been stapled to each rat's front feet.

As he approached the rats, the black markings on the white index cards became clearer. The card stapled to the tail of one rat said:

Andy P. Hart, Esq.
January 19, 1975–April 25, 2013
Annuit Coeptis
Novus Ordo Seclorum

Written on the card stapled to the rat's feet: "I tried to warn LT Matt Davis, JAGC, USNR."

The card stapled to the feet of the other rat said, "RIP, Lieutenant Matt Davis, JAG Corps, US Navy."

The card stapled on that rat's tail proclaimed, "I rattled the cage. Now I am a dead rat. Signed, LT Matt Davis, JAGC, USNR."

Matt felt an instant rage. He ripped one of the rats off the string and flung it across the room, against the concrete wall. It splatted against the wall and dropped to the floor, feet up with the note still stapled to its tail.

He released several expletives, then stormed out into the hallway and marched down to the chief's desk in the entryway. "Chief!"

"Yes, sir?"

"How long have you been on duty?"

"About an hour, sir."

"Did you see anybody go into my room?"

"Sir, I haven't seen anybody in the passageway."

"You sure?"

"Yes, sir. Custodial staff comes by in the morning. Somebody may have gone in your room this morning. I can check with the morning duty officer, if you'd like, sir."

Matt released another expletive. "Forget it, Chief. You got a knife or scissors?"

"I got a pocketknife, sir."

"Can I borrow it?"

"Yes, sir." The chief reached into his pocket and retrieved a red Swiss Army knife and handed it to Matt.

"Thanks, Chief."

Matt took the knife and headed down the passageway to his room.

He whipped out the blade and sliced the string holding the other dead banana rat.

He pulled the white plastic trash liner from the wastebasket in the corner of the room and dropped the two rat carcasses in it. Tying down the plastic bag, he headed out of the room and down the passageway to the chief's station. "Is there a dumpster around here, Chief?"

"Out behind the barracks, sir. You want me to take something back there?"

"No, thanks. I'll take care of it. What's the best way to get there? Out front and around the back?"

"Straight through this passageway behind me. Door's unlocked. You can't miss it."

"Thanks. And here's your knife." Matt walked down the hallway to the double doors behind the chief's desk and out into the late-afternoon sunlight.

He opened the trash can, tossed in the bag with the rats, and slammed the lid closed with a crash that echoed against the back of the concrete building.

If these cowards thought they could intimidate him, their shenanigans were going to backfire in their good-for-nothing faces.

CHAPTER 13

. . .

EMILY GARDNER'S APARTMENT
HALSTEAD TOWER
ALEXANDRIA, VIRGINIA

What to wear to dinner with one of the most powerful men in the country, who also was a member of the president's cabinet?

With her heart still heavy for Diane, Emily decided not to belabor her decision, selecting an above-the-knee black designer dress and simple white pearls.

She decided, too, on a whiff of perfume, Ralph Lauren Romance Summer Blossom from Macy's.

"That should do it."

Emily stepped out of her apartment, locked the door, and entered the waiting elevator on the fourth floor of Alexandria's snazzy Halstead Tower. Her mind whirling, she punched the button for the lobby. The elevator hummed and started dropping.

A moment later, the door opened to the marble-floored lobby.

The black stretch limousine was waiting out front, and she walked quickly across the lobby, her pumps *click-click-clicking* across the floor.

As she reached the revolving glass door to exit the building, her phone rang.

She stopped short of the door and fished in her purse. Perhaps Secretary Strayhorn was postponing the meeting.

She looked at the caller ID: "RADM Jeffrey Lettow, USN."

Diane!

"This is Emily Gardner."

"Emily? Jeff Lettow here."

"Is she okay, Admiral?"

"We don't know yet how serious it is. She is suffering from smoke inhalation. The doctor says the next twenty-four hours will be key."

Emily's breathing quickened. She wanted to be at the hospital with Diane. "Please tell me that she's going to make it, Admiral."

No immediate answer.

"Admiral?"

"Like I said. The doc says the next twenty-four hours will be key. I can tell you I'll be here with her the whole time, and I'll be praying for her."

"Is anybody else there with her?"

"Not now. Admiral Brewer had to return to the Pentagon for an emergency meeting with SECNAV. I expect him back anytime. But I've promised Zack I'll stay here until her condition clears."

"How's Zack holding up?"

"You know Zack. He's a tough guy. Doesn't show much emotion. He's all about duty. Duty to God. Duty to Diane. Duty to country. I know how much he loves her. I pray the Lord doesn't call her home. That's a lot to bear."

"I have a meeting I have to be at, Admiral. I have to go. Thanks for calling, and please let me know if there's a change."

"Will do."

The phone went dead.

Emily stepped through the revolving doors, and as she did, a man in a dark pin-striped suit with dark shades stepped out of the front of the limo. "Miss Gardner?" the man said.

"That's me."

"We're from the Homeland Security motor pool. Secretary Strayhorn sent us for you this evening." He opened the back door of the limousine. "If you'll have a seat, ma'am."

"Thank you." He took her arm and guided her into the plush and comfortable leather backseat and closed the door.

The dark tint over the windows, combined with her pupils having been shrunk from the sunlight, made the interior seem dark and chilly.

The limousine rolled forward, and a cold, nervous chill swept her body. How and when would all this end? She closed her eyes and prayed.

• • •

GUANTÁNAMO BAY DETENTION CENTER
CAMP DELTA
UNITED STATES NAVAL BASE
GUANTÁNAMO BAY, CUBA

The light.

It had disappeared again. The sole source of light, the small trap-door at the bottom of the back door of his cell, had been closed, leaving him in total darkness.

The darkness was their passive mode of torture between other more active methods of torture. They were trying to drive him mad, to frighten him or break down his resistance to a false confession.

The deep, maddening darkness had returned. But to a degree, Hasan took solace in it.

Was he too good or somehow too special in the eyes of God to be tortured for his faith? Jonah had gone into the belly of a whale. They threw Joseph into a dark pit. King David hid in dark caves, running from Saul. Peter and Paul were thrown into prisons. The Lord Jesus himself descended to the gates of hell before bursting forth from the tomb in the most glorious resurrection in all of history.

Was he somehow better than Jonah? Or less of a sinner than Joseph? Or holier than Paul and Peter? Should he not suffer like his own Savior?

He closed his eyes and recited the words of Paul to the church at Philippi. "I want to know Christ, and the power of his resurrection, and the joy of sharing in his suffering."

He repeated the phrase again: "and the joy of sharing in his suffering."

Tears rolled from his eyes. But not sad tears. Tears generated by a warm joy in his soul.

He waited for a few moments. In silence. Waited on the voice of the Lord.

A moment later, the words of the Scottish lawyer James M. S. Tait came to his lips, and he whispered:

"Oh for the grace, in every earthly loss, to bow the head to God, as Christ did on the cross!"

A sharp clanging from outside the cell.

A voice came through the darkness.

"Hasan Makari. We are coming for you. You can end this all, end all this pain, if you will confess."

• • •

LA CHAUMIÈRE
FRENCH RESTAURANT
GEORGETOWN AREA
WASHINGTON, DC

"Here we are, ma'am." The chauffeur pulled up on the right side of the street and parked.

The small, simple-looking restaurant in the posh residential section of Georgetown bore a large red awning above a bay window. On the awning was the restaurant's name, *La Chaumière*.

She remembered enough French to translate. *La Chaumière* meant "the cottage" or "the small house."

The place did have a cottage-like, unassuming look to it. Not the type of five-star restaurant that one would expect a member of the president's cabinet to frequent.

But perhaps that was the point.

The driver got out and opened the door for her, and she stepped out onto the sidewalk.

The security guard who had been riding in the front passenger seat got out and opened the front door of the restaurant for her.

"Thank you." She smiled and stepped inside.

"Miss Gardner, I presume?" The elderly host wore a black evening jacket and formal pants.

"That's me," Emily replied.

"We've been expecting you, madam."

"Thank you." She glanced around.

"This way, madam," the host said. He led her down a short hallway, past a quaint dining room with a stone fireplace, and into a private dining area with a single round table draped in a white tablecloth and with two chairs.

She had seen no patrons in the restaurant. Only waitstaff.

"Welcome to *La Chaumière*, madam," the host said. "This is our terrace room, complete with a good view of Georgetown. The secretary enjoys the view out on the street and always reserves the room when he dines with us."

"Very nice." The white-haired man's name tag said "Albert." "Tell me, Albert, does the secretary dine here often?"

"Yes, quite often."

"Forgive me, but is he usually alone when he dines here?"

The man smiled. "Sometimes if he has an important meeting, he reserves the whole restaurant for privacy considerations." Albert changed the subject. "His staff called and said he would be here momentarily. Could I bring you something? Wine perhaps? We have a marvelous selection from the Normandy region."

"Perrier water will be fine for the time being. We'll see what the secretary wants to do when he gets here."

"Of course, madam."

The host walked away. His posture was that of a man used to waiting on and dealing with the upper crust of society.

She gazed out onto the street, long shadows darkening the brick sidewalks and quaint roadways of Georgetown.

A young couple walked by the restaurant, hand in hand, their eyes sparkling with the clear intoxication of romance, their look wistful.

Emily's eyes followed them down the sidewalk until they disappeared around the corner.

Why, in the transitional moments of twilight, when the shadows elongate, when the sun surrenders first to the tree lines and then to the horizon, and when the first handful of stars dare to dance in a sky still possessing a weakening bluish hue, why, at this time of day, did she think of love?

And why, when she thought of love, did she think of love lost, of love never attained, of love sacrificed on the altar of a stellar military and wildly successful legal career?

Even amid the aftermath of the day's events, of facing death, of not knowing Diane's fate, of wondering about the motivations of powerful men like Billy McNamara and the even more powerful Fallington Strayhorn, she felt the faint strain of loneliness, of sadness, of love lost.

Perhaps she should go ahead and order a glass of pinot noir. Or something stiffer.

She turned her gaze from the street when she heard voices outside the dining room.

"She's right in here, Mr. Secretary."

"All right."

Two men in dark-blue suits with squiggly hearing devices in their ears stepped into the room, followed by a middle-aged woman in a black suit, holding a clipboard. Then a robust, slightly overweight middle-aged man, or a bit older, whose visage was familiar to every bureaucrat in the federal government.

"Well, lookity who's already here!" Fallington Strayhorn belted this out in a jovial laughing manner, in a voice that oozed politician through and through.

"Mr. Secretary."

She started to stand, which prompted a "Keep your seat, keep your seat" from Strayhorn, motioning her to sit.

Strayhorn approached the table, and one of his bodyguards rushed to pull out his chair. Strayhorn sat, grinning with apparent delight. This grinning seemed odd, considering Strayhorn headed a massive federal agency whose mission was to respond to the carnage from today's terrorist attacks.

"Y'all can take your posts," he said, which brought a chorus of "Yes, sirs" from the bodyguards and other staff members accompanying him.

Emily watched as Strayhorn's posse scattered. One bodyguard posted himself outside the dining room in the hall. Two others walked outside and posted themselves on each side of the bay window, looking out on the street.

The woman with the clipboard disappeared, at least for the time being.

Emily and Strayhorn, alone for the moment, looked at each other across the small table by the window.

Strayhorn broke the ice. "If I must say, the TV cameras don't do you justice."

She smiled. "Thank you, sir. At least I think that's a thank you."

"Oh yeah. That's a compliment, all right, because you look fabulous on TV."

She felt herself blush. Strayhorn looked better in person than he did on TV. Adequate looking for a big man. Not overly attractive, but not repulsive either, and charming.

"Well, thank you, sir."

The reemergence of Albert in the room alleviated the awkwardness for her.

"Good evening, Mr. Secretary," Albert said. "Your usual?"

"Absolutely," Strayhorn said. "And anything the lady would like. What would you like, Emily?"

"Well . . ."

"My usual is straight-up bourbon. You can try that. You can try anything. I don't care."

"Ah . . ." She thought for a second. "I'll have whatever your house white is."

"Certainly, ma'am." Albert nodded and turned and stepped out of the room again, leaving Strayhorn alone with Emily.

"So," he said, "I know it's been a long day. How are you feeling?"

"I'm feeling okay, sir, I suppose, considering the circumstances."

"Anything new on your friend?"

"Still the same. The chief of Navy chaplains, Admiral Lettow, is keeping me informed."

"Ah, yes, Lettow," Strayhorn mused. "I've heard of him. First Baptist they've had in that position in a long time, as I recall."

"I wouldn't know."

"I know this is hard for you, Emily"—his face morphed from grinning to serious—"but I felt that we should meet despite the circumstances."

Emily nodded.

"Your libations, sir." Albert arrived holding a silver tray containing a glass of white wine and a glass of liquor. He set the wine in front of Emily, then the liquor in front of Strayhorn.

"Thanks, Albert," Strayhorn said.

"Would you care to order, sir?"

"Not now, Albert. We need a few minutes to talk. Keep your eyes on the drinks though."

"Yes, sir."

Strayhorn waited until Albert left the room. He turned to Emily. "Okay, let's talk." He took a sip of bourbon. "It's been a tough day for the country, don't you think?"

"Yes, sir."

"I've been impressed by your performance." Another sip of bourbon. "Both before the attack and, even more so, after the attack."

She sipped her wine. "Thank you, Mr. Secretary."

"I know how you feel about your friend Diane."

"You do, sir?"

"I do. Did you know Jerry Myer?"

"General counsel for Homeland Security?"

Strayhorn nodded. "He was a patriot, a great lawyer, and a friend.

Massive heart attack one day. Gone the next. He was one of the best friends I had in Washington in a town where you have to be careful about who you trust."

"I'm sorry for the loss of your friend, Mr. Secretary."

"His death was also a blow to Homeland Security."

"Yes. I'm sure. Did he have a history of heart problems?"

"Not that anyone knew about." Strayhorn fiddled with the lapel of his jacket. "Just fifty-one years old. In decent shape—in better shape than this ole guy. Went to the gym every day. He keeled over with a heart attack one Friday."

Emily studied the man's face. Part of his countenance seemed sad when he talked about Myer. But his piercing brown eyes seemed steely, almost dispassionate about it all. Maybe it was all political bull.

"I guess we never know." She sipped on Perrier water. "I can't remember. Did Mr. Myer have family?"

"Sure did. A wife, two boys in college, and a girl still in high school."

"So sad."

A lull in conversation.

"Anyway," Strayhorn continued, "my general counsel's office hasn't been the same since he died. Hoyt McGovern is acting general counsel, but the problem is lack of vision, lack of leadership, and lack of visionary legal thinking."

Emily wasn't sure how to respond. In the small Washington legal community of federal general counsels, she never bad-mouthed other lawyers she might have to work with.

"I'm sure it will work out, Mr. Secretary. I don't know Hoyt McGovern that well. But sometimes transitions take a little while to get ironed out. I mean, it's only been a couple of weeks since Mr. Myer passed away, hasn't it?"

"Robert!"

"Yes, sir?" The guard posted outside the dining room stepped in in response to Strayhorn's call.

"Go tell Albert to bring more bourbon, will ya?"

"Yes, Mr. Secretary."

Strayhorn's brown eyes bored into Emily's, and he let his gaze linger. He eyed her up and down in a manner that gave her the creeps. "Yes, my dear. It will have been two weeks this Saturday. When Jerry died, I appointed Hoyt to serve as acting general counsel, and I explained that this position would be interim.

"But at this point, we are at war. I don't have any more time to waste . . . Thank you, Albert." He waited until the host replenished his liquor glass and left. "As I said, a time of war is not a time for experimentation. I've got to get this department shipshape."

Where was he going with this? "I'm sure that you will serve the country and serve the president well," Emily said.

"I can only serve the country and the president well if my department is firing on all cylinders. That's why I want you as general counsel of the Department of Homeland Security."

What? Did he just say . . . "I'm . . . sorry, sir?"

"I've been watching you, Emily. When you came up with the fraudulent enlistment theory on Najib Makari, I thought, 'What a brilliant solution!' And then, when you were so smooth and photogenic in handling questions from the national press, I knew I'd found Hoyt McGovern's replacement." He sat back and smiled at her.

As for Emily, the import and the idea of Strayhorn's words had a numbing effect. Had she heard him right? "Excuse me, sir. You want me to be general counsel for the TSA?"

He belted out a laugh. "Now, Emily, you know that the late Jerry Myer wasn't general counsel for TSA."

"Homeland Security? You want me as general counsel for Homeland Security?" She sat back, stunned. "But, sir, I'm not even general counsel for TSA yet."

"I know that. But the good news is that Billy McNamara shouldn't have a problem with it, since I'm not snatching his general counsel. Although I am snatching his best lawyer." Another sip of bourbon. Another chuckle. "If he doesn't like it, tough. I'll fire him if he gives me any lip." More chuckling. More drinking.

She sat still for a second. "I'm flattered, sir. I don't know what to say." She sipped her wine, trying to get a grasp on all he had said. If she had heard all this right, she had been offered the promotion of a lifetime, to become the top lawyer in the largest agency of the federal government. Her head swirled. This was hitting her like a gushing fire hose. What should she do? She never expected this. "I have some sensitive projects over at TSA. Billy wants a legal position paper defending the TSA plan to deploy in malls and at train stations and to conduct searches. Should I get that done first?"

"Heck, no. Billy can assign another lawyer to that. Who's the general counsel over there?"

"That would be Nick Miller, sir." Nick Miller was the guy she'd been rumored to possibly replace upon his retirement.

"Oh yeah. Him. Well, let Nick figure it out. Better yet, tell ya what. You know TSA is part of Homeland Security. So we'll let you bring that project with you, and we'll announce the legal position from the mother ship. Ole Nick Miller will be working for you!" He smiled and held up his glass, obviously waiting for her to clank hers against his.

She forced a smile, held up her wine, and allowed the clank to happen.

"A toast! To Emily Gardner. General counsel of the Department of Homeland Security!"

CHAPTER 14

• • •

The tropical morning sun burned across the tops of the palm trees. Two banana rats ran out in the jeep's path. Rusotto tapped the brakes, allowing the yellow-furred nuisances to cross the two-lane road unscathed.

The sign came into view as Rusotto slowed the jeep.

Office of Military Commissions
Expeditionary Legal Complex
Guantánamo Bay, Cuba

Another sign, a white sign on a brick wall, proclaimed:

Camp Justice
Guantánamo Bay, Cuba
Established September 11, 2007

Above the Camp Justice sign, the American flag flapped in the morning breeze. And beside it to the right was the black POW-MIA flag. On each side of Old Glory were the flags of the five branches of the armed services, with the Army and Navy flags closest to the American flag, and the Air Force, Marine, and Coast Guard flags flanking the others.

Behind the barbed wire surrounding the perimeter were a dozen Quonset huts covered with khaki canvas covers that flapped in the wind.

Past the Quonset huts was the two-story courthouse, a khaki-colored rectangular stucco building as bland looking as a typical high school gymnasium, except for the observation tower rising above the building with two tall antennas on the tower.

"Strange-looking place, isn't it, sir?"

"I'll say," Matt said. "Where'd the Camp Justice thing come from?"

"They had a contest, and some technical sergeant came up with it. The Bush administration wanted to build a more permanent complex, but Congress rejected that, so you still have these Quonset huts. You're lucky. They used to put the lawyers up in these huts. I'm not sure why they've got you over on the Leeward Side."

"Maybe so they could hang more rats from the ceiling of my quarters?"

"Say again, sir?"

"Nothing, Rusotto."

Rusotto gave Matt a quizzical look, then returned to tour-guide mode. "President Obama campaigned on closing the place and never did. So we have a permanent facility here that looks like a MASH unit or something."

"Looks more like a Nazi concentration camp to me."

"Agreed, sir," Rusotto responded. "Here's your drop-off. You'll have to clear through the metal detectors and all that, but they're expecting you, so you should be okay." He stopped the jeep.

"Thanks, Rusotto." Matt stepped out, brushed off his summer white uniform, picked up his briefcase, and leaned back into the jeep. "I'm

214

thinking this will last an hour or two. Are you going to pick me up when I'm done?"

"You bet, Lieutenant. Just give me a call."

"Super." Matt checked his watch. Ten minutes until court. "Can I ask you one other favor before you leave, Rusotto?"

"Sure. Anything, Lieutenant."

"Would you check with the master at arms back at the RLSO about getting me a sidearm issued?"

"Aye, sir. But I doubt if they're going to let you take it in there." He nodded at the Military Courthouse. "Security's unbelievable."

"I don't care about in there. Just see what you can do, will ya?"

"Aye, sir. Do you have a preference?"

"Nine millimeter. With a couple of fully loaded clips."

"I'll see what I can do, Lieutenant. I don't see that as a problem."

"Appreciate it, brother."

"Aye, aye, sir."

Matt returned Rusotto's salute, turned around, and heard the jeep drive away.

He walked toward the first guard station of the heavily fortified outer compound.

"Morning, sir." A US Marine sentry snapped to stiff attention and shot a salute. Two other Marine corporals also shot salutes.

"Lieutenant Matt Davis, Navy JAG, reporting for court, Sergeant."

"Aye, sir. We've been expecting you, sir. But we're going to have to search your bag and ask you to step through security, sir."

"Not a problem, Sergeant." Matt stepped into the full-body scanner and responded to the "Hands on your head, sir" command. Off to the side, two Marines rummaged through his briefcase.

The government had no business searching a defense attorney's papers. What if he had sensitive evidence that was "eyes only" material for the defense attorney and his client?

"You're all clear, sir." Matt looked at the sergeant's name tag: Swanson.

"Are you my escort today, Sergeant?"

"Swanson, sir. Staff Sergeant Todd Swanson. Aye, aye, sir. You've got me for the day. I'm ordered to escort you to the courtroom, to stay with you while you're in court, and to bring you back out when you're done."

Matt studied the Marine's face for a second. His was the face of a good man whose duty was to his country and not to some power-grabbing political agenda.

"Very well, Sergeant Swanson. Let's rock and roll."

"Aye, sir. If you will follow me, please."

Matt followed the sergeant out of the guard shack, making quick strides down the sidewalk as they headed up to the gymnasium-looking courthouse building.

They came to another checkpoint, prompting more enlisted Marines to throw sharp salutes at the sign of an approaching naval officer.

"He's with me," Swanson said, which seemed to be enough to allow them to pass the second checkpoint without another pat-down.

Swanson opened the doors leading into the main entrance of the building.

The inside hallways were like nothing Matt had ever seen in a courthouse. Marine guards, armed with M-4 rifles, were posted every twenty feet or so down the main hallways.

The place resembled an armed encampment more than a courthouse.

"The courtroom is right this way, sir." Swanson led Matt down another hall, then stopped and pushed open a wooden double door.

The empty courtroom looked like a congressional investigation hearing room, not a traditional courtroom. At the front, where one would expect a judge's bench to loom high above the spectators, a long rectangular wooden table, like a conference table, sat with a navy-blue skirt hanging from it to the floor. On the table were microphones and laptop computers in front of each of five black chairs. At the center of the table, a small sign, gold-plated with a black inscription, proclaimed: "Chief Judge, US Military Commissions." Four other gold-plated signs each proclaimed: "Judge, US Military Commissions."

Behind the table, behind each of the chairs, were five flags, one for each of the armed services of the United States military. Matt noticed the US Navy flag in the center, which gave him an odd sense of pride. The blue flag of the Air Force flanked the Navy flag on the left, and the red-orange flag of the Marine Corps was on the right. The white flags of the Coast Guard and Army stood as bookends to the other military flags.

The American flag, normally front and center in most courtrooms, stood oddly to the left of the military flags.

In the well of the empty courtroom, past the visitors' gallery, two rectangular wooden tables were positioned several feet apart and in front of the center table. One table bore a sign that said "Defense Table." The other table's sign said "Prosecution Table."

Matt walked down the center aisle between the empty gallery of seats, stepped into the well area of the courtroom, put his briefcase on the counsel table marked for the defense, pulled out a chair, and sat down.

He checked his watch. Two minutes until nine.

Where was everybody? No prosecutor. No judges. No court reporters. No reporters. No anybody.

A minute later, a door opened behind the long table, just to the right of the US Army flag.

A sergeant major in battle fatigues walked in. "All rise. Oyez, oyez, oyez, this military commissions tribunal for the United States of America is now in session. The honorable Chief Judge, Colonel Michael Karpel, United States Marine Corps, presiding. God save the United States, and God save this honorable court."

Matt stood as a United States Marine colonel in green service uniform, which the Marines call their "alpha uniform," stepped into the courtroom. The colonel had a bulldoggish look about him and at first glance bore a strong resemblance to Colonel Nathan R. Jessup, the fictional Marine colonel played by Jack Nicholson in the classic movie *A Few Good Men*, which, ironically, was about another military court-martial at Guantánamo Bay.

From the left side of the courtroom, the prosecution team slipped in, led by the lead prosecutor, a full colonel in the Air Force.

The assistant prosecutor was a woman, a US Navy JAG officer . . . What?

Her eyes caught his, causing his chest to pound and his hands to sweat.

The military judge called the court to order. "Please be seated. Call *United States of America versus Hasan Makari and Najib Makari.*" Matt sat in his chair as the judge continued, "Counsel, please state your names, ranks, and branch of service, if applicable. Start with the government."

The Air Force officer rose. Tall, slim, and with white hair, he looked more like a diplomat than a prosecutor. "Good morning, Your Honor. Colonel Tom McGrary, United States Air Force. I've been assigned as lead prosecutor in this matter."

"Good to see you again, Colonel McGrary," the judge said.

"Always a pleasure, sir." McGrary responded in a tone that reeked of familiarity and mutual admiration.

"And I see that you have an assistant at counsel table today?"

"Yes, Your Honor. And I'll let her introduce herself."

McGrary nodded at the woman, and she rose, and Matt's heart nearly bolted from his chest. Definitely psychological warfare from the drop of the gavel!

"Good morning, Your Honor. Commander Amy Debenedetto, United States Navy. I've been assigned as Colonel McGrary's co-counsel." She kept her blue eyes looking straight ahead, as if determined to avoid even an inadvertent glance.

"Welcome to Guantánamo, Commander. I hope that you find your stay a pleasant one."

"Thank you, sir."

"Counsel for the defense?"

So this was his punishment.

Rather than an admiral's mast or a court-martial for fraternization, they would pit him against the object of his dalliance in a fierce, life-or-death legal battle to be played out in front of the world!

"Counsel for the defense? Are you going to introduce yourself?" Judge Karpel's tone had transformed from congenial joviality poured out on the government's table to an irritated snappiness.

"My apologies, Your Honor." Matt pushed himself to his feet. "Lieutenant Matt Davis, United States Navy, Judge Advocate General's Corps, for the defense, sir."

"Is your mind on something else, Lieutenant?"

"Only on my job, sir." His first lie to the court rolled from his lips, and his conscience bothered him.

"Very well. We haven't seen junior officers serving as lead counsel in these proceedings. But if Navy JAG thinks you're up to the task, that's JAG's choice."

"Thank you, Colonel."

"All right. I understand the defense has filed a motion and wishes to be heard."

"That's correct, Your Honor."

"Are you prepared to proceed, Lieutenant?"

"Ah. Yes, sir. If the court would allow me to retrieve a few notes from my briefcase."

"Get whatever you need and let's get moving. I don't have all day, mister."

"Aye, sir." Matt fumbled through his briefcase and found a legal pad and a pen, all the while feeling the eyes of everyone in the courtroom boring into him. And her eyes, hers were the hottest of them all.

There. His legal brief. He pulled out the brief and his legal pad and pen, plopped them on the table, and looked up at the judge. "The defense is ready to proceed, Your Honor."

"Very well. Then let's get on with it."

"Aye, sir." Matt locked eyes with the bulldoggish-looking colonel and tried putting her out of his mind. "Your Honor, our first motion that we've filed is a motion that the government be required to give me expedited contact with my clients. As you know, Your Honor, the Sixth Amendment to the United States Constitution guarantees an accused the right to effective assistance of counsel."

"You think the Constitution applies down here, Lieutenant?" Karpel interrupted him midstream. "My bet is that Colonel McGrary over here"—he gestured at the prosecution table—"will argue that the Constitution does not apply because we're dealing with alleged foreign terrorists and we're not on US soil."

"Actually, Your Honor," McGrary said, "Commander Debenedetto will argue the government's position on the issue."

"Commander Debenedetto will argue the government's position on the issue."

The words rang in Matt's ears like an echo in a torture chamber.

"Ah." Judge Karpel raised an eyebrow. "We'll be hearing from Commander Debenedetto first." Karpel spoke as if he was anticipating a treat.

"Okay, Lieutenant. So my guess is that Commander Debenedetto"—the judge nodded at the defense table—"is likewise going to make the argument that the Constitution does not apply here." Karpel drilled his stare straight at Matt.

Matt swallowed hard. He reached down and poured himself cold water in a Styrofoam cup, took a sip, and set the water down.

"Your Honor, I take the position that the Constitution, and thus the Sixth Amendment, does apply. First of all, we're on a United States naval base even though we technically are not on United States soil, since GITMO has been leased from the Cuban government. Courts-martial take place on US naval vessels all the time, and these vessels are at sea, and the Constitution and the UCMJ and the Rules for Courts-Martial apply. Not only that—"

"All right. I get it." Karpel waved his hands in the air. "Hold that point for a moment, Lieutenant, and I'll get back to you and let you finish your arguments." Karpel shifted his gaze to the prosecution table. "But first I'd like to get Commander Debenedetto's position on this." The judge's voice transitioned from the sound of a yapping bulldog to a lovesick puppy. Who could blame him? "Commander, we are going to do this piecemeal, and so I want you to limit your response only to Lieutenant Davis's argument that the Constitution should apply here at GITMO."

She stood facing the judge, fitting impeccably into her service-dress white skirt and blouse. What a sight to behold—his Kryptonite in the flesh. Someone was toying with his mind.

"Your Honor," she said in the velvety voice that nearly got him court-martialed, "with respect, Lieutenant Davis's analysis is flat-out wrong. First, we are not on US soil, and there's nothing in the Constitution mandating that it be applied outside the geographic borders of the United States. Second, the Lieutenant's argument about the Constitution applying on naval vessels at sea doesn't fly either."

"What do you mean, Commander?" Karpel asked. "You would agree, would you not, Commander Debenedetto, that the Constitution would apply in a military court-martial on an American warship at sea."

"Yes, of course, Your Honor."

"Well, what's the difference? Doesn't your fellow naval officer, Lieutenant Davis, have a point? I mean, the North Arabian Sea isn't United States territory. And you just said the Constitution would apply in the North Arabian Sea. Why not here in GITMO?"

"Well, there is a distinction, Your Honor."

"Oh yeah? What is it?"

"A United States warship is owned by the United States of America. Wherever that ship is, at any given time, is considered United States territory. By contrast, the naval base here at Guantánamo Bay is on territory leased from the Cuban government. We're on leased territory here, Your Honor. The *Carl Vinson*, by contrast, is owned by the United States, whether it's in the North Arabian Sea, the Persian Gulf, the South Pacific, or anywhere else in the world. Also, Your Honor, these terrorists are not United States citizens and, thus, are not entitled to constitutional protection and are not entitled, therefore, to effective assistance of counsel under the Fifth Amendment."

"Hasn't this all been decided already, Commander? Didn't the Supreme Court in *Boumediene v. Bush* declare that detainees have constitutional rights? Isn't Lieutenant Davis right when he claims that these defendants have rights under the Bill of Rights because the Supreme Court already decided it?"

"No, Your Honor, the *Boumediene* case, along with the cases of *Hamdi v. Rumsfeld* and *Hamdan v. Rumsfeld* are limited in scope and address only the issue of habeas corpus. Those cases say that detainees have habeas corpus rights. But that's it, Your Honor. There's nothing in those cases that expands detainees' rights."

"But isn't habeas corpus part of the Constitution, Commander? And if that part of the Constitution applies, can't I extrapolate that, say, the constitutional right to effective assistance of counsel would apply?"

Amy hesitated. Karpel, for all his seeming fascination with her, was asking the right questions.

"No, Your Honor," Amy said. "The Supreme Court has had the opportunity on at least three Bush-era cases to expand a detainee's rights and has not done so. The Supreme Court has said that habeas corpus applies at times, but it has never said anything else applies. Therefore, since the court is aware of these issues, then it's fair to say that it declined to expand anything else beyond habeas corpus."

Karpel nodded, then looked back at Matt, as if relishing having pitted the two of them against each other. "What do you say, Lieutenant? The commander has a point. We're on leased property, and the court hasn't specifically expanded detainees' rights beyond habeas corpus."

Matt paused and glanced over at Amy. She glanced back, and his heart skipped a beat. He knew her well. She made the argument she had been ordered to make, and she argued it well. But she didn't mean it.

"With respect, Your Honor, to my colleague, Commander Debenedetto, this court is right in its analysis. Habeas corpus is indeed from the Constitution, which undermines their argument that the Constitution doesn't apply here. Clearly, it does. The *Boumediene*, *Hamdi*, and *Hamdan* cases prove it.

"Plus," Matt continued, "the whole distinction between a warship owned by the United States and a naval base leased by the United States is form over substance. And the argument about not being United States citizens doesn't fly either. First off, one of these defendants, Najib Makari, is a petty officer in the United States Navy, and thus entitled to all constitutional protections, including the right to effective assistance of counsel. The other, Hasan Makari, was arrested in the United States and detained in the United States. I would argue that his right to a trial under American law attached at the point of his arrest. Had he been arrested outside the United States, that might have been different. But because he was arrested in Philadelphia, I would argue that his constitutional rights attached at that point."

"Okay," Karpel said, "so your position, Lieutenant Davis, is that the Constitution applies. Even here in Communist Cuba?"

"Of course, Colonel," Matt said. "The rule of law must apply, even in a military proceeding. And with respect, sir, all American law, even military law, is under the Constitution."

"Now wait a minute." Judge Karpel threw his hands up. "They just shipped you down here from Norfolk, right?"

"Yes, sir."

"Who was your commanding officer in Norfolk?"

"Captain Al Rudy, sir."

"I know Captain Rudy," Karpel said. "Good man. So, Lieutenant, tell me what you think would happen to you if one day you disagreed with your CO about something and you walked into Captain Rudy's office and started screaming at him, and cursing him out, and telling him he can stick it where the sun don't shine." Karpel glanced toward the prosecution table, then stared at Matt. "What do you think would happen to you, Lieutenant?"

Matt hesitated. "If I did something like that, I imagine I'd be taken to captain's mast or court-martialed for insubordination."

"But wait a minute." Karpel flailed his hands. "Don't you have a right under the First Amendment to say whatever you want to say?"

Matt saw what was coming. "Your Honor, obviously disrespect cannot be tolerated in a military chain of command."

"But you said the Constitution applies in the military. Now you're saying the First Amendment doesn't always apply in the military. So which is it, Lieutenant? Does the Constitution apply? Or does it not? And maybe this is the reason, say, the *Boumediene*, *Hamdi*, and *Hamdan* cases did not expand any constitutional rights beyond habeas corpus."

"Your Honor, with respect, I meant to say that while the full panoply of constitutional rights available in the civilian world may not always apply within the military chain of command, nevertheless, the distinction here is that the Constitution always applies in military courts-martial. And every officer here in this courtroom has taken this oath to support the Constitution of the United States against all enemies, foreign and domestic. That is at the heart and soul of the officer's oath. Colonel McGrary has taken that oath. Commander Debenedetto has taken it. You've taken it, Your Honor. I've taken it. The Constitution is never suspended in an American court of law. Not now. Not ever."

Karpel leaned back in his chair, crossed his arms, and rocked back and forth for a moment, as if considering Matt's argument. He glanced at Amy, then back at Matt.

"Lieutenant, how long have you been on the island?"

"Thirty-six hours, sir."

More rocking. More apparent contemplation.

"Let's say, for the sake of argument, that I agree with what you're saying, or even partly agree. Let's say I agree that your clients, even though they're foreign, and are accused of acts of terrorism, and are being held in Cuba, let's say I agree that they have the right to effective assistance of counsel. You've been here thirty-six hours, and that's not even two days yet. Lieutenant, how long a delay in your seeing them would cause ineffective assistance of counsel?"

"Your Honor, there's no bright-line test. I'm entitled to see them, and they are entitled to see me, immediately upon arrest or as soon as I can get to them after their arrest. Otherwise, without legal advice, they might say something that could undermine their case or my ability to defend them."

Karpel uncrossed his arms. "Immediately, huh?" Then he crossed his arms again and rocked some more. "Commander Debenedetto."

"Yes, Your Honor."

"Whether the Constitution applies or not, what would be the harm in letting Lieutenant Davis go ahead and see his clients?"

Amy leaned over and started a whisper session with Colonel McGrary.

"Are you going to answer my question, Commander?"

"Sorry, Your Honor. To answer your question, if this were an ordinary case, I suppose there would be no harm in letting Lieutenant Davis go ahead and talk to his clients. But this is not an ordinary case. It's a case that involves national security. These defendants have been implicated in planting terror cells in the United States that led to widespread terror and murder in four American cities.

"We have a compelling national interest in preventing that. We need to interrogate these terrorists more to get all the information we can to save lives on the homeland, Your Honor. I mean, this is why these trials were moved to Cuba to begin with. The interrogations allow us to get information that's crucial to national security, while at the same time fully protecting the Constitution back home."

"Some would say we're not doing such a hot job of protecting it back home," Karpel quipped.

"I understand those arguments, Your Honor. But the point being that it's on a completely different level here for national security purposes."

Karpel took a sip of water. "Let's say I agree with you, Commander. Or say I partially agree with you." He put on a pair of wire-rimmed glasses. "How much time do you contend you need to interrogate these defendants before you think it's okay for them to see their lawyer?"

Karpel's question started another brief whisper session between Amy and Colonel McGrary. "Your Honor, our interrogators need to continue their questioning uninterrupted for at least a week before the defendants are given access to counsel."

"A week?" Karpel whipped his glasses off his nose.

Matt sprang to his feet. "That's ridiculous."

"Sit down, Lieutenant. I'll get to you in a minute." He looked at Amy. "Constitution or no Constitution, a week sounds like a long time, Commander. You have gotten enough evidence for an arrest. What more do you need?"

Again, more whispering between Amy and McGrary.

"Your Honor, what we're looking for is evidence of sleeper cells. It's true that we have enough evidence to make the arrest of these terrorists. What we don't know is who else is out there. We've seen attacks on four civilian malls in the United States in the last twenty-four hours by a terror group claiming affiliation with these defendants and demanding their release.

"Your Honor, if we can identify other sleeper cells, maybe we have a chance to make arrests and shut those sleeper cells down and save lives. Your Honor, this is a matter of national security. We need another week to interrogate these men to avert more terror attacks."

"Your Honor," Matt interrupted.

Karpel held up his hand. "Save your argument, Lieutenant. I'm ready to rule."

"But, Your Honor."

"Sit down, Lieutenant."

"Sorry, sir." Matt swallowed hard.

"All right, here's what I'm going to do. Recognizing the need for national security, and with appreciation of the government's need to protect the public from terror attack, I nonetheless agree that the Constitution applies here. At least to a degree.

"I note, having served as staff judge advocate to at-sea commands, that it is US Navy policy, when it captures a suspected terrorist on the high seas, to read that suspected terrorist his rights. The court takes judicial notice that this happened, for example, when US Navy SEALs shot three pirates and took a fourth into custody off the coast of Somalia after their attack on the freighter *Maersk Alabama*. If you saw the movie *Captain Phillips*."

Judge Karpel paused, then continued, "Now, I don't know what the TSA does, and I don't care. But this is a military court. And in the Navy, the Fifth Amendment right against self-incrimination applies. Even to suspected terrorists. And therefore the Sixth Amendment right to effective assistance of counsel applies.

"And while I'm at it, Lieutenant Davis is right. We've all taken an oath to defend the Constitution. And if the actions of terrorists force us to abandon the Bill of Rights in the name of national security, then the terrorists will have won, and America will no longer be America."

Another pause.

"Having said that, I do recognize that there is merit to Commander Debenedetto's argument that there's a legitimate need to investigate and protect the public. So here's what I'm going to do." He looked at the prosecution team. "Commander Debenedetto?"

"Yes, sir."

"I'm going to work with you, but only to a degree. I'm going to give the government twenty-four hours to question these suspects if they want to answer questions. But here's the deal. You can question them all you want. But federal investigators, whether TSA or military or whoever, must inform them, prior to any interrogations, of their right to an attorney and their right to remain silent."

"But, Your Honor—"

"Hang on." Karpel held up his hand again. "Now, as a military judge, I recognize that I do not have direct control over any civilian interrogators, such as TSA investigators or anyone else not in uniform. So I can't order TSA investigators to Mirandize these men. However"—he held up a wagging finger—"however, I sure as heck can suppress evidence against these defendants if I find that it has been acquired illegally."

Yes! Finally something positive.

"Lieutenant Davis."

Matt rose to his feet, feeling vindicated. "Yes, Your Honor?"

"Congratulations. You've won the battle. At least in a sense. I find that your clients do have a constitutional right to effective assistance of counsel. I also find that your clients have a constitutional right to a speedy trial under the Sixth Amendment. And therefore, they're going to get their speedy trial."

"Sir?"

"Effective tomorrow morning, at zero nine hundred hours, I will call this case to trial. At that time, you can have all the access to your clients that you want."

"But, sir!"

"I'll give you two hours in the morning in the courthouse holding cell to interview them. You can spend an hour with each. Two hours with them both, however you want to do it. Then we call the case at zero nine hundred hours."

"But, Judge, I need more than two hours' prep time."

"Says who? Look on the bright side. Some defense counsel might welcome this ruling. It gives the government less time to interrogate your clients before trial."

Matt stood there, searching for a response. Perhaps he'd won the battle but lost the war, like he'd thrown an effective cross and gotten sucker-punched in the stomach. The judge had a point. Getting his clients to trial faster would expedite getting them out of the hands of the TSA torture monsters.

"Anything else, Lieutenant?"

What should he say? Instinct told him to zip it. "No, Your Honor."

"Anything from the government?"

Amy and Colonel McGrary started whispering again. A tinge of jealousy crawled down Matt's neck that the colonel had her on his side of the table. Even in the midst of all the legal electricity and dramatic turmoil, the sight of her jolted his attention.

This time, McGrary rose.

"You had something, Colonel McGrary?"

"Your Honor, I rise to inform the court, and to inform defense counsel, that the government will be seeking the death penalty against both of his clients."

Silence.

"Very well. So noted. The record should reflect that the government will be seeking the death penalty against Hasan Makari and Najib Makari. The court will stand in recess until zero nine hundred hours."

CHAPTER 15

• • •

The black limousine pulled up in front of the modern-looking five-story glass-and-cement building with an American flag flying front and center. At street level, a navy-blue rectangular sign with the department seal in one corner had inscribed in white:

Homeland Security
3801 Nebraska Avenue NW

A chauffeur stepped out of the car and opened the back right door.

The woman seated in the back was wearing a red dress. She felt a gust of wind swirl around her well-toned calves and flap at her hemline. She pushed her dress down and started to step out onto the sidewalk.

The chauffeur took hold of her arm and helped guide her out of the limo. "Welcome to Homeland Security, Miss Gardner."

"Thank you." Emily looked up at the flag fluttering in the breeze. Chills of patriotism descended her spine.

Three men were walking toward her. Two of the men, one on each side of the man in the middle, were armed TSA ELITE Special Forces guards. The one in the center was a trim, graying, middle-aged man in a gray suit and a red tie. He smiled and stepped in front of the guards with his hand extended.

"Miss Gardner, I'm Max Porterfield, deputy general counsel. Welcome to Homeland Security."

His grip was strong, his smile disarming. "Thank you." She wondered if this was all a dream. "It's a pleasure to meet you."

"Congratulations on your nomination, ma'am."

"Thank you."

"These gentlemen are Officers Blount and Taylor. They're your assigned security guards. They will be near you at all times and will be available for your security needs 24/7."

"I have a security detail?"

"Yes, ma'am. Their job is to keep you safe in the building and escort you to and from your residence. They're available to travel with you to events, public appearances, and even on vacation."

"Well, okay. Nice to meet you, gentlemen."

"Ma'am." The ELITE Forces guys nodded.

"As for me," Porterfield continued, "aside from serving as your principal assistant, Secretary Strayhorn has assigned me the pleasurable task of showing you around the building, showing you to your office, and then helping get you prepped for your confirmation hearings."

Porterfield's words nearly stopped her in her tracks. Of course. How could she have forgotten? The general counsel's position required confirmation by the United States Senate. In all the conversation she had with Strayhorn last night, that one little factoid was not mentioned. Strayhorn must have assumed she knew it. And, of course, she did know it but hadn't thought of it . . . until now.

"Well, all right, Mr. Porterfield. Let's get started. I'll follow your lead."

"Yes, ma'am." Porterfield gestured toward the building as he turned, inviting her to walk with him. They walked through the automatic sliding doors. Four or five armed guards, wearing TSA or

Homeland Security uniforms, manned the lobby. Porterfield pointed to the elevators.

Officer Blount punched in several numbers on a keypad, and the elevator doors slid open.

"This is a secure elevator that goes straight up to the GC's offices. The entry code is 14178." Porterfield directed her into the elevator. "But we'll get you a pack with all that."

"Thank you."

The doors closed, and the elevator started rising. They ascended rapidly and said nothing on the way up.

The doors slid open. "The general counsel's suite," Porterfield said. "After you, ma'am."

Emily stepped out of the elevator to a reception committee of about twenty men and women in business attire, all smiling and applauding.

A banner over their heads said "Welcome, General Counsel Designate Gardner!"

"Ms. Gardner," Porterfield said, "meet your personal legal staff."

Emily smiled, once again overwhelmed by the unexpected. She stepped over to the applauding semicircle, her hand extended. "Hi. I'm Emily Gardner."

"I'm Beth Hodges."

"Irving Watson, Miss Gardner."

"Miss Gardner, I'm Nancy Bunker-Ward."

Others introduced themselves. Their excited voices were jumbled together.

"All right. All right," Porterfield interrupted. "I hate to bust up the party, but I have to take the boss to get her ready for her Senate confirmation hearing. There'll be plenty of time for chitchat later."

Emily waved. "Thanks for the warm reception, everybody. I look forward to meeting you all one-on-one."

"Okay, Miss Gardner." Porterfield's hand found the middle of her back and steered her off to the right.

They walked across the large red-carpeted foyer that was full of mahogany furniture and ornate gold-plated lighting. Across the foyer, a smiling blonde woman sat at a desk. Behind the woman was an open doorway with a flag on each side, the American flag and the Department of Homeland Security flag. Above the doorway, a sign read "General Counsel's Office."

"Miss Gardner," Porterfield said, "your personal appointments secretary, Jean Griffith."

The blonde stood, smiled, extended her hand, and said in a southern accent, "A pleasure to meet you, ma'am."

"Nice to meet you, Jean," Emily said.

"My pleasure. Could I get you coffee or anything?"

"That's sweet. I'm fine. I think Mr. Porterfield here has to work with me on getting me ready for my Senate hearing. Maybe later."

"With pleasure, ma'am. I've taken the liberty of leaving a few fruits and other snacks, like granola bars, on the table beside your desk."

"Thank you, Jean. I love eating healthy."

"I can tell, ma'am."

Emily smiled. Her staff seemed so kind, her new secretary so thoughtful.

"Okay," Porterfield said, "let's check out your office."

"Let's do it."

They stepped into a corner office befitting the CEO of a Fortune 500 company or the senior partner of a major law firm.

"This is my office?"

"Yes, ma'am, assuming we can clear Senate confirmation in seventy-two hours."

"I have to appear before the Senate in three days?"

"Before the Senate Homeland Security and Governmental Affairs Committee."

"Ah, yes. Senator Rosen's committee."

"You got it, ma'am."

"You don't foresee any problems, do you?"

"Not with your record, ma'am. But . . ." He seemed to be thinking. Then he pointed to the huge dark wood desk in front of the large bay window. "I've got a stack of papers in a binder for you to go through to help you get ready."

She walked over and sat in the comfortable black leather chair. For a few seconds, she just sat there and took in the atmosphere. "I believe I asked you if you foresee any problems with the nomination process."

"May I sit?"

"Of course."

He sat in a chair in front of her desk and fiddled with his tie. "Not all the senators on the committee are Homeland Security fans. You can expect a grilling from Tea Party types who claim we want to trash the Constitution. Also, we've gotten a heads-up from staffers on the Hill about rumblings over your experience level. Some of our opponents plan to make an issue of that."

She raised an eyebrow. "What's wrong with my experience level?"

"Nothing, as far as I'm concerned. But some wonder why Secretary Strayhorn reached down and tapped a midlevel attorney from the TSA general counsel's staff to become the lead lawyer for the nation's largest and most important agency in the federal government. Again, you can expect a line of questioning designed to embarrass, but if you can hold your own, you should be confirmed."

"Okay. I think I can deal with those questions. Anything else?"

"Well, we've got these crazy conspiracy theories floating around out there, and you could get a question or two about those."

"Oh, really?" She paused. "Now you've piqued my curiosity. What kind of conspiracy theories are you talking about?"

"Stuff floating around on the Internet. The craziest one has to do with your predecessor, Mr. Myer. Some of these conservative wacko blogs claim he didn't die of natural causes. It's the same stuff. Every time someone high-profile dies, rumors fly that he was bumped off. It's crazy out there. Ya know?"

"How would I know about Jerry Myer's cause of death?"

"You wouldn't. But that won't stop some grandstanding senator from asking you."

She thought about that. "Okay. Where do we start?"

"Here's the White House press release on your nomination." He opened a briefcase that he had been carrying and handed her a piece of paper. "After you take a look at that, I need you to go through those papers I left on your desk and study them. I'm afraid you'll have a bit of homework the next couple of days. I'll need to meet with you again tomorrow, and we'll drill some of this stuff." He paused as she glanced at the press release. "What do you think of the press release?"

Department of Homeland Security, Washington, DC
For Immediate Release to All Media Outlets:

The White House has announced President Douglas Surber's intention to nominate Emily Elyea Gardner to the post of general counsel for the Department of Homeland Security. The announcement follows the recommendation of Homeland Security Secretary Fallington Strayhorn, whose department has been searching for a general counsel to replace former General Counsel Jerry Myer, who died unexpectedly from heart complications two weeks ago. Secretary Strayhorn explained the need to fill the post with expedience, given the domestic terror attacks suffered by the nation this week.

"We had anticipated a longer search process in filling this, one of the most important senior positions within the department. While some expected the search to take months," Secretary Strayhorn explained, "this week's terror attacks against our nation expedited the urgent need to have every major position in the department filled to be ready for the battle before us. By good fortune, Emily Gardner was in the right place at the right time and is available to begin serving immediately.

"Her work in the general counsel's office in the Transportation Security Administration has been nothing short of extraordinary, and she has proved to be one of the brightest legal minds in the nation. She will be a great asset in the War on Terror, helping the department navigate the sometimes tricky legal waters and obstacles in that war.

"We look forward to her hearings before the Senate Homeland Security and Governmental Affairs Committee, and we encourage the United States Senate to confirm this outstanding nominee."

End of Release

She looked up at Porterfield. "Looks good. Nice comments by Secretary Strayhorn."

"I wrote the release," Porterfield said. "But I know these are Secretary Strayhorn's comments. The papers are on your desk in that black binder." He nodded at a three-ring binder that looked to have several hundred pages in it. "I'll leave this briefcase if you want to take papers home tonight to prep for the hearings." He placed the briefcase on her desk. "But make sure the papers stay secure, and don't leave anything at home. There's sensitive material in there that must remain confidential for obvious reasons."

He reached into his jacket pocket. "Here's my card. Call me anytime, 24/7. I'll instruct the staff to leave you alone. But you can let me know or let Miss Griffith know if you need anything." He nodded and smiled. "Before I go, is there anything else I can do for you?"

She gazed at Porterfield for a second, examining his face for the first time. His jaw protruded with a cleft chin, and his piercing black eyes contrasted sharply against his thick and wavy graying hair. His looks proved to be both scary and hauntingly handsome all at once. Porterfield resembled an ex–Navy SEAL more than a lawyer.

"No, I'm fine. I see I've got a lot of work to do."

"Good luck, ma'am." He turned, walked out of the office, and closed the door.

She reached for the black binder and noted the label on the outside.

CLASSIFIED
Senate Confirmation Debriefing Papers
General Counsel-Designate Emily Gardner

She started to pinch herself when her cell phone rang. She checked the caller ID that she had preprogrammed into her phone: "RADM Jeffrey Lettow, USN."

Her heart pounded. "Admiral Lettow?"

"Emily?" His voice sounded somber.

"Yes. Is everything okay? How is Diane?"

"You asked me to call you if there was any change with Diane. I'm afraid she's taken a turn for the worse."

"What do you mean?"

"They've called Admiral Brewer back to the hospital. She coded. That's all I know."

"Oh, dear Jesus, no."

"I'm sorry. Zack just arrived. I've got to go." The line went dead.

"Dear Jesus!" Emily's body started shaking. Tears splashed on her new mahogany desktop, on the word CLASSIFIED on the binder. "Please help her, Lord. Help me get control of myself. I'm no good to anybody like this."

CHAPTER 16

• • •

Matt couldn't sleep. Wearing a white T-shirt and skivvies, and covered by only a sheet, he turned one way, then the other way. He turned over and tried plowing his face into the pillow. But that didn't work either.

His mind raced in a blurred swirl. How could he defend two capital cases on the fly, with no time to prepare?

What was the military judge, Colonel Karpel, up to? At first he had come across as a guy bent on rubber-stamping whatever the government wanted. And then Karpel swung in the direction of the defense when he ruled in favor of Matt's motion. But it wasn't a clean victory. Matt should have been given immediate access to both clients.

But then again, the ruling wasn't a clean victory for the prosecution either. Perhaps Judge Karpel was saying, "Okay, look, government, I'm giving you another twenty-four hours to do whatever you're going to do to these guys, then we're going to try this case, whether you are ready or not."

Perhaps there was a method to Karpel's madness. Then again, perhaps not.

The scene had flashed through Matt's mind a hundred times. It was like facing a locomotive in the courthouse from the first drop of the gavel.

The thing that seemed to slow the locomotive? He'd replayed it in his mind a dozen times—his spontaneous, impassioned reminder that each officer in court, as a member of the United States military, had taken an oath to defend the Constitution.

He had not preplanned those comments. But with those words, Karpel had looked up, slowed his cadence, and injected a more balanced flavor in his tone. Even Amy and Colonel McGrary seemed speechless.

Indeed, the Constitution evoked power for the perseverance of liberty.

But then came the ruling that the trial would be fast-tracked. That would never happen in a capital case back in the United States. They tried the Fort Hood terrorist, Major Nidal Hasan, four years after the fact.

But then again, Nidal Hasan's delay violated every principle of the military's speedy trial clock. And he got the death penalty anyway, which he deserved.

Matt knew enough military history to know that some of the most famous courts-martial in the military had been fast-tracked.

The famous court-martial of Private Eddie Slovik for desertion, which led to his execution for desertion in World War II, commenced in November of 1944, one month after his deliberate desertion from the Army.

The court-martial of Army Air Corps Colonel Billy Mitchell commenced in November of 1925, one month after the Army preferred charges against him for violating the Articles of War by criticizing his superiors.

The tragic court-martial of Captain Charles McVay, the commanding officer of the USS *Indianapolis*, the cruiser that transported the atomic bomb to Tinian Island and was then sunk by a Japanese submarine on its return voyage, commenced in November of 1945, about ninety days after the *Indianapolis* sank.

Of those three cases, Slovik and Mitchell were convicted. McVay was acquitted but later committed suicide. All demonstrated the historical swiftness of the military justice system.

But going to trial on a capital case only a few days after being arrested?

Matt twisted and turned, then twisted some more.

He rolled over on his back and gazed at the ceiling. A streetlight outside flickered, sending a faint, slim stream of fluorescent light through the top of the windows and casting a narrow band on the ceiling.

At least there had not been any more threats since court, either overt or implied, and Rusotto had helped him secure the 9mm pistol from the arms locker. This brought him a little bit of peace and comfort, although not much.

This much he knew. If he didn't get some rest, he would be worthless, and his clients might get the death penalty because their lawyer fell asleep at the wheel.

He checked the digital clock: 1:20 a.m.

Matt rolled back on his stomach and closed his eyes. Even if his mind was racing at a thousand miles per hour, he would force rest upon his body.

There. That was better. A deep, satisfying breath.

Perhaps sleep would be waiting by the top of the hour.

Another yawn.

He felt it coming.

Sweet sleep.

He closed his eyes. His breathing grew rhythmic. Finally. Thank God.

Three sharp raps on the door sent his heart racing. Thoughts of the threatening e-mail from someone posing as the dead Andy Hart rushed to his mind, along with Rusotto's repeated warnings of "Watch your back."

Matt reached over into the drawer beside his bed and pulled out the 9mm pistol and worked the lever, chambering a bullet into firing position. He turned off the safety, making the gun ready to fire.

More raps on the door.

His feet hit the floor and he stood, holding the pistol straight up. Quietly, he moved toward the door. He brought the pistol out front, ready to fire.

Against the dim light out in the passageway, shadows appeared at the base of the door—the shadows of the boots of his assailant.

"Matt."

The voice from the other side sent his heart thumping.

"Matt." The second time he heard his name, he put the gun down. He turned the knob and cracked open the door.

Against the full light from the hallway, her figure was stunning, even in a T-shirt, navy running shorts, and white tennis shoes.

"Amy?" he whispered. "What are you doing here?"

"I wanted to see you before tomorrow started."

"It's already tomorrow."

"You know what I mean." She flashed those same blue eyes that had melted his resistance on his sailboat. "Please."

"You're crazy," he whispered. "Haven't we gotten into enough trouble already?"

"Somebody's going to see me out here if you don't let me in."

"Did somebody follow you here?"

"I don't know." She locked eyes with him. "I don't care."

"Man, oh, man." He looked down the empty hallway both ways. "Come on." He waved her in and closed the door and locked it.

He wasn't sure if he had pulled her to him or if she had rushed into his arms. Not that it mattered. Their kiss was long and satisfying.

"Okay, okay. That's enough." He pulled away from her. "You're crazy."

"Maybe so. If I ever get out of this place, I'm resigning my commission so we don't have to sneak around in the dark like this and worry about getting prosecuted for fraternization."

He put his arms around her waist, looked into her face, and leaned in and kissed her again.

"Okay, I'm enjoying this, but this isn't right." His heart was pounding for a different reason. "We can't be doing this. Admiral Brewer would string us up. And if the media caught wind of this . . ." His voice trailed off.

"I'm sorry," she said. "I wanted to see you so bad."

"I know, Commander," he said. He pulled her in for a hug but did not kiss her this time. "We both have a job to do."

"I know," she whispered. "I want you to know, Matt, that I've been ordered to do this."

"I know."

"I've got to do it," she said. "I don't have a choice. I don't believe in these arguments."

"I'd almost rather be court-martialed than have to do this," he said.

"Me too," she said. "How did we get ourselves into this?"

"I don't know," he whispered. "But you'd better go before we both get arrested for aggravated fraternization. I hear the prisons aren't too inviting in this neck of the woods." He looked at her, then pulled her to him and kissed her once more. "Okay, ma'am. I'm going to have to ask you to leave."

"Yes, Lieutenant." She smiled, and he opened the door.

She stepped out quickly, walking away down the hall, not looking back.

He let his eyes linger a moment, enjoying the outline of her figure until she was out of sight.

CHAPTER 17

• • •

With her mind swirling like the wall at the eye of a hurricane, thinking about her US Senate confirmation hearings looming, Emily had gotten out of bed, put on a pot of French vanilla roast, and set up office on the coffee table in her living room.

For hours she had pored through the reams of information Porterfield had given her. Of course, anticipating what the senators would ask had proved problematic. She had tried starting with a broad approach, sifting through department position papers on counter-terrorism, then border security. Immigration remained a hot topic. Of course, those types of policy questions would be best directed at the secretary, as opposed to a nominee for general counsel. But that wouldn't stop publicity-hungry senators from asking her anyway.

And then there would be the typical legal questions from senators convinced that the federal government, and particularly Homeland Security, had become increasingly heavy-handed on constitutional issues.

Emily expected to be pounded about her perceived lack of experience, having been suddenly promoted from a deputy general counsel's position at a subsidiary agency. But the best way to reduce the inexperience factor was to demonstrate command of her subject matter under intense questioning.

Beefing up on all the possible issues on such short notice had proved daunting, if not impossible, like plugging a thousand holes in a dam with three fingers.

As midnight had approached, her knees and back and joints bone-tired, she had decided she needed sleep.

She had crawled into her queen-size bed, pulled the comforter over her, and tried to doze. But the mental mind churning had gotten out of control. By one thirty she was up again. She hit the button on her single-cup coffeemaker and, within a couple of minutes, was back in business.

Porterfield had warned her that she would be hit by a couple of the libertarian, pro-military senators on her legal theory of "fraudulent enlistment" that she had devised to justify prosecuting Najib Makari at Guantánamo instead of before a military jury.

She sat on the couch, sipped her coffee, and leaned over the coffee table, leafing to the next page in the three-ring binder.

The headline on the page caught her eye.

WEB LINK—SECRET

Notes on SITUS Project
Secure Login: *www.situsproject.gov/gencounsel/classified*
Username 1: hsgencounsel126Loblolly
Username 2: hsgencounsel204Latham
Username 3: hsgencounselusmom0717
Password 1: 3145&ff%54north
Password 2: hampton0717lionspaw

"What? Secret web link? The what project?" Emily put on her reading glasses and reread the strange reference. "What's that all about?"

Her laptop was on the coffee table beside the three-ring binder. She looked at the laptop, then at the three-ring binder containing 375 pages. She had gotten through about half on the first read through.

She looked at the page again and picked up her laptop.

She started to type: "www.situsproject.g . . ."

Then she glanced at the binder again. "I've got to get through that binder before the hearing. This can wait until later. No time to get side-tracked on a wild-goose chase through the Internet."

She put the laptop back on the coffee table and turned to the next page in the binder.

Summary of Recent Fourth Amendment Cases Relating to Search-and-Seizure in National Security Matters

CASE 1. *Florida v. Riley, 488 U.S. 445, 109 S. Ct. 693, 102 L. Ed. 2d 835 (1989)*

Fact Summary: Based on anonymous tip, a law enforcement helicopter conducts surveillance of a greenhouse at an altitude of 400 feet. No warrant was issued. An officer on board the helicopter spots marijuana growing in the partially covered greenhouse, leading to defendant's arrest and conviction.

Holding: No search warrant required, conviction affirmed.

Facts: Acting on an anonymous tip . . .

Something made her flip the page back.

Secure Login: *www.situsproject.gov/gencounsel/classified*

"Oh, what the heck." She picked up the laptop, opened Google Chrome, and typed in the secure login: "www.situsproject.gov/gencounsel/classified." "There." She hit the Enter button.

The computer went into search mode.

A second later, a message popped up:

You have entered a classified website maintained by the US Department of Homeland Security. Access to this website is on an "eyes only" basis and requires a security clearance of TOP

SECRET. Unauthorized entrance may result in felony criminal prosecution. To maximize security against cyber-attack, you will be required to enter three different usernames followed by two passwords. These five prompts will come up individually, and you will be required to enter each prompt before proceeding. Remembering that you are subject to criminal prosecution for unauthorized entrance into this site, you may now proceed at your own risk.

"Wow," she said. "All right, if they want a felony prosecution, then let's get this show on the road."

She typed the first username, "hsgencounsel126Loblolly."

Then the second.

Then the third.

A red message flashed on and off:

Username Sequence Successfully Processed!
Caution—Unauthorized Entry Will Result in Criminal Prosecution!
If You Have Authority to Visit This Site,
Please Enter Password Sequence

"Why do I feel like I'm entering the nuclear launch codes or something?"

She looked back at the first password, then proceeded to type: "3145&ff%54north."

Then the second: "hampton0717lionspaw."

Another flashing red sign:

Classified Site Successfully Entered!
Do You Wish to Abort?
Abortion of Site at This Point Will Avert Criminal Prosecution for
Unauthorized Users!
Do You Wish to Abort?
___ Yes, I wish to abort.

___ No, I do not wish to abort. I understand that I may be criminally prosecuted for unauthorized entry of this site.

A thought struck her. She had not yet been confirmed by the Senate. She wasn't yet general counsel. Was she subjecting herself to prosecution by entering the site?

"Play it safe, Emily."

She started to click "Yes, I wish to abort."

But . . . she was handed the binder and ordered to study it to prepare for the hearing. It seemed like explicit access was granted.

On the other hand, she had not been given specific permission to go beyond the physical binder.

Still, the physical binder contained the notification of the site and had specific login instructions, including usernames and passwords.

On impulse, she clicked "No, I do not wish to abort."

Another flashing warning:

Entering the SITUS Project Website
TOP SECRET

Below that flashing sign, another instructional option: Click Here to Enter.

She had gone this far. Why not continue?

She clicked the Enter button.

Information started scrolling down the screen. A moment later, the screen was filled with information about the top-secret SITUS project.

She put on her reading glasses, took a sip of coffee, and started from the top.

"What?" She squinted and read again. "Wait a minute."

She reread the first paragraph. Then she read the second paragraph, and the third. Her body felt as if someone had dumped a bag of ice over her head and shoulders.

Her heart quickened and she felt restless, suddenly short of breath.

She got up and walked over to the window to look down on King

Street. A few cars zipped by, their headlights and taillights shining off the street.

This had to be a nightmare.

By morning, if not sooner, they would know that she had opened the document.

Maybe that's what they had planned all along, to expose her to the truth, then test her loyalty. Or perhaps it wasn't true. Maybe they planted the information to see how she would react.

No, it had to be true. Her predecessor, Jerry Myer, had died from a "heart attack" as much as Andrew Breitbart had died from a "heart attack."

Maybe Myer had left the log-in instructions to the classified site buried deep within the briefing papers for a reason. Or maybe someone else had slipped the instructions into the binder.

But did Max Porterfield know? How could she know for sure if he knew? Could she trust him? Could she trust anyone?

She turned from the window and eyed the bottle of Argentinian Malbec, unopened, on the kitchen counter. Tempting, but not a good idea.

Maybe she had read it wrong.

That must be it. After all, it was late. Or perhaps early, depending on whether one's definition of two thirty in the morning was early or late.

She sat down on the couch, rubbed her eyes, and started reading again. "Oh dear." She put her hand over her mouth.

"Dear Jesus, what have I gotten into?"

Emily stood up. Her body felt clammy. She walked across the room and plopped down on the love seat. She brushed her hand across her forehead, wiping cold sweat from her brow.

What to do?

Where to go?

She felt the sensation of a giant, cold steel fist squeezing her body.

Who to call?

Who could she trust?

"Think, Emily!"

Two names came to mind: Diane and Zack.

She could trust either with her life. Zack was a man of honor. And unlike so many women obsessed with gossip and meaningless chitchat, Diane could be trusted with the deepest secrets. Diane would know what to do.

But Diane remained in critical condition, and this was no time for Zack to have to deal with all this.

Not now.

"Lord! Help me!"

Where were the wise when they were needed? Where were the strong when she needed a shoulder to lean on?

She thought of her Grandma Edna Elyea, a quiet woman of faith known for the world's best Italian cream cake and affectionately known by everyone as "Mamma E." Emily remembered Mamma E's death like it was yesterday. With a host of contraptions around her and needles stuck in her arms, Mamma E was almost comatose, under the influence of morphine. Her breathing had slowed. Then, almost supernaturally, Mamma E raised her head and a beatific smile crossed her face, as if she was witnessing something from another world.

It had been a week since Mamma E had spoken to anybody. But when she raised her head and looked off into space, she began to recite her favorite psalm, "The Lord is my shepherd . . ." She kept reciting the psalm with a supernatural, velvety beauty, as if her words were propped up by the Spirit. And then she reached these words, which were her last words: "He restoreth my soul."

Emily looked across the room at the old black King James Bible, left to her by "Mamma E, sitting atop the old buffet, also an inherited grandmotherly relic of days gone by.

She walked over and, with reverence, picked up the Bible and held it against her heart. The book was a lifeline in the midst of a tempest. And after she caressed it for a moment, she kissed it and opened it.

"Let's see. Proverbs. Go back one. Psalms." She turned back the pages, then two more until she found it. "There. Psalm 23."

Her eyes fell on these words:

*Yea, though I walk through the valley of the shadow of death, I
will fear no evil: for thou art with me; thy rod and thy staff
they comfort me.*

*Thou preparest a table before me in the presence of mine enemies:
thou anointest my head with oil; my cup runneth over.*

She closed the Bible.

What would Mamma E do?

The answer came quickly. Mamma E would pray. Emily closed the
Bible and got on her knees in front of her coffee table.

"Lord, I don't understand any of this. But you've brought me into
the valley of the shadow of death. I have enemies out there. Or I will
soon have enemies. Protect me and give me wisdom."

CHAPTER 18

· · ·

"The Lord is my shepherd; I shall not want. He maketh me to lie down in green pastures: he leadeth me beside the still waters. He restoreth my soul: he leadeth me in the paths of righteousness—"

"Sorry to interrupt, gentlemen."

Zack and Jeff both looked up. Dr. Berman was smiling.

"Doc, what have you got?" Zack cut to the point.

"Well, she's not out of the woods, Admiral, but she wants to see you."

"She's conscious?"

"Yes, sir. But I don't know how long she will be alert. If you want to see her, sir, you'd better come now."

"What do you mean, if I want to see her? Lead the way."

"Certainly, Admiral."

Zack turned to Jeff. "Come with me."

"No, go ahead, Zack. You need this time alone."

"Jeff, you're my best friend, and she would want you there. Besides, I may need prayer support."

Jeff seemed hesitant, half wanting to come, half wanting to hang back.

Zack grabbed the chief of Navy chaplains by the arm and pulled him to his feet. "Come on, man. We don't have time to lose."

"Okay," Jeff said.

They followed Dr. Berman past the nurses' station, through the swinging doors under the "Intensive Care" sign. Walking down a brightly lit hall, passing a platoon of white-uniformed nurses and orderlies, the doctor pushed open the third door on the left.

A forest of stainless-steel contraptions, dangling IV bags, and beeping and blinking instruments rose above the bed.

A white blanket covered her from the neck down, but the auburn red locks of her hair against the white pillows reminded him of a thousand sunsets he'd seen at sea, like the sunset glistening in a broad orange carpet across rippling wavelets.

The slow *beep-beep-beep* of the heart monitor proved disconcerting, but thank God, her heart was beating.

"Diane?" He said her name in a gentle tone that he hoped would convey his love for her. She opened her eyes, not fully, but enough for him to see a sparkle—a weak sparkle—but nonetheless a sparkle. The edges of her lips curled into the resemblance of a smile.

He bent down and caressed her hair and kissed her forehead. "I love you."

She looked up at him and whispered, "Come closer."

He bent down and put his ear by her lips. "Zack . . ." Her whispered voice trailed off. "Zaahh . . ."

"I'm here, baby cakes. I'm here."

"Closer. I love you."

He kissed her on the lips. "I'm not leaving you."

Her eyes opened, and the magnetic green and hypnotizing sparkle that had captured him in an odd twist the first time they fought bitterly on opposite sides of the courtroom returned—for a second. "No . . . Zack. Listen. Our country is in trouble. The president . . . needs you!"

She reached for his hand. "Go to your duty station and serve. We all need you."

Her eyes closed and her head turned on the pillow.

"Diane? Di?" Zack whispered.

"She's under heavy medication, Admiral." An intensive care nurse entered the room.

Zack leaned over and kissed Diane on the forehead again.

A hand touched his shoulder. "She's a remarkable lady," Jeff said.

"I'm fortunate. And blessed."

"I'm going to step out and give you a few minutes of privacy with her," the doctor said.

"Zack." He turned around. Her eyes were open. "Do . . . your . . . duty . . . Go!" Her eyes closed.

He kissed her on the cheek. "Wow."

"Wow, indeed," Jeff said.

"You heard the lady?"

"I did," Jeff said.

"Well, what should I do?"

"You're asking me?"

"You're the chaplain, aren't you?"

Jeff winced, as if thinking. "What exactly are you asking me?"

"I'm asking you if I should stay here."

"Let's go for a walk."

"Where to?"

"Back to the waiting area."

"Okay."

Jeff put his hand on Zack's shoulder and started to step out of Diane's room.

"Hang on, Jeff."

"Sure."

Zack took one last look at her and allowed his eyes to linger a moment. From the beginning, it was always hard for him to take his eyes off her, in good times and bad, for she was the most beautiful creature he had ever seen. And even now, struggling in the intensive care ward of a large naval hospital, she remained the most beautiful creature he had ever seen.

"Okay, I'm ready," he told Jeff.

"Are you sure?" Jeff asked. "We can take all the time you want."

"She's sleeping. She needs to save her strength."

"You asked what I think you should do?"

"That's what I asked."

"Diane is strong," Jeff said. "She wants you to go do your duty and has given you the freedom to do just that. There's nothing you can do here, so, as strange as this may sound coming from me, as a pastor, I think you should honor her request. I'll stay here. Crystal will alternate with me. But I think she's right."

"Right about what, Jeff?"

"Right about this. Something is wrong out there. This attack against these malls could be the tip of the iceberg. In this time of so much uncertainty, when there are so few in Washington who can be trusted, your country needs you, Zack. I think your wife is right. We need you at your duty station. And I have a feeling that she's right that the president may need you before this is over with." Lettow put his hand on Zack's shoulder.

Zack looked him in the eye. "You're a good friend, Jeff."

"And you're a strong man, Zack. Go do your duty."

CHAPTER 19

• • •

What should she do?

She had received no peace about who would be safe for her to call—no peace about whether she should talk to someone.

But beyond all that, what about this evidence? How best to preserve it without anyone knowing she had it?

Download it on a flash drive?

Bad idea. That would create an internal record of the download. She could explain opening the site. After all, they gave her the classified notebook that contained the web address and passcodes. But downloading top-secret information on a stick drive could be a prosecutable offense even if the information were not so politically explosive. No, that was too risky.

She pressed the Control and *P* buttons. The screen went gray, displaying the message "Loading Preview."

A few seconds later, the screen read: "TOP SECRET—SITUS Project."

"Let's see." She checked the printer for paper. "Looks like enough."

She sat back down and moved her cursor to the gray Print button on the screen. She started to click it when something stopped her.

"Can they tell if I print it?"

She took a deep breath, then opened Google and typed "remote printing detectable."

A ton of stuff popped up, all of it technical, like "Manual Printer Configuration" and "Printer Configurations Dialogue."

She tried deciphering the confusing technical explanations but could never get any straight guidance on whether the Homeland Security monitors could tell if she printed the information from her screen.

"I can't take a chance on it," she said, as if to convince herself.

Should she even touch it? Would anybody pay attention? Would the press even run with it?

Maybe Fox News would run with it. But would it do any good? As a trial lawyer, she understood the importance of preserving evidence. She also knew that in some cases, possession of the wrong type of evidence could prove fatal.

Now she knew why Jerry Myer died. He had opposed the SITUS project.

If she didn't step carefully here, she would be next.

A chilling fear crawled down her neck, then all through her body.

"Lord, help me."

Funny how her prayer life had gotten so active in the last twenty-four hours. "Lord, if you get me out of this alive, I won't neglect my prayers or Bible reading ever again."

Emily stood up and walked around, fretting. She went to the kitchen to make another cup of coffee and noticed her iPhone charging on the counter. Then it hit her.

"Why didn't I think of that earlier?"

Forgetting about the coffee, she went to her bedroom and opened the top drawer of her dresser. The digital Nikon camera lay in the drawer.

She powered up the camera and went back into the living room, sat down, centered the viewfinder, and pressed the shutter. The first shot of the screen went off with a bright flash, and when she checked the digital image, the bright flash had wiped out the picture.

She blurted out a curse word and felt immediate guilt, since she was about to utter another prayer. "Lord, help me figure this out."

Emily fiddled with the digital menu. She scrolled down to the option for "flash on/flash off." She pressed the "flash off" option and held the camera up to the screen and tried again. She tried holding the camera still, but her hands kept trembling.

She snapped the shot, then checked the image. A bit blurred.

"Lord, help me keep my hands still." She breathed in deeply, then exhaled, trying to relax.

She opened her eyes. "Okay. Let's try again." She held up the camera and again snapped the image on the computer screen.

She checked the image. Much better.

Moving to the next screen, she snapped another photograph. Then another.

The whole process took almost fifteen minutes.

She spent another five minutes reviewing the screen shots, then logged off the website.

Now what? She removed the memory card from the camera and put it in the side pocket of her purse.

She was supposed to be preparing for her confirmation hearing before the Senate. But how could she face questions from senators, knowing what she now knew? Suppose they asked her about any of this? Or if she had knowledge of any Fourth Amendment issues that would be of concern?

And even if she was confirmed, how could she take the job, knowing what she knew?

Her heart started pounding again. Her hands shook.

Should she go public or remain silent?

She opened another window on her laptop and started typing a search term, then changed her mind and decided to type the search on her smartphone: "international visa requirements."

CHAPTER 20

• • •

When the red phone rang on the desk in the office adjoining the master bedroom, the secretary of Homeland Security was shaving in the bathroom. He laid down his razor and wiped his face with a towel.

He walked out of the large tile-floored master bathroom, across the spacious bedroom, and into the mahogany-paneled office, where the red phone was still ringing. He picked up the phone.

"Secretary Strayhorn."

"Mr. Secretary, this is Max Porterfield."

"Porterfield! I've been expecting you. But not so soon. You caught me in the middle of my morning shave."

"My apologies for the timing, Mr. Secretary."

"No problem, Porterfield. Whatcha got?"

"Sir, she took the bait."

"Talk to me, Porterfield."

"Well, I gave her the notebook. Told her to memorize it for the Senate confirmation hearing. She said she would, and I have no doubt she did. She's a voracious reader, that's for sure. A little before two this morning, an internal alert in the Homeland Security computer system triggers that someone is trying to access secret data on the SITUS project. We trace the invading computer to Ms. Gardner's laptop. She obviously found the memo buried deep in the notebook."

"She's sharp," Strayhorn said. "That's why I picked her to begin with. Did she try anything after that?"

"You mean like an attempted download of info, sir?"

"That's exactly what I mean."

"No, sir. She took the bait, but she didn't fall into the trap. No indication of anything downloaded. No indication that she tried to print anything from the site."

"Hmm. Okay," Strayhorn said. "How long was she on the site?"

"Forty-seven minutes altogether, Mr. Secretary. Then she logged back off it at quarter to three."

"Hmm." Strayhorn thought. "That might be long enough to read through the materials once."

"Agreed, sir," Porterfield said.

"Has she been back on the site?"

"No, sir."

"Let me know if anyone tries accessing that site or if Ms. Gardner tries accessing it again."

"Of course, sir."

"Are you picking her up to bring her to the office?"

"I'll have the security detail pick her up at 8:00 a.m., and I'll start working with her over at the general counsel's office."

"Okay," Strayhorn said. "I want you to let me know if she breathes one word about the SITUS project."

"Yes, Mr. Secretary."

"We'll find out real quick if we can trust her, or if she's going to try something stupid like her predecessor."

CHAPTER 21

. . .

The night had yielded to a dull gray dawn over the nation's capital.

Emily looked out of her fourth-story window, down at King Street coming to life with commuter traffic, full of cars driven by bureaucrats, diplomats, and government workers, clogging the roads to the Rochambeau and Arland D. Williams Memorial Bridges, the backed-up choke points spanning the Potomac from Arlington into Washington.

Her night had been sleepless, her soul restless.

What to do?

What if they were monitoring her laptop?

At this point, she had to assume they were monitoring her laptop, her desktop, and her cell phone.

She looked down to the street again. Out to the right, women wearing spandex workout suits and men in jogging shorts and T-shirts, some wearing tank tops, were going in and out of the XSport Fitness Center, the popular workout joint that occupied the first floor of the building next to the Halstead Tower apartments.

Two men wearing shades and dark warm-up suits were loitering on the sidewalk outside the fitness center.

Why would they be wearing shades this early? And on an overcast day?

One kept glancing over in the direction of her luxury apartment complex.

Were they Homeland Security?

TSA ELITE?

Perhaps FBI?

Maybe her mind was playing tricks on her.

But wearing shades at 6:30 a.m.?

Maybe they were just a couple of supercool fashion dudes. Maybe male models or something. All types lived in Alexandria.

There! Again! The one on the right with the navy-blue warm-up threads. He glanced toward the Halstead Tower.

"What's he looking at?"

Her heart pounded like a battering ram pulverizing her inner chest.

She stepped away from the window. They had to be feds of one sort or another.

What now?

A hundred ideas swam through her mind as she envisioned a thousand possible scenarios. The thought of the upcoming Senate hearing orbited as a distant moon around the epicenter of a million angry solar flares.

By now they probably knew that she had logged on to her computer and read about the SITUS project. They knew that she knew.

Maybe they had laid out the bait for her to see if she would nibble, or bite the hook. That had to be it. They wanted to know if she was for them or against them.

Of course!

And she'd fallen for the bait—hook, line, and sinker!

She could kick herself!

How could she be so stupid?

Ignorance is bliss, and now she could not plead ignorance!

She had to stay a step ahead of them.

Best not to use her laptop anymore.

She grabbed her bottle of Perrier water off the table and took a swig of it as she headed out into the hallway. She pressed the Down button on the elevator.

A *ding*.

The doors opened.

The man standing there in a warm-up suit sent her heart into a frenzy.

"Are you okay, ma'am?" the man asked.

When she saw his wedding band and looked into his face, she recognized him as a neighbor from the sixth floor.

"Yes, I'm fine."

She stepped into the elevator.

"Where to?"

"Lounge level."

"You got it."

The elevator dropped, *dinging* past the third floor, then the second floor.

"Have a good day," the man said as the doors opened on the first floor.

"You too." Emily stepped out and headed to the resident lounge.

Thank God. The room was empty. She had to hurry.

She sat at the computer terminal and swirled the mouse, bringing the screen from sleep mode to the Google homepage.

She typed her first query: "Russian Embassy Washington DC."

The screen responded with a website: "www.russianembassy.org."

Now on the Russian Embassy's website, she clicked a dropdown menu titled "Consular Issues," and then, from there, another dropdown titled "Visas."

"Let's see." She parroted the words on the screen. "General Visa, Business Visa, Tourist Visa. Hmm."

She started by clicking the General Visa section. "Let's see." Should she call the embassy? Or just pay a visit?

How would she be received? What if they were tailing her?

Of course they would be tailing her.

She went back to the Google search bar and typed another query, "Ed Snowden," and clicked the result.

Edward Joseph "Ed" Snowden, born June 21, 1983, is an American computer specialist and ex CIA employee, who worked as an NSA contractor. Snowden is best known for disclosing top-secret and classified information of the United States government, revealing spying by the US government against other allied governments, including Germany, Britain, and Israel. After felony warrants were issued for Snowden's arrest, he fled United States authorities and sought temporary asylum in Russia. Charges remain pending in the United States for espionage, which is a capital offense.

Now wanting to vomit, she scribbled down the phrase "espionage," then wrote "temporary asylum."

If she were given to suicide, if blowing her brains out were a possibility . . . she did have a gun upstairs.

"Stay strong, Emily. This is hard. Don't back down."

She checked her notes. What was missing?

She typed in the Russian embassy website, found the telephone number, and scribbled it down.

Maybe she should just go upstairs and take her gun and end it all.

CHAPTER 22

• • •

With the sun rising over the aqua-blue waters of the eastern Caribbean and white seagulls swirling in two peaceful, lazy circles overhead, the armed Humvee pulled up in front of the courthouse and stopped. Two jeeps were now in front of it, and two were behind it.

As soon as the Humvee stopped, armed US Marines in full combat gear and bearing rifles jumped out of the jeeps and surrounded the Humvee.

A Marine Corps captain walked to the Humvee and opened the back door.

"I need you to step out, please, Mr. Makari."

With his hands cuffed behind his back and his feet chained together, Hasan Makari put his feet down on the asphalt pavement in front of the courthouse.

The refreshing coolness of the early-morning Caribbean breeze brushed against his orange jumpsuit.

"Sir, we're going to lead you over into the courthouse building and take you to a holding cell. I think the plan is that you will meet with your lawyer there before the trial starts later this morning." The Marine captain's voice reflected neither anger nor excitement. Only the sound of consummate professionalism.

Why did Hasan trust the Marines as much as he distrusted the TSA thugs? It felt like both good and evil were working under the banner of the American flag. And unlike the TSA agents who had brutalized him since his arrest in Philadelphia, the Marines seemed to have no dog in the fight.

"You will not have to worry about me not cooperating, Captain."

"Thank you, sir," the captain said. "Please go with Sergeant Martin here." He held his hand out toward the stucco courthouse.

Surrounded by four armed Marines and a battery of television cameras and strobe lights, Hasan shuffled forward, up a short curved sidewalk leading to the side entrance of the courthouse. The fresh air soothed his lungs, and as one of the Marines took hold of his left arm to guide him up the steps of the courthouse, he caught a glimpse of the American flag flying over the courthouse.

Somehow, in spite of the false accusations and the torture he had endured, the sight of the flag and the professionalism of the Marines calmed his nerves. He prayed silently as they walked with him into the courthouse.

"To the right," the Marine said. Hasan squinted and blinked, trying to get his pupils adjusted after stepping in out of the light.

"This way," the Marine said. The entourage turned again, off the main hallway, leaving the American reporters behind. They walked down a narrower hallway to the end to a closed steel door under a small sign that said "Holding Cell."

"Sir, you'll have to wait here for a while. Your lawyer should be here soon. Step into the cell and face the back wall. Don't turn around until you hear the door close behind you. We're going to uncuff you to make you more comfortable. Please don't try anything."

"You have my word, Sergeant." Hasan stepped into the cell. A

Marine guard took hold of his hands behind him. The steel clamps of the handcuffs popped loose.

"Stay still, sir."

"Yes, Sergeant."

The door slammed behind his back. Next came the jangling of keys and the sound of dead-bolt locks sliding into place. He was alone again. He looked around the spartan cell, its cinder-block walls painted a dull gray.

At least there was no trapdoor for them to slip in rats or snakes. And his hands were no longer cuffed. He rubbed his wrists.

He sat on the steel bench and bowed his head and considered the great men of the faith, like the apostles Paul and Peter who were jailed for their faith. He remembered the American pastor Saeed Abedini, sentenced to prison in Iran because of his Christian faith.

Now, for reasons Hasan did not understand, his time for persecution had arrived.

He did not blame the Americans. He did not hate the TSA. For he knew that the Lord had called him here to suffer for Christ.

He closed his eyes and recited the Bible verse that Eugene Allison had taught him all those years ago from Philippians: "I want to know Christ, and the power of his resurrection, and the joy of sharing in his suffering."

His mind turned to Najib. "Lord, do whatever you will to me, for your glory. But, Lord, whatever you do"—tears streamed down his cheeks as he gazed up at the ceiling—"whatever you do, please protect my son. And, Lord, if it be your will, allow me to see him again someday. But if you must take me to protect him, then take me."

He wiped his eyes and recited the words of King David that brought him so much comfort. "The Lord is my shepherd; I shall not want. He maketh me to lie down in green pastures: he leadeth me beside the still waters. He restoreth my soul."

. . .

With Rusotto scheduled to pick him up in five minutes for the ferry ride and drive to the Military Commissions Courthouse, Lieutenant Matt Davis stepped in front of the dresser in his dorm room and looked into the mirror for a final uniform check.

Summer whites were the uniform of the day most days in Cuba. And while US Navy summer whites may have been the world's best-looking military uniform, the white uniform, unlike the wintertime service-dress blues, could show the tiniest flaws. Every little dust particle. Every little smudge. And as often happened with JAG officers wearing them, every little ink mark.

Matt did a quick once-over. So far so good.

Medals in alignment. Check.

Name tag in alignment. Check.

Shirt and zipper gig line lined up with edge of belt buckle. Check.

Matt checked his watch. It was time.

"Lord, give me strength and wisdom for this day. Let's do this."

He put on his cap, grabbed his briefcase, opened the door, and stepped into the hallway.

When he turned around to lock the door, he saw it dangling there.

A dead banana rat had been stapled by its tail to the outside of the door, just above the doorknob. It hung upside down, its nose touching the doorknob.

Below the doorknob, hanging by a piece of black electrician's tape, was a white envelope with "Lieutenant Davis" written in blue ink.

Matt snatched the envelope from the door and opened it.

"Do you understand that the Constitution has no place here? Lawyer friends of terrorists won't be tolerated. Your friend the rat never understood this. Your friend Andy Hart never understood this either. Tread lightly, Lieutenant."

Matt started to slam his briefcase against the wall but remembered that his laptop was inside. He stuffed the note in the envelope, then pulled the iPhone from his pocket and took a picture of the rat with the envelope and e-mailed it to himself.

So angry that he wanted to break something, or break someone, Matt stormed down the hallway, past the duty station, where the chief of the watch nodded and smiled.

No point in even mentioning this to the chief. Whoever did this, there would be no witnesses.

He stepped out into the morning sunlight. Rusotto was waiting in the jeep.

"Good morning, sir," Rusotto said.

"Rusotto, do you know anything about defense lawyers being threatened down here?"

Rusotto went blank, his face seeming to match the color of his summer white uniform, as if the topic paralyzed him. "What do you mean, sir? Has someone threatened you?"

Matt whipped out his phone and pulled up the image of the banana rat. "This is what I mean, Rusotto. This little dead rat I discovered two minutes ago stapled to the outside of the door to my quarters. And on top of that I get this note saying the Constitution doesn't apply here, and I should tread lightly or I'll wind up like the rat."

Rusotto sat there for a second. "Unbelievable."

"Well, Rusotto, when you first met me, you told me to 'watch my back.' Is this sort of thing a surprise to you?"

Rusotto looked at him. "No, sir. The gossip grapevine has been full of these kinds of stories about threats to defense counsel. But it's not something that's openly talked about. No, I'm not surprised at all, sir. I'm sorry you're having to go through it."

Matt studied Rusotto's face. This topic clearly frightened him. "Who do you think's behind this, Rusotto?" Matt asked as he tossed his briefcase in the back of the jeep and took a seat next to the driver.

Rusotto hesitated.

"It's okay, Rusotto. Don't feel obligated to answer the question."

"Sir, could I answer off the record?"

"You bet, Rusotto. Stays here."

"Sir, I'm pretty sure that whoever's behind this intimidation of counsel is not military."

"No? Why do you say that?"

"Have heard scuttlebutt from the senior JAG guys on both sides. Nobody wants defense counsel intimidated. Trial command doesn't want it. The senior prosecutors are disgusted by it too. But for some reason, there's an unwritten rule that nobody talks about it. It's like the senior command down here is intimidated or something. It's odd."

Matt scratched his head. "Somehow, I didn't think this junk came from within the military. If I know Admiral Brewer like I think I know him, then I know for a fact that Admiral Brewer would have none of it."

"No, sir. I wouldn't think so, sir."

"I've got one more question, Rusotto."

"Anything, sir, as long as I have your word as an officer that what I tell you stays here."

"You got it, Rusotto."

"Thank you, sir. Fire away."

"If these threats are not originating from anyone inside the military, then where are they coming from?"

Rusotto seemed to hesitate, as if wondering whether he had said too much. "Sir, I overheard Commander Petronio talking about this the other day. I can tell you that there's a lot of distrust regarding this new TSA ELITE Force, or whoever they are. The commander thinks they're a front for the CIA. Kind of a different face out front so the CIA can do whatever it wants in terms of torture while remaining in the background."

"Where'd Petronio come up with that?"

"I don't know, sir. Just passing along what I heard."

Matt crossed his arms. "Does Petronio think they had anything to do with Andy Hart's death?"

Rusotto looked outside the driver's window. "I thought you said only one more question, sir."

"You're right, Rusotto. My apologies. You've been kind enough to share enough stuff off the record. Let's rock and roll."

Rusotto swung his head around and looked straight at Matt. "Yes, Lieutenant. Commander Petronio does think they're responsible for Andy Hart's death. So do some other senior officers. That's why I told you to watch your back."

Matt nodded. "Well, from what I've seen, I'm not surprised. But you know what?"

"What's that, sir?"

"They picked the wrong junior officer to intimidate. Because the more they try this bull, the harder I'm pushing back. They can kill me if they want, but I'm going to kick some butt before they do."

Rusotto looked at him, sporting yet another stunned look. "You are a brave man, Lieutenant."

"I don't know if it's brave or just plain crazy. But if they want to mix it up, then, baby, let's mix it up."

Rusotto sat there behind the wheel. A smile crawled across his face.

"Well, don't just sit there, Rusotto. Let's get this jeep moving. We've got a ferry to catch and some butts to kick."

"Aye, sir!"

CHAPTER 23

• • •

In a dark warm-up suit, gray running shoes, and dark glasses and carrying a purse with her credit card and $10,000 cash and a carry-on, Emily stepped out in front of Halstead Towers.

She looked over to her right, toward the XSport Fitness Center.

The two strange-looking weirdos were gone, at least for the time being. She looked down King Street and tried to wave down the first taxi as it zoomed by.

"Taxi!" She held out her hand. The older yellow Crown Victoria pulled over to the side of the street. Painted on the outside was "Alexandria Cab Company."

The driver looked out the driver's side window as she crossed the street. "Where to, ma'am?"

"Dulles International Airport."

CHAPTER 24

. . .

How long had it been since they'd locked him up in this cell?

Hasan could only guess. But his hunger pangs suggested that at least an hour had passed.

Where was his lawyer?

He had trusted the Marines when they told him that his lawyer would arrive soon. Unlike the TSA ELITE guards, or whoever they were, the Marines had never—at least not yet—brutalized him or mistreated him or been anything other than professional with him.

They did tell him that his lawyer would be here soon, didn't they? He had heard that right. Hadn't he?

Or had he imagined all that? In the midst of all the torture, his mind had started playing tricks on him.

Nonsense. He heard what he heard.

Yes, they said that his lawyer was coming soon. And Hasan needed a good lawyer to help him get this cleared up, if it was even possible to clear it up.

He remembered watching television reports about the Guantánamo Bay Prison Camp—about prisoners being held more than a decade without ever being charged. One report on the BBC was about a British citizen who had been held more than eleven years. Hasan could not remember the prisoner's name but remembered he claimed, "We were treated like animals." In that case, the former British prime minister, David Cameron, had requested that the American president, Barak Obama, release the British national.

But Obama refused.

If the president of the United States could refuse a request from the British prime minister to release an uncharged prisoner from this place, was there any hope for him?

Christ always provided hope.

Hasan knew that his God was the God of the impossible. The Father of the universe, the Creator of all things, the God of Abraham and Isaac and Jacob, and the Father of the Lord Jesus Christ, who loomed larger and greater and more powerful than David Cameron or Barak Obama or any other earthly ruler or king who had ever lived.

But still, even Jesus himself took the burden of the world's oppressions. In the garden, Jesus prayed, "Father, if it is possible, may this cup be taken from me." Another time, on the cross, Jesus prayed, "My God, my God, why have you forsaken me?"

Hasan's heart and spirit were broken. And the heaviest burden was not knowing if he would see Najib again.

These crazy people thought because he had an Arabic-sounding name, he was Muslim. Didn't they know that thousands of persecuted Arab Christians in the Muslim world had Arab-sounding names?

Not that they cared about the truth. Simply make up a story, create a scapegoat, and perpetrate a lie.

Where was the truth?

He prayed aloud. "If it be your will, Lord, somehow use the truth to set me free."

A jingling sound from the door. Keys unlocking the door.

His lawyer had arrived! Thank God!

"Stand away from the door. We are about to open the cell."

Hasan stepped to the back of the cell.

The door swung open. Two Marines stood outside. One turned and looked over his shoulder. "Bring the prisoner."

A couple of seconds later, two more Marines walked into view with a prisoner.

Hasan's delayed reaction of about two seconds came from the short beard growing on the prisoner's face and from the mental struggle to determine if this was only a dream.

"Najib!"

"Papa!"

"Najib!"

"Stand back, sir."

Hasan ignored the Marine and charged forward, grabbing his boy in a bear hug as the Marine tried gently to pull him back. But Hasan would not let go of Najib and started kissing his face and forehead.

"I love you, Najib." Tears flowed faster than words. "I love you, my son. I love you so much. Thank God, you are alive."

"Stand back so we can uncuff him, please."

Hasan did not stand back, and the Marines did not force him to.

Najib's handcuffs slid off, and he put his arms around Hasan. They embraced each other, neither one wanting to let go, and Hasan silently thanked his Maker for the moment and wept for reasons that he could not understand.

He heard the cell door close.

Hasan stepped back and looked at his son. He noted the scruffy appearance of the black beard starting to grow. He saw that Najib's black eyes sparkled with a glint of defiance, which brought energy to Hasan's spirit. "What are you doing here? They arrested you too?"

"It's bad, Papa. No basis for it. It's infuriating. We had a plane from the ship crash in the Atlantic, and when the ship came back into Norfolk, as I stood on the side of the ship looking for you, they came and pulled me out of line and accused me of trying to sabotage the flight deck. And then they started asking about you and insinuating that we were involved in some terrorist group. What about you, Papa? What have they done to you?"

"I am sorry, my son. I never arrived in Norfolk. They arrested me in Philadelphia—these TSA ELITE agents. They took me into an interrogation room and accused me of being involved in the murder of the American ambassador all those years ago."

"What? I was there that day. That is ridiculous!"

"I know, son. But that is how they twist things. They videotaped you and me standing along the sidewalk when the ambassador was killed. As I waved to the ambassador, they claimed that I was signaling the attack on him."

"Who, Papa? Who said this?"

"Those TSA ELITE agents. They were the ones making the accusations. The Marines and sailors haven't said anything."

Najib shook his head and sat down on the bench at the back of the cell. Hasan sat beside him. "Why are they doing this, Papa?"

Hasan put his hand on Najib's shoulder. "I do not know the Lord's purposes in all this, Najib."

"You think this is of the Lord, Papa? These people seem like they are the sons of Satan to me."

"The Lord has his purposes. These people are manipulated by lies, and they use lies, and Satan is the father of lies. But Satan flees at the name of the almighty Lord Jesus! Yes, God the Father has allowed this for his purposes. Just as he allowed Job to lose all he had, and allowed Peter and Paul to be cast into prison, and allowed the Lord Jesus to be crucified on a cross. I don't know his purposes, but we must trust him, Najib."

Najib looked down and for a moment did not respond. "You know, Papa, they say that no one ever gets out of this place."

"Whoever they are," Hasan said, "they do not know our God. For our God is the God of the impossible."

"I want to believe, Papa. My faith is in him. But I'm not feeling it. I hope they send us a lawyer who can help—a lawyer who isn't working for the TSA."

DON BROWN

• • •

US GOVERNMENT LIMOUSINE
LICENSE: US GOVERNMENT HLS-1
SOUTHEAST BOUND, MASSACHUSETTS AVENUE
WASHINGTON, DC
8:30 A.M.

The black US government limousine, traveling with two DC police squad cars, one in front of it and one in back, slowed to a crawl as traffic backed up on the approach to Ward Circle Park, at the intersection of Massachusetts and Nebraska Avenues.

"Holy smokes," Strayhorn muttered. "Thank God for traffic jams." He turned a little in the backseat, his eyes focused on the red-hot American University coed in the short yellow dress walking along the sidewalk.

Powerful politicians liked young, hot-looking women. JFK, Clinton, Gary Hart, Johnny Edwards. How splendid to be in such good company, he thought. Perhaps he would take a job teaching over there when he retired from the government.

A smile crossed his face.

The secure phone ringing in the backseat of the limo interrupted the prurient images dancing about in his mind.

"Secretary Strayhorn," he said.

"Mr. Secretary, this is Max Porterfield. I'm afraid we've got a problem."

"What kind of a problem?"

"It's Emily Gardner, sir. She's disappeared."

"What do you mean, disappeared?"

"We sent a limo over about a half hour ago to pick her up, and she's nowhere to be found."

Fallington Strayhorn unleashed a string of profanity as veins started popping out on his head. His driver and the TSA security guard, both in the front seat, looked back. "Is everything okay, sir?" the TSA guard asked.

"Yes," Strayhorn snapped. "Roll up the glass, will you?"

"Yes, Mr. Secretary."

Strayhorn waited as the electric motor powered up the wall of glass separating the back of the limousine from the front section, then turned his attention back to his phone call.

"And how is it that we lost sight of her, Porterfield?"

"I'm sorry, sir. That's not clear. We had a couple of guys stationed outside, but people were going and coming. It's sometimes easy to lose track. You know how it is."

"No, Porterfield, I don't know how it is. But I'm sure you're about to tell me." He caught his thoughts. "When and how did we discover she's missing?"

"When the Homeland Security limo went to pick her up. She wasn't waiting at the pickup point. The driver called, and she didn't answer her cell phone."

"Have you tried tracking the GPS on her cell phone?"

"Yes, sir. She left her cell phone in her apartment."

"You've searched her apartment?"

"Yes, sir."

"Anything in there to give us any clue as to where she is?"

The limousine moved forward, swinging through Ward Circle Park.

"Not yet. We're searching the place now, sir."

"Any indication of foul play?"

"No. Not in the apartment anyway."

Strayhorn unleashed another string of profanity.

"Do you want us to notify Alexandria PD, sir?"

"Absolutely not." Strayhorn snorted. "Keep this in-house, at least for a bit longer. If and when we finally notify the local police, we need to do some advance legwork to make sure they're on board with our official position, whatever I decide that position will be. Do you understand?"

"Yes, sir."

"And, Porterfield?"

"Yes, sir."

"If she wants to act like Jerry Myer, if she wants to go all clean and pure and honest on us—" He caught himself. "You catch my drift, don't you?"

"Loud and clear, Mr. Secretary. This will be taken care of."

"Good. Update me as soon as you have something."

"Yes, sir."

Strayhorn exhaled. "That's what I get for thinking that a younger, less experienced attorney could be easily swayed."

"I'll call you as soon as we know something, Mr. Secretary."

• • •

CAMP JUSTICE
GUANTÁNAMO MILITARY COMMISSIONS
MILITARY COURTHOUSE
GUANTÁNAMO BAY, CUBA
8:40 A.M.

Hasan paused for a breath, then put his hand on Najib's back as he continued to pray. "And, Father, we know that our lives are in your hands, and this being the case, we do ask for your protection in this strange and foreign place, a place we never dreamed we would be. We thank you that you have given us each other. But, more importantly, we thank you for your Son, Jesus, who died on the cross for our sins, who was buried, and who you resurrected from the dead—"

Jingling keys interrupted Hasan's prayer. He looked up at the cell door.

"Perhaps they are coming for us, Papa," Najib said.

"I don't think so, son. Not yet."

More jingling and the door cracked open.

"Stand back, please." An authoritative voice from the other side.

Hasan and Najib stood against the back wall.

The door cracked open, then opened more. A trim American

naval officer stood there. The officer wore an all-white uniform with a short-sleeved shirt. At the ends of the black felt shoulder boards were two gold stripes, indicating the officer's rank. Hasan wasn't sure what they meant.

The officer stepped forward and extended his hand. "Good morning, gentlemen." His handshake was firm, his smile confident. "I'm Lieutenant Matt Davis. I'm your lawyer."

The young officer did not seem much older than Najib. But he exuded an instant warmth and a confidence that Hasan considered an answer to prayer.

"I am Hasan Makari. This is my son, Najib. You are—how is it you Americans say it?—a sight for sore eyes."

"Well, I hope you feel that way when we are done." The officer pointed to the bench. "Please, have a seat."

Hasan sat first. Najib sat beside him but said nothing. Davis sat to the left of Hasan, which put Hasan in the middle. "The first thing I want to know," Davis said, "is how have they been treating you?"

Hasan looked at Najib.

"In other words," Davis said, "have you been mistreated?"

Hasan turned and looked at the officer. "Can we trust you, Lieutenant?"

"With your life," Davis said.

"Somehow, I believe it, Lieutenant."

"Gentlemen, we don't have a lot of time. They're going to be hauling us into court soon. We have to work fast." He looked at Hasan, then at Najib. "So have you been mistreated?"

"Let me start," Hasan said. "I will tell you what they have done, and I will leave it to you to decide if it is mistreatment."

"Let's hear it, Hasan."

"It appears that they have been hoping for a confession. Therefore, they tried electric stimulation, they tried waterboarding, and they tried this little trick whereby they released several hundred rats into the cell with me."

Davis bit his lip. He got up off the bench and walked toward the cell door, his back to Hasan and Najib. He slapped the cell door and turned around. "These Nazis are not what America is about."

"I understand that they do not represent the spirit of America, Lieutenant. I have held America high as an ideal for freedom here on earth since I was a boy. I taught my son the same way." Najib nodded. "That's why he joined the US Navy. To serve the country we have revered from afar."

"This is true, sir," Najib said.

Davis nodded his head. "What about you, Najib? Did they try this stuff with you too?"

"Yes, Lieutenant. They tried electric-shock treatment. They tried waterboarding."

"Did either one of you give them any type of confession?"

"No, sir, Lieutenant," Najib answered first. "We cannot confess to something we did not do."

"Of course you can't," Davis said. "But before we go any further, I have a confession to make."

Hasan looked at Najib, then back at the officer. "A confession? I do not understand, Lieutenant. They tried to make you confess something?"

"No. They've tried to intimidate and threaten me into not defending you like you deserve. But it won't work."

"You seem sincere, Lieutenant."

"I plan to fight hard for you. But here's what you need to know. And I want to disclose this so there's no question about it, and so you can make an issue of it if you want."

"I'm confused, Lieutenant," Hasan said.

"Okay." Davis ran his hand through his hair. "One of the two prosecutors in this case is a woman. Her name is Commander Amy Debenedetto. She was assigned to the prosecution team this week, about the same time I became defense counsel." He ran his hand through his hair again. "You should know that the prosecutor and I have been romantically involved."

Silence. Confusion.

"I do not understand, Lieutenant," Hasan said.

"What you need to understand is that it could be considered a conflict of interest for the prosecutor and the defense attorney to have a romantic relationship. Some might accuse me of not trying as hard as I need to try if ticking off my girlfriend in a trial might cause her to, say . . . withhold affection. Do you understand?"

Hasan nodded. "I suppose."

"Not only that, but it's improper under the American military justice system for a junior officer to have an affair with a senior officer."

"Is this commander your senior officer?"

"Yes. Most of the time when this affair was going on, she was a midgrade officer, as a lieutenant commander, only one rank ahead of me. But right before they sent her here, they promoted her to commander. That's two ranks ahead of me."

More silence.

"Lieutenant, do you believe this relationship will affect your ability to represent us?" Hasan asked.

Davis looked him squarely in the eye. "Absolutely not. If anything, it will inspire me to work harder."

Hasan studied his face for a moment. "I believe you, Lieutenant. I believe that you will do all you can to protect us. So why are you even telling us this?"

"For two reasons," Lieutenant Davis said. "First, because as a lawyer, it's my duty to inform you, as my clients, of possible conflicts of interest. And second, because they are seeking the death penalty."

That announcement socked Hasan and Najib like a brick to the gut.

"And if the death penalty is handed down, I want to give you every reason you can find for an appeal. Even if you have to throw me under the bus and appeal based on a conflict of interest by your lawyer." Lieutenant Davis stopped. "As a matter of fact, it is a potential conflict of interest for me to be representing both of you under American law. But for whatever reason, they've assigned me to represent you both. But again, if you get convicted, I want you to use all this to your advantage, even if that means publicly embarrassing me in front of the world. Do you agree?"

Hasan was stunned. Najib clearly had no idea what to say. "We may have never found out about this relationship with the prosecutor. Why would you tell us all this, Lieutenant?"

"Because it's the right thing to do. I believe in America. I believe in the principle of innocent until proven guilty. I believe that you have the right to effective assistance of counsel. I believe in this system. And if it turns out that I have to fall on my sword to protect your rights under the Constitution of the United States—rights that you have whether they say you have those rights or not—well, then, I'm prepared to do that."

Something stood out about this Lieutenant Davis. Hasan was not sure what. "Lieutenant, your honesty and boldness are refreshing. You did not have to tell us these things. I think I can speak for my son in saying that our confidence is in the Lord, and our confidence is in you."

The officer nodded his head and looked at them both with steely blue eyes. "Well, all right then. And you can cut the 'Lieutenant' stuff. Behind closed doors, my name is Matt." He looked at Najib. "And that goes for you too, Najib."

"Yes, sir." Najib shook the officer's hand.

Lieutenant Davis then extended his hand toward Hasan. "Is that okay?"

"It's a deal, Matt." That brought a smile to the officer's face. "We are in your hands."

"Well, all right then," the officer said. "Now that we've got all that settled, let's get to work."

• • •

ALEXANDRIA CAB COMPANY CROWN VICTORIA
APPROACHING DULLES INTERNATIONAL AIRPORT
STERLING, VIRGINIA
8:45 A.M.

From the backseat of the cab, Emily heard the signal light clicking. The cab slowed, shifting to the right lane.

She had been counting her cash to double-check that she had enough. She noted $9,500 as she looked up and saw the exit sign for Dulles International Airport.

She resumed counting the hundred-dollar bills, silently mouthing the amount so as not to alert the driver. "Ninety-six hundred, ninety-seven hundred, ninety-eight hundred, ninety-nine hundred, ten thousand."

"Which airline did you say, ma'am?"

"Um, Aeroflot, please."

"Ah. Going to Russia?"

Why do people ask questions that are none of their business? Or maybe it was good that he asked the question. It was only a matter of time before they tracked down the cabbie and interrogated him.

"Yes. I'm headed to Russia on business."

"Oh yeah?" The cab pulled up in front of the well-known terminal with the sweeping blue glass that resembled a large tidal wave cresting over a beach. "Well, here's the drop-off for Aeroflot."

"Super. How much do I owe you?"

"Eighty bucks."

"Here." She handed him a hundred-dollar bill. "Keep the change."

"Thanks, lady! Can I help you with your bags?"

"No, thanks. I've only got one carry-on."

"Ya sure I can't help?"

"No, thanks." Emily stepped out, picked up her carry-on and her purse, and stepped up on the curb. She walked through the main entrance to the airport and looked around as she headed toward the gates.

Had she been followed?

The terminal swarmed with early-morning travelers, some walking quickly with bags in their hands, some loitering about, some attending to small children. Nothing unusual. But no matter. Even if she had been followed, she had no choice.

She hoped they would start a local search around the apartment in Alexandria before expanding the search. Still, she had to move before they put two and two together and alerted TSA at all airports to be on the lookout for her.

She looked up and checked the flights. Thirty minutes before Aeroflot Flight 4325 boarded for Moscow.

Thirty-five minutes before United Flight 8893 boarded for Fiumicino.

She had to move fast.

No line yet at the Aeroflot desk. She beelined it to the sign that said "Wait Here."

"May I help you, madam?" The tall blonde woman spoke with a Slavic accent.

"Do you have any seats on the 9:30 flight to Moscow?"

"Yes, we do have a few seats left."

"What is the best rate you can give me?"

"One moment, please." The woman punched at her terminal screen. "Round trip or one way?"

"One way."

More typing. "Are you a member of our Aeroflot international travel club?"

"No. And I'm in a hurry, if you don't mind."

"The best rate I can give you in our coach section is $3,500."

"That's one way?"

"Yes. This is a last-minute booking."

"Okay, I'll take it."

"Do you have identification?"

Emily pulled out her passport and driver's license and slid them across the counter.

"And what credit card will you use for your purchase today?"

"I'm using cash."

"Cash?" The woman raised an eyebrow.

"Is that a problem?"

"No, madam. The total price, with taxes, user fees, and the entry fee required by the Russian government, is $3,672."

"Okay. Fine." She reached into her purse and counted thirty-seven hundred-dollar bills and slid them across the counter to the woman.

The woman counted the money. "I believe you are a hundred short, madam."

"What? How could I have missed that?"

"Would you like to recount the money?"

"No. Hang on." Emily wasn't sure if she'd undercounted or if the woman was trying to steal from her. But there was no time to find out. She grabbed another hundred-dollar bill and slipped it across the counter. "Here."

The woman nodded. "I'll get you your change and print your boarding pass."

"Thank you."

Emily's heart pounded harder with every passing second.

"Here, madam. Your change—it should all be there—and your boarding pass for Aeroflot Flight 4325 to Moscow." She slid the boarding pass across the counter. "Do you have bags to check?"

"No bags. Just a carry-on."

"Oh, really?" A raised eyebrow. "Well, you had better get moving. Your flight boards in thirty minutes."

"Thank you for your help." Emily grabbed her ticket and headed over to the TSA line. This would be her first real test, and she uttered a prayer. "Lord, buy me time. Keep them blind until I'm out of here."

Three people stood in front of her waiting for the TSA agent. But so far no armed TSA ELITEs were in the area. But that didn't mean they couldn't call for help at a moment's notice.

The initial TSA ticket scanner, an angry-looking woman, snarled and glared at each traveler passing by. Not good.

Finally, Emily stepped forward.

"Boarding pass and ID," the woman snapped.

Emily complied without speaking.

The woman scanned her boarding pass. "Moscow, huh? Why are you going there?"

Emily noted her name tag, Norman. "Just some business, Officer Norman."

The woman responded with a quick, contemptuous smirk, marked the boarding pass, and gave it back. At least she wasn't wasting time. "Take off your shoes. Put your bag on the belt. Anything metal, put it in the bin."

"Yes, ma'am."

A sigh of relief, and a *Thank you, Lord.*

She cleared through the body scanner without incident, picked up her purse and carry-on bag on the other side of the metal detector, got herself together, and headed down toward the Aeroflot gate. She noted her gate, 14C, then stepped into the ladies' restroom just before it.

With bag and purse in hand, she walked down to the last stall on the left, went in, and locked the door behind her. Thank God the government had not yet installed cameras in the stalls.

But it was only a matter of time.

She took off the gray running shoes, then stripped off the blue warm-up suit.

The air-conditioning system cooled her bare stomach and back, causing goose bumps from the sudden temperature change. She slid her left foot into the leg of a yellow warm-up suit, then her right foot. Then she put on the top. She zipped up the suit and switched from gray to white running shoes.

Stashing the blue suit and gray shoes in her bag, she brought up the hoodie to cover her hair.

She stepped out of the stall, then walked out of the restroom, turned left, and moved toward the signs for the baggage claim area.

A moment later, she was outside the air terminal section, walking quickly past moving conveyor belts with baggage.

Not looking to the left or the right, she headed to the escalator and slowly stepped on, then kept walking to accelerate her ascent.

Straight across from the top of the escalator was the United Airlines desk. Three attendants were at the desk, and Emily stepped up to the "Please Wait Here" sign. The clock on the wall showed less than twenty-five minutes to boarding. Up in front, the passengers on the left and right appeared to be in animated conversations with the ticket agents, while the passenger in the middle was checking four bags.

"Come on." These people were never going to shut up.

"Next, please."

To Emily's left, another ticket agent had stepped behind the counter. Thank God. She quickly walked to the counter. "I need a ticket on your next flight to Fiumicino."

"So you mean the 9:35 flight?"

"Yes, ma'am."

"That flight might be booked. Let me check."

Please, Jesus.

"It looks like that flight might be full. We have an eleven o'clock flight. Will that work?"

The attendant's words were like a bag of rocks hitting her stomach.

"Are you sure?"

"Yes, ma'am."

Dear Jesus. What do I do?

She still had the ticket to Moscow. What option did she have? She could pray that somehow the Russians wouldn't turn her over upon her arrival.

"Okay. Thank you, ma'am." She stepped back from the counter and looked for the nearest entry checkpoint.

"Ma'am!"

Emily turned around.

"We've had a cancellation," the United agent said. "I've got one seat if you want it."

"I'll take it." She rushed back to the ticket counter. "How much?"

"Round trip or one way?"

"One way."

"Okay, that's $3,350, which includes taxes and fees."

"Super. I've got cash."

"Cash?"

"Right here. Is that okay?"

"That's fine, but I may have to get change."

"Don't worry about change. Here's $3,400."

"Your identification, please?"

"Sure." She slipped her driver's license onto the counter.

"I'll be quick." The woman typed on her keyboard. A few moments later, she handed Emily the boarding pass. "Here you are, Miss Gardner. Good luck."

"Thank you."

Now to clear TSA once more. The angry woman, Officer Norman, had been at Checkpoint 1. Emily headed to Checkpoint 3, as far away from Officer Norman as possible.

She stepped into the line at Checkpoint 3 and prayed that she wasn't yet on the TSA watch list. The line snaked through the velvet-roped labyrinth, moving in a human S.

Twenty minutes.

Other passengers filed in behind her as the line snaked along. Two more people were in front of Emily as she eyed the TSA officer checking tickets. He was an elderly agent with a white mustache and wavy white hair. He was acting friendly with ticket holders. Emily was next.

"Are you ready for your break?"

Emily looked up. Officer Norman had walked up behind the man and was waiting to take over his line.

The man got up and smiled, then Officer Norman sat on the stool where he had been sitting. "Next in line!"

What to do?

To step out of line now, to walk all the way back through the roped corridor, past the twenty-five or thirty passengers standing in line behind her, would call attention to her.

"Next in line!"

Officer Norman's black eyes glared at Emily. There was no turning back.

Dear Jesus, help me.

"Your boarding pass and your identification."

Emily did not say a word. Why risk voice association? She handed the boarding pass for Leonardo da Vinci–Fiumicino Airport and her driver's license to Officer Norman.

The TSA agent picked up Emily's license and examined it. Then she looked at Emily. She reexamined the license. Then another glare at Emily. Her angry eyes glistened like a rattlesnake's.

"Do I know you?"

Emily lowered her voice. "No, Officer. I don't think we know each other."

"You sure about that?"

"I don't know how we would know each other."

"Have you flown recently?"

"No, ma'am."

"You sure?"

Keep the answer short. No opportunity for voice recognition.

"Yes, ma'am."

The woman looked up. Then down again. Up. As if trying to remember something. Down again.

Finally, she took her magic marker and circled the code on the boarding pass for Da Vinci–Fiumicino and handed it back to Emily. "Have a good flight."

Emily nodded and smiled and uttered a silent prayer that they would not search her. She put her bag and purse and shoes on the conveyor belt and stepped into line for the scanner.

"Okay, step out," the next TSA officer said to her.

"Thank you," she said with a quick, faked smile. She grabbed her things off the conveyor belt and stepped out of the search area before Officer Norman could change her mind. She found the sign pointing to the Aeroflot gate, then hopped on the moving walkway and walked quickly along it to catch the boarding for Flight 4325 for Moscow.

• • •

PULMONARY INTENSIVE CARE UNIT
BETHESDA NAVAL HOSPITAL
(WALTER REED NATIONAL MILITARY MEDICAL CENTER)
BETHESDA, MARYLAND
9:00 A.M.

A long, sustained swishing sound. The soothing sound of the ocean at Coronado Beach, down by the Hotel Del. The reassuring sound of freedom generated by the Navy Seahawk helicopter flying by over the ocean, parallel to the beach, headed to the North Island Naval Air Station a mile away.

The sun was on its downward trek, soon to be setting over the Pacific.

She put her feet into the cool sand and smiled. Zack was such a romantic. No spot on earth could soothe her soul like returning to the site of their honeymoon. Zack got it.

Zack got her.

"Got it for you, baby!"

She turned around. There he stood, all svelte in his Carolina blue Tar Heels T-shirt and dark blue running shorts. He was even hotter looking as a three-star admiral than he was as a young JAG officer. The sight of him still charged her in an instant!

He was holding a silver tray with one peach margarita and one lemonade—Zack didn't drink alcohol—with pineapples and cherries on plastic sticks in the drinks. He set the tray down on the wooden table between their two Adirondack chairs, then sat down.

"This what you wanted?" His face sported a thickening five o'clock shadow. He winked at her and flashed a pearly white smile over that devilish dimple of his. Oh, thank God, he was her husband.

"You're what I want, baby," he said.

She blushed hot. After all these years, he still did that to her.

The *beep-beep-beep* was getting louder. Something was wrong.

"Zack? Zack? Where am I?"

She opened her eyes to white sheets, stainless steel, and that insistent beeping.

"Are you okay, Diane?"

She turned her head. Jeff was standing there. Zack's old friend, her friend. Rear Admiral Jeffrey Lettow.

"Jeff, I'm okay. I was dreaming." She remembered what had happened. The thought of Emily, her leg pinned under the table, sent a wave of panic through her.

"Is there anything I can do for you? Anything I can get you?"

"Yes," Diane said.

"What is it?"

"My friend . . . Emily is in trouble. I need you . . . to pray for her."

CHAPTER 25

• • •

Navigating a line of flashing cameras, Matt rushed down the main hallway of the courthouse and through the back door of Courtroom 1.

He stopped for a moment to absorb the sight before him.

Unlike during his first appearance before the tribunal yesterday, the courtroom now was packed. Military members and select members of the media from around the world and from NATO countries that had contributed military forces and monies to the global War on Terror were all jammed into the courtroom.

In the back row to his right, two sketch artists sat. One had drawn a colorful rendition of the front of the courtroom, showing the flags and prosecution team already in place. The other was drawing a side view of his client, Hasan Makari, with a sinister-looking slant, showing a scruffy beard and mean, piercing eyes—nothing at all like the warm man with whom he had spent the last thirty minutes.

Matt stole a glance at the prosecution table at the front of the courtroom. Amy was hunched over in her service-dress blue uniform at the left side of the counsel table, sitting beside the lead prosecutor, Colonel

291

Tom McGrary. She was taking notes on a legal pad, keeping her head down. Amy did not look back and did not notice him.

Neither did Colonel McGrary or anyone else, for that matter. Not until he started to walk down the center aisle toward the front of the courtroom. His arrival set off a sudden hush in the courtroom. Then a collective murmuring. Then louder mumbling. Heads turned. Their stares drilled into him.

He stole a glance at her when she turned to look at him. He could not help himself.

Those blue eyes. *Dear God, help me to focus.*

Focus. He had to focus! For he was beginning the most important assignment of his life, an assignment that meant life or death for two men.

Walking down the center aisle, he looked over to the right, into the faces of his clients. They sat at the defense counsel table in orange jumpsuits. Their legs and arms were chained as if they were animals. For indeed, they were already considered animals, already indicted in the court of world opinion without a word yet spoken in their defense. Even in the eyes of the sketch artists, drawing them to appear with a devilish flair, they were terrorist animals.

The long faces of Hasan and Najib showed fear, hope, and faith. He saw it in their eyes. They were trusting their lives to him.

Dear God, help me.

He stepped up to the counsel table, to the left of Hasan. Matt laid his briefcase down, then nodded at them and smiled. He walked over behind the father and son, knelt down, and put a hand on each of their backs. He wanted the media to see that he considered them to be human, worthy of a defense.

He whispered, "It's going to be okay. I don't know how yet, but it's going to be fine."

"We trust you, Lieutenant Davis," Hasan whispered. "And we trust God."

Out of genuine affection and to prove a point, Matt leaned over and gave Hasan a hug.

"All rise!"

...

DULLES INTERNATIONAL AIRPORT
AEROFLOT GATE AREA
STERLING, VIRGINIA
9:02 A.M.

Emily arrived at the gate area, where the long line of passengers stood in front of Aeroflot Gate 4. Over the ticket station, manned by two pale Russian-looking types with high cheekbones, the black electronic strip flashed in red letters "Flight 4325—Moscow."

The woman with long blonde hair behind the Aeroflot desk spoke into the microphone, her voice amplified out in front of the desk. "Continuing our boarding of Aeroflot Flight 4325 to Moscow. All passengers seated in Section C, please board at this time."

Emily checked her boarding pass: Sec C. Row 35. Seat B.

"That's me."

She filed into the line for "Section C" passengers. The line moved along efficiently. She moved up to the gate agent, handed her the boarding pass, and held her breath.

The gate agent smiled at her and ran the ticket under the electronic scanner. "Enjoy your flight."

"Thank you." She stepped into the Jetway tunnel. The backup started about thirty feet down the way, as passengers bottlenecked at the front entrance of the jet.

Emily looked back toward the terminal.

More passengers filed into the Jetway.

She checked her watch.

It was now or never.

She turned around and with several "excuse mes" started walking against the flow of human traffic crowding into the Jetway. When she reached the entrance, she lowered her head, did not look toward the ticket lady, and hoped that she would not be noticed as she moved behind the line of passengers still waiting to get on the plane.

Now back in the terminal, she checked the overhead flight board for the status of flights.

United Flight 8893 for Rome-Fiumicino—now boarding Gate D14.

Emily checked her watch and broke into a jog.
"Jesus, help me make it."

CHAPTER 26

• • •

"Call the case of *United States of America versus Hasan Makari and Najib Makari*," the chief judge said. "The record should reflect that all parties and counsel are present, and the prosecution has indicated that it will be seeking the death penalty in this case. Is that correct, Colonel McGrary?"

Decked in his service-dress blue Air Force uniform, resplendent with colorful medals across his chest, the lead prosecutor stood and spoke with a regal bearing and stately voice. "That is correct, Your Honor. The United States will be seeking the death penalty against both defendants on charges of murder, conspiracy to commit murder in the death of Ambassador George Madison, United States ambassador to Lebanon, and for terrorism and conspiracy to commit terrorism by the establishment of sleeper cells within the United States and the United States Navy, and now in connection with numerous deaths in the sleeper cell mall attacks in four cities in the United States."

Burning anger flushed up Matt's neck and into his face. He rose to his feet. "Your Honor."

"Have a seat, Lieutenant." The military judge, Colonel Karpel, held up his palm in the wait-a-minute gesture. "You'll get your chance."

"Aye, sir." Matt glared over at the prosecution table. Amy stared at a legal pad, keeping a poker face and taking notes. Colonel McGrary displayed a sarcastic smugness of self-satisfaction.

The judge said, "Very well, the court notes the charges and further notes the government's intention to seek the death penalty." He slipped on a pair of wire-rimmed glasses. "Does the government have any other motions or other preliminary matters?"

"Not at this time, Your Honor."

"Very well." Karpel looked at Matt. "Lieutenant Davis, I believe you were about to say something?"

Matt rose back to his feet. *Keep your cool, Matt.* "Your Honor, Colonel McGrary just announced that the government is charging my clients, that is, both of them, with the murder of Ambassador Madison. Aside from the fact that neither of my clients was involved with the ambassador's death, I'd note that, for the record, Najib Makari was a little boy when the ambassador died and could not possibly have been involved!"

Karpel nodded his head.

"And not only that, but—"

"Hang on, Lieutenant. Your point about Mr. Najib Makari sounds like a jury argument to me. And this is not the proper time for that."

"I understand, Your Honor. But—"

"But"—Karpel wagged his finger—"as I said, Lieutenant, this is not the time for that argument. Now do you have anything else?"

Matt exhaled. *Lower your voice. Slow your pace.* "Well, yes, Your Honor. As a matter of fact, I do."

"What, Lieutenant Davis?"

"Well, this is the first time we've heard anything about a charge against my clients in connection with the mall attacks back in the States. Your Honor, those attacks occurred just yesterday. And they occurred while my clients were incarcerated here at GITMO. Your Honor, my clients are entitled to an effective assistance of counsel under the Sixth Amendment to the United States Constitution. I can't effectively defend them against a charge that I'm hearing about for the first time, even as we speak."

Judge Karpel whipped off his glasses and raised an eyebrow. "So are you making a speech, Lieutenant, or are you attempting to make a motion?"

Matt checked his notes, then acknowledged Karpel. "Yes, Your Honor. First, the defense moves that the charges alleging murder relating to the mall attacks in the United States be dismissed."

"On what grounds, Lieutenant?"

"Your Honor, under the Sixth Amendment of the United States Constitution, my clients have an absolute right to be informed of the charges against them. The government can't drop a bomb on my clients at the last second, when the trial starts. That's not meaningfully informing them of anything." Matt jabbed his finger in the air. "The Sixth Amendment guarantees that an accused has a right to confront the witnesses against him. Given the short-fused time frame, my clients cannot confront their accusers, those accusing them of alleged involvement in these shopping mall terror attacks. Also, there's no probable cause that these defendants caused all these deaths, and they have a right under the Fourth Amendment not to be tried unless the government can show probable cause. Your Honor, this is an unacceptable attempt at trial by ambush, and this charge should be dismissed."

Silence.

"Colonel McGrary," Karpel said.

"Yes, Your Honor."

"When was the charge sheet drafted to add the murder charge?"

"Just last night. But I would point out that the conspiracy to engage in terrorism charges had already been drafted, and these murder charges are a natural outflow of the conspiracy charges. Therefore, there's nothing surprising about these charges. Besides, the government drafted the charges almost immediately after the events. And, Your Honor, I'd point out that you've already ordered this case to be prosecuted on a fast track. So in the scheme of things, this delay doesn't mean much at all."

Only the *tick-tick-tick* of the clock on the wall behind the bench. Matt wanted to respond to McGrary, but his instincts told him to remain silent until Judge Karpel ruled.

Karpel sat on the bench toying with an ink pen. "The court will take a brief recess to consider the motion to dismiss. The court will stand in recess for fifteen minutes."

"All rise."

• • •

DULLES INTERNATIONAL AIRPORT
UNITED AIRLINES GATE AREA
STERLING, VIRGINIA
9:15 A.M.

Emily jogged down the corridor, her eyes fixed on the United gate area, about a hundred yards down the way. She was starting to feel out of breath when the announcement came over the PA system.

"This is the final call for United Flight 8893 with service to Rome-Fiumicino. All passengers with boarding passes for United Flight 8893 with service to Rome-Fiumicino, please report to the ticketing area at this time. Repeat. This is the final call for United Flight 8893 with service to Rome-Fiumicino."

Emily shifted her jog to a sprint, arriving at the gate as the ticketing agent was closing the door to the Jetway.

"One more!"

The ticket agent turned around. "Are you Miss Gardner?"

"Yes. Here's my boarding pass."

"We've been paging you."

"Sorry. Circumstances beyond my control."

"Carol, call the flight attendant and see if they've closed the jet."

"Sure."

The ticket agent held the boarding pass under the automatic scanner. It beeped. She looked at Emily. "If they've closed the jet, we're going to have to put you on our next flight in two hours."

Emily winced. "Is there nothing that can be done? The plane is still here. I see it sitting right there. And I need this flight."

"Sorry, ma'am. New FAA regs. I know it doesn't make sense. But once they close the doors to that jet, in the eyes of the government, it's already in the air, even if it's sitting on the ground."

The phone rang and the ticket agent picked it up. "Okay. Okay, thanks." She hung up the phone. "This is your lucky day, Miss Gardner. They were about to shut the cabin door, but they'll hold it open for another thirty seconds, but that's it."

"Praise God."

"Here, let me open the Jetway." The ticket agent stepped to the door, punched an electronic code, and opened the door to the Jetway. "You'd better get moving before the captain changes his mind."

"Thank you." Emily rushed into the Jetway, jogging down to the open hatch of the United jet.

"Have a good flight."

CHAPTER 27

• • •

CAMP JUSTICE
GUANTÁNAMO MILITARY COMMISSIONS
PRISONER HOLDING CELL
MILITARY COURTHOUSE
GUANTÁNAMO BAY, CUBA
9:25 A.M.

His hands and feet chained together, Hasan sat on the bench in the holding cell and stared at the gray cinder-block walls.

Najib sat at the other end of the bench, his head hanging low, a look of dejection on his face. Hasan wished that he could put his arms around his son to soothe and encourage him, but the chains prevented it.

"I believe that this Lieutenant Davis is fighting hard for us, my son."

Najib nodded. "Yes, I agree, Papa. But I worry that the system may be rigged against him. I feel like I am in a Communist country or something. This wasn't my vision of America."

Hasan pondered that. "Remember, my son, evil knows no boundaries. Even in a great republic like America, evil slips in, sometimes masquerading as government officials, with the purpose of destroying freedom from within.

"The system might be rigged against Lieutenant Davis, but it is not rigged against God. God will not allow his name to be mocked. And besides, this judge at least appears to be considering Lieutenant Davis's arguments."

Two knocks on the door. "Stand back!" someone yelled. As if the chains on their legs would give them a plethora of options on where to stand.

Hasan said, "Remember. The Lord promised to be with us always. Even until the end."

The door swung open. Two armed US Marine guards stood outside. "Okay, gentlemen. I'm Sergeant Parker, US Marines. I'm assigned as chief of our security detail the rest of the day. They're ready to start court again. You know the drill. Same as earlier this morning. We'll bring you in the front of the courtroom. Everyone is in place. They're waiting for you. Walk to counsel table and stand beside your attorney, Lieutenant Davis, until they tell you to sit."

Hasan nodded.

"Follow me. Single file. You first." He pointed to Hasan, and Hasan and Najib shuffled out of the cell and through a small open area. They stopped at a steel door. The sign said "Courtroom Entrance." The sign was in English and Arabic. "Here we go, gentlemen," the Marine said.

He opened the door.

Bright lights flooded in almost like floodlights. Hasan followed the Marine into the courtroom through the side door, and as his eyes adjusted, a sea of faces appeared in the gallery. And then he focused his eyes on Lieutenant Davis, standing alone at the defense counsel table.

Following the Marine's lead, their chains clinking against the floor, Hasan and Najib shuffled their way over to stand beside Lieutenant Davis at the counsel table. The military judge, a Marine Corps officer, said, "You may be seated."

More shuffling and scraping of chairs could be heard throughout the courtroom as dozens of spectators and all the lawyers took their seats.

"Very well," Judge Karpel said. "The court has considered the defense motion to dismiss the charge of murder in connection with the recent mall attacks in the United States, with the defense motion resting upon the Sixth Amendment of the Constitution, wherein the defense is raising the Sixth Amendment's Confrontation Clause and its Effective Assistance of Counsel Clause as the basis for the motion."

Karpel removed his glasses. "In any military tribunal—and this is a military tribunal—an accused may be tried in short order because of the operational requirements of the military.

"Because military operational requirements are unique in a military justice system, we often must move more quickly than in the civilian system. Even still, we take pride in noting that our efficiency and accuracy and justice are generally superior to the civilian system.

"Now, in this case, the government chose to try both of these defendants together as co-conspirators. That is the government's choice. One of the two defendants, Petty Officer Najib Makari, is an active-duty sailor aboard the USS *Abraham Lincoln*, which is about to set sail again.

"So I have fast-tracked this case because of operational necessity, because we can't put the *Abraham Lincoln* and its sailors in limbo because of the trial of Petty Officer Makari. The court notes that the USS *Abraham Lincoln* is in port for thirty days, then is scheduled for deployment to Sixth Fleet in the Mediterranean."

"But, Your Honor." Matt rose to his feet.

"Sit down, Lieutenant. I haven't issued my ruling on your motion yet."

"Aye, sir."

"As I said," Karpel continued, "this case was fast-tracked out of operational necessity. However"—the judge waved a finger in the air—"that doesn't mean that the government can have its cake and eat it too. Even though the case has been fast-tracked, the charges of murder and conspiracy to commit murder of Ambassador Madison were referred and were part of the charge sheet before this case was called to order. It is also true that the charge of conspiracy to commit acts of terror against the United States was also preferred and referred prior to trial.

"Now, understanding the close timing on all this, the court must draw a line in the sand. While there appears to be at least probable cause underlying the other charges, the last-second addition of these murder charges in the mall attacks does not even give the defendants the opportunity to explore whether probable cause exists." Silence. *Tick-tick-tick.* "And frankly, the court cannot see probable cause to support these charges. Therefore, the court will dismiss the charges of murder and conspiracy to commit murder with regard to the mall terrorism activity."

Mumbling in the back.

"But, Your Honor!" Colonel McGrary rose to his feet. "A dismissal might preclude the government from recharging this on double-jeopardy grounds!"

More mumbling in the gallery.

"Order in the court!" Judge Karpel whapped his gavel down twice, bringing instant silence in the courtroom. "That's not my problem, Colonel, and it's not my job to speculate on all that. But perhaps you should have considered that before you referred these charges at the last second."

"But, Your Honor, this is highly unusual. I'm sure the government isn't going to approve of this."

"The government isn't going to approve?" Karpel whipped off his glasses in an angry move and followed that with an angry tone. "Colonel, do you think this court gives a rat's derriere as to whether or not the government approves? Unlike some courts, this court is not a kangaroo court to rubber-stamp whatever the government wants. I will remind you that it is my duty, as an officer in the United States military and as an officer of the court and as a military judge, to make my rulings consistent with the Constitution. And I'll remind you that you still have charges pending against these defendants, and you are still seeking the death penalty. I have not thrown out your entire case. If you don't like my ruling on these particular charges, take me up on appeal."

"My apologies, Your Honor." McGrary stood there biting his lip, his black eyes ablaze with anger.

"Very well. Do we have any further pretrial motions?" Judge Karpel demanded. "Colonel McGrary?"

"No, Your Honor. Reserving rights to appeal, based on the court's decision to dismiss the most recent charges, the government is nevertheless prepared to proceed with trial."

"Very well. Does the defense have any more pretrial motions?" Karpel directed his gaze at Matt. "Lieutenant Davis?"

Matt rose to his feet. "Yes, as a matter of fact, we do."

"What now?" McGrary threw up his arms.

"Hang on, Colonel," Karpel said. "What other motions do you have, Lieutenant?"

"Your Honor, my clients wish to assert their right to habeas corpus."

"Habeas corpus?" McGrary blurted out.

"Lieutenant, have you petitioned any federal court for habeas corpus?"

"No, Your Honor," Matt said. "I haven't had a chance. But I intend to file with the US District Court in Columbia, South Carolina, of which I am a member."

"Your Honor, this is an unnecessary stall tactic," Colonel McGrary thundered, increasingly agitated. "Lieutenant Davis is trying to deny the government's day in court. First the motion to dismiss, and now this. He admits he hasn't even filed a habeas corpus action. And this is not the forum for filing such an action."

"With respect, Your Honor," Matt thundered right back at the superior officer, "Colonel McGrary's allegations are ridiculous. My clients have an absolute right to file habeas corpus, and that was settled by the US Supreme Court in the 2008 case of *Bush v. Boumediene*, that a Guantánamo detainee may file for habeas corpus to a federal court in the United States and have his rights heard by a federal court."

Judge Karpel leaned back in his chair, seemed to think for a moment, then, for the first time, stared at Hasan.

What was he thinking? Hasan wondered. And what was this habeas corpus that Matt was talking about?

This marked the first extended eye contact from Judge Karpel. Hasan studied the man's face. He seemed hard, yet under the hard surface, he also seemed to be fair.

Karpel looked away from Hasan. "I think it's clear that you have a right to petition for habeas corpus, Lieutenant Davis. But as Colonel McGrary points out, you haven't filed the petition, and this isn't the place to file it. And even if you had filed it, that petition would have to be granted for it to have any effect on this court."

Matt responded quickly. "True, Your Honor. I haven't had time to file it because this case was spun up so quickly that I cannot in good faith say that I can provide effective assistance of counsel. So I'm asking the court for a forty-eight-hour continuance to allow me to file this petition."

"What?" McGrary asked.

Matt glanced at Hasan and Najib. He put his hand on Najib's shoulder.

"It's their right under the Constitution, as Judge Karpel stated in the court's opinion."

"This is ridiculous, Your Honor!" McGrary again. "If Lieutenant Davis had already filed, that would be different. But we're at the stall-tactic stage."

Matt responded, "Please, Your Honor. Forty-eight hours won't prejudice the government's case, and it will help the record on appeal."

"But, Your Honor."

"That's enough, Colonel." Karpel held up his hand. "Deny motion to continue. However, I will place the court in recess for forty-eight hours to allow you to file whatever you want to file. But be forewarned. Because of the operational requirements I mentioned earlier, I do not anticipate any more recesses or continuances. Is that clear, Lieutenant?"

"Aye, sir."

"All rise."

• • •

Fallington Strayhorn paced back and forth across the large office, then stopped in front of the bay windows and peered out across the Potomac into Virginia. If it weren't for the towers at Reagan airport, he could almost see her apartment from here. How had they lost track of her? And where was Porterfield?

He checked his watch.

This was unacceptable. This whole thing had been poorly timed and poorly executed.

Part of it was his mistake, assuming that a young lawyer would be starry-eyed and swooned into the program if he dangled the carrot of the general counsel's position.

What should he do about notifying the local authorities? What about the press? What should he tell the White House?

Now, to make matters worse, word came from Guantánamo Bay that the military judge in the terror trials was not fully cooperating.

Partially cooperative. Just not totally cooperative.

For this to work, Homeland Security needed to get that conviction and needed to keep Emily Gardner under wraps!

Strayhorn slammed his hand on the windowsill and cursed.

His desk phone rang.

"Mr. Secretary, Mr. Porterfield is on the line for you, sir."

"Porterfield! What's going on with our hot little fugitive?"

"I'm afraid she's pulled a Snowden, sir."

"What do you mean, pulled a Snowden?"

"Sir, I've been out at her apartment, where we've started an investigation. Surveillance video outside the building showed her getting into a cab around 7:30 a.m. We tracked the driver down and found that he took her out to Dulles."

"Well, get out there and get that place locked down! Now!"

"Too late, sir."

"What do you mean?"

"She told the cabdriver she was going to Moscow. We followed that up and checked with Aeroflot. She bought a ticket with cash, then boarded a jet. Looks like she's in the air now. I'm concerned she may request political asylum."

"What! Somebody's head is going to roll over all this!"

Porterfield did not respond.

"What flight number?"

"Aeroflot flight number 4325 to Moscow."

Strayhorn scribbled the flight number on a legal pad. "Listen, Porterfield, I want you to go straight to Andrews and jump on the department's jet, the 777 designated for my use, and make a beeline straight to Moscow. I want you to pick her up, arrest her, and bring her back here."

"I'm already ahead of you on that, sir. We're pulling into Andrews right now, and the jet is on the runway, ready to go. But what if the Russians won't cooperate?"

Strayhorn stewed in anger. What utter incompetence to have let Emily Gardner escape!

"Just get to Andrews and get on the plane. Let me worry about how to handle the Russians."

"Yes, Mr. Secretary."

The line went dead.

This thing had the potential to backfire and blow up big-time on him. He couldn't let that plane land and have Emily Gardner showing up at the Moscow airport and calling a press conference.

If only there were some way to shoot down that plane over the ocean and blame it on something else.

If he were the secretary of defense, that's exactly what he would do.

But could he persuade the president to order a shoot-down? He could tell the president that Homeland Security had learned that the Aeroflot flight was going to be flown into the United States Embassy in London.

Of course, the president would be reluctant to shoot down a Russian airliner, especially one with American citizens aboard. That might provoke World War III. But he might be willing to force it down. Perhaps in the Canary Islands or in Spain. But that might not work. Fallington Strayhorn knew he needed Emily Gardner dead.

If they could force the plane down on allied territory, Homeland Security agents could pull Emily off the jet, arrest her, destroy whatever evidence she carried, and make sure that she never spoke with anyone.

But then again, how would all that be explained to the Russians? They would never believe that an Aeroflot pilot would be involved in a sinister plot to drive a plane into the United States Embassy in London.

He kept running through his options. It might work if they told the Russians that they had received information about a passenger who was involved in the plot. Then, after the problem with Emily had been eliminated, they could issue a formal apology to the Russians based on bad intel.

Of course, that would mean burning a lot of capital with the president, which might, in a worst-case scenario, cause the president to relieve him of his responsibilities. But realistically, that probably wouldn't happen.

Still, better to take a chance on being relieved of his duties over a false alarm than to have Emily sing like a canary.

Who could he trust on this other than Porterfield? The joint chiefs would want to see proof.

He picked up the phone. "Carol, call Willie Roberts over at TSA. Tell him to get to my office, now."

"Yes, Mr. Secretary."

• • •

PULMONARY INTENSIVE CARE UNIT
BETHESDA NAVAL HOSPITAL
(WALTER REED NATIONAL MILITARY MEDICAL CENTER)
BETHESDA, MARYLAND
10:30 A.M.

Rear Admiral Jeffrey Lettow sat in the chair in the corner of the hospital room, keeping a watchful eye on Diane as he had promised. He glanced up at the clock: 10:25 a.m.

Jeff glanced at Diane. She was still sleeping. He decided to call a friend who needed a few words of encouragement. Then he'd call Zack to check on him, although he halfway expected Zack to stop by the hospital at lunchtime.

He got up and walked softly out into the hallway outside the room, pulling Diane's door partially closed.

He pulled out his iPhone and dialed his friend Bobby Brown's number.

The phone rang three times and went to voice mail. Jeff hung up and stepped back into the room.

Diane was sitting up in bed, eyes glaring at him, a feisty look on her face.

"I'm right here," he said. "Is everything okay?"

"Where's Zack?"

"He's gone to work. You insisted on it. Remember?"

"I remember. Just wanted to make sure he's doing what he was told."

"Yes, ma'am," Jeff quipped.

"I need you to do something for me."

"Sure. Anything."

"Get me my clothes, then step out and close the door."

"What?"

"You heard me. I'm feeling great, and my country is at war, and I might not be active duty anymore, but I can still serve my country, even if that means being Zack's closest confidant. I can still defend the Constitution. I'm blowing out of this place."

"How about if I call Zack first?"

"Call Zack all you want. Call Dr. Berman. I don't care who you call. But if you don't get me my clothes, I'm walking out of this place in my hospital gown. And that's not a sight I think anybody wants to see."

"I think a lot of people would love to see that."

Jeff turned around. The judge advocate general of the Navy was standing at the door.

"At least I for one would like to see that." Zack stood there with a grin.

"I wasn't expecting you for another hour or so," Jeff said, "but I'm sure glad you're here."

"Yes, well, I missed my good-looking better half," Zack said.

"You arrived in the nick of time," Jeff said. "I was about to call you."

"I overheard what she said," Zack said. "She sounds like her ole feisty self. Good thing nobody has to face her on the witness stand today. She'd slice 'em up like a sharp knife on a roll of salami."

"Why are the two of you talking about me like I'm not here?" Diane protested. "Zack, I'll tell you like I told Jeff. Please get my clothes. I'm ready to go home."

Jeff and Zack exchanged glances. "Don't look at me, sir. You've got one more star on your collar than I do. Plus you live with her."

"Yeah, but you're a man of the cloth," Zack said. "And that connection with the Almighty means a lot more than the extra star on my collar."

"Okay, that did it. I'm getting up." Diane twisted around and dangled her legs over the edge of the bed.

"Hang on, baby." Zack sat on the bed and gently restrained her. "What's the hurry?"

"I might be an admiral's wife, but if I'd stayed in, I might be the admiral myself."

"You are the commander in chief in our house."

"Don't patronize me. I feel great, and we've been attacked."

"What's the hurry? Can't we get Dr. Berman to check you out first?"

"The hurry is Emily."

"Emily?"

"I keep dreaming about her, Zack. Something's wrong."

"What do you mean, something's wrong? She survived that mall attack and didn't even require medical treatment. She's scheduled to appear before the Senate Homeland Security Committee for confirmation hearings this week to become general counsel for Homeland Security."

"I don't know, Zack. I have this horrible feeling. I can't explain it."

Zack raised an eyebrow, as if looking for spiritual advice.

"Don't look at me," Jeff said.

"Zack!"

"Okay, baby. How about if we let Dr. Berman check you out so I can feel better about this. Will you do that for me?" He leaned over and kissed her on the cheek.

"You can call Larry if you want. But I'm asking you to please go get my clothes. Because Larry or no Larry, I'm out of here."

• • •

DEPARTMENT OF HOMELAND SECURITY
OFFICE OF THE SECRETARY
WASHINGTON, DC
10:30 A.M.

"Mr. Secretary, Willie Roberts is here."

"Send him in." Fallington Strayhorn stood up as the door opened. The blue-eyed lawyer with the pretty-boy look walked into the office and shook Strayhorn's hand.

"Close the door, Willie, and have a seat."

"Yes, sir."

Roberts sat in the chair in front of Strayhorn's desk.

"Willie, you're a great team player. We've entrusted you with the keys to the kingdom, and you've performed brilliantly. And that includes the surveillance you gave us on Emily Gardner. From everything we've seen, she thought it was a budding romantic interest and had no clue we were sizing her up for the general counsel spot. The sky is the limit for you in this organization, and your rise could be faster than you ever thought."

"Thank you, sir."

Strayhorn studied the eager look on the young lawyer's face. If only Emily Gardner and Jerry Myer had gotten on board.

"Listen, Willie, we've got an extremely sensitive, time-sensitive matter that I need you to move on now. This must remain top secret within the confines of this department."

"I understand, Mr. Secretary."

"Unfortunately, we still don't have a general counsel."

"Emily didn't take the bait?"

"No. And it's even worse. Looks like she's trying to pull a Snowden."

"A Snowden?"

"Yep. It looks like she downloaded sensitive information and jumped on a plane to Moscow before we could stop her. We've got to get that plane out of the sky before it lands."

"How can I help, sir?"

"We've got to convince the president and the Defense Department to bring that plane down before it lands. I need documentation that the plane is a terror threat to the US Embassy in London. That plane's in flight now. We need interceptors up, and we have no time."

Willie nodded. "Understood, Mr. Secretary. I can do that."

"How long will it take to get me documentation? The president's gonna want proof."

"If you let me borrow your computer, it will take a couple of hours to feed in the data, then to feed in the buffers to simulate e-mail traffic from multiple sources, and then to put in the codes so that the sources are not traceable."

"Two hours?"

"Yes, sir. Possibly three, Mr. Secretary. I understand that this is for the good of the country. And if you want plausible deniability, we have to dot our i's and cross our t's."

"Now you're saying maybe three hours?"

"Could be, Mr. Secretary. It's not like popping an Egg McMuffin in the microwave. I don't think it will take longer than that. But the last thing you want is DOD or somebody tracing these false flags back to this office."

Strayhorn checked his watch and wiped sweat off his forehead. "Well, okay, but hurry. The whole flight is about ten hours, so we don't have much wiggle room."

"Yes, Mr. Secretary."

CHAPTER 28

• • •

CAMP JUSTICE
GUANTÁNAMO MILITARY COMMISSIONS
PRISONER HOLDING CELL
MILITARY COURTHOUSE
GUANTÁNAMO BAY, CUBA
10:33 A.M.

Hasan and Najib sat together on the back bench of the holding cell, waiting to be moved back to their individual cells. Hasan hoped the delay would be longer, because at least he was with Najib. When they took them back to their cells, they would be separated again.

Hasan lowered his head and prayed, and as he did, he heard three raps on the door. "Stand back."

"If they separate us again, my son, stay strong in the Lord."

"I am trying, Papa. But my faith is weakening."

The door opened.

"Lieutenant Davis!"

"Call me Matt." The JAG officer stepped into the cell and the door closed behind him.

"My apologies, Matt." Hasan allowed himself a smile.

"I wanted to stop by and check on both of you and to talk to you about legal strategy."

"You were magnificent, Lieuten . . . excuse me, Matt . . . you were magnificent. Although I do not fully understand what happened."

"We have an old saying in the defense bar: 'Delay, delay, delay.' If you delay, you don't go to trial. If you don't go to trial, you don't lose. Meanwhile, something good may happen."

"What do you mean, Lieutenant?" Najib asked.

Hasan was pleased that Najib seemed engaged enough to ask a question.

"I don't know where this judge is coming from," Matt said. "On the one hand, he's ramming through the case for trial. On the other hand, the government might not be ready for trial, which could lead to an acquittal. But the problem is that acquittals are rare here in GITMO.

"Now, this judge has given us some positive rulings. But the problem is, they're pushing for the death penalty. My first goal is to block that. The more issues we are able to raise at trial, the greater the chance that the Supreme Court, eventually, might find a reason to overturn the death penalty if they hand it down in either of your cases."

Hasan wasn't sure how to interpret that.

Najib spoke up. "Lieutenant?"

"Yes, Najib."

"You speak about avoiding the death penalty. And we appreciate that. But what about getting us out of here? We did not do anything."

Matt's face contorted. "That's another story."

"What do you mean?"

"There have been people held here for years. Sometimes people who aren't even charged with a crime. Some held without trial for years. In your case, at least you're getting a trial. But I'm concerned that the case is going to trial too fast. Not only because I don't get enough time to prepare like I want, but it also looks like a shift in strategy by the government."

"How so?" Hasan asked.

"This is a gut feeling, Hasan. But they seem to be shifting from arresting and holding these so-called terrorists forever—I'm using their description when I say 'terrorist'—to arresting, quickly prosecuting, and quickly executing."

"Why the change?" Hasan again.

"I'd guess for several reasons. First, because it's cheaper to execute someone than it is to feed them. Second, because of public criticism of the long delays in taking someone to trial. And third, because once they execute someone, they can never dispute the government's version of what happened. Like Lee Harvey Oswald. He'll never get a chance to say what happened with Kennedy."

"In other words," Hasan said, "kill off the witnesses, and you can rewrite history however you would like."

Matt nodded. "That's how I read it, Hasan. And that's why I've got to do everything in my power to make sure that you aren't their guinea pig case."

Silence.

Najib said, "As far as I'm concerned, I'd rather they kill me than hold me here forever."

. . .

DEPARTMENT OF HOMELAND SECURITY
OFFICE OF THE SECRETARY
WASHINGTON, DC
1:35 P.M.

Fallington Strayhorn walked back into his office, stood beside his desk, crossed his arms over his rotund belly, and watched the whiz-kid lawyer, Willie Roberts, typing all kinds of code on his computer. Three hours had passed, and the whiz kid had worked furiously.

In that time, Fallington had walked in and out of his office, gotten something to eat, canceled all his appointments for the day, and worried about how and when to announce Emily Gardner's disappearance.

Strayhorn didn't like the idea of placing his entire fate into the hands of a thirtysomething-year-old bright-eyed attorney like Willie Roberts. But greatness involved taking chances. Only a riverboat gambler could win the lottery. What they were about to achieve, the great governmental machinery over which he would preside, would transform America forever—if he could persuade Doug Surber to bring that plane down.

Roberts punched a button on the keyboard. "Done, Mr. Secretary."

"Tell me what we've got, Willie."

"We've got multiple sources with anonymous warnings that Aeroflot 4325, currently over the Atlantic and bound for Moscow, will be commandeered by terrorists and forced to fly into a high-profile target in London, namely, the American embassy."

Strayhorn nodded. "And we've got plausible deniability built into this?"

"Yes, sir. We have multiple anonymous sources from foreign computers that will have been eliminated by the time DOD or anyone else tries tracking these sources down. In the midst of all that's going on with all the mall terror, this will provide the perfect cover."

"Excellent," Strayhorn said.

He picked up the phone on his desk and punched the button for his secretary.

"Yes, Mr. Secretary?"

"Carol, get me the president. Tell the White House the situation is urgent."

CHAPTER 29

• • •

President Douglas Surber sat on the sofa in front of his desk, chatting with both the chairman of the joint chiefs of staff, Admiral William Cameron, and the secretary of defense, Erwin Lopez.

Two television screens were on mute, one showing live footage of the Fashion Valley Mall in San Diego, where security forces were working in the aftermath of the mall terror attack. Another showed video footage, again live, from the Shops at Legacy near Dallas, still smoldering from the mall attacks.

"Gentlemen," the president said, "I need to make sure that we have sufficiently beefed up our defense so that we don't get whacked again. We cannot allow another terror strike against civilian targets here in the US. We have had too much bloodshed already. This attack alone will take years to recover from."

"Mr. President," Secretary Lopez said, "part of the problem here is that we aren't dealing with conventional military forces. This is a tactical intelligence war, whereby the enemy blends into the woodwork and could appear at any time, anywhere."

The buzz from the president's phone interrupted the defense

secretary. "Excuse me, gentlemen. This must be important for Gail to interrupt me like this."

Surber stood up and walked over to his desk to answer the secure phone. "Yes, Gail?"

"Sorry to interrupt, sir. It's Secretary Strayhorn. He says it's an emergency."

"Put him through."

"Yes, sir." A pause. "Mr. President, Secretary Strayhorn is on the line."

"Fallington. What's up?"

"Mr. President, I'm sorry to interrupt, but we have a problem."

"What? Dear God, what can go wrong now?" Surber caught the eyes of Admiral Cameron boring into him. "Fallington, hang on. I've got Erwin Lopez and Admiral Cameron right here with me. Let me put you on speaker so they can hear."

"Sure, Mr. President."

Surber pressed the Intercom button on the secure phone. "Okay, Fallington."

"Gentlemen, Homeland Security has intercepted e-mail traffic from several sources that terrorists on a Russian Aeroflot airliner that took off from Dulles this morning are planning to crash the jet into the US Embassy in London."

"Did you say the US Embassy?" Admiral Cameron said.

"Yes, Admiral."

"Fallington. Erwin Lopez here. How solid is your intel?"

"Hard to say, Erwin," Strayhorn said. "We can't say for sure if it's a hoax or it's real. The information has come in so fast that we haven't been able to fully cross-verify everything. But we've got it pouring in from several sources, and that plane is already in the air. So with a missile potentially bearing down on our embassy, we're putting the threat as high priority."

"Mr. Secretary. Admiral Cameron here. What's the flight number of that Aeroflot flight, and when did it take off?"

"Give me a second, Admiral. I want to make sure we are precise." A second passed. Then another. The president exchanged looks of concern with Admiral Cameron and Secretary Lopez. "Admiral, that's Flight 4325, and we show a takeoff time from Dulles at 9:30 a.m."

Cameron grunted. "They're well over the Atlantic by now."

"What if the info isn't right?" the president said.

"It might not be, Mr. President," SECDEF Lopez said. "The problem is, we don't have time to fully verify before they're on top of London. After Benghazi, we can't not act, sir."

"Agreed, Erwin. But I can't just shoot down a civilian airliner, either," Surber said. "We've got civilians on board." He paused. "Fallington, any Americans on that plane?"

"Yes, Mr. President. Primarily Russians, but some Americans, as we understand it."

"I mean, am I supposed to take out American citizens to save our embassy?"

"Not just our embassy, but civilians in London, including Americans, Mr. President," Erwin Lopez said. "I'd remind you, sir, that on 9/11, Vice President Cheney gave the order to take out Flight 93, but that never happened because Todd Beamer and his buddies took the flight down before it reached Washington. And Vice President Cheney was operating under a tight time constraint. Even tighter than what we have here."

"I remember," the president said. "And President Obama took no action to protect our consulate in Libya, which turned out to be a disaster. But in this case, we're talking about shooting down a Russian airliner. That could start World War III. At the very least, we need to immediately evacuate the embassy."

"Definitely, Mr. President," Lopez said.

Doug picked up another phone and punched the direct line for his chief of staff, Arnie Brubaker.

A second later, "Yes, sir, Mr. President."

"You still in New York, Arnie?"

"Yes, sir. Should be home tonight."

"Arnie, we've got a situation brewing, which I'll brief you on later. But listen. I want you to call Secretary of State Mauney and order our embassy in London evacuated immediately."

"What should I say if the ambassador asks why, sir?"

"Elevated terror threat. Get on it now, Arnie. And let me know when it's done."

"Yes, sir."

The president hung up the phone and returned to the sofa.

"Mr. President," Strayhorn said, "maybe the Russians would never know what hit the airliner. Airliners can disappear over the ocean. When they shot down KAL 007, that didn't start a war."

"Different circumstances, Fallington," Surber said. "KAL was a Korean airliner. Plus the Russians claimed it violated their airspace and thought it was a bomber. Besides, there's no guarantee they wouldn't find out about it. Maybe I should call President Zalevsky and turn the problem over to the Russians."

"With respect, Mr. President," Secretary Lopez said, "I'd advise against that. You can't trust the Russians, and they might send aircraft out to challenge us."

"Mr. President, there's a possible alternative."

"I'm all ears, Admiral."

"Sir, depending on where the plane is, we could force them down before they reach Britain. I'd suggest Iceland. But we have to hurry. If they won't cooperate, then you could order it shot down."

A pause.

Lopez nodded. "Not a bad idea, Mr. President. I think I'd brief Prime Minister Mulvaney. After all, the Brits are the targets here. Persuade them to take part in the military mission so it's not all on us if this goes south. But that would be it. Mr. President, we've got to get moving or that plane will be in London."

The secretary of defense was right. There was no time for delay. "What's your recommendation, Mr. Secretary?"

"I'll defer to Admiral Cameron."

"Admiral?"

"Sir, we've got the George Bush Strike Group in the North Atlantic. I say let's send a couple of fighters up and order that plane down in Iceland. Jam it so they can't get a distress call out. Get the Brits involved too. If the Aeroflot jet won't land, we've got to splash it."

Surber nodded. He twisted in his chair and felt sick. Perhaps he should call the White House physician for something to soothe his stomach.

No time for that.

If he'd known in advance what he would have to endure the last couple of days, he would not have run for president. But he asked for the job, and now another world-changing decision was on his shoulders.

"Okay, Admiral. I concur. Let's get our jets up there, order that airliner down, and if it won't cooperate, splash it."

• • •

UNITED FLIGHT 8893
SOMEWHERE OVER THE ATLANTIC
1:42 P.M. EST
1842 HOURS ZULU TIME

From her window seat in row 42, under the tranquilizing hum of the jet's four engines, Emily peered down at partial cloud cover that cast spotted shadows on the sun-glistened ocean below.

What had she done?

Had she thrown her life away?

How had she wound up in this situation? She had wrestled with this question ever since Strayhorn's proposition.

It was clearer now. Strayhorn had tried swooning her by offering her one of the top legal jobs in the country. He sweetened the bait because she was a long-shot candidate and would leapfrog over at least a half dozen other government lawyers more senior to her. Strayhorn banked on her becoming so enthralled with the position of power that she would find a way to legally justify his plans.

From the Teapot Dome scandal, to Watergate, to Operation Fast and Furious, this was how government corruption worked. Bureaucrats and corrupt politicians dangling golden carrots of power with the understanding that the recipient would turn a blind eye to the corruption and, when the corruption was exposed, defend such corruption legally with a straight face.

That's what Strayhorn wanted from her. If this was exposed, she had the legal mind to defend it. He had seen that when she devised the TSA legal strategy for declaring Najib Makari to be outside of the protective procedures of the Uniform Code of Military Justice, based on the fraudulent enlistment theory. Yes, his motives were becoming clearer by the second.

But what choice did she have? To play ball with them. Or die.

"Could I get you anything, ma'am?"

The smiling flight attendant interrupted her thoughts.

"No, thank you."

She looked out the window, down at the ocean.

The ocean.

Seeing it now, from thirty thousand feet, rekindled the question that every naval officer who had left before retirement asked at one point or another: "Why did I leave the Navy?" She had asked this question many times. The idyllic years of service in the United States Navy were the best years of her life

Against those thoughts, the words of Thomas Wolfe saddened her. "You can't go home again."

But if she saw him again, would she feel like she had come home?

Their affair was electric, incomparable to anything she had ever experienced. When she announced that she was leaving active duty to join the TSA, they reached an irreconcilable fork in the road. He would "never leave the Navy for a government-bureaucrat job" and encouraged her to reject the offer.

She should have listened. But ambition and a thirst for new

adventure got the best of her. Their last night together followed her hail and farewell, then the Navy processed her out of the service and sent him to Europe.

Should she try to contact him? Why get him involved? For that matter, could she trust him anymore? Maybe he had found someone else.

He had professed his love for her, and they'd even discussed marriage. But both remained stubborn. He wanted to stay in the Navy, and she wanted something else.

How she hated bad timing.

No, she would not involve him with this.

But what choice did she have? Besides, he didn't have to help her. He could say no.

And why not? She said no to him when he needed her most. Maybe he'd shove it right back at her by saying no when she needed him.

Was there hope for them?

Was there hope for her?

Soon, she would know.

She closed her eyes to get her mind off things. As the jet streaked east across the Atlantic, the memory of his kisses dominated her thoughts and, like an incredible wonder drug, distracted her mind from Fallington Strayhorn and Max Porterfield, and thoughts of following Jerry Myer to a certain death.

• • •

DEPARTMENT OF HOMELAND SECURITY JET
BOEING 777 (DHS 1)
SOMEWHERE OVER THE ATLANTIC
1:45 P.M.
1845 HOURS ZULU TIME

From the plush first-class cabin leather seats directly behind the cockpit, Max Porterfield checked his laptop screen, watching the flight trajectory as the Boeing 777 rocketed over the ocean to the east.

Because of prevailing tailwinds, and with the plane lightly loaded, the pilots promised they could shave from thirty minutes to one hour off the flight to Moscow.

"Based on their takeoff time, it may be difficult, but still possible, to beat the Aeroflot flight there," the pilot had said.

But even if they landed on the heels of the Aeroflot flight, they could arrest Emily, detain her, and fly her back to the US aboard the 777.

No matter what, they could not allow her to survive long enough to stand trial. Porterfield had considered how to dispose of her. The most efficient means would be an unsolved missing person report.

They would handcuff her, bring her aboard the 777, take off, and then execute her in the plane. They could drop the body from five thousand feet over the Atlantic, and local police could issue a missing person report for her.

The DHS aircrew and TSA ELITE agents had been briefed— Emily Gardner, now an enemy of the United States, could damage the country more than Ed Snowden. The role of DHS and TSA ELITE was one and the same—to stop enemies of the US government at all costs.

Everyone understood: for the good of the country, she had to be silenced.

The big plane banked left and the secure telephone rang. Porterfield reached down into a black leather bag and picked up the phone.

"Yes, sir."

"Change of plans, Porterfield," Fallington Strayhorn said.

"How so, Mr. Secretary?"

"Tell the pilot to change course. I've convinced the president to either shoot the Aeroflot jet down or force it down in Iceland."

"Iceland?"

"That's it. Set your course for Reykjavík. I hope the Navy does the dirty work for us and splashes that jet. But if not, I want you to arrest her in Iceland and execute the plan as discussed."

"We'll get her, Mr. Secretary."

• • •

2 US NAVY F/A-18 HORNETS
STRIKE FIGHTER SQUADRON 87
"GOLDEN WARRIORS"
CARRIER AIR WING 8
USS *GEORGE H. W. BUSH* STRIKE GROUP
ALTITUDE 41,000 FEET
SOMEWHERE OVER THE NORTH ATLANTIC
1859 HOURS ZULU TIME

Lieutenant Commander Michael A. "Mikey" Garcia, code named "Maverick," nudged the control stick to the right, sending the powerful war bird into a bank. Garcia, a second-generation Navy pilot, grew up living, breathing, and drinking naval aviation. His father flew an F-14 Tomcat, one of the greatest fighters ever built. Indeed, naval aviation was in Garcia's blood from birth.

As the jet continued in its bank, turning to zero-four-zero degrees, leveling out for its trajectory back to the supercarrier *George H. W. Bush*, Garcia looked out at the choppy blue waters of the North Atlantic. The thrill of banking the fighter into a turn, opening up a wide view of the ocean below, still sent a rush through his body.

Garcia loved flying combat air patrol and would fly twenty-four hours a day if they would let him. But the wide swoop thirty miles off the southern tip of Greenland meant that Garcia and his wingman, Lieutenant Seth Angel, were on the back side of their patrol and would soon yield this section of the airspace to two other jets from Strike Squadron 15.

Garcia depressed the mike, opening communication with the ship. "Bush Control. Golden Warrior One. Lined up at zero-four-zero degrees. Range four-niner-four. We'll see you in about forty minutes."

"Golden Warrior. Bush Control. Copy that. See you in a few."

Out to the right of Garcia's cockpit, Seth Angel's jet flew a hundred yards off his wingtip. Garcia shot Angel a thumbs-up, signaling the final return flight to the *Bush*, and Angel reciprocated.

With the attacks against the malls back home, Garcia wanted to unleash his jet's firepower against whoever was responsible.

But in the War on Terror, these cowardly yellowbelly terrorists hid in the shadows and blended in with the civilians. Few were brave enough to fight like men.

No point in worrying about that now. The air wing's job was to keep this section of the skies, and the sea below, safe for democracy. And in this section of the world, that's exactly what they were doing.

"Golden Warrior. Bush Control."

"Bush Control. Go ahead."

"Be advised that we have received orders to intercept a Russian Aeroflot passenger jet, Airbus 330A, flying in this sector bound for Moscow. Stand by for coordinates."

"Bush Control. Roger that. Standing by. Bush Control, I now have coordinates on my monitor. Awaiting further orders."

"Very well. Stand by for further orders."

Electricity shot through Garcia's body. Nothing excited a fighter pilot more than an intercept order. "Bush Control. Golden Warrior One. Copy intercept coordinates for Aeroflot airbus. Standing by for further orders."

Garcia adjusted the control stick to bring the Hornet in line for intercepting the Russian airliner. Probably some dignitary was aboard and the government wanted to provide fighter escort over the Atlantic, in light of the terror attacks on the US.

"Golden Warrior One. Bush Control."

"Go ahead, Bush."

"Stand by for orders."

"Standing by."

Three seconds passed.

"Golden Warrior One. Your orders are as follows: You are to jam communications with the Russian jet upon approach, then order the plane to land in Reykjavík. If the plane refuses to land, you will then consider the plane to be a hostile target and eliminate it."

Garcia jerked his head back. "Say again? Bush Control? Did you just order me to shoot down an airliner?"

"Golden Warrior One. Roger that. Repeat. If the plane refuses to land, you will then consider the plane to be a hostile target and eliminate it."

They wanted him to shoot down an airliner? The last time that order was given to a US pilot was September 11, 2001. And although that order was never executed, that order came from the vice president of the United States.

Garcia depressed the Talk button. "Bush Control. Roger that. Understand my orders. If the plane refuses to land, consider the plane to be a hostile target and eliminate it."

"Roger that, Golden Warrior. Set vector for intercept and go to afterburners."

"Roger that, Bush. Setting vector for intercept and going to afterburners."

• • •

AEROFLOT AIRBUS 330A
FLIGHT 4325
SOMEWHERE OVER THE NORTH ATLANTIC
BETWEEN GREENLAND AND ICELAND
1859 HOURS ZULU TIME

Commander Dimitry Petrokov, the first officer of the Aeroflot airliner, in the right copilot's seat, checked his instrument panel and gazed out at the open sea below. The ten-hour flight from Washington to Moscow was a long one, and the routine could be boring.

But still, it beat the Red Air Force. At least the pay beat Red Air Force pay.

"Would you like coffee, Giorgy-Alexeevich?" he asked the pilot.

"What I would like is a shot of vodka," the pilot said. "But I haven't been able to persuade the big guys at Aeroflot Control that because the airbus flies itself, the pilots should be able to take a vodka break at the midway point."

"Love your thinking, Giorgy-Alexeevich. Only six more hours to Moscow, and the vodka is on me."

The pilot laughed. "Good enough. For now, coffee will do. Yes, order a pot from the stewardess."

"Yes, sir." Petrokov started to get out of the copilot's chair when the electronic alarm buzzed on the control panel.

A message flashed:

Электронные зажатые передачи!

"Captain, our transmissions are jammed."

"What?" The pilot looked over. "Check alternate frequencies."

"Yes, sir." Dimitry punched in four alternate frequencies. Then five. Six. "Sir, I've tried six, now seven alternate frequencies. All jammed."

"Check long-range radar. Let's see what's out there."

"Yes, Captain." He punched a button to draw back to a view three hundred miles around the aircraft. "Looks like we have visitors approaching at high speed, Captain."

"I knew it," Giorgy-Alexeevich said. "Can you get a make on the approaching aircraft?"

"Stand by, sir." He programmed the computer for an identification read. "Computer shows two McDonnell Douglas F/A-18s approaching at Mach speed."

"Americans," the pilot said. "Probably carrier based."

"Agreed, sir. Besides the Americans, only Spain, Canada, and Switzerland own the F/A-18. At least in this region. And this one's too far out to be anything other than carrier based. What is going on, sir?"

"I don't know, but I don't like it. Probably something to do with the mall attacks in America. But . . . who knows."

. . .

US NAVY F/A-18 HORNETS
STRIKE FIGHTER SQUADRON 87
"GOLDEN WARRIORS"
CARRIER AIR WING 8
USS *GEORGE H. W. BUSH* STRIKE GROUP
OVER THE NORTH ATLANTIC
1902 HOURS ZULU TIME

"Bush Control. Golden Warrior. I've got him on my screen. Preparing to open communication."

"Golden Warrior. Roger that. Initiate communication sequence."

Garcia switched to a universal frequency designed to cut through the American jamming, opening a channel to the Russian aircraft.

"Russian Airbus. This is US Navy F/A-18. Do you copy?"

Static. Nothing.

"Russian Airbus. This is US Navy F/A-18. Please respond."

More static. "US Navy F/A-18. Why are you jamming my communications?"

Garcia hesitated. He was a fighter pilot. Not a diplomat. "Russian Airbus. US Navy F/A-18. You've been jammed because we've been ordered to jam your communications. We've also been ordered to instruct you to land in Reykjavík."

. . .

AEROFLOT AIRBUS 330A
FLIGHT 4325
OVER THE NORTH ATLANTIC
BETWEEN GREENLAND AND ICELAND
1905 HOURS ZULU TIME

"Did he tell me to land this plane in Reykjavík?" Giorgy-Alexeevich looked at Dimitry with a puzzled look.

"That is what I heard, Giorgy-Alexeevich," Dimitry said.

"Is he crazy?"

The pilot depressed the Transmit button. "US Navy F/A-18. This airliner is owned and operated by Aeroflot, which is primarily owned by the government of the Russian Federation. I do not work for the US Navy. I do not report to the US Navy, and until I receive orders from my superiors to deviate from my flight plan, I see no reason to engage in such a deviation."

• • •

US NAVY F/A-18 HORNETS
STRIKE FIGHTER SQUADRON 87
"GOLDEN WARRIORS"
OVER THE NORTH ATLANTIC
1907 HOURS ZULU TIME

"Bush Control. Golden Warrior. I've told him to land, but he's giving me some lip. He says he'll land only if ordered by Aeroflot or the Russian government. Please advise."

"Golden Warrior. Stand by."

"Roger that." Garcia switched to a frequency enabling direct communication with his wingman piloting the other Hornet, Lieutenant Seth Angel.

"Golden Warrior Two, Golden Warrior One. Let's move to a formation straddling his cockpit. I want to get a good look at him, and I want him to see us. You take a hundred yards to starboard. I'll take the shotgun seat a hundred yards to his port. Let's see if letting him have a look at US Navy supersonic fighters will knock some sense into him."

"Golden Warrior One. Roger that, sir. Moving into formation one hundred yards starboard."

"Warrior Two, copy that." Garcia feathered the control stick to the left and increased airspeed, veering off to the left side of the giant airbus. A few seconds later, he had pulled even with it. Wearing his crash helmet and with his oxygen mask strapped to his face, he looked out to the right, through his glass bubble cockpit, toward the cockpit of the airbus.

Through the window of the Russian cockpit, Garcia saw the silhouette of a man wearing a civilian captain's cap.

Garcia brought his binoculars to his eyes.

Both planes rocked slightly, so Garcia had a problem adjusting his binoculars on a straight fixed line to the other cockpit. A second later, he got a fix on his defenseless adversary.

The Russian's chin jutted out like a rock. His broad shoulders wore a white long-sleeved uniform shirt. Like most Aeroflot pilots, he was probably ex-military.

The Russian looked straight ahead, as if ignoring the F/A-18. But then he turned his head and looked toward the fighter. He brought his binoculars up to get a closer look at the Hornet.

The seconds became an eternity, with the two pilots, the Russian and the American, engaged in a stare down at forty thousand feet above the ocean, each looking down the lenses of the other's binoculars.

"Warrior One. Bush Control."

Garcia put down the binoculars. "Go ahead, Bush."

"Inform Aeroflot that US intelligence has discovered that terrorists are aboard his aircraft, that there is a plot to commandeer the aircraft for terrorist activity, and if he won't land, we will open fire. Bear in mind, we are showing you fifteen minutes from Reykjavík, so his time is short."

"Bush Control. Roger that. Switching to air-to-air." Garcia punched in the frequency for the airbus. "Aeroflot Airbus. This is US Navy F/A-18. Be advised. US intelligence has learned of terrorist activity aboard your aircraft with plans to commandeer your aircraft. Please land your aircraft at Reykjavík or we have orders to fire on you."

• • •

AEROFLOT AIRBUS 330A
FLIGHT 4325
OVER THE NORTH ATLANTIC
BETWEEN GREENLAND AND ICELAND
1908 HOURS ZULU TIME

Giorgy-Alexeevich looked at Dimitry. "I think he is bluffing."

"Why would he bluff, Captain?"

"Whether he is bluffing or not, I will not set this plane down unless there is a reason to or unless I am ordered by Russian authorities to land the plane."

Dimitry felt queasy. "Perhaps we should continue talking to better gauge his intentions."

"Dah. Open channels."

"Channel open, Giorgy-Alexeevich."

"US Navy F/A-18. This is Captain Giorgy-Alexeevich Butrin. Captain of the Aeroflot Russian airbus 330A, Flight 4325, en route to Moscow Domodedovo International Airport. We are under a strict time schedule, imposed on us by Aeroflot and the Russian government, to land this plane in Moscow on time. Unlike many of the domestic carriers in the United States, Aeroflot takes pride in punctuality.

"This aircraft contains no terrorists. And even if it did, I can assure you that we Russian pilots, unlike many US airline pilots, are more than capable of defending our cockpits, for we have no aversion to weapons in the cockpit. US Navy, do you copy?"

Static.

"Aerobus 330A. US Navy F/A-18. We copy and note our great respect for the professionalism of Aeroflot pilots. However, we have our orders. And based on your trajectory at this point, you have ten minutes to prepare for landing in Reykjavík. I say again. Land in Reykjavík or prepare to be shot down."

Giorgy-Alexeevich's face turned red. Veins popped out on his forehead.

Dimitry had flown with the crusty Red Air Force veteran for over a year, and while he was considered to be the best captain in the Aeroflot fleet, he had a reputation for being hot-tempered.

"US Navy F/A-18. This aircraft is carrying the Russian national women's gymnastics team, following their successful tour in the United States. You would want to risk an international incident and start a war by shooting down a plane carrying the national women's gymnastics team?"

Static. No answer.

"Captain," Dimitry said, "if they shoot us down, without witnesses, it will be difficult for our government or anyone else to prove. We would go down as a plane missing over the Atlantic, as others have done. It would be impossible for anyone to even find us out here."

"They won't shoot us down, Dimitry," Giorgy-Alexeevich snarled. "That serves no purpose. This is some propaganda ploy by the US government. They want to force down a Russian plane, claim they have arrested terrorists off it who are responsible for their mall bombings, and make it appear that they have everything under control, at the expense of embarrassing the Russian government and implicating Aeroflot in helping terrorists escape."

"Russian Airbus. US Navy F/A-18. You have nine minutes."

Dimitry rubbed his forehead. "What if he is right, Captain? What if someone is on board planning to commandeer the aircraft?"

"And what if I am right?" Giorgy-Alexeevich said. "What if this is a propaganda ploy?"

"US Navy. Russian Airbus. This plane not only carries the Russian national gymnastics team, but also a number of American citizens. There are innocent women and children on board this aircraft. *American women and children.*" Static. Giorgy-Alexeevich looked at Dimitry. "Surely they won't kill their own people."

"I don't know, Giorgy-Alexeevich. Rumor has it that Vice President Cheney ordered the shoot-down of Flight 93."

"But that never happened," Giorgy-Alexeevich said. "Passengers on board that plane brought it down."

"Or so the Americans claim," Dimitry said.

"Russian Airbus. US Navy F/A-18. You have eight minutes."

Giorgy-Alexeevich reached under his seat, retrieved a bottle of vodka, and took a swig. "No American will defeat me at poker!"

"It's not a game of American poker I'm worried about, Giorgy-Alexeevich."

"No?" The pilot glared angrily at Dimitry. "Then what are you worried about, Dima?"

"I'm more concerned about Russian roulette than American poker."

The pilot took another swig, defying Aeroflot regulations against drinking in the cockpit. "Okay, Dima. Call Oxana into the cabin, review the flight manifest, then do a quick walk-through of the cabin to see if anyone looks like a terrorist. If so, I will land in Reykjavík."

Dimitry nodded. "Very well, Giorgy-Alexeevich." He picked up the microphone for the flight attendant station. "Oxana, report to the cockpit with the flight manifest. It is urgent."

Three knocks on the cabin door. Dimitry stepped up and opened the door for the high-cheeked, blue-eyed flight attendant. Oxana stood there with a fearful look on her face and the flight manifest in her hands.

"Let's check to make sure everyone is in their seats and nothing looks unusual."

"Yes, Dimitry."

Dimitry stepped back into the cabin. The Russian national gymnastics team and their coaches filled the first-class section. Several were snoozing, their heads against the bulkhead or leaning back in a reclined position. Some of the girls on the team, their hair pinned up in blonde buns, wearing blue jumpsuits, could not have been more than thirteen or fourteen years old, the age of Dimitry's daughter.

Some slept.

Some played games on their iPods.

Some thumbed through magazines.

One girl, Natasha Batsakova, a gold medalist in last summer's Olympics, smiled at him as he walked by.

The rest of the gymnastics team occupied seats halfway down the aisle. Starting at row 25, a family of six was spread across the seats—a mother, a father, and four children.

A little girl with blonde locks rested her head on her mother's shoulder.

"Is everything okay, Captain?" the father asked as Dimitry walked by.

"Yes, sir. All is well." But Dimitry lied.

An elderly couple sat behind the family, sleeping. Behind them was an American businessman, working on his laptop.

More families and businessmen, women and children filled the plane. No one was remotely suspicious.

These were passive-looking people. No Arabs. No Chechens.

Dimitry headed back to the cabin.

As he walked back up the center aisle through the first-class cabin and was nearing the cockpit, a hand tugged his right arm. He stopped and looked down.

"Thank you for taking care of us, Captain." It was Natasha Batsakova, the darling of the Russian gymnastics team, whose sweet smile was angelic. Like Svetlana Khorkina, the sensational Russian gymnast who won multiple world championships before retiring, Natasha was Russia's international sensation. Natasha radiated an attractive magnetism and beauty that matched her incredible talent.

"My pleasure, Miss Batsakova. And thank you for the glory you have brought to Russia. I am a huge fan."

He stepped back into the cockpit, locked the door, and took his seat.

"Well, Dimitry, did you find any terrorists?"

"Captain, I saw no one who looked suspicious."

"US Navy F/A-18. This is Russian Airbus. We have checked our manifest. This plane has the Russian gymnastics team aboard, including

DON BROWN

the most famous gymnast in the world, Natasha Batsakova, and a mix of harmless citizens that includes women and children.

"Now if you will patch me through to my Russian superiors, and if they order me to land, I will land. Otherwise, I have orders to get this team back to Moscow on time, and I intend to do exactly that."

• • •

US NAVY F/A-18 HORNETS
STRIKE FIGHTER SQUADRON 87
"GOLDEN WARRIORS"
OVER THE NORTH ATLANTIC
1913 HOURS ZULU TIME

"Bush Control. Golden Warrior."

"Go ahead, Golden Warrior."

"Sir, he claims he's got the Russian national gymnastics team on board. He claims Natasha Batsakova is one of his passengers. He says he's checked his manifest and has no terrorists on board. He says he's on a deadline to land the team in Moscow on time and will land in Iceland only if we patch him through to the Russian authorities and the Russians order him to land."

"Golden Warrior. Stand by."

"Stand by. Roger that."

The fighter struck hard turbulence, bumping into it like striking a slew of air potholes at five hundred miles per hour. The airbus was also bouncing from the turbulence.

But Garcia's queasiness was not about turbulence. He became a fighter pilot for high-altitude fighter-against-fighter aerial dogfights, with winner-take-all, life-or-death consequences. But the notion of splashing an unarmed airliner?

Not what he envisioned when he joined the Navy.

But if an airliner were going to be used as a huge missile, in a 9/11 kamikaze attack, the airliner became a target.

337

But that didn't soften the task. The thought of killing innocent women and children for the greater good made him want to vomit.

"Warrior One. Bush Control. Issue another warning, then drop back and lock on. If he does not initiate landing procedures in three minutes, take him out."

"Roger that. Dropping back to lock on."

A frequency switch. "Warrior Two. Warrior Leader. Drop back five hundred yards. Stay on my wing. Prepare to lock onto target."

"Warrior Leader. Roger that, sir. Preparing to drop back."

Another frequency switch. "Russian Airbus. This is US Navy F/A-18. Your request for direct communication with Russian authorities is denied. Prepare to land in Reykjavík or you will be shot down."

• • •

AEROFLOT AIRBUS 330A
FLIGHT 4325
OVER THE NORTH ATLANTIC
BETWEEN GREENLAND AND ICELAND
1918 HOURS ZULU TIME

"These Americans are the world's worst bluffers." Giorgy-Alexeevich was fuming. "They never mean what they say. Remember? Obama said using chemical weapons was a line in the sand. Then Assad thumbs his nose at Obama. Or when we invaded Ukraine? They do nothing! I've studied the Americans," he snarled. "They're all talk."

"But, Giorgy-Alexeevich, Obama was a politician. Politicians say things and don't deliver. This is the American military. The US Navy does not bluff and bluster."

"Nonsense!" the captain snapped. He swigged more vodka. "They are bluffing. And if they think they can intimidate me, they can think again!"

"Captain, look!" Dimitry said. "The American jets are falling back behind us. Probably maneuvering into firing position."

"More bluff and bluster. Increase speed to full power."

"Increasing speed. Yes, sir." Dimitry pushed forward on the throttle, his hands feeling clammy, his forehead sweaty. The Pratt & Whitney turbofan engines responded, whining, bringing the airbus to full speed.

"Russian Airbus. This is US Navy F/A-18. Your increase in speed is not consistent with our instructions. You have one minute and thirty seconds to initiate landing sequence."

"US Navy F/A-18. This is Russian Airbus. If you fire upon us, you commit an act of war. Our position is unchanged. Lower your jamming frequencies so that I can radio my superiors. If they approve, then will we land in Iceland."

No response. More static.

A beeping alarm sounded on the control panel.

"Captain. The Americans have locked their missiles onto us!"

"It is all theater!" Giorgy-Alexeevich screamed. "I will not blink."

"Captain. We should reconsider our position."

"Are you questioning my leadership, Dimitry?"

"No, Captain. My apologies, sir."

• • •

US NAVY F/A-18 HORNETS
OVER THE NORTH ATLANTIC
1919 HOURS ZULU TIME

His hand reached over to the missile launch button. Cold sweat beaded on Garcia's forehead. "Lord, if it is possible, take this cup from me."

He switched back to air-to-air. "Russian Airbus. US Navy F/A-18. Our fire control radar is locked onto you. Please don't make me shoot you down. I am initiating countdown to missile launch. T minus thirty seconds. Twenty-nine. Twenty-eight . . .

. . .

AEROFLOT AIRBUS 330A
FLIGHT 4325
OVER THE NORTH ATLANTIC
BETWEEN GREENLAND AND ICELAND
1919 HOURS ZULU TIME

The American pilot's countdown sounded like a deathwatch. Dimitry's hands shook. His breathing quickened.

Giorgy-Alexeevich was playing a dangerous and deadly game to prove that his manhood was greater than the American's.

What if Giorgy-Alexeevich was right?

"Fifteen . . . fourteen . . . thirteen . . ."

No, Giorgy-Alexeevich could not be right. Dimitry had heard the American's voice. He knew in his gut.

Suddenly, their faces flashed through his mind.

The girls on the gymnastics team. The elderly couple asleep in the back. The American family. The eyes of Natasha Batsakova, her sweet voice thanking him for taking care of her.

"Giorgy-Alexeevich. Please!"

"Shut up, Dimitry!"

"Eight. . . seven . . . six . . ."

Dimitry reached for the pistol in his holster. He worked the action and pointed it straight at the pilot's head. "Giorgy-Alexeevich! Land the plane!"

. . .

US NAVY F/A-18 HORNETS
OVER THE NORTH ATLANTIC
1920 HOURS ZULU TIME

"Three . . .

   "Two . . .

"One.

"Jesus, forgive me."

Garcia pressed his thumb against the missile launch button.

He felt a burst. Two AIM missiles streaked out in front of the jet, slicing across the skies toward the Russian airbus.

Static over the loudspeaker.

"US Navy, hold your fire! We are landing! We are landing!"

The blinding fireball lit the sky like an exploding sun. Static blared over the air-to-air.

Garcia steered the fighter into a right bank. From over his shoulder, flaming debris from the blown-up aircraft streaked toward the ocean below.

Loneliness blanketed his cockpit like a heavy, steel curtain. His arms felt immobilized, his hands frozen. Garcia prayed, silently, to the heavens. He wiped tears from his eyes and switched frequencies.

"Bush Control. Golden Warrior One. Be advised. Target is eliminated."

"Warrior One. Roger that. Return to ship."

• • •

DEPARTMENT OF HOMELAND SECURITY JET
BOEING 777
OVER THE ATLANTIC
1940 HOURS ZULU TIME

"When we land in Reykjavík," Max Porterfield said to the small squad of TSA ELITE agents gathered around him in the aisle, "we will board the Russian airbus. We will identify the subject, handcuff her—"

The phone rang. Homeland Security headquarters.

"Excuse me, gentlemen." He answered the phone. "Yes, Mr. Secretary."

"Porterfield. No need to land in Iceland. We can pop the champagne, Porterfield. The Navy has eliminated the problem for us."

Porterfield understood what Strayhorn was saying. The Aeroflot jet carrying Emily Gardner had been shot out of the sky. He felt instant relief, but also instant disappointment. He wanted to be the one to solve the Emily Gardner problem, which would have benefited him professionally.

"Acknowledged, Mr. Secretary. We're standing down and flying back to Washington."

• • •

PULMONARY INTENSIVE CARE UNIT
(WALTER REED NATIONAL MILITARY MEDICAL CENTER) BETHESDA NAVAL HOSPITAL
BETHESDA, MARYLAND
2:45 P.M.

"It's about time you got here," Diane said, half teasing and half irritated. The target of her verbal jab was Commander Larry Berman, Medical Corps, United States Navy, her attending physician, who, in Diane's estimation, had taken too long to appear in her room to discuss the prospect of her immediate discharge from this place.

"My apologies," Berman said with a chuckle. "A couple of emergency procedures with the thoracic surgeon I practice with, and the next thing you know, the day is gone. So, I hear you want out of this place."

"I can't do anything with her, Doc," Zack said from the corner of the room. "She's harder headed than a brick."

"You're one to talk about being hardheaded, Zack Brewer."

Berman flipped through the reports he had in his hand. "Okay, vitals are good and you're getting good oxygen flow through your lungs, but I'm still a little skeptical about cutting you loose today." Berman and Zack exchanged "what are we going to do with her?" glances. Then Berman looked at Diane. "You know, since you aren't active duty anymore, I can't stop you from leaving if you want to get real stubborn about it. And I see you've changed into your jeans and boots, which isn't exactly our standard patient attire."

"I know, Doc. I made Zack get my clothes. But I promised him I'd at least hear what you have to say before I walk out of this place."

342

"Hmm." Berman scratched his chin. "If I release you today, will you promise that you'll come back and let us check you day after tomorrow? And that you'll let Admiral Brewer bring you back if you feel the slightest bit queasy or have any shortness of breath?"

Diane smiled. "You've got a deal, Doc."

"Okay." Berman nodded. "For the record, this is against my better judgment, because in my opinion it's kind of a fifty-fifty call in your case, but I'm going to go ahead and sign the discharge papers."

"Thanks. I love you, Doc!" She stood up and gave him a big bear hug and kissed him on the cheek, then turned to her handsome hunk of a three-star husband. "Let's get out of here, Zack!"

"Yes, ma'am."

CHAPTER 30

· · ·

President Surber sat alone, reviewing a memo from his chief of staff, Arnie Brubaker, outlining updated casualty reports from the barbaric mall terror attacks that besieged the United States.

The weight of his office was not only on his shoulders but also in his throat, in his stomach, and through his arms and legs. The sobering report of climbing casualties encompassing more than two hundred dead Americans, including women and children, from the four mall terror attacks around the country was compounded by the fact that he had just authorized the shoot-down of a Russian airliner that was about to rain destruction on the capital city of America's closest ally.

He had hoped that the British would have been more active in the operation, but they had no warplanes in the area, and the conservative British prime minister, David Mulvaney, had asked that the US take care of it. They could not wait until that plane got past Iceland.

Britain was not only America's closest ally but a fellow NATO member, and the seventy-year mantra of NATO was that an attack against one is an attack against all. And Britain was under terrorist attack, or about to be, if America had not acted.

Still, the knowledge that Britain and the US Embassy in London had been saved from the terror that America had experienced in the last two days did not lessen the indescribable sick feeling of guilt and sorrow that gripped him.

He wanted to weep. But he could not weep. At least not in public. He was the elected leader of the free world. He had to project an outward mantle of strength.

"Mr. President."

"Yes, Gail?"

"Admiral Cameron and Secretary Lopez are back. They need to see you."

He laid down the casualty report. "Send them in."

Both men entered the Oval Office, walking past the black-suited Secret Service agents. Their faces were grimmer than ever before.

"What's wrong?" the president demanded.

"Sir," the four-star admiral began, "naval intelligence has been monitoring the transmissions that Secretary Strayhorn claimed tipped off Homeland Security about the Russian airliner that we shot down, and frankly, sir, the military has concerns."

Cameron looked at Lopez, and Lopez nodded. "Sir, this is preliminary, but we no longer believe that the Russian airbus was a terror threat."

"What?" The president raised an eyebrow. "Did you just tell me that the Russian airliner that I ordered shot down was not a terror threat to smash into our embassy in London?"

"Yes, sir. Naval intelligence has been able to backtrack the source of those e-mails, and we highly doubt their authenticity."

"So I killed three hundred innocent passengers because of an intelligence failure? Is that what you're telling me?"

More contorted glances between the high-ranking military men. "Mr. President," Cameron said, "this is hard to say, sir."

"Spit it out, Admiral. I don't have time for bull."

"Sir, we believe we killed three hundred innocent civilians. But not because of an intelligence failure."

"What? You're talking in circles, Admiral! Spit it out!"

"Sir, the reason I said it was not because of an intelligence failure. We believe it may be the result of intelligence fraud."

"Intelligence fraud? Admiral, what the heck are you talking about?"

"Sir, we've determined that the so-called threats concerning this airliner originated from Department of Homeland Security computers. There were seven e-mail messages. All claimed to be from groups in different locations around the Middle East. Two from Pakistan, two from Afghanistan, two from Yemen. And one from Somalia in Africa. They all supposedly had inside information about the same Russian airbus. On the surface, if you believe that, the threat looked credible.

"The problem is that the Navy's tracking codes traced the origination of all of these messages to a single computer at the Department of Homeland Security back here in Washington. It appears that someone in Homeland Security wanted you to order the attack on that airbus based on phony information."

"What? Does Secretary Strayhorn know about this?"

"No, sir. And we recommend that we hold off informing him, at least for the time being."

"Why, Admiral? This is his department. He should be the first one to know."

"Sir, this is preliminary, but we believe he already knows."

"He knows? Then why hasn't he informed me?"

Cameron waited a few seconds before answering. "Sir, we've traced the false flags concerning the Russian airliner to the secretary's office."

"To what secretary? . . . To the secretary of Homeland Security?"

"Yes, sir. We believe somebody sent the false flags from Secretary Strayhorn's office."

Douglas Surber stood up, folded his arms, and walked over to the bay window of the Oval Office. He looked out on the South Lawn and beyond that to the National Mall. The American flags were fluttering in the circle around the base of the Washington Monument. On the outside, from a distance, all looked well.

But appearances could be deceiving. In reality, Douglas Surber, the president of the United States, was living one of those worst-night-mare moments. The whole country seemed to be out of control.

"How did the Navy crack this?"

The answer came from over his shoulder. "Sir, someone tried to put encryption codes on these messages to make them impossible to break. What the programmer didn't know is that the Office of Naval Intelligence has software to break those codes that not even Homeland Security knows about. Someone tried building in a foolproof encryption code that would be untraceable. Fortunately, it failed."

"What are your recommendations, gentlemen?"

"The first is obvious, Mr. President." This from the secretary of defense. "First, we can't let the Russians or anyone else know, aside from the British, that we were involved in the shoot-down. That airbus has disappeared off the radar screen, and no one knows why it disappeared at sea."

"So I can't let anyone know, but the blood will forever be on my hands," the president said.

"We can't let anyone know," Erwin Lopez said. "Too much is at stake, and it won't do any good."

"What else?"

"Sir"—again Secretary Lopez—"we can't play our hand with Secretary Strayhorn yet. If he's somehow involved with this, now is not the time to let him know. We need a bit more time to investigate a couple of other things. There's an outside possibility that he's not involved, but if he is, and I suspect he is, we need to play it cool to get to the bottom of this."

Douglas Surber turned around, his back now to the outside. He had ordered the portraits of three presidents hung in the Oval Office. The greatest president of the eighteenth century, George Washington. The greatest president of the nineteenth century, Abraham Lincoln. And the greatest president of the twentieth century, Ronald Reagan.

What would they tell him if they were here? What would they advise?

He already knew. They would advise him to preserve the republic and to defend the Constitution at all costs. That's exactly what he was sworn to do.

If members of his administration were subverting either the Constitution or the republic, he had to act, and he had to act decisively. But he had to act when the time was right.

"Very well, gentlemen. I'm ordering the Department of Defense to monitor this situation under top-secret conditions. Report to me every two hours, or sooner if needed."

"Yes, Mr. President."

CHAPTER 31

. . .

"This calls for a celebration, Willie." Fallington Strayhorn poured champagne into the flute and slipped it across the desk to the young, starry-eyed sycophant. "You were brilliant."

"Thank you, Mr. Secretary. I'm glad to do it for the safety of our country and for the best interests of the department."

"A toast," Strayhorn said, "to present successes and to future successes!"

"I'll drink to that, Mr. Secretary."

Glasses clanged. Strayhorn chugged down half the champagne and refilled his glass.

"Another toast," Strayhorn proclaimed, raising his glass, watching Willie Roberts raise his in response. "Here we go. *Sic semper evello mortem traditorem*. Do you know what that means, Willie?"

"Let's see, *sic semper* is . . . "thus ever to" . . . Sorry, sir. My Latin is rusty."

"Well, get used to it. It is the future motto of the elite leadership of Homeland Security, of which you will be a part. It means 'Thus ever shall I always kill the traitor.' Or, more succinctly, 'Death to the traitor.'

I'm thinking about shortening it to *Sic sempter traditorem*. 'Death to the traitor.' What do you think?"

"I like it, sir."

"Yes, well, Emily Gardner and her predecessor, Jerry Myer, were traitors. So let us raise our glasses to our new and future motto, 'Death to the traitors.'"

The bubbles percolated to Strayhorn's head. The weight of the world lifted from his shoulders, thanks to the US Navy. Soon, under his plan, all the armed services, including the US Navy, would reorganize under Homeland Security—under his command.

Indeed, the plan to have the military moved under Homeland Security had already begun. The United States Coast Guard was moved under Homeland Security in 2003. That was only the beginning. All of the departments of defense and transportation and agencies like TSA, the FBI, and even the IRS should be consolidated under Homeland Security.

Strayhorn's US Coast Guard forces, including Coast Guard cutters, were already deployed to the Guantánamo Bay Naval Base, which, along with the presence of TSA ELITE Forces, was a step in the right direction.

Once all the branches of the armed forces joined the Coast Guard under the control of Homeland Security, that consolidation of power would make security enforcements within the United States that much easier.

The phone rang. "Mr. Secretary." The voice of Carol Gibson came over the speaker.

"Yes, Carol."

"Max Porterfield is calling from the air phone of the Homeland Security jet, sir."

"Ah. Speak of the devil." Strayhorn sipped more champagne. "Porterfield, my boy. Your ears must have been burning. We were just talking about you."

"Mr. Secretary." Porterfield sounded anything but jovial. "We have a problem."

"A problem? No problems here. The US Navy has taken care of the problem."

"No, sir, Mr. Secretary. I'm afraid there's been a mistake."

Strayhorn put down his champagne glass and sat up straight. "What kind of mistake?"

"Sir, our ELITE Forces have gone back and reviewed video surveillance from Dulles. Emily Gardner pulled a fast one on us."

"What the heck are you talking about, Porterfield?"

"Well, sir. She bought a ticket to Moscow and got in line and checked onto the flight. Aeroflot reported to us that she had checked in. We assumed she was on board. But she slipped out of the line, and we didn't catch that on tape at first. She bought another ticket to Rome."

"Rome! What are you telling me, Porterfield? Are you telling me I persuaded the president to blow up a Russian plane over the ocean and Emily Gardner wasn't even on it?"

"I'm sorry, sir. It happened so fast. Sometimes it takes awhile to verify and cross-check data."

"Porterfield!" Strayhorn launched into a profanity-laced tirade. "You let a woman lawyer outsmart the whole DHS and our ELITE Forces?"

"I'm sorry, sir. I—"

"When is her plane landing in Rome?"

"Right about now, sir."

"Great! That's just great! What time is it over there?"

"Just after midnight, sir."

More cursing. "Porterfield, you turn that plane around, and you get to Rome, and you get our people to snatch that traitor out of the airport there, or wherever she is, or don't bother coming back to the United States! Because if you come back here and Emily Gardner is still alive, I'll bring in some of our Saudi allies and have them do a little sharp-blade Muslim justice to the area between your head and your shoulders, then I'll have your head mounted like a stupid twelve-point buck, and I'll have the taxidermist staple a set of twelve-point deer antlers on your head, because you'd be as stupid as a deer in the headlights, and I'll mount your dead head on the wall so I can remind our future ELITE agents not to be as dumb as that guy on the wall! Do you understand my instructions?"

"Yes, sir, Mr. Secretary. I'll take care of it, sir."

CHAPTER 32

• • •

"What the heck?" Lieutenant Commander Brady Kash, JAGC, USN, rolled over and looked at the digital clock—12:25 a.m. The incoming call showed an unlisted number. "This better be good." He hit the Talk button. "Lieutenant Commander Kash."

"Brady?"

The voice on the other end melted his anger. "Em? Where are you?"

"At Fiumicino Airport."

"You're in Rome? Why are you in Rome?"

"No time to explain. Look, Brady. I'm in trouble, and I need help. I don't have time to go into it. I know it's been a long time, and I feel horrible for how things ended. I understand if you don't want to or can't help me. Plus you could be putting yourself at risk."

He sat up and rubbed his eyes. Was this a dream? "Em, what's this all about? I mean, last time I saw you, you were on the trial team at Sigonella and I was staff judge advocate, and we were all

353

hot and heavy and even talking marriage. Then you decided to get out of the Navy, move to Washington, and that was that. So what's going on?"

"I'm sorry, Brady, I shouldn't have—"

"Hang on. Are you safe?"

"For the time being. But I can't stay at the airport long. They'll be looking for me."

"Who? Who's looking for you?"

"No time to explain right now, but I'm sure if they find me, they'll kill me."

"What are you talking about? You know, after the way we ended, after you left—"

"I'm sorry, Brady. I shouldn't have called. I've got to go."

"Wait a second."

"I don't have time, Brady."

"Okay. Not sure about this, but I'll help you."

"Thanks, Brady. But I have to get out of here. Now."

"Okay." He wiped his forehead. "You have plenty of charge on your phone?"

"I'm not sure. This is a travel phone that I keep as a spare, and I didn't have a chance to charge it before I left the States."

"Okay, listen. After we hang up, take the battery out of your phone. This saves the battery and makes it tougher for them to track you. Then take a cab to a coffee shop called Caffè Domiziano. It's open all night. It's right across from Four Rivers Fountain. The cabdriver will know where it is. Wait there for me. I'm about a hundred forty miles away. It will take me about two and a half hours. If you see anyone suspicious, go into the streets and blend into the dark. Put the battery back in at 3:00 a.m. and call me. Ya got that?"

"Got it."

. . .

Max Porterfield decided that if he could get his hands on Emily Gardner, he would cut her heart out himself. He'd never been outsmarted before. But she had pulled a fast one on him, embarrassing him on a high-stakes stage, embarrassing him in front of the big boss. He had to hand it to her. She was slick. Too bad she had taken all that talent to the other side.

She'd declared war, in a way that her predecessor Jerry Myer never did. Fine. The department had special friends in Italy. Her demise would not be pretty—or painless.

"Excuse me, Mr. Porterfield?"

A TSA ELITE agent stood in the aisle beside his front-row seat.

"Whatcha got, Bob?"

"We've established that call to your contact in Rome."

"Excellent. I'll take it."

The ELITE Forces agent handed him the phone. "Guido?"

"How may we be of service to you, Mr. Porterfield?"

"Guido, we've got a rogue operator who just landed in Italy."

"What's his name? We'll take care of him for you, boss."

"Not a him. A her. Her name is Emily Gardner. Thirty-eight-year-old lawyer type. She's gone rogue from Homeland Security and has information with her that would make Snowden look like a harmless pussycat."

"Dang." The Italian chuckled. "And so you want the family to take care of what the great new TSA super ELITE Homeland Security types dropped the ball on." More snickering.

"Guido, Homeland Security doesn't keep the family on retainer to be the subject of jokes."

"Sorry, boss." Another chuckle. "Okay, so I take it you want us to track her down, cut her up in a thousand pieces, and feed her to the sharks off Sicily?"

"Do what you have to do. I want to see her dead body."

"Okay, okay, boss. But hey, it's late! We're not only going to need time-and-a-half for this little project, but I need to know what this babe looks like."

"Stand by. I'll have my staff e-mail photos and contact information for you and your boys."

"Super."

"And, Guido."

"Yes, boss?"

"I'm depending on you. I'm depending on the family."

"No problem, boss. You've got Sicilians on the case now, and she's on our turf. I'm calling my team at the airport now. We'll track her down if she's anywhere in Italy. If you sweeten the pot enough, we'll even let your Homeland Security bosses think that your TSA boys got her." More laughing.

"Okay, Guido. What does 'sweeten the pot' mean?"

"I'd say an extra $10 million. That's $5 million in advance, $5 million when the job is done. That's chump change for the US government."

"Okay. Fine," Porterfield snapped. "Homeland Security has a discretionary account for this sort of thing. I'll wire the first part immediately. Just take care of it, Guido."

"Will do, boss."

• • •

VIA LABICANA
ROME, ITALY
2:24 A.M.

The black Maserati Ghibli cruised northwest on the lighted boulevard of Via Labicana, passing the Mercure Hotel on the right. Up ahead, to the left of the road, spotlights lit up the rounded facade of the ancient Roman Colosseum, the most famous of the great Roman landmarks.

The driver slowed, not wanting to deal with the hassle of some whippersnapper *agent de poliẓia* who might not recognize the Maserati as part of the family fleet.

Most officers recognized the family vehicles and left them alone.

But occasionally he had to indoctrinate a rookie policeman on understanding the pecking order of respect to be afforded the various classes of vehicles on the streets of Rome.

"Never mess with the family, young man" would be the message accompanied by an Uzi up the nose of any young cop who tried to interfere by making a traffic stop. Not that the driver minded delivering that message. But he did not have time for that kind of nuisance tonight. There was too much money on the line to get sidetracked.

The Maserati slowly approached the Colosseum, and as it swung left onto Via Celio Vibenna, the phone rang.

"What do you got, Sal?"

"Where are you, Guido?"

"Approaching the Colosseum. Why?"

"Maybe a break, my brother. We offered money, and an airport cabbie sang like a canary. Says he dropped Emily Gardner off at Piazza Navona about an hour ago."

"Where did he drop her?"

"He said she wanted to be dropped at Piazza Navona."

"Probably Caffè Domiziano. Okay, I'm headed over there. Get me backup. We'll comb the area and be ready to collect the rest of the bounty at daybreak."

"Got it, boss."

•••

Emily sat at a small table in a corner of the café. Like New York and, to a lesser extent, like Washington, Rome never slept at night. But unlike Washington or New York, Rome reached back to before the time of Christ, bringing the ancient world back to faintly touch fingers with the modern world.

The Caffè Domiziano, located in the ancient oval-shaped Navona Plaza, was built on the site of the Stadium of Domitian, the long oval stadium once used for chariot races, that dated back to about AD 86. Sitting alone at her wrought-iron table, Emily gazed through the windows of the café and into the Italian night. Off to her right, at the north end of the oval plaza, stood a spotlighted white-marble statue of the Roman god Neptune.

Outside the café, against the backdrop of the spotlighted white-marble fountain statue of the "Four Rivers," a white obelisk resembling a miniature replica of the Washington Monument, a constant stream of people moved about, many flowing in and out of the café.

The sound of rushing water spewing from the three spotlit fountains in the square formed a soothing backdrop. The late hour did not seem to deter the Roman nightlife. Young lovers, homeless people, police officers, taxicab drivers, strange-looking freaks with pink hair and multiple nose and face piercings all moved about, as if Rome had no bedtime.

If her soul were not so knotted, the Domiziano would make a fascinating venue for people-watching.

But on this night, her only target for people-watching was suspicious-looking characters dispatched by Homeland Security.

Sooner or later, her renegade bosses at Homeland Security and the new TSA ELITE agents would discover which flight she had boarded. And there was no limit to their reach.

"Vorrebbe la signora, di caffè?"

The handsome young black-haired waiter had approached her twice, asking if she wanted coffee.

"No. *Ma grazie,*" she said.

He nodded his head, smiled, and stepped away.

She could use some coffee. But she had not exchanged her dollars into euros yet, and she was not about to use a credit card, which would be like putting a bull's-eye on her back.

She checked her watch. Another half hour before she could call Brady.

"God, give me wisdom on what to do."

A sick feeling overcame her. She didn't know why, but she had to get up and move.

She stepped into the dark alley beside the café that led out to Corso del Rinascimento, the street running north and south and bordering the east side of the plaza. As she stepped out onto the sidewalk beside Corso del Rinascimento, she looked over her shoulder, back toward the café.

Four men in dark suits were jogging into the café, one behind the other, with the air of Nazi storm troopers.

"Dear Jesus. They're on to me. Help me, Lord!"

She turned, hurried across Corso del Rinascimento, and ran off into the night, through the ancient streets of Rome.

• • •

CAFFÈ DOMIZIANO
PIAZZA NAVONA 88
ROME, ITALY
2:35 A.M.

Guido walked into the old landmark, the Caffè Domiziano, with three of his associates, fellow members of the family, so to speak. From the inside entry area of the café, he surveyed the scene.

"What do you think, Guido?" Tony asked.

"This place is weird enough in the daytime," Guido said. "But at two thirty in the morning, they look like a bunch of miscreant fruitcakes from outer space."

"I don't know, boss," Vinnie said. "I don't see nobody that looks like our girl."

"That's the truth," Gio said. "Looks more like a flophouse than a coffee bar."

"Hey, Vinnie. Give me that picture."

"You bet, boss." Vinnie handed Guido an eight-by-ten color photo of Emily Gardner.

"Hey!" Guido snapped, holding the picture high in his right hand. A few people broke from their conversations and looked up.

"Hey! Hey! Everybody, listen! Anybody with info on this woman? I'll make it worth your while!"

Silence.

All the room's eyes were locked on him. But no one said a word.

"Hey, boss," Gio said. "Over in the corner."

A young black-haired man wearing the white shirt and black pants of a waiter had raised his hand.

"You!" Guido said. "You got something?"

The man nodded.

"Step outside!"

"But I . . ." The man hesitated. "My customers."

"Don't worry about your customers."

"But I—"

"Vinnie, you know how to serve coffee?"

"Yeah, boss. I can serve a mean hot coffee."

"Excellent. Stay here and serve coffee for this fellow's customers 'til I'm done with him. Will ya?"

"Sure, boss."

"You! Outside!"

"Yes, of course." The waiter hung his head and hurried across the café and out into the night where, against the gushing sound of the three fountains, he was joined on the plaza by Guido, Gio, and Tony.

"You know who we are, son?"

"Well, sir, I think . . . I . . ." His voice shook.

"Well, let me tell you. Who we are . . . we are the people you don't want to mess with. Because lying can be hazardous to your health. So I need you to shoot it straight with me. Did you see this woman?"

The waiter nodded. "I . . . yes."

"When?" Guido grabbed his shoulder. "Where?"

"She was here earlier tonight. For about two hours. She sat over in the corner by herself. She didn't order anything. I asked several times. Her Italian was understandable, not good."

"You sure it was her?"

"Positive."

"When did she leave?"

"About ten minutes before you arrived."

"Did she leave with anyone?"

"No. She left alone. She walked out quickly."

"What was she wearing?"

"Well, that was odd. She came in wearing a yellow warm-up suit. But I noticed that soon after she arrived, she went into the bathroom and changed into a dark blue warm-up suit. I did not pay much attention. People sometimes change clothes."

Guido reached into his pocket and handed the waiter one hundred euros. The waiter's face lit up.

Guido grabbed the waiter by the collar and slammed him against the outside wall of the café and then pushed his face hard against the wall.

He reached into his belt and pulled out a stainless-steel serrated utility knife from its sheath. "You feel this, punk?"

"Ah . . . I . . ."

"You feel the cold steel of this razor-sharp knife on your throat?"

"Please? I . . ."

"You took my money, you slimeball. Now you belong to the family."

"Per favore! Signore! Per favore!"

Guido removed the knife from the waiter's throat and pressed the tip of the blade against his left cheek, gently at first, then harder, cutting his flesh and drawing blood.

"Aaahhh!" Blood dripped from the small cut.

"Congratulations, sir," Guido said. He swiped his finger across the waiter's blood and smeared it all over his cheek. "We're now blood brothers. And that means we're officially family."

The waiter was shaking. Tears streamed from his eyes, mixing with the blood on his face.

"And you know that family is always there to help family. Right?"

"Si, signore."

"And you know what happens if you double-cross the family?"

"I'm telling the truth. I . . . Please."

Guido shoved the waiter to the ground and went back into the café. "Vinnie! She's in the area. Let's go."

• • •

VIA DEL SALVATORE
ROME, ITALY
2:50 A.M.

Emily darted into a small alleyway, revealed by the streetlight to be Via del Salvatore. The alleyway was long, narrow, dark, and paved with cobblestones. Brick walls rose high on each side of it.

As she moved through the alleyway, dim lighting seeped in from each of the two connecting streets.

How far until she was out of the alley? Perhaps a hundred yards, although it was difficult to judge. She moved as quickly as she could, but not so fast as to risk tripping over the uneven cobblestones.

A whiff of urine and beer wafted in the night air, and a glass-like *clank* echoed off the walls.

She stopped.

Was somebody there?

Her heart pounded.

Jesus, help me.

She took another step. Another *clink*. Her foot had kicked something. She looked down.

A bottle. Her foot had kicked a bottle.

She exhaled, feeling relieved for a second anyway, and started walking again.

Then she stopped and turned around. She went back and kneeled down, reaching out in front of her.

There.

She reached down and picked up the empty beer bottle and stuffed it in her bag. "I've got to get out of here."

She started walking again, faster and faster. She kept her eyes on the opening at the end of the alley and prayed that whoever they were would not trap her in the alley. She was almost there when a beam of light hit her in the back of the head.

She turned around. Someone was in the alley with a high-beam flashlight.

"Fermarsi! Non si muove!" a man's voice boomed in the alley. He was running, the flashlight beam making weird arcs against the buildings.

Emily ran out of the alley and sprinted into the night.

• • •

VIA DELLA DOGANA VECCHIA
ROME, ITALY
2:55 A.M.

"Hey!" Vinnie yelled as he sprinted through the alleyway. The alleyway, known as Via del Salvatore, spilled into a larger north-south street, Via della Dogana Vecchia.

Vinnie looked to the left, down toward the Piazza San Luigi and the French Library. Nothing.

He looked to the right, in the direction of Via Giustiniani, the east-west street that ran toward the Pantheon area.

Still, nothing.

Which way did she go? He had looked down for a split second when he started running, to avoid tripping in the dark, and when he looked up, she was gone.

He pulled his walkie-talkie out of his pocket. "Hey, boss, this is Vinnie."

"What do you have, Vinnie?" The voice of Guido.

"I spotted her, but she disappeared again."

"Whereabouts?"

"She cut through Via del Salvatore and came out at Via della Dogana Vecchia."

"Which way did she turn?"

"Sorry, boss. I lost a visual on her for a second. I can't say. But she's somewhere over in this area. I have a feeling she's headed toward the Pantheon area."

"What makes you think that?"

"Well, I can't swear to it, but I thought she turned right. For some reason, my gut tells me she may be headed that way."

"Okay. Follow up on that, and we'll get reinforcements."

The sound of smashing glass echoed from somewhere across the street. "What the—"

"What's going on, Vinnie?"

"I heard something, boss. Sounds like somewhere across the street and down toward Via Giustiniani. I'm going to check it out."

• • •

PANTHEON AREA
ROME, ITALY
3:05 A.M.

Emily jogged down a dark alley, past a row of cars parked in front of a row of townhouses. Off in the distance, she could see the columns of the ancient Roman Pantheon. She looked back over her shoulder.

Nothing.

No one there.

Emily checked her watch. It was after three. She needed to call Brady.

She stepped over between the back bumper of an Alfa Romeo and the front bumper of a Fiat and crouched down. She pulled her phone from her bag and powered the phone up.

Down at the end of the alley, about a hundred yards behind her, a flashlight beam cut through the dark.

"Dear Jesus."

She powered off the phone and kept her hand over the face of it, praying that she would not be spotted.

The flashlight swept the alley in a crisscrossing pattern, first to the left, then to the right.

She froze in position, crouched down between the two cars, next to the right front tire of the Fiat to avoid the beams.

But the beams were getting brighter. Closer.

Now she could hear voices. First in the distance, then growing louder.

Her heart pounded like a jackhammer so hard that she heard a faint *thump-thump-thump* in her chest.

She tried to catch her breath and fought the powerful instinct to take off and run. After all, she had been a distance runner and jogged thirty miles a week back home. Maybe she could outrun them.

But even if she could run faster than these guys, no one could outrun a bullet. When in doubt, remain still.

Was it her imagination?

Wait a second.

No, not her imagination. The voices seemed more distant.

The flashlight beams disappeared.

Like a diminishing musical decrescendo, the voices faded, faded.

A moment later, the only sounds were from the wind as it whooshed through the alley and the distant beeping of car horns.

"Thank you, Jesus," she whispered.

She reached down into her bag for her cell phone and powered it up. A moment later, she hit the speed dial that she had programmed in for Brady.

Two rings.

"Where are you?" His voice felt like a lifeline to a soul lost at sea.

"In an alley. Somewhere near the Pantheon."

"Okay. I'm in the area. Can you make it to the Pantheon?"

"Yes, I think so."

"I'm in a black four-door Mercedes. What are you wearing?"

"Navy warm-up suit. White running shoes."

"I'll pick you up in front of the Pantheon in five minutes. Jump in the car and let's get the heck out of here."

"Got it."

She stood up, picked up her bag, and hung the straps over her shoulder.

She glanced at the dimly lit columns of the Pantheon and kept moving toward them. Once she reached the Pantheon, she would feel safe. She would be with Brady.

The hand came out of the night like a thunderbolt from the black. He grabbed her face and held it, like in a vise, squeezing her so that she felt excruciating pain. His arms were powerful, and he pulled her back against his body. She caught a whiff of expensive cologne as she was nearly choking from his grip. She pushed his arm with her hands, but his powerful muscles would not be budged.

"Thought you could outsmart us, my voluptuous little goddess?" The man's deep voice spoke English in a heavy Italian accent. "Your government might be incompetent, but Italian free enterprise is efficient."

The blade in his right hand glistened under a streetlight. "What a horrible waste of a lovely woman. Close your eyes. This will be painless."

Emily closed her eyes and slumped.

"That's right, my dear. This won't take long."

She reached into her bag, grabbed the jagged beer bottle, and jammed it into his neck.

"Aaahhhhhhh!"

He loosened his grip and dropped the knife on the sidewalk.

She turned around.

He leaned back against the alley wall, grabbing his neck, flailing in pain.

She grabbed her cell phone, lit it up. The knife lay on the sidewalk. She picked it up and shoved it into the other side of his neck.

The big man slumped over and fell to the ground, his neck gushing blood, his eyes and mouth wide open, black pupils staring into the heavens. Blood flowed from his mouth.

She bent over and opened his jacket.

The pistol was holstered on his right side.

She lifted the pistol from the holster, stuffed it in her bag, and took off in a wild sprint down the alley, her eyes on the Pantheon.

. . .

PANTHEON AREA
ROME, ITALY
3:07 A.M.

Static burst through Guido's walkie-talkie. "Guido. It's me, Gio. Where are you?"

"At Via Giustiniani. Sitting in the car with the motor off."

"Did you hear that?"

"No. I didn't hear nothing. What are you talking about?"

"I heard something, Guido. Like a yell or something."

"Guido, it's me, Tony."

"What's going on, Tony?"

"Vinnie and me, we was walking down an alley, heading toward the Pantheon. Then we split up. He ain't answering his walkie-talkie, boss. I heard some kind of scream, too, that didn't sound like no woman."

"Tony, how far away are you from where you left him?"

"I ain't far. A couple blocks."

"Go check on him. I'll try to raise him on my walkie-talkie."

"On my way, boss."

Guido switched to the band frequency for Vinnie. "Vinnie, this is Guido. What's up, man?"

Static.

"Vinnie. Guido here. Answer me. Where are you?"

More static. No response.

"Guido! This is Tony! Vinnie's dead!"

"Dead?"

"Somebody stabbed him in the neck! He's got a beer bottle jammed in one side of his neck and a knife in his throat. It's bad, boss!"

Guido cursed so loud that his voice echoed off the old stucco and brick buildings on the street. "Do you see anything or anybody, Tony?"

"No, boss. Whoever done this must've took off toward the Pantheon, because I've been at this end of the alley and I ain't seen nobody."

"It ain't a matter of whoever done it, Tony. That American witch! She's responsible!"

"You're probably right, boss. She's pretty good if she pulled this off."

"Okay. Tony. Gio. Fan out and sweep the area. If you see the witch, shoot her in the head first and ask questions later. I'm driving toward the Pantheon to cut her off. Enough fooling around! Let's find the witch and kill her!"

• • •

APPROACHING THE PANTHEON
ROME, ITALY
3:12 A.M.

The great eight-columned building with the broad triangular front roofline bore a striking resemblance to the United States Supreme Court in Washington. But unlike the Supreme Court, there was no great staircase leading up to the columns of the Pantheon. The base of the columns was down at street level, making it a less imposing structure.

The old Roman streets had been laid out all around it and even up close on each side, giving the Pantheon the odd appearance of a great classical building plopped down in the middle of a neighborhood.

Emily stood in the shadows, waiting.

Headlights flashed up to her left.

The black Mercedes slowed at the front entrance.

"Emily!" the voice called from the car.

The front passenger door swung open, and she sprinted to the car—and to the sound of the voice of the man who almost became her husband.

• • •

APPROACHING THE PANTHEON
VIA DEI PASTINI
ROME, ITALY
3:13 A.M.

The Maserati eased up to the square in front of the spotlit Pantheon. The driver scanned the area with his eyes. Nothing. Then, right beside the east portico of the Pantheon, a woman jumped into the front seat of a black Mercedes and slammed the door. The Mercedes moved out to the south, and the Maserati pulled in behind it.

"I've got her!" Guido blurted on the walkie-talkie. "She jumped into a black Mercedes on southbound Via dei Cestari. We're moving south past the Pantheon. They won't get far."

• • •

PANTHEON AREA
SOUTHBOUND VIA DEI CESTARI
ROME, ITALY
3:14 A.M.

"Looks like we've got company." Brady pressed the accelerator. "You might want to strap in. Here he comes."

Emily turned and looked out the back window. The sports car was speeding up, matching the Mercedes' acceleration, closing the distance. Brady sped up again, and the car matched the acceleration, again closing the distance to the Mercedes.

The car started flashing its headlights off and on in rapid fire.

"This guy's not a happy camper," Brady said. "Hang on. I'm getting ready to hang a right."

The Mercedes swung a hard right in a squealing skid, slinging Emily to the left, her shoulder leaning against Brady's.

"Is he still back there?"

Emily looked back. "He's swinging around the corner."

"Looks like he's in a Maserati." Brady glanced in the rearview. "This should be interesting. What'd you do to hack these people off?"

"I don't know. Larceny? Murder in self-defense?"

"I'm not sure I want to hear it."

Now the sound of the horn blaring from the car behind them.

"This guy's serious," Brady said. "Hang on, we're swinging left."

The Mercedes swung hard again, pushing Emily against the door.

"Is he still back there?" Brady asked.

"Here he comes."

Brady pushed harder on the accelerator, and the Mercedes picked up his speed. The accelerator showed 60 mph, then 63 mph. Her heart pounded. She remembered Princess Diana, who was killed in a car race through another European city. Had she come this far to die in a car crash?

Whoever he was, he kept flashing his lights and beeping his horn. The horn blaring stopped.

Suddenly, gunshots pierced the night.

"Brady! He's firing at us!"

She looked back again. The man's arm was out the window. Two bright flashes were accompanied by two more sharp cracks of gunfire over the sound of the car engines.

"Okay, get down on the floor and keep your head down! We're gonna swing right again! Hang on!"

The sound of more gunshots cracked the air as Emily ducked her head down low.

"Hang on, Em!"

Tires squealed. They were going to flip!

"Okay, okay!" Brady said. The Mercedes emerged from the turn and leveled out.

"Is he still back there?"

"He's still there," Brady said.

The car accelerated again, coming out of the curve.

She heard another shot fired. Then another.

The next shot was followed by an instant explosion of the glass. Shards of glass sprayed into the front seat. The bullet had smashed the back window and drilled a smaller bullet hole through the front windshield, under the rearview mirror.

"That was too close for comfort!" Brady said. "Hang on!"

The speedometer showed 70 mph.

Emily reached down into the bag and grabbed the pistol that she had taken off the thug she had stabbed in the neck. She worked the action to put a bullet in the chamber, then rolled down the passenger's side window.

"What are you doing?" Brady said.

"Fighting fire with fire."

"Em, stay down!"

She leaned her head out the window, and with the night wind whipping her hair, she aimed the pistol back at the pursuing Maserati and pulled the trigger in rapid succession, firing first at the grill, then at the tires. Sparks erupted on the pavement under the Maserati.

Another shot from the Maserati. This bullet smashed the rearview mirror, missing Brady's head by inches.

"Em, get down! You're gonna get shot!"

She ignored Brady's order and pulled the trigger again, this time firing at the Maserati's windshield.

The Maserati veered, spun, then smashed into a streetlight and burst into flames, flipped over, and came to rest on the sidewalk.

"Dear Jesus, help me." Emily slipped back into the passenger's seat.

"Nice shooting," Brady said. "Where'd you get the gun?"

The wind was whistling in through the bullet hole in the front windshield. Emily breathed heavily, trying to get her adrenaline rush under control. She heard Brady's question and thought about her answer. It had to be the truth.

"I took it off a dead guy."

"I don't want to know." A pause. "I need to slow down before the Rome *polizia* are all over my rear."

"Thank you."

The Mercedes started onto a bridge over the Tiber River. Emily paused for a moment to take in the dazzling beauty of lights strung along both sides of the ancient river. The sight was a surreal peaceful contrast to the storm she found herself in.

On the other side, the Mercedes turned left, this time making more of a smooth, angled turn following the base of a Y.

The next sign proclaimed the name of the broad boulevard: Via della Conciliazione.

As the car swung onto the boulevard, the grand architectural marvel rising into the night ahead of them was breathtaking. Dozens of ornate lights flanked the boulevard. Standing at the end, like a masterpiece at the center of a great oil painting, was the cathedral, its bluish-green dome brilliantly lit with spotlights. Below the dome, magnificent white columns reached down to the street.

So magnificent was the architecture in front of her, with the many lights setting it off, that for a fleeting moment, Emily forgot what had just happened. She felt like a girl again, like Dorothy approaching the Emerald City.

Brady slowed the Mercedes as he turned into the broad circular plaza in front of the cathedral.

"You know where you are?"

The sound of sirens in the distance.

"Yes. Pictures don't do it justice."

"Once you cross that threshold, you're in another country. They won't follow you inside. This is the safest place for you right now. I want you to get out of the car, cross that threshold, go inside, find a priest, and ask for help. This is the best guarantee I have right now for keeping you alive." The sirens were getting louder. "I've got to get out of here. I'll look for you when things settle down. But you need to go, for your own safety and protection."

"Thank you, Brady." She kissed him on the cheek. "I hope to see you again." She got out of the car, closed the door, and walked across the international border into the Vatican.

She turned around and watched as the Mercedes, its back window a jagged hole, drove out the boulevard, turned left, and was gone.

• • •

DEPARTMENT OF HOMELAND SECURITY JET
BOEING 777
FINAL APPROACH TO FIUMICINO INTERNATIONAL AIRPORT
ROME, ITALY
3:28 A.M.

"We'll be touching down in two minutes, Mr. Porterfield," the pilot said over the loudspeaker. "You may want to strap in, sir."

"I don't have time to strap in!" Porterfield snapped. "Not until I find out what's going on on the ground." He stood up in the aisle as the plane bumped from last-minute turbulence. "Bob, have you gotten Guido back on the phone yet?"

The lanky TSA ELITE Force agent lumbered up from the back of the plane, holding a phone in his hand. Another hard bump. Porterfield grabbed the seat but did not sit.

"I'm sorry, Mr. Porterfield," the agent said. "I've tried raising him on his cell phone about twenty times in the last twenty minutes. He's not answering, sir."

Porterfield cursed. "For the $5 million we paid him as a down payment, he'd better answer the phone! Try him again. If he doesn't answer, call somebody else. Try Gio; tell 'em the United States Department of Homeland Security demands action."

"Yes, sir."

Porterfield slumped down into his seat and looked out at the ocean of white lights sprinkled across the great Eternal City. The plane dropped again, then some more. As the ground lights of Fiumicino International Airport swooshed by in a blur, the jet's wheels bumped onto the runway, followed by a whooshing sound as the pilots threw the jet engines in reverse to slow it.

"Yes, this is Bob Rosenfeld. United States Transportation Security Administration ELITE Force. Mr. Porterfield would like to speak with Guido Antonelli, please."

Good, Porterfield thought. *At least Rosenfeld appears to have someone on the phone.*

"Say again?" Rosenfeld's voice sounded shocked.

"What's going on, Rosenfeld?" Porterfield turned around.

"Mr. Porterfield. I have Gio Valento on the phone. He says they found Guido dead, sir."

"What? How? Give me that phone!" Porterfield snatched the phone. "This is Max Porterfield, federal agent with United States Homeland Security. Where is Guido?"

"We found him dead, boss. All shot up in a car chase."

"Dead? Who killed him?"

"Don't know, sir."

"Where's Emily Gardner?"

"Don't know, Mr. Porterfield. We're still looking."

"Look, Valento. I'm in town now. And we wired your organization five million bucks. You'd better turn this city upside down and deliver me Emily Gardner, or I'll have the president drop a nuclear bomb on this place, or even worse, I'll recommend that he turn SEAL Team Six loose on your organization. Is that clear?"

"We're working on it, sir."

"Working on it's not good enough. Now find Gardner, or I'm coming after you myself!"

CHAPTER 33

• • •

The dark night had turned to a gray haze. Outside the walls of the great city-state, the awakening sounds of Rome, the beginning roar of car and bus engines and honking horns, floated to Emily's position in front of the Vatican.

She had spent the last three hours crouched behind shrubbery near the entrance to the gardens. Every fluttering of a dove hopping from bush to bush, every solitary squawk of a seagull had convinced her that Brady was wrong when he promised that the Mob wouldn't come looking for her here. But thank God, the sounds of the night had done nothing except accelerate her already racing heart.

Activity was beginning to stir. Human activity.

They wore black berets and baggy but colorful purple and orange vertical-striped uniforms. Two members of the Swiss Guard stepped to the front door of the great basilica and swung open the doors. Two others, wearing conquistador-looking chrome helmets topped with red plumes, posted guard, one on each side of the open doors.

Emily walked across the cobblestone plaza, up the steps, past the Swiss Guards, and into the ornate and spacious ancient cathedral. The

375

floor was white marble with inlaid precious-stone patterns of orange and green.

A sign, standing near the entrance, proclaimed in Italian: *Il Sacramento di Penitenza e Conciliazione.*

Under the sign, an arrow pointed to the right.

Along the walls on the right side of the great cathedral were dark wooden confessional booths, which looked almost like giant china cabinets without the glass. On the outside of the booths hung simple white signs for the language of the priest inside.

Italiano.

Italiano.

Français.

Русский.

Deutsch.

Then, finally, English.

She strode across the floor, her eyes fixed on the English-speaking booth, her running shoes squeaking across the marble floor. She picked up her pace, certain that someone was following her, even though the nervous glance over her shoulder revealed no one.

Her heart thundering again, she stepped into the booth and pulled closed the screen behind her.

"Forgive me, Father, for I have sinned."

"How have you sinned?"

"In many ways. For masquerading as a Catholic when I'm Protestant. For stealing property that isn't mine. For killing a man, then for killing another man. For betraying my country, or for trying to save it. I don't know. For all these things."

Silence.

"That's quite a list, my child. Christ died for your sins. And God can forgive you for them all because Christ died and rose again. But what is it that I can do for you?"

Emily collected her thoughts. "I need your help, Father. I would like to request political asylum from the Holy See."

• • •

The secure phone rang on the table beside the bed, prompting Zack to slide his arm from around Diane and roll over toward the table.

The flashing letters revealed the source of the call: the White House.

"The White House?" Zack picked up the phone. "This is Admiral Brewer."

"Admiral, could you hold for the president, please?"

"Certainly."

Zack slung the sheets off his side of the bed, sat up, and swung his legs to the floor.

"What's going on, Zack?" Diane said.

"Call from the president."

"What? At this time?"

He held his hand up to stop her questions. He had to focus.

"Zack. You there?" The voice of the most powerful man in the world.

"Mr. President?"

"Sorry to wake you up so early, but I need your help," the commander in chief said.

"Anything you need, sir."

"Glad to hear it. Listen, Zack . . ."

The alarm sounded as the clock reached 4:00 a.m.

"Excuse me, Mr. President." He reached over and killed the alarm. "I was about to get up, and I should have cut that off when you called."

"No problem. Listen, Zack. We've gotten an asylum request."

"An asylum request, sir?"

"Yes. From the Holy See."

"The Vatican?"

"That's right. I found out a few minutes ago."

"Who's requesting asylum, sir?"

"Emily Gardner."

"Emily!"

"Yes. She wants to talk to you, and Pope Francis is requesting that we send you as the emissary to negotiate with her. And I agree and Secretary Mauney and Secretary Lopez both agree that you're the man for the job."

Zack thought. "When would you like me to leave?"

"Pack your bags and head out to Andrews immediately. There's a State Department jet waiting to fly you to Rome."

"Aye, aye, Mr. President."

• • •

RESIDENCE OF THE SECRETARY OF HOMELAND SECURITY
MASSACHUSETTS AVENUE NW
WASHINGTON, DC
4:15 A.M.

"What do you mean you can't find her?" Fallington Strayhorn demanded. In dark-blue pajamas, he was pacing in the study of his large Georgetown townhouse and screaming into the secure phone. Sweat beaded on his forehead. He wiped it off with a white napkin, tossed it on his desk, and grabbed another. "Porterfield, I didn't get a wink of sleep all night!"

"I'm sorry, sir."

"And now you're telling me you can't find her? That your Mafia buddies lost track of her? And this after I authorized a $5 million down payment to those clowns?"

"They had her. They were in pursuit, but the guy chasing her took a bullet to the head and his car crashed into a light pole. Burned. They're still looking."

Strayhorn picked up a book, then slammed it down on the desk. "That's not acceptable, Porterfield. While they're running around over

378

there, what am I supposed to do back here? We haven't even announced that Emily Gardner is missing!"

No answer.

"Do I need to send an army of TSA ELITEs over there to help you and your Mafioso friends do their jobs?"

"That might not be a bad idea, Mr. Secretary. We could set up a command post over here to make sure this job is done right."

Strayhorn cursed. "How many do you need?"

"Twenty-five may raise too many questions. But I think I can manage that number pretty much under the radar. They can supplement the efforts of our undercover allies here on the ground."

"By undercover allies," Strayhorn said, "you mean those Mafioso guys who let Gardner escape?"

"If you prefer that description, Mr. Secretary. I'd feel a lot better about this if we had our own TSA ELITEs on the ground."

More cursing. "Okay. I'm gonna call Willie Roberts and get him on it. Make sure nobody finds any flight records of her leaving the country. Then we'll go out with a routine missing persons report on Gardner. What else?" He checked his watch. "Okay, listen, Porterfield. You've got to find that woman. Both of our futures depend on it. Do you understand?"

"Yes, sir."

• • •

THE WHITE HOUSE
THE OVAL OFFICE
7:15 A.M.

President Surber was at his desk, going over updated casualty reports from the mall terror attacks with his chief of staff, Arnie Brubaker. Casualties had risen overnight to fifty more deaths. They were discussing the need for a national day of prayer when the phone rang.

"Mr. President, the secretary of defense."

"Thanks, Gail." Surber picked up the hotline to the Pentagon. "What do you have, Erwin?"

"Mr. President, Homeland Security has filed a missing person report with the Alexandria PD for Emily Gardner, and they've issued a brief press release saying she did not show for work. They're asking all persons with information on her whereabouts to contact the Alexandria PD. The press release says that two suspicious black men were seen in the vicinity of Gardner's apartment before she disappeared. They even included photos of these two black men."

"So let me get this straight," the president said. "Yesterday we track down the bogus e-mails claiming terrorists are on the Aeroflot liner to Homeland Security. Early this morning we get a call from the Vatican saying Gardner is there, is requesting asylum, and wants Zack Brewer to go there to negotiate. And now Homeland Security is putting out a press release claiming Emily is missing? And they are even suggesting that a couple of black men kidnapped her?"

"Obviously Strayhorn doesn't know what we know about Emily being at the Vatican."

"Obviously." The president leaned back in his chair. "Is this guy trying to pull off some kind of coup?"

"I'm not sure, sir. But whenever you're ready to move, you have the support of the military, and I'm sure the Justice Department too."

"Not yet, Erwin. We're not there yet. I don't have enough evidence tying this to Strayhorn. Let's give him a little more rope. See what he does. But I want you to order all US military bases on lockdown until further notice."

• • •

DEPARTMENT OF HOMELAND SECURITY
OFFICE OF THE SECRETARY
WASHINGTON, DC
11:15 A.M.

"Is there anything else I can do, Mr. Secretary?" Willie Roberts, his eyes sparkling, was still intoxicated by his sudden baptism into the presence of power.

"I'm not sure what we can do over there until the ELITE agents get there," Strayhorn said. "Those Mafiosos have proven useless." He checked his watch. "It's a ten-hour flight to Rome. You did a great job rounding up our ELITEs. That took some time. They've been in the air for five hours, so another five hours puts them on the ground at 5:00 p.m. our time, 11:00 p.m. Rome time. You can do the math. Unless Porterfield and his minions strike gold before then, we'll just have to wait until reinforcements arrive."

The phone rang. Strayhorn checked the caller ID. "Whatcha got, Porterfield?"

"Possible break, Mr. Secretary."

"Talk to me."

"We finally traced her cell phone calls. We couldn't earlier because of computer problems. She also used her other phone. She called an ex-boyfriend. A JAG officer in Naples. Lieutenant Commander Brady Kash."

"Excellent. Find out if he knows anything."

"We will, sir. But he's at the naval station in Naples, and they've just gone to lockdown by the president's order."

"Strange. Why did he wait until today to do that?"

"I don't know, sir. We may have to wait for reinforcements before we can get to Kash and hope that either Surber ends the lockdown or Kash leaves the base."

"All right. Keep me posted."

• • •

APPROACHING THE VATICAN
9:30 P.M.

Wearing his summer white uniform with the gold insignia of a three-star admiral on his shoulder boards, Zack got into the backseat of the Range Rover the Vatican had dispatched to Fiumicino International Airport. As the Rover pulled away from the curb, he took out his cell phone.

Two rings later, he heard the voice that could melt him from half a world away.

"How are you, baby? . . . Good. We're driving up to the Vatican. The lights and the architecture are incredible. St. Peter's Basilica is right in front of me. It takes your breath away."

"You take my breath away, Zack."

"Same here. I wish you were here."

"I do too. What time is it there?"

"Almost 2130."

"It's still afternoon here," Diane said. "Sounds like it's almost your bedtime."

"No bed for me tonight. Too much work to do."

"I understand."

"Look. They're stopping this Range Rover. I've gotta go."

"Good luck. I'll pray for you. Love you."

"Thanks. Love you too."

The Range Rover pulled up to the circular entrance of the Vatican, in front of a row of towering round columns.

"Welcome to the Apostolic Palace, Admiral," the driver said.

Two Swiss Guards approached the Rover. One opened the door, then they both came to attention and shot salutes. "Welcome to the Vatican, Admiral."

Zack got out, put on his cover, and returned the salute.

"I'm Captain Canan, Swiss Guards. I shall be accompanying you on your stay."

"Thank you, Captain. I hope I won't be tying you up too long."

"If you will come with me, sir."

"Certainly." Zack followed the officer into a columned walkway, where they were joined by another officer and a priest with closely cropped white hair, fiftyish, wearing a flowing reddish robe.

"I'm Cardinal McClure, Admiral," the priest said in a Scottish brogue. "I advise the pontiff on geopolitical matters when the situation calls for it. This seems to be such a matter. Miss Gardner is waiting for you in a conference room in the Vatican library. We have set up a secure phone for you to call Washington, along with computers. If there is anything else you will need, just ask."

"Thank you, Cardinal," Zack said. "Has the Holy See granted asylum to Miss Gardner?"

They stepped into the foyer of the grand library with its black-and-white checkered marble floor. Golden archways stretched down a long hall, with golden chandeliers hanging one after the other for lighting. Elaborate biblically themed paintings covered the long ceiling.

"My understanding is that the Holy Father has not decided. He is hoping and praying that you might be able to defuse the situation."

"I'll try, Cardinal," Zack said. "But I don't know yet what there is to defuse."

"Let's find out," the cardinal said. "She is right in this room. Captain?"

"Yes, sir." The Swiss guard opened the door.

Emily sat at the far end of a conference table. She stood up and smiled when she saw him. "Admiral! Thank God!"

"Emily. Are you okay?"

"I'm fine. At least I think I am. I don't know." Tears streamed down her cheeks. "There's so much I have to tell you."

• • •

13 HOURS LATER
THE WHITE HOUSE
THE OVAL OFFICE
4:30 A.M.

"Don't you ever sleep, Zack?"

"With respect, I could ask you the same question, Mr. President."

"Please, have a seat. What do you have?"

Zack paused. Emily had given him proof, but he felt sick having to recite it. "We've got a big-time problem with Homeland Security and TSA, sir."

"Talk to me."

"An unconstitutional power grab based on lies, deception, and murder."

The president leaned back. "Let's hear it."

"As Emily was preparing for her Senate confirmation hearings, she ran across evidence that was internally classified as top secret by Homeland Security—a plan to grow Homeland Security into the most powerful agency in the government. If it had worked, Fallington Strayhorn would have become almost like a shadow president, maybe with enough power to effectively act as president."

Surber nodded. "And how was he planning to do this?"

"Strayhorn and some of his subordinates cooked up a grand scheme to grow Homeland Security and to make TSA its principal enforcement arm. They came up with their own top-secret plan called the SITUS project.

"SITUS stands for Subway, Interstate, Train, US Highways, and Shopping Centers. The idea was to get an army of TSA agents, run by this new TSA ELITE Force they came up with, all over the highways, the interstates, in the train stations, the shopping malls—you name it.

"They wanted federal agents all over the highways to supplant the authority of state troopers. They were proposing that TSA agents at shopping malls randomly search customers entering the malls with naked body scanners and pat downs, all in the name of national security.

"They were lining up five czars, one for each of the areas of SITUS, all to report to Strayhorn as secretary of Homeland Security."

"Wait a minute," Surber said. "They wanted a highway czar and an interstate czar—all that, reporting to Strayhorn?"

"That's right, Mr. President. And a subway czar. They were going to call them the Five Horsemen."

"And how were they going to convince anyone to support all that?"

"They needed a terror event to whip up public fear, convince people that we need more protection. So they had their subordinates rig and coordinate these mall explosions. They manufactured evidence linking the bombings to the Council of Ishmael and framed the Makaris. They staged this arrest of Hasan Makari at the Philly airport, carefully timed with all the cameras to show up, and claimed he was conspiring with his son to commit acts of terror. They claimed that the son, Najib, was responsible for an F/A-18 crashing into the Atlantic, although the Navy found no evidence of it. Then they blamed the Council of Ishmael for retaliating for our arrest of these two terrorists."

"So the Makaris were framed?"

"Yes, sir. Hasan Makari is a Christian. So is his son. They aren't Muslim. But part of the plan was to have them transported by these new TSA ELITE agents to Guantánamo where they could be in charge of interrogations."

"They wanted TSA assigned to GITMO?"

"Yes, sir. Under the plan, TSA ELITE Forces would target domestic terrorists and transport them to GITMO, where they would interrogate them and gather evidence for conviction. The CIA would keep jurisdiction over foreign terrorists. But any so-called 'domestic terrorists' would fall under TSA and Homeland Security."

"A classic power grab."

"Yes, sir. And the Makaris were their first test case. They needed to have the Makaris convicted and executed to bolster public support for the effectiveness of TSA. Of course, after that, anyone arrested in a shopping mall, on a highway, almost anywhere by TSA, would be classified as a domestic terrorist and placed under their jurisdiction."

The president shook his head. "Unbelievable. How many TSA agents were they hoping to hire?"

"An army, sir. To fan out over the country. Initially a hundred thousand. False terror flags like the mall bombings were part of the strategic plan."

"And they thought Emily would go along with this?"

Zack nodded. "They did. But that's where they miscalculated, sir. They needed a general counsel to build a constitutional defense for the millions of random stops and searches they were planning, on national security grounds. They gambled, hoping that Emily, being a lower-ranking agency lawyer, would be starstruck when offered the general counsel's position. Emily is the one who came up with the legal theory for TSA to justify prosecuting Najib Makari at GITMO as a terrorist, arguing that he was not entitled to protection under the Uniform Code of Military Justice because his enlistment contract with the Navy was void. Based on that aggressive stance, they thought she would play ball on their team. They miscalculated, and it backfired."

The president sat in silence. A minute passed. Then another. "You're sure about all this, Zack?"

"I've seen the evidence myself, Mr. President. Emily photographed it from the secure site and smuggled it out of the country."

"Good work, Zack. And thank Emily for me. We'll get a warrant for Strayhorn's arrest. We'll have federal marshals arrest him at 10:00 a.m. at Homeland Security headquarters. I know I've asked a lot of you, Zack, but I'd like you to be there to make sure this gets done right."

Zack nodded. "I'll be there, Mr. President."

• • •

DEPARTMENT OF HOMELAND SECURITY
NATIONAL CAPITAL REGION HEADQUARTERS
WASHINGTON, DC
9:30 A.M.

Alone in his office, Fallington Strayhorn poured himself a shot of bourbon in a glass, then walked over to the refrigerator in the corner of the office and popped a can of Coke and poured it in with the bourbon.

He needed a drink and took a sip.

Still nothing in terms of locating Gardner.

The Coke and bourbon trickled down his esophagus, providing instant relief for his nerves. But he needed more. He set the drink down and extracted a Marlboro 54 from his pocket and lit it. He inhaled deeply.

Much better.

A knock on the door.

"Come in."

The door cracked. Carol Gibson stood there, wearing a nicely fitted green dress. "Sir, Willie Roberts is here for you."

"Send him in."

Willie Roberts stepped in a bit hesitantly. A skinny, scrawny nerd and a definite visual downer after his secretary. "Close the door, Willie. What's going on?"

"Bad news, Mr. Secretary."

"Spit it out."

"This is supposed to be hush-hush, but our sources at the State Department say that Emily Gardner is at the Vatican."

"What?"

"She's at the Vatican, sir. And she's applied for asylum."

"Asylum? What the—"

The phone buzzed. "Sorry to interrupt, Mr. Secretary, but it's Max Porterfield, and he says it is urgent."

"Put him through." Strayhorn picked up the phone. "Where's Emily Gardner, Porterfield?"

"I'm sorry, sir. But we're hearing through back channels that she's asked for asylum from the Vatican."

Strayhorn sat down at his desk and eyed the bourbon and Coke. His first inclination was to pick up the glass and sling it across the office. He picked it up but changed his mind and gulped it down. He put Porterfield on speaker.

"All right, gentlemen." He refilled his glass, this time with straight bourbon. "I don't care what else you do at this point, but I want every record dealing with the SITUS project destroyed." He took a big swig of bourbon. "Can you do it?"

"Definitely, Mr. Secretary," Roberts said, "but time is of the essence."

"Okay. Willie, I'm putting you in charge of it. Get rid of all SITUS files. Now. Let me know when you're finished. Porterfield, get your butt back to Washington."

"Yes, Mr. Secretary."

Strayhorn slammed down the phone.

"Get to it, Willie."

"Yes, sir." Willie Roberts left the office and closed the door behind him as Strayhorn's lips once again found the rim of the bourbon-filled glass.

• • •

DEPARTMENT OF HOMELAND SECURITY
NATIONAL CAPITAL REGION HEADQUARTERS
WASHINGTON, DC
9:45 A.M.

In the elevator riding up to the secretary's suite, Zack had engaged in small talk with the attorney general, Tom Anderson. They had been joined by the secretary of defense, three FBI agents, and five federal marshals.

Two platoons of United States Marines were positioned downstairs and outside, around the building, in case a problem arose from TSA ELITE Force agents who might come to the aid of Strayhorn.

They planned to arrest Strayhorn, cuff him, and lead him down the secure elevator to a Justice Department van, to be driven to the United States Courthouse for arraignment.

The elevator door opened into the secretary's suite, and Zack, closest to the door, stepped out first and was followed by the rest of the party.

Strayhorn's personal secretary, Carol Gibson, glanced up with a look of shock.

"Miss Gibson, I'm Attorney General Tom Anderson. This is Defense Secretary Erwin Lopez and Vice Admiral Zack Brewer. These gentlemen are FBI agents and federal marshals. We'd like to see Secretary Strayhorn."

"Yes, sir." Gibson picked up the phone. "Mr. Secretary, you have visitors." She paused. With a sound of concern in her voice, she said, "The attorney general, the defense secretary, Vice Admiral Brewer, and several FBI agents and US marshals." Another pause. "Yes, sir."

"He'll be right with you, gentlemen."

The loud gunshot shook the walls.

Carol Gibson screamed as the marshals burst into Strayhorn's office.

"Get an ambulance!" one marshal shouted.

Zack rushed in behind the agents. Strayhorn was sprawled on the floor, a revolver next to his hand. Blood gushed from his head, or what was left of his head, and pooled on the carpeting.

"Secure the area!" a marshal shouted.

Outside the office, Carol Gibson could be heard wailing and moaning.

Attorney General Anderson stepped into the office and looked down at the body. "Secretary Lopez, Admiral Brewer, I think our work is done here. Let's get Miss Gibson out of here and leave this crime scene for the professionals.

"Let's go see the president."

• • •

GUANTÁNAMO BAY DETENTION CENTER
CAMP DELTA
UNITED STATES NAVAL BASE
GUANTÁNAMO BAY, CUBA
NOON

Hasan sat alone in a corner of his cell, his head down, praying. The grip of loneliness was setting in again, and he recalled that even God's servants sometimes became despondent and tired. It had happened even to Elijah, even after the great miracle of fire called down on Mount Carmel.

Hasan wasn't concerned about himself. He had lived a long, fruitful life, and if God took him home, so be it. His mind and heart were heavy for his son. Najib was young and still had most of his life before him.

Someone was at the door.

"Stand back, please."

When the door cracked open, his heart leaped, and he stood, his eyes suddenly flooded with tears. "Najib!"

"Papa!"

The son rushed to the father and they hugged as the prison cell door clanged shut behind them.

"What are you doing here?"

"I don't know, Papa. They came and got me, and I assumed that we were returning to court. But they brought me here."

"Whatever, son, I am so glad to see you." Hasan wiped tears of joy from his eyes. He loved no one on the face of the earth as much as his son. He wrapped his arms around Najib again and held him tight, still weeping. The Lord was good, and no matter what, for the moment at least, they still had each other.

"It will be okay, Papa. I'm fine."

More clanging at the door. Hasan released Najib and turned toward the door again. Keys jingled in the lock. The door swung open.

"Lieutenant Davis!" The JAG officer stood there in his summer whites.

"Hasan. Najib. I have someone I'd like you to meet." He turned around. "Amy?"

The attractive officer from court stepped next to Matt. She was wearing a white summer officer's uniform with white skirt and white pumps. The black shoulder boards had three gold stripes across the end. She had an envelope in her hand.

"This is Commander Amy Debenedetto, Judge Advocate General's Corps, US Navy. She is the assistant prosecutor in your case, and as I disclosed to you, she is very special to me."

"It is a pleasure, ma'am," Hasan said.

She smiled and nodded.

"Commander Debenedetto has a message for you." Matt looked at her. "Amy?"

The commander opened the envelope and took out a sheet of paper and started reading:

"From Douglas Surber, President of the United States.

"To Commander, United States Naval Base, Guantánamo Bay, Cuba; Commander, United States Military Commissions, Guantánamo Bay, Cuba; Commander, United States Naval JAG Corps Trial Command; Commander, United States Air Force Trial Command; Commander, United States Air Mobility Command; Commanding Officer, USS *Abraham Lincoln*; Commander, United States Fleet Forces Command; Commander, United States Seventh Fleet."

Her voice was firm yet feminine. She looked up at Hasan and seemed to smile for a second, then looked back down at the paper. Why was she here? And why was she here with Lieutenant Davis? Had they been betrayed?

"Subject: Presidential pardon and dismissal of charges.

"I, Douglas Surber, president of the United States, do hereby declare that Hasan Makari, a citizen of Lebanon, currently in the United States by legal visa, and Boatswain's Mate Third Class Najib Makari, United States Navy, and currently assigned to the USS *Abraham Lincoln*, are hereby, and from this moment forward, fully pardoned for any crimes that they have committed against the United States or may have committed against the United States.

"No evidence exists that they committed any criminal acts in either the assassination of US Ambassador George Madison, or aboard the USS *Abraham Lincoln*, or that they ever engaged in any act of terror or conspiracy to commit any act of violence against the United States or its citizens.

"And furthermore, based upon newly discovered evidence which proves that they have been involved in no criminal activity against the United States, and based upon my constitutional powers as commander in chief of all United States military forces worldwide, which includes the United States Military Commissions Tribunal and all United States courts-martial, I do hereby order that all charges against the defendants Hasan Makari and Petty Officer Najib Makari be dismissed with prejudice, and that they be immediately released from custody from the United States detention facility at Guantánamo Bay, Cuba."

"What? Papa!" Najib looked at Hasan, his eyes wide open.

Matt grinned from ear to ear, wiping tears from his eyes.

"Furthermore"—Commander Debenedetto held up her hand—"the commander, US Naval Air Forces Atlantic, is directed to transport Petty Officer Makari and Mr. Makari back to Norfolk, Virginia, immediately, where they may travel freely and without inhibition as guests of the United States government and as guests of the president of the United States. To help defray the costs of his visit to the United States, Hasan Makari is awarded a special stipend of one hundred thousand dollars ($100,000), with payment to be arranged through the Navy Federal Credit Union upon his arrival in Norfolk, Virgina. And upon the expiration of his leave, at the end of thirty days, Petty Officer Najib Makari shall report back to his duty station on board USS *Abraham Lincoln*.

"It is so ordered by my direct command as commander in chief of all United States military forces worldwide.

"Douglas Surber, President of the United States."

Commander Debenedetto slid the papers back in the envelope. She looked up with a huge smile. "Congratulations, gentlemen. You are free to go."

Hasan threw his arms around Najib and wept and whispered in his son's ear, "Our God is faithful. No matter what storms we face, he is always with us."

EPILOGUE

· · ·

The soft afternoon breeze rolled across the warm, sun-drenched wooden deck. The smell of salt from the sea brought a feeling of relief, and of finality, and of promise of brighter days ahead. In a pair of white shorts and his red Gamecocks T-shirt, Matt leaned back in the Adirondack lounge chair, pulled out a lighter, and flicked it on.

"You sure you don't mind?" He fired up the end of the cigar even before Amy could answer.

She laughed. "After what we've been through, I might even join you."

It was just the two of them, together, out on the cigar deck outside the officers' club, and that was fine with him. He liked alone time with her.

He had decided that Amy just might be the candidate for love of his life. But for now, he would keep such thoughts to himself. Too much talking too fast and things could get out of control. "Can I order you a drink?"

"No, thanks," Amy said. "Besides, I'm still your senior officer, and I make more money than you. Maybe I should be ordering you a drink."

393

"Maybe I'll take you up on that later," Matt said. "And since you're still my elder and my superior, maybe we could get ourselves into some more trouble?"

"Oh, stop it, Matt." She giggled. "You're trouble. Besides, I lost my case. You won. Maybe they'll promote you to commander, and we won't have to worry about getting in trouble anymore."

He drew in on the cigar. "I didn't win. We all won. And nobody would've won if it weren't for Emily Gardner."

"So true." She turned toward him and smiled. "You know, Emily and I were in Justice School together."

"I know." Matt took another drag. "I've heard it all before. The two of you are legendary." He reached over and patted her knee.

"Careful, Matt. You're going to get us in trouble again."

"So?" He laughed. "What are they going to do? Send us back to GITMO and pair us on opposite sides of another high-profile terror trial? Besides. Nobody's watching us out here."

"Admiral Brewer called." She touched his hand, igniting lightning under the setting Caribbean sun. "He said they're going to give Emily the Presidential Medal of Freedom."

"She deserves it. Speaking of presidential, isn't it about time for President Surber's address?"

"I think it's at five." A cool late-afternoon breeze swept across the deck. "Do you want to go inside the bar and watch it?"

"Not if we can get it out here on your iPhone. I'd rather be alone with you."

"Good idea." She removed her hand from his to get her phone.

"Hang on." She punched the phone and went online. "Okay, I have it on Fox. Looks like he's about to start." She held up the phone so they could both see the screen.

He doused the cigar and snuggled up close to her as the image of Fox White House correspondent Tom Miller appeared on the screen.

"Hang on." She plugged in a pair of earphones, gave him one, and put the other in her ear. Another excuse to get up close to her as they listened.

What a great way to end a great day, he thought.

The screen switched to their commander in chief, sitting in the Oval Office, and the volume came up.

"My fellow Americans.

"Thomas Jefferson once said that the price of freedom is eternal vigilance. Some years later, the British parliamentarian Lord Acton said that 'absolute power corrupts, and power corrupts absolutely.'

"This week, unfortunately, we have seen that both of these statements ring true.

"We have seen an attempt inside our own government, by certain men, to usurp power for themselves in a way that would destroy and discard all the noble principles on which our sublime Constitution has stood. These men wanted power for themselves, and they were prepared to burn the Constitution and to kill and destroy.

"They concocted an evil plan to usurp civil liberties while feeding their own power. But I am pleased to report that their constitutional coup has failed. In their evil travesty of justice, we have seen bloodshed, the blood of the innocent and the blood of the guilty.

"But today our republic still stands.

"What they have done, however, is a reminder that we must guard against expanding power within the government and against the expanding egos of people who would place their own thirst for power, their own thirst for money, and their own self-aggrandizement above all else. Our government has gotten too big. It has gotten unmanageable. We have too often come to a mind-set, in this War on Terror, that we are willing to sacrifice liberty on the altar of a perceived need for protection.

"But if we as a nation throw out our Bill of Rights for the sake of so-called protection, if the right of privacy set out in the Fourth Amendment is trashed by government spying, if the right against unreasonable search and seizure without a warrant is thrown away, if we are willing to surrender our freedoms and liberties under the guise of wanting to be protected, then we have become spineless as a nation, and America will no longer be America, and the terrorists will have won.

"My fellow Americans, that surrender will not happen on my watch. I have sworn to uphold the Constitution, which includes the Bill of Rights, and I intend to do it.

"Effective today, I am taking the following actions. First, I am ordering the acting secretary of Homeland Security to abolish this newly created TSA ELITE Force program and to surrender the more than two billion rounds of hollow-point bullets it purchased in 2012 to the United States military. Homeland Security does not need more bullets than the United States Army and the United States Marine Corps combined.

"Second, I am ordering the acting director of TSA to immediately cease the practice of invasive and intrusive full-body scanners at United States airports, which amount to an unconstitutional search without a warrant and without probable cause. Passengers in America who have done no wrong should not be treated like criminals under the freedom-grabbing excuse of personal protection.

"Third, I am ordering the director of the National Security Agency and the acting secretary of Homeland Security to cease all monitoring of American phone calls and e-mails, and to stop the collection of data that violates Americans' privacy under the Fourth Amendment. And I will ask the Congress to pass legislation that makes it a felony, punishable by prison, for any federal official to violate the Fourth Amendment rights of an American.

"Fourth, I will ask the Congress for a 70 percent funding reduction in the following agencies, all of which have gotten out of control and affect our civil liberties: the Environmental Protection Agency, the Internal Revenue Service, the Transportation Security Administration, the federal Department of Education, and the Department of Homeland Security. All these agencies have gotten so big and unwieldy that they have caused more harm to the country than whatever good they have served.

"Fifth, and finally, the United States Naval Base at Guantánamo Bay has, for over a century, been a valuable lynchpin in assuring American military security in the Caribbean. The Guantánamo Bay naval base will remain as a lynchpin to our naval superiority in the area. But the military prison at Guantánamo Bay that has housed international detainees has outserved its usefulness. As commander in chief, effective immediately, I am ordering that the prison facility be closed."

Cheers erupted from all over the base—from inside the officers' club, from the streets outside, from the beaches.

The president continued, "We must understand, now and always, that the freedom of the individual and the power of government are inversely proportional to one another. An all-powerful government is a tyrannical government.

"Not on my watch, ladies and gentlemen. Not on my watch.

"Those who violated the law in this attempted power grab, to the extent they have survived physically, will be prosecuted fully under the law. I have taken an oath to defend the Constitution, and I intend to do just that.

"God bless you, and God bless the United States of America."

For a moment, it was as if time had stopped. The silence in the wake of the president's words was profound.

The breeze whipped up again.

Matt started to light his cigar but changed his mind. He stood up and reached for her hand. "Let's go for a walk."

She got up out of the chair, the breeze blowing her hair, a curious look on her face and a capricious sparkle in her eyes. "Where are we going?"

"The beach," he said. "Trouble or not, I can feel the warm sand under my toes and the lapping aqua waters of the Caribbean calling our names."

She smiled and gave him a quick kiss on the cheek. "It's a date, even if we get in trouble." She took his hand and led him off the deck, across the lush green grass and across the road toward the broad, sparkling white beach. "I can't think of a better way to end our day than a swim with you in Guantánamo Bay."

ACKNOWLEDGMENTS

...

Special thanks to my "West Coast Editor," US Army Veteran Jack Miller of La Mesa, California, who, along with his lovely wife Linda, has served as a benevolent benefactor for the Lambs Theater of Coronado, California; the San Diego Zoo and Wild Animal Park; the First Baptist Church of Lemon Grove, California, and various other worthy charitable causes organizations.

DISCUSSION QUESTIONS

• • •

1. What inner struggles was Emily Gardner facing that ultimately caused her to decline the professional opportunity of a lifetime?
2. Like Emily, have you ever confronted an opportunity in life that seemed too good to be true, but you ultimately declined to embrace that opportunity? Why? Do you have regrets, or are you satisfied that you did the right thing?
3. Is Emily governed in any way by her personal faith and her personal convictions in making the decision she makes? Why or why not?
4. In *Detained* both Hasan Makari and his son Najib are falsely accused of something they did not do. Do you know someone who has been falsely accused, or can you relate to the feeling of being falsely accused? How do you think Hasan and Najib handled these false accusations?
5. When Hasan arrives in Philadelphia, his hopes and dreams very quickly turn into an unexpected nightmare. Have you ever encountered a situation in life where something so bright and promising—like Hasan's hopes for coming to America—suddenly became so dark and disastrous in what seemed like an instant?

How did Hasan rely upon his personal faith to get through this very dark cloud he was facing?

6. What do you think of the decision by the Navy to pit Matt Davis against Amy Debenedetto at the terror trial in Cuba? Do you think this made it more difficult for Matt to defend his clients? Why or why not?

7. Discuss the character of Fallington Strayhorn, Secretary of Homeland Security, who is involved in a power-play in the highest levels of the US government and is willing to break the law and even kill to get his way. Do we as a country really face this kind of danger from within our own government? Or is this type of situation only realistic within the confines of the author's imagination? Why or why not?

8. When Matt Davis arrives in Cuba, he receives an e-mail from Andy Hart, a deceased former GTMO lawyer who represen some detainees at Guantánamo Bay. Who do you think wa behind this e-mail, and how do you think Matt would have reacted to receiving this type of e-mail?

9. Who was Andy Hart? Was he a real person or a figment of the author's imagination? Based on what you learned about Andy Hart, does this make you consider the novel in a different light? If so, how?

10. *Detained* reintroduces Zack Brewer and Diane Colcernian (Now Diane Colcernian Brewer), the stars of the original Navy Justice Series. Now Zack is a three-star admiral and Judge Advocate General of the Navy. When Diane is nearly killed in the terrorist attack, Zack insists on remaining with her in the hospital, but she insists on him going out and doing his duty. What does this say about Diane's character? Do you agree with Zack's decision to honor her request? What effect does this decision have on the outcome of the book? Discuss times when, like Zack, you have

been faced with a dilemma on what to do, and have had to do something you were not comfortable with.

11. How do you feel about President Douglas Surber's decision to shoot down the Russian plane? Can you empathize with what President Surber was going through both before the decision was made, and then after he had learned the truth, that Strayhorn had lied to him? How so? What do you think of the president's decisions at the end of the book, in light of all that happened, after the truth had been exposed?

12. Aside from the longstanding relationship between Zack and Diane, *Detained* introduces two new couples, namely Matt and Amy, and then Emily and Lieutenant Commander Brady Kash, JAGC, USN. Which couple do you think has the best chance of making it? Why? Who would you like to hear more about in the future?

The Navy Justice Series

Defiance

Don Brown

From a murder in Paris to a courtroom in California to a terrorist camp in the Gobi Desert, Don Brown's follow-up to *Treason* and *Hostage* plunges into a suspense-filled journey of danger, duty, and hope.

The commander's bodyguard is Shannon McGilverry, a crack NCIS agent assigned to protect Navy JAG Officer Zack Brewer. Zack is being hunted by terrorists, stalked by a psychopath, and is working his way through a perilous, politically-charged trial. When another Navy JAG officer is murdered, it's clear that Zack is in harm's way.

As his bodyguard, Shannon must do more than protect Zack. She also must set aside her growing feelings for the brilliant attorney and investigate rumors that the love of his life, Diane Colcernian, may still be alive. Zack finds himself in need of his faith more than ever as Navy SEALs launch a daring rescue attempt that has the potential to trigger World War III.

Available in stores and online!

Hostage

Don Brown

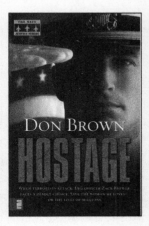

JAG Officer Zack Brewer's prosecution of three terrorists posing as Navy chaplains was called the "court martial of the century" by the press. Now, with the limelight behind him, all Zack wants to do is forget. But the radical Islamic organization behind the chaplains has a long memory—and a thirst for revenge.

Now the Navy has a need for Zack that eclipses all else. When an unthinkable act of aggression brings Israel and its Arab neighbors to the brink of war, Zack and co-counsel Diane Colcernian are called to the case of a lifetime. As leading nations focus their gaze upon these two, other eyes are watching as well.

Zack and Diane are in harm's way.

A kidnapping, an ultimatum…and suddenly, Zack faces an impossible choice. If he loses this case, the world could explode into war. If he wins, his partner—the woman he loves—will die.

And Zack himself may not survive to make the decision.

Treason

Don Brown

The stakes are high . . . and the entire world is waiting for the verdict.

The Navy has uncovered a group of radical Islamic clerics who have infiltrated the Navy Chaplain Corps, inciting sailors and marines to acts of terrorism. And Lieutenant Zack Brewer has been chosen to prosecute them for treason and murder.

Only three years out of law school, Zack has already made a name for himself, winning the coveted Navy Commendation Medal. Just coming off a high-profile win, this case will challenge the very core of Zack's skills and his Christian beliefs—beliefs that could cost him the case and his career.

With Diane Colcernian, his staunchest rival, as assistant prosecutor, Zack takes on internationally acclaimed criminal defense lawyer Wells Levinson. And when Zack and Diane finally agree to put aside their animosity, it causes more problems than they realize.

Black Sea Affair

Don Brown

It's a mission that could bring the world to the brink of nuclear war.

Now time is running out.

It starts with a high-stakes theft: weapons-grade plutonium is stolen from Russia. The Russian army is about to attack Chechnya to get it back, but U.S. intelligence discovers that the stolen shipment is actually on a rogue Russian freighter in the Black Sea manned by terrorists.

It turns into a global nightmare: a secret mission gone awry. An American submarine commander is arrested and hauled before a military tribunal in Moscow, starting a game of brinksmanship so dangerous that war might be its only possible conclusion.

A submarine mishap escalates in international crisis. With the world watching, JAG Officer Zack Brewer is called to Moscow to defend submarine skipper Pete Miranda and his entire crew. It is a heart-stopping race against the clock. With Russian missiles activated and programmed for American cities, Brewer stalls for time as the U.S. Navy frantically searches the high seas for a floating hydrogen bomb that could threaten New York Harbor.

Available in stores and online!

The Malacca Conspiracy

Don Brown,
Author of the Navy Justice Series

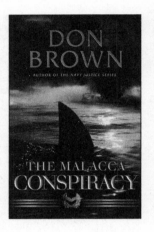

Set in Singapore, Indonesia, Malaysia, and
the United States, *The Malacca Conspiracy*
is a bone-chilling tale of terrorism on the
high seas, political assassination, and nuclear
brinkmanship. And for Zack and Diane—your
favorite JAG characters from Don Brown's
popular Navy Justice Series—a story of hope
for a long-standing romance that is now or never.

When a dastardly plot is hatched in the Malaysian seaport of
Malacca to attack civilian oil tankers at sea, to drive up the price of
crude oil futures, to assassinate the Indonesian president, and use fat
windfall profits to finance a nuclear attack against American cities,
Navy JAG officers Zack Brewer and Diane Colcernian reunite in a
sizzling race against the clock to foil the conspiracy before disaster
strikes.

But as President Mack Williams sends ships of the U.S. Seventh
Fleet towards the Malacca Straights to reassert control over the sea
lanes, will Zack and Diane survive this dangerous and final high-stakes
drama of life and death?

You won't be able to put this thriller down until you find out.

Available in stores and online!

ABOUT THE AUTHOR

• • •

 Don Brown is the author of *Thunder in the Morning Calm*, *The Malacca Conspiracy*, the Navy Justice Series, and *The Black Sea Affair*, a submarine thriller that predicted the 2008 shooting war between Russia and Georgia. Don served five years in the US Navy as an officer in the Judge Advocate General's (JAG) Corps, which gave him an exceptional vantage point into both the Navy and the inner workings "inside the Beltway" as an action officer assigned to the Pentagon. He left active duty in 1992 to pursue private practice, but remained on inactive status through 1999, rising to the rank of lieutenant commander. He and his family live in North Carolina, where he pursues his passion for penning novels about the Navy.

Visit his website at www.donbrownbooks.com
Facebook: Don-Brown